The suspenseful tales in this new collection take intrepid readers of all ages into that unexplored world where the darker and more dangerous powers of man and nature reside. Edgar Allan Poe, Sir Arthur Conan Doyle, and other masters of the mystery story lead us to the terrifying brink of the unknown.

STEWART H. BENEDICT, with degrees from Drew University and Johns Hopkins, has taught German at New York University, English and French at Michigan Tech and Jersey City State College. He has also worked as a technical editor and an advertising copywriter. His articles, most of them dealing with modern American, English, and European literature, have appeared in leading magazines.

THE LAUREL-LEAF LIBRARY brings together under a single imprint outstanding works of fiction and nonfiction particularly suitable for young adult readers, both in and out of the classroom. This series is under the editorship of M. Jerry Weiss, Distinguished Professor of Communications, Jersey City State College, in association with Ned E. Hoopes, Associate Professor of English, Pace College, and Charles Reasoner, Associate Professor, Elementary Education, New York University.

TALES of TERROR AND SUSPENSE

EDITED BY STEWART H. BENEDICT

Published by DELL PUBLISHING CO., INC.
750 Third Avenue, New York, N.Y. 10017

Copyright © 1963 by Dell Publishing Co., Inc.

Laurel-Leaf Library ® TM 766734

DEDICATION: To E. S. B.

First printing—October, 1963
Second printing—November, 1966
Third printing—June, 1967
Fourth printing—October, 1967
Fifth printing—March, 1968
Sixth printing—March, 1970
Seventh printing—August, 1971

Printed in U.S.A.

ACKNOWLEDGMENTS: "The Small Assassin" is reprinted by permission of Harold Matson Company from *Dark Carnival*, copyright 1946 by Ray Bradbury. "The Vanishing Lady" is reprinted by permission of The Viking Press, Inc., from *While Rome Burns*, copyright 1934 by Alexander Woollcott, Copyright renewed 1962 by Joseph P. Hennessey. "The Escape" is reprinted by permission of Mrs. Hereward Carrington. "The Adventure of the Speckled Band" from THE COMPLETE SHERLOCK HOLMES SHORT STORIES is reprinted by permission of the Trustees of the Estate of Sir Arthur Conan Doyle and John Murray, the publishers.

CONTENTS

PREFACE

As the title suggests, all of the short stories in this collection have two features in common: they involve suspense and they arouse terror in the reader. Now, of course, every story or novel or play (or even something as short as a joke or an anecdote) involves suspense; if it did not, we would never become interested in hearing it through to the end. But the special effect that a so-called suspense story has on us is different. As we begin to read it, the impression starts to build in us that events out of the ordinary are about to take place, events that we want very much not to happen, yet events that we feel we must find out about. Thus we see that what many writers have said about suspense stories as "thrillers" and "chillers," implying that they appeal only to our emotions, is not entirely true. Actually, what they show is a victory of the mind over the emotions: our intellectual curiosity is stirred to such a degree that we have to keep reading, even though we realize perfectly well that what we read will terrify us. When Helen Stoner tells Sherlock Holmes of her life in the lonely house at Stoke Moran with her cruel and violent stepfather, Dr. Roylott, or when Judge Bermutier tells his guests about the hand which Sir John Rowell kept hanging in his drawing room, we feel the presence of terror, but continue in spite of it.

Two things are capable of arousing terror in almost all of us: first, the unfamiliar, especially if we cannot find a logical explanation for it, and, second, death. At this point some may object, saying that there are people who not only are not afraid of the unfamiliar, but who go out in search of it. True enough, yet the point that is different about stories of terror and suspense is that the unfamiliar comes upon a victim at a time and in a form in which he does not want it. Others may point out that not everybody is afraid of death either; some men face it with courage, some with resignation, some even with joy. That, too, is true when we are talking about the *fact* of dying, but not when we consider the *manner* of dying. Reading about the gruesome end of Elias Hutcheson in "The Squaw" or the shocking source of Alice Leiber's death in "The Small Assassin," we find it hard to hold back a shudder.

It almost goes without saying that fear is an emotion and so stories of terror and suspense appeal primarily to our emotions. As many authors have written, tales of this type offer us a sort of self-torture or self-punishment, but self-torture held within bounds by the knowledge that the horrifying events of the story are not happening to us, and probably never will happen to us. As a result, we torture ourselves while we are learning about these events, but after the story is over there remains for us a deep sense of relief—we have escaped them.

Since the emotional impact of these stories is so strong and so universal, they have always had, and continue to have wide popular appeal, along with the related types of the ghost story and the detective mystery. They are found in both Greek and Roman literature, in the Middle Ages, and in that seventeenth-century literature called baroque. But they did not really begin to flourish until about 1800 and it is only for the past hundred years or so that they have been recognized as a special class of literature.

Of the writers included in this collection, the earliest and one of the most important is E.T.A. Hoffmann (1776-1822), called "the German Poe"; his influence in establishing the tale of terror as a respectable type of story was very important in Europe. The French writer Prosper Mérimée (1803-1870) was fascinated all his life by the violence which is a part of primitive societies and especially of Corsica, as "Mateo Falcone" shows. The master of this type and one of America's artistic geniuses was Edgar Allan Poe (1809-1849); his book *Tales of the Grotesque and Arabesque* contains some of the great masterpieces of horror. Very little known in the United States is the Irish author J. Sheridan LeFanu (1814-1873), whose book *In a Glass Darkly* is a fine collection of stories that deal with the "borderlands of the mind." W. Wilkie Collins (1824-1899) is most famous for his two suspense novels, *The Woman in White* and *The Moonstone*, but "The Traveller's Story of a Terribly Strange Bed" is widely known, too, and has been recently dramatized on television. Bram Stoker (1847-1912) is remembered today as the author of *Dracula*, familiar to all American movie-goers; his specialty was the so-called Gothic story, with its trappings of eerie castles, vampire bats, black cats, and the like. Guy de Maupassant (1850-1893), generally considered France's greatest short story writer, turned only occasionally to tales of terror, but when he did he proved himself a master of them, too, as "The Hand" proves.

The best writer of detective stories up to the present time has been Sir Arthur Conan Doyle (1859-1930), the creator of Sherlock Holmes. Although "The Adventure of the Speckled Band" is really an adventure in detection, it is a horror story as well, considering the fiendish murder instrument. Rudyard Kipling (1865-1936) is notable as a Nobel Prize winner and author of many novels, stories and poems about India, including *The Jungle Books* and "Gunga Din." Marie Belloc Lowndes (1868-1947), although she began in other areas, turned to fictionalized versions of true crime cases and to mystery novels and attained her greatest success with "The Lodger." Hereward Carrington (1880-1958) was one of the twentieth century's leading authorities on psychic phenomena. Alexander Woollcott (1887-1943), drama critic and radio personality, did some of his best writing in the field of true mysteries. The successor to Jules Verne and H.G. Wells as a master of science fiction, Ray Bradbury (1920-   ) scored his first success with *Dark Carnival*, a book of unusual horror stories.

So much by way of introduction. Now to the tales of terror and suspense.

STEWART H. BENEDICT

MADEMOISELLE DE SCUDERI

BY E. T. A. HOFFMANN

(Translated and abridged by Walter E. Reichelt)

IN THE RUE ST. HONORE STOOD THE SMALL
house which Magdaleine de Scuderi, known for her charming verse, occupied through the favor of Louis XIV and the Marquise de Maintenon.[1]

Late, around midnight—in the fall of 1680—a loud and violent knocking at the door echoed through the hall. Baptiste, who in la Scuderi's small household acted as cook, servant, and doorkeeper, had gone to his sister's wedding in the country, and so it happened that only old Martiniere, the maid, was awake in the house. Hearing the continuous rapping, suddenly very much aware that she and Mademoiselle were in the house without protection, she remembered tremblingly the many recent thefts, burglaries, and killings. She remained in her chamber convinced a murderous gang was seeking admittance.

Meanwhile the blows kept thundering against the door and it seemed to her as if a voice were calling, "In Christ's name, open up!" Cursing Baptiste and his sister's wedding, filled with increasing fear, she grabbed a candleholder and ran into the hall; there she heard the voice clearly: "In Christ's name, open up!"

Surely, she decided, a robber doesn't speak like this. Perhaps someone was seeking refuge, someone aware of her lady's generosity. Trying to make her voice sound as masculine as possible, she opened a window to ask who it was raging at the door so late at night. In the shimmering of the moon's rays which were just breaking through the dark

[1] The second wife of Louis XIV.

clouds, she saw a tall figure, muffled in a grayish cloak, a broad-brimmed hat pushed down over his eyes. She called out loudly so that the person standing by the door could hear, "Baptiste, Claude, Pierre, get up and find out what good-for-nothing is down there."

A soft voice spoke gently, "Ah, Martiniere, I know it is you, dear woman, trying to disguise your voice. I know Baptiste has gone to the country to his sister's wedding. Don't be afraid to let me in. I must speak with Mademoiselle this very moment."

"What are you thinking of?" replied Martiniere. "Don't you know she has been fast asleep for some time? And that I wouldn't wake her from the sleep she needs so much at her age?"

"I know," countered the man in gray, "I know that your lady has just laid aside the manuscript of her romance *Clelia* and is still writing some verses which she means to read tomorrow in the chambers of the Marquise de Maintenon. I beg of you, Madame Martiniere, be merciful and open the door. It is a question of saving an unfortunate person from disaster. The honor, freedom, and even the very life of a man depend upon my speaking to your lady! Think of Mademoiselle's anger if she were to discover it was you who turned someone asking for help away from her gate."

"But why do you appeal for help at this hour of the night? Can't you come back tomorrow?"

"Does fate announce the hour when it strikes like deadly lightning? Can help be denied if it is of avail only at the instant? Open the door. Fear nothing from a miserable person, one who is defenseless, deserted, and hard pressed by a monstrous destiny."

Martiniere heard him sigh and moan. His voice was so youthful and gentle that she was deeply moved. Without further thought, she fetched the keys. As soon as she opened the door, the gray-clad figure pushed by her violently, calling out, "Take me to Mademoiselle!"

Startled, Martiniere lifted the candleholder high; the shimmering light fell on a deadly pale, horribly distorted, youthful face. She nearly fainted in fear when the man drew his cloak apart and revealed the shiny handle of a stiletto. His eyes flashed at her and he called more wildly than before, "Take me to Mademoiselle!"

Martiniere now sensed her lady to be in extreme danger. All her love for Mademoiselle flared up, giving her a courage she had never thought possible. Quickly shutting the door to her chamber, she said firmly, "Your violent behavior here inside the house does not agree with your mild words outside. I will not let you speak with Mademoiselle now. If you have no evil in mind, you shouldn't fear daylight. Come back tomorrow. As for now, get out of the house!"

A dull sigh escaped the muffled figure. He stared at Martiniere and reached for his stiletto. She silently commended her soul to God, but remained steadfast, pressing herself against the door through which the stranger had to pass to get to la Scuderi. Again he shouted, "Take me to Mademoiselle!"

"Do what you will. I shall not move from this spot. Carry out your intentions and you'll end up on the Place de Greve[1] along with your accomplices."

"Yes," he answered, "you're right. I am armed like a thief or a murderer, but my accomplices have not been condemned." Saying this, he drew out his stiletto.

"Jesus save me," she cried, expecting the blow. But at that moment the clanking of weapons, the hoofs of horses could be heard. The Marechausee[2] was outside. "Help! Help!"

"Woman, do you want my ruin? Take this and give it to Mademoiselle." Murmuring this, he seized the candleholder from Martiniere, put out the candles, and put a small casket into her hand.

Slowly she groped her way through the darkness to her room, where she sank exhausted into an armchair. She heard the rattling of the keys which she had left in the

---

[1] The site of executions in Paris.
[2] The armed police patrols of Paris.

door. The house was being locked. Then slow, uncertain steps neared her room. Fixed to the spot, she awaited the unknown; but when the door was opened she saw honest Baptiste by the light of the night lamp. He was pale and bewildered.

"By all that's sacred, Madame Martiniere, what has happened? I left the wedding because I had a premonition. And, as I was coming down the street a patrol suddenly bore down upon me. Fortunately Desgrais, the Marechausee lieutenant, was with them. He recognized me as soon as the lamp of an armed man shone upon my face and said, 'Why aren't you guarding your mistress' house? Things are risky out here. We're planning a good catch tonight.' You don't know how his words hit my heart. And then, as I stepped across the threshold, a muffled figure, bare dagger in hand, leaped by me and threw me aside. The house was open—the keys in the door. What does it mean?"

Relieved of her extreme anxiety, Martiniere told him everything that had taken place. Together they went into the hall; there lay the candleholder which the stranger had tossed aside while fleeing. "I think," said Baptiste, "we ought to throw the casket into the Seine, for how do we know that our lady on opening it will not die from some fiendish poison as did the old Marquis de Tournay when he opened a letter sent to him by an unknown person."

After a long discussion, these two loyal servants finally decided to tell Mademoiselle everything in the morning and to hand the casket over to her with all possible warnings. Their worries were well founded, for Paris at that time was the stage of the most horrible acts.

Glaser, a German apothecary, the best chemist of his time, had occupied himself with alchemical experiments in the search for the philosopher's stone. He was joined by Exili, an Italian, for whom the art of transmuting base metals into gold was only an excuse for learning the master's chemical secrets. He wanted to learn the art of mixing, boiling, and sublimating poisonous substances, and he did succeed in preparing a poison so subtle that it killed without leaving a trace or an odor. And no physician could tell that a person had not died of natural causes.

But even though he worked carefully Exili was eventually caught mixing poisons. In his cell was put Captain Godin de Sainte Croix, whose affair with the Marquise de Brinvillier had brought shame on her entire family. When her husband would not intervene, her father obtained the court order which separated the adulterous pair. The passionate, revengeful captain, capable of every vice, attached himself to the Italian. Soon the pupil equaled the master.

The Marquise de Brinvillier, a corrupt woman to begin with, was turned into a monster by Sainte Croix. He brought her to the point at which she poisoned not only her father but also her brothers and sister, the father as an act of revenge, the others for the rich inheritance. Poisoning eventually became a passion with her. The sudden death of several beggars to whom she had been accustomed to hand out bread finally centered suspicion on her, and Sainte Croix was killed one day when a glass mask he always wore when mixing poisons slipped. As he died without leaving an heir, the courts seized his belongings, thus finding his entire stock of deadly poisons.

Paris breathed more easily once the monster was gone. But soon it became evident that the terrifying art of Sainte Croix had been passed on. Like an insidious spirit of evil, murder slipped into the most intimate circles and swiftly carried away its victims. He who was in the best of health one day tottered to his deathbed the next, and no physician's skill could save him.

Wealth, a desirable position, a too youthful wife were enough to incite murder. Distrust severed the most sacred ties. The husband trembled before his wife, the father before his son, the sister before her brother. Meats remained untouched, wines untasted. In vain did fathers go far into the country to buy food and prepare it themselves.

To control these secret crimes, the king named a special court to investigate and to hand out punishment. This court, named the Chambre Ardente, met in the Bastille with Regnie as its president. His zealous efforts were long to remain fruitless. It remained for Desgrais, the Marechausee lieutenant, to discover the secret hideout of the poisoners.

He ferreted out an old woman, la Voison, in the suburb of St. Germain, who told fortunes and called up spirits. Like Sainte Croix, Exili's pupil, she had mixed the poisons which helped sons to inheritances, degenerate wives to younger husbands. Desgrais dug into her secrets. She confessed everything and the Chambre Ardente ordered her to the Place de Greve.

A list found on her caused many others, some of them in high positions, to become suspect. Even François Henri de Montmorenci, Boudebelle, Duke of Luxembourg, Peer and Marshal of France, did not remain untouched. The dreadful Chambre Ardente had him locked up in the Bastille, where Regnie's hatred caused him to be thrown into a six-foot hole. Months passed before it was discovered that the Marshal's name had been on la Voison's list only because she had once cast his horoscope.

Regnie's blind zeal led to arbitrary acts and to cruelties. The tribunal took on the air of the Inquisition. The most trifling suspicion led to the closest confinement, and it was often only a matter of chance that saved an innocent victim from execution. Moreover, Regnie's repulsive appearance and malicious nature soon brought upon him the hatred of those he was supposed to protect. The Duchess of Bouillon, whom he asked during an interrogation whether she had ever seen the devil, replied, "I see him now."

While on the Place de Greve the blood of both guilty and innocent flowed and secret poisonings became rarer and rarer, a calamity of another nature was spreading new consternation. A band of criminals seemed intent on seizing all jewels. Precious pieces disappeared in unexplained fashion immediately after their purchase. Those who dared to carry jewels with them late at night were either robbed or killed on the streets. Those who escaped with their lives said a blow on the head had knocked them unconscious before they were robbed. Those who were found dead all had similar stab wounds in the heart.

What cavalier at the wealthy court of Louis XIV was not involved in a secret love affair? As if the bandits were in league with evil spirits, they knew exactly when a courtier was to visit his mistress furtively at night. Often the unfortunate victim was caught on the very doorsteps of his love.

In vain were suspects arrested. In vain did Regnie try to force confessions. In vain were guards and patrols strengthened. The criminals could not be traced. Only the practice of going armed and preceded by torchbearers seemed to be of any help. Even then servants were often scared away by rocks while at the same time the masters were murdered.

Desgrais foamed with rage. Whenever he appeared in one section of Paris, a murder took place in another. Infuriating too was his inability to locate the stolen jewels at any of the customary spots. He even used the trick of having many Desgraises walk the streets of Paris, agents who imitated his dress, his walk, his speech, so that not even the police knew where he was at any given moment.

One morning Desgrais came to President Regnie pale and excited. "What news? Did you find any trace of the criminals?"

"Sir," began Desgrais, stammering angrily, "sir, last night near the Louvre the Marquis de la Faie was attacked in my presence."

"Great Heaven," rejoined Regnie. "We've got them!"

"Listen," Desgrais interrupted, "just listen to what happened. I'm standing at the Louvre watching for the devils who are taunting me. Suddenly I recognize the Marquis de la Faie sneaking by in the moonlight. He is scarcely twelve steps past me when a figure appears from nowhere, throws him down, and falls upon him. Without thinking, I cry out and jump at the murderer. I trip on my cloak. I jump up and follow, blowing my horn. From the distance I hear the whistles and shouts of my men. 'Here,' I cry, 'here, Desgrais, Desgrais!' My quarry suddenly turns into the Rue Nicaise; his strength seems to be failing. I increase my pace. He seems scarcely fifteen steps ahead of me."

"And you seized him. Your men surrounded him." Regnie

grabbed Desgrais as if he were the fleeing killer.

"Fifteen steps," continued Desgrais dully, "fifteen steps ahead of me, the figure leaps into the shadow of a wall and disappears through it."

"Through the wall? Are you mad?"

"Call me mad, say that I am seeing things. But it is just as I'm telling you. I stood staring at the wall when my men came rushing on the scene. We tapped along its length, back and forth. There was no trace of a door, a window, or any opening. It is a sturdy stone wall surrounding the yard of a house in which live people beyond the slightest suspicion."

Desgrais' story became known in Paris. Heads were filled with tales of black magic, pacts with the devil, and the raising of spirits. Superstition conquered reason. The devil was soon believed to be protecting evildoers. The people were intimidated and the police officers themselves walked the streets in fear, wearing amulets to ward off the devil.

The efforts of the Chambre Ardente were useless. Louis XIV was asked to name a new court with expanded powers to search out the killers and punish them. The king, convinced he had already given too much power to the Chambre Ardente, shaken by the many executions carried out by the bloodthirsty Regnie, rejected the suggestion. However, in an attempt to convince him of the need for a new court of inquiry and punishment, he was handed a long poem while he was working with his ministers in the chambers of the Marquise de Maintenon, according to his custom. The verses lamented the fate of the lovers who risked their lives whenever they ventured on journeys of gallantry bearing rich gifts to their loves. It was honorable, claimed the poem, to risk one's life in a chivalric encounter for the sake of love, but it was not honorable to be slain by thieves at night. Louis, the polestar of love and gallantry, was called upon to radiate the light which would destroy the terror of the dark, the monster who was turning sweetest love into deepest tragedy.

The poem, witty in its description of the lover's nightly journey to his beloved, and its praises of the king, was read with pleasure by Louis. He turned to the Marquise, asking her what measures should be taken to protect the lovers of Paris. But she, true to herself, answered piously that secret lovers ought not to be protected. Not satisfied, the king next turned to Mademoiselle de Scuderi, who was sitting in an armchair close by, and said to her, "The Marquise does not want to hear of the gallantries of our noble lovers. But you, mademoiselle, what do you think of this poetic request?"

She rose deferentially from her seat; a touch of red came upon her cheeks as she replied softly,

> *"Un amant qui craint des voleurs*
> *n'est point digne d'amour."*

Surprised by the courtly spirit of these few words which so thoroughly refuted the mile-long tirades of the poem, the king called out, "By St. Denis, you are right, mademoiselle. No blind measures will be taken which might strike innocent and guilty alike."

It was during the following night that the strange intruder appeared at the house of la Scuderi. In the morning Martiniere described the incidents of the night in lively tones to her mistress and handed her the casket. Baptiste and she stood by fearfully as Mademoiselle weighed the box in her hand. "You two are seeing ghosts. These murderers know I'm not rich. I have no treasures to make murder profitable. And who could possibly be seeking the death of a seventy-three-year-old woman who has never persecuted anybody except the villains in the stories she writes? No matter in what frightful language you describe the intruder, I can't believe he meant to harm me. Therefore!"

Martiniere jumped back three steps, Baptiste nearly fell to his knees as she pressed a tiny metal button and the lid of the case flew open noisily.

How astonished she was to see two golden, jewel-encrusted armbands and a superb necklace sparkling in the sunlight. Eying these pieces with awe, Martiniere exclaimed that not even the Marquise de Montespan possessed such adornments.

"What does this mean?" asked la Scuderi. Just then she saw a small piece of paper which lay folded at the bottom of the casket. She had scarcely finished reading the note when she sank back into her chair. Tears came to her eyes. "What have I done to be insulted in this manner at my age? Oh, God! Are the words which I uttered in such a light-hearted way capable of being interpreted so dreadfully?"

Martiniere picked up the slip of paper and read,

> *Un amant qui craint des voleurs*
> *n'est point digne d'amour.*

Your subtle mind, most gracious lady, has saved from persecution those of us who exercise the right of the strong upon the weak and who take treasures which were to be wasted frivolously. As evidence of our thankfulness accept this trifling gift of jewelry. It is the best we could collect at the moment, even though much more worthy gems should be showered on you. We beg that you will not deny us your continued friendship.

The Invisible Ones

Horrified by the precious stones, to which the blood of the victims still seemed to cling, Mademoiselle de Scuderi walked silently back and forth in her chamber. Finally she ordered Baptiste to fetch a sedan chair, for she had decided to take the jewel case to the Marquise de Maintenon.

Having heard the story, the Marquise asked to see the jewels. After admiring even the smallest golden link, she said, "Do you know, Mademoiselle, that no one but Rene Cardillac could have made these pieces?"

Rene Cardillac was at that time the most skillful goldsmith in Paris and one of the oddest persons of the age. Although short, he was nonetheless broad-shouldered and muscular. Despite his advanced age, he had the strength and flexibility of youth. If he had not been known throughout the city as a man of honor who was completely unselfish, his strange, greenish, deep-set eyes would have given rise to the suspicion of deceit and secret malice. He knew how to set precious stones so that every piece of jewelry, no matter how insignificant it had seemed beforehand, was a precious masterpiece once it left his workshop. He accepted every assignment with a burning desire and set prices so low that they were not consonant with the quality of his work. Having accepted a task, he worked night and day, hammering away in his workshop. But as soon as a job was completed, he found it impossible to part from the piece and kept putting off the person who had given him the order. When he was at last forced into handing the jewel over, he could scarcely hide his rage at having to do so.

Yet as soon as somebody ran after him shouting, "Master Rene, would you like to make a bracelet for my sweetheart?" or "Please take these inexpensive stones and set them into a necklace for my bride!" Cardillac would stop with sparkling eyes and almost tear the stones away. Rushing happily to his goldsmithy, he would hammer out a masterpiece, working long hours. But as soon as the customer appeared, Cardillac turned surly again.

"Master Cardillac, tomorrow is my wedding day."

"What's your wedding day to me? Come back in two weeks."

"I can see it's finished. Here's your money. Let me have it."

"And I say improvements must be made. I can't give it to you."

"If you don't hand it over I'll go get some men from the Marechausee."

"The devil take you and your bride. May the necklace strangle her!" Saying this, Cardillac might shove the case into the hands of the patron and then throw him downstairs.

There were times when the goldsmith begged individuals to take back their orders. On one occasion he threw himself at the feet of the king and begged as a special favor from Louis that he not require him to perform any more work. He also refused to accept any assignment from the Marquise de Maintenon.

That is why the Marquise now said, "If I send for Cardillac he'll refuse to come because he'll think that I want to have him work for me."

Mademoiselle, who earnestly wanted to have the jewels returned to their rightful owner, replied, "Why not tell him we only want his evaluation of some jewelry?"

A short time later the goldsmith entered the chamber. He seemed embarrassed when he saw la Scuderi, and, like one who has met the unexpected, he bowed to her before turning to the Marquise, who asked him whether the jewels in the case were his workmanship.

"Indeed, Madame Marquise, one can't know Cardillac's work without realizing immediately that no other goldsmith could have produced these."

"For whom," asked the Marquise, "did you make these?"

"Only for myself. You may think it strange, but it is so. Just for the sake of the work, I picked out my best gems and created these pieces. They disappeared from my shop a short time ago."

"Heaven be praised," cried la Scuderi as she jumped from her chair with the sparkling eyes of a young girl. "Master Rene, take back the treasure which was stolen from you."

But Cardillac rubbed his chin, sighed, took the casket, and then sank to his knees before la Scuderi. "Fate, gracious lady, has destined these to be yours. I remember now that I thought of you while I was working on them. Don't scorn the best that I have produced in a long time. Take them and wear them."

"Come now, Master Rene, if I were young and beautiful, these jewels might be suitable for me. But what am I to do with them on my faded arms?"

"Mademoiselle, accept the jewels. You little realize how I venerate your virtues. Please take them."

The Marquise took the case from Cardillac's hand. "By heaven, Mademoiselle, you're always talking about your advanced years. What have we to do with old age? Take these like some young girl who would love to have the sweet fruit if only someone were to put it into her hand."

During this speech Cardillac kissed the hem of la Scuderi's dress and then ran out of the room knocking down chairs and tables.

Maintenon laughed. "There we are. The goldsmith is in love with you and is paying court by giving you rich treasures according to the ancient custom of chivalry."

The two expanded upon the joke of the goldsmith's being in love, but when Mademoiselle finally left she said, "Madame Marquise, I can't wear these jewels. I am horrified by the thought that they were in the bloody hands of criminals. There is even something mysterious about Cardillac's behavior. I can't help feeling there is a terrible secret back of all this; and yet, when I review all the circumstances, I can't possibly imagine what the secret is nor how Cardillac, the very picture of an honest and decent citizen, could be involved in any evil."

Several months went by when by chance one day la Scuderi happened to be riding across the Pont-Neuf in the glass carriage of the Duchess de Montsanier. At this time the glass coach was still a fairly recent invention so that when one appeared on the street the curious pressed about it. Thus it happened that la Scuderi's carriage was stopped on the bridge by a large crowd. She suddenly heard loud cries and curses and saw a young man forcing his way through the press using fists and elbows. As he came closer she found herself fixed by a penetrating glance from a deadly pale youthful face that seemed afflicted by some deep-set grief. His glance remaining on her, he fought his way through to her side, opened the door, threw a letter on her lap, and, dealing out blows, retreated into the crowd.

Martiniere, who was in the carriage with her mistress, fainted with a cry of horror on seeing this young man. In vain did la Scuderi pull the cord to the coachman. He, like a madman, whipped his horses, which reared, then plunged forward, foam squirting from their jaws. La Scuderi poured the contents of her smelling bottle over her unconscious companion, who finally opened her eyes. Nervously clutching her mistress, fear and horror apparent in her face, she moaned, "By the Blessed Virgin, what did that terrible per-

son want? He is the one who brought you the casket of
jewels on that terrible night!"

Her mistress calmed her, pointing out that nothing terrible had happened; only a note had been thrown. She now
opened the folded sheet and read.

A terrible fate weighs me down and only you can ward it
off. I implore you, like a son to his loving mother, to return to Master Cardillac the necklace and the armbands
you received from me. Your welfare, your very life depend upon it. If you do not do so by the day after tomorrow, I shall force myself into your chamber and kill myself there before your eyes.

Mademoiselle de Scuderi was certain now that the mysterious stranger planned nothing against her even though
he may have been a member of the criminal gang. "If only,"
she told her maid, "he had seen me on that night, what
obscure relationships might have been clarified for me. But
no matter what the facts of the case are, I shall do what is
asked of me in this note, even if it is only to rid myself of
those infernal symbols of evil. Once he has the jewels securely in his hands, Cardillac will hardly let go of them
again."

She wanted to return the jewels on the following day.
Yet it seemed as if all the literary figures of Paris had cho-
sen that very morning to besiege her with verses, anecdotes,
plays. Noon came. Mademoiselle then had to wait upon the
Duchess de Montsanier, and so the visit to Master Cardillac
was delayed.

She felt herself tortured by unrest. The youth kept ap-
pearing before her, and a memory out of the past tried to
emerge. Her slightest slumber that night was disturbed by
agonizing dreams. As soon as day came, she had herself
dressed and driven to the goldsmith's.

On the Rue Nicaise where Cardillac lived, a large crowd
was attempting to storm his house. Only the efforts of the
police kept them away. From the crowd came shouts of
"Tear the murderer apart!" Finally Desgrais arrived with a

large armed detachment which cleared a path through the
raging throng. The door of the house was pushed open. A
man in chains was brought out and carried away amid the
terrible curses of the mob.

At the moment that Magdaleine de Scuderi came upon
the scene, a loud scream reached her ears. "Drive up," she
called to the coachman, who with skillful handling of his
reins scattered the crowd, allowing the carriage to stop in
front of Cardillac's house. There she saw a beautiful girl
clutching the knees of Desgrais and crying out, "He is innocent! He is innocent!" In vain were the attempts by Desgrais
to tear himself loose, to get her up from the ground. Suddenly a strong, bulky fellow seized her arms, dragged her
away from the police lieutenant, stumbled with her, and
dropped her down several stone steps at the bottom of
which she remained lying silent—seemingly dead.

La Scuderi could contain herself no longer. She opened
the carriage door and alighted. Respectfully the crowd
made way for the venerable lady. Seeing a few women lift
the girl and rub her forehead with a restorative, she
stopped before Desgrais to ask, "In the name of Christ,
what is going on here?"

"A terrible thing has happened," answered the lieutenant. "Master Cardillac was found murdered this morning.
His apprentice Olivier Brusson is the murderer. He has just
been taken away to jail."

"And who is the girl?"

"She is Madelon, Cardillac's daughter. The infamous
youth was her lover. Now she screams and sobs that he is
innocent. In the end she may turn out to have been his accomplice and like him will have to be taken off to prison."
As Desgrais said this, he threw Madelon a maliciously gloating glance before which Mademoiselle de Scuderi shivered.
Just then the girl began to breathe again but without making a sound or moving. No one knew what to do with her.
La Scuderi, deeply touched and with tears in her eyes,
looked at the innocent angel; she was struck with horror by
the lieutenant and his rough assistants. Quickly deciding,
she called out, "I'll take the girl with me."

A murmur of approval ran through the crowd. The women lifted the girl into the carriage, with everyone pushing forward to help. Blessings came from all lips for the kind lady who was saving an innocent girl from Desgrais' bloody vengeance. Back home, la Scuderi called in Seron, the most famous physician of Paris, who brought the girl back to consciousness.

After several hours in the presence of Mademoiselle de Scuderi, Madelon found herself able to recount what had happened. At midnight she had been awakened by a soft tapping on her door and had heard Olivier's voice begging her to get up, for her father was dying. Terrified she jumped up and opened the door. A pale Olivier, sweat dripping from his face, lighted her way to the workshop. Her father lay there with dull eyes, gasping in the throes of death. Throwing herself upon her father, she noticed for the first time his bloody shirt. Olivier gently drew her away and tried to clean a wound on the left side of her father's chest. In the meantime Cardillac's consciousness returned. He took her hand and placed it in Olivier's, pressing both. They fell on their knees before him. He arose partially but sank down again and died with a sigh. They now lamented loudly. Olivier told her how the master had been murdered during an errand that night and how he had strained himself to carry the heavy man back home. As soon as day broke, the other occupants of the house, who had heard the disturbance during the night, came up and found them kneeling by the side of her father. There was a cry of alarm. The police arrived and Olivier was immediately dragged away as the murderer.

Madelon added to her story a touching account of Olivier's piety and loyalty. He had venerated the master, who had returned his love, selecting him above all others to be her future husband despite his poverty, because his skills were as great as his nobility of heart.

La Scuderi, who had been deeply moved by this, found Madelon's statements about Olivier confirmed by the neighbors. They were unanimous in praising the moral, pious, loyal, and industrious behavior of the young man. No one knew anything evil about him. Yet when the conversation turned to the bloody murder, they shrugged their shoulders and muttered that there was something mysterious behind it.

Olivier, placed before the Chambre Ardente, steadfastly denied any guilt and insisted that his master had been attacked in the streets and that he had carried him home still alive, where he died shortly afterward. All this agreed with what Madelon had told Mademoiselle.

Again and again la Scuderi went over even the most insignificant details of the terrible event. She inquired whether there had ever been any trouble between master and apprentice, whether Olivier was not completely free of sudden fits of anger which at times befall even the most good-natured individuals, leading them to sudden deeds of violence. Yet the more Madelon spoke of the quiet household in which lived three people united by love, the more did any shadow of doubt about Olivier vanish from her mind. Weighing all the evidence, disregarding whatever might incline her favorably toward Olivier, she could find no motive for Cardillac's murder on his part. He is poor but capable. He succeeds in winning the favor of his famous master; he loves the daughter; the master favors his love; happiness and wealth lie before him. Of what fiendish hypocrisy would he have to be capable to kill his master and then to act the way he did after the murder? La Scuderi became firmly convinced of his innocence and decided to save him from the Place de Greve.

It seemed best for her to go to President Regnie before turning to the king himself. Regnie received her with great respect. He listened quietly to everything she could advance in support of Olivier. A slight, malicious smile indicated that he was at least paying attention to her plea that a judge must not necessarily be an enemy of the accused but ought also to listen to whatever favors him. When la Scuderi was finally drying her tears, Regnie began his answer: "It is commendable for your honorable heart that you believe everything a young girl in love tells you, and that you are not capable of thinking such a vile deed possible, but it is otherwise with a judge who is accustomed to tearing the mask of hypocrisy from criminals. Mademoiselle, I do my duty, caring little for the opinion of the world. Let evildoers tremble before the Chambre Ardente, which knows no punishment except that of blood and fire. But, dear lady, I do not want you to look upon me as a monster of cruelty. Therefore, let me convince you in a few words of the guilt of this young criminal. Your perceptive mind will then surely reject a leniency which does you honor but which would not become me at all.

"Now, then, in the morning Master Cardillac is found murdered by a dagger thrust. No one is with him but his apprentice Olivier Brusson and the daughter. A blood-covered dagger which fits the wound is found in Olivier's room. 'Cardillac,' says the apprentice, 'was killed in my presence on the street.'

" 'You went with him and yet you couldn't defend him against the murderer or hold him or call for help?'

" 'The master walked fifteen to twenty paces ahead of me.'

" 'Why so far ahead of you?'

" 'That's the way he wanted it.'

" 'What business did the master have on the street so late at night?'

" 'I don't know.'

" 'But didn't he rarely leave the house after nine?'

"At this point Olivier looked down, sighed, cried, and swore that Cardillac had really gone out that night. Yet, Mademoiselle, it has been proved that Cardillac never left the house on the night in question. The door of his house is provided with a heavy lock that makes a piercing noise when opened or closed. Moreover, the hinges of his door creak so loudly they can be heard on the top floor, as we have found out. On the ground floor, right next to the door, lives old Master Claude Patru with his aged housekeeper, quite a spry woman despite her eighty years. These two heard how, according to his nightly custom, Cardillac came down exactly at nine o'clock and barred the door, making a great deal of noise, went back up the stairs, read the evening paper, and then retired to his bedroom.

"Master Claude, like so many people of his age, suffers from sleeplessness. His housekeeper, therefore, lit a candle in the kitchen, where the two sat in silence for several hours. At some time after midnight they heard distinct steps, a fall, and shortly afterward moans."

"But," interrupted la Scuderi, "can you, by all that's holy, tell me why Olivier should have committed the crime?"

"Well, Cardillac wasn't poor. He owned some valuable gems."

"Wouldn't all his wealth have gone to his daughter and wasn't she about to become Olivier's wife?"

"Perhaps he had to kill for others."

"Others? What others?" asked la Scuderi surprised.

"You must know," replied President Regnie, "that Olivier would long ago have been executed on the Place de Greve, if his crime were not connected to that mysterious band which has carried out its crimes despite all investigations and courts. Cardillac's wound is similar to that suffered by those murdered in the streets. Most decisive for me is that since Olivier's arrest all murders have ceased. The streets have become as safe during the night as during the day, evidence enough that he headed the band. He may not have talked yet, but we have ways to make him speak."

"And what of Madelon," cried la Scuderi, "that innocent dove?"

"Well," said Regnie, with a deadly smile, "who'll guarantee she wasn't a partner in the plot against her father? Her tears are only for the murderer. I may soon be forced to drag her from your protective arms."

"Be humane," was all Mademoiselle could reply. While the president of the Chambre was conducting her to the staircase, a strange thought came to her. "Might I see Olivier Brusson?"

"Certainly, my dear lady. If you are not afraid to enter the gloomy abode of crime, if you do not hesitate to see all

stages of corruption, you will find the doors of the Conciergerie[1] open to you in two hours."

Having arrived at the Conciergerie, she entered a large,
bright room. Not long afterward she heard a rattling of
chains. Olivier Brusson was being brought to her. But as
soon as she saw him she fainted and when she awoke he
was gone. She demanded to be taken to her carriage immediately. At first glance she had recognized Olivier Brusson to be the young man who on the Pont-Neuf had thrown
the note into her carriage and who had brought the jewels
to her. Now all doubt was gone. He must belong to that
terrible gang of killers. He had certainly slain Cardillac.
And Madelon? Mademoiselle felt herself deceived by all
those forces of Hell that she had never believed in. She began to doubt all truth. She even entertained the horrible
suspicion that Madelon had been part of the plot. Many details which seemed proof of Olivier's innocence now seemed
redolent of evil, studied hypocrisy. She decided to remove
this vicious adder from her bosom.

Yet when she entered her chamber, Madelon fell at her
feet, looking at her with the divine eyes of an angel. La
Scuderi composed herself as much as possible. "Go, go take
comfort in the murderer whose deed will find its just punishment. May the Virgin Mary prevent any guilt from lighting
on you." Leaving the care of the girl to Martiniere, she retired to another room.

She heard Martiniere take Madelon away. Disjointed
cries came to her—"Unhappy Olivier"—"She too has been
beguiled." The cries went straight to Mademoiselle's heart
and again she sensed a secret and felt Olivier to be innocent. She wondered in despair, "What demon of Hell has
involved me in this affair which may cost me my life?"

At that very moment, a pale and frightened Baptiste entered with news of Desgrais' presence outside the door.
Since la Voison's trial, Desgrais' appearance at a house
foreshadowed a formal accusation. La Scuderi smiled at
Baptiste, "My name was on la Voison's list?"

[1] The pretrial prison in Paris.

"For heaven's sake," replied Baptiste, "how can you possibly say that? But Desgrais, a terrifying Desgrais, is outside acting mysteriously."

"Go and get the man who seems to be worrying you so much."

"The president," said Desgrais as soon as he entered, "sends me to you with a request which he would not make unless he were sure of your virtue and your courage. Olivier Brusson, who seemed so near a confession, has been almost violent after having seen you. He swears he is innocent of the murder even if he deserves to die. We can get nothing else out of him. Even threats of torture have remained fruitless. He begs us to grant him an interview with you and swears he will confess everything to you. Please, dear lady, say that you will hear Olivier Brusson's confession."

"What," la Scuderi cried, "am I to be a tool of the secret court? Am I to betray the confidence of an unfortunate being? Am I to send him to the Place de Greve? No, Desgrais!"

"Perhaps," answered Desgrais with a slight smile, "you will change your mind after you have heard Brusson. Didn't you yourself ask the president to be humane? He is being so in agreeing to Brusson's request before he orders him tortured. Now, Mademoiselle, we don't expect you to enter the dismal cells of the Conciergerie. Brusson will be brought to you at night as a free person, even though well guarded. No one will listen to anything he may have to say to you. I'll pledge my life that he plans nothing against you. And then it will be up to you to tell us as much as you want of what he has confessed to you."

La Scuderi decided to obey the higher power which seemed to demand that she uncover the terrible mystery. That night there was a knock at the door. She shivered when she heard the steps and the muted mutterings of the guards bringing Brusson to her. Finally her door opened. Desgrais entered and with him Olivier Brusson, freed of his chains and decently dressed. "Here is Brusson," Desgrais said, bowed, and left the room.

Brusson sank down on his knees before her. The longer she looked at him, the clearer did memories of a beloved person arise in her. All fear left her. Forgetting that Cardillac's murderer knelt before her, she addressed him quietly and with sympathy in her voice: "Now, Brusson, what do you have to tell me?"

"Oh, my dear lady, have all memories of me escaped you? Have you entirely forgotten Anne Guiot? It is her son, the boy whom you often took on your lap to fondle and feed with sweets, who is kneeling before you."

La Scuderi sank back in her armchair. Anne Guiot, the daughter of an impoverished citizen, had been reared by her from early childhood as if she had been her own child. When she was grown up, a decent young man, a watchmaker, gained her love. A boy, the image of his mother, was born to the couple. La Scuderi made a little idol of the tiny boy, who grew to look upon her as a second mother. After three years Brusson took his family back to his native Geneva. Anne wrote a few letters to her foster mother, but then remained silent. That had been twenty-three years ago.

"How horrible! How horrible! Are you Olivier, Anne's son?"

"Yes, Mademoiselle, you could never have foreseen that the little boy whom you held on your lap would as a grown youth stand before you accused of murder. I am not beyond reproach. The Chambre Ardente can justly accuse me of a crime, but, as I hope to gain eternal salvation, Cardillac did not die by my hand." Saying this, Olivier began to tremble. La Scuderi pointed to a small chair next to her. He sat down slowly.

"Listen quietly and I shall uncover for you a secret you will not have suspected, which will surprise you and fill you with horror. As far back as I can remember we lived in misery at home. Father was disappointed in all his hopes. He died shortly after obtaining an apprenticeship with a goldsmith for me. Mother often talked about you and about writing you, but overcome by misery and a false shame, she kept from writing. A few months later she followed father to the grave."

"Poor Anne," la Scuderi exclaimed, overcome with anguish.

"Thank God," Olivier cried loudly, "she isn't here to see her son so close to the hangman, branded with shame."

There were noises in the hallway. The guards were stirring.

"My master kept me very short even though I soon surpassed him at his work. One day a stranger came to buy some jewelry. When he saw a necklace I had made he praised me and said that there was only one man, Rene Cardillac, who could do better work. 'Go to him. He'll take you into his workshop. Only you can help him and only he can teach you.' I went to Paris. Rene Cardillac received me coldly, brusquely. I kept after him to give me a job to do, no matter how small. He finally gave me a ring to make and when I finished it he hired me. I was with him several weeks before first seeing Madelon who had been in the country.

"She often came into the workshop. I noticed her love for me with pleasure. No matter how closely her father watched us, many a quick touch of hands gave evidence of our silent vows. Cardillac seemed to notice nothing. I thought of gaining his favor, becoming a master craftsman, and then asking him for the hand of his daughter. One morning as I was about to begin work Cardillac came to me with anger in his eyes. 'I don't need you anymore,' he began. 'Get out of the house within the hour. The fruit for which you are reaching is beyond your grasp.' I wanted to reply, but he seized me and threw me out the door. Aroused, pained by a bloody bruise, I walked the streets of Paris, finally finding refuge with a friend in the suburbs.

"I found no peace. At night I sneaked around Cardillac's house looking up at Madelon's window. A high wall with niches containing decaying stone figures surrounds the home. I was standing close to such a figure one night and looking up at the windows facing the wall when suddenly I noticed a light in the workshop. It was midnight. Never before had Cardillac been up at this hour. He was accustomed to retire at nine. Suddenly the light vanished. I pressed myself against the stone figure but jumped back terrified when I felt a counterpressure as if the figure had come alive. In the dimness I could barely see the statue move slowly. A dark figure stepped out from behind it and into the street. I jumped back to the wall and saw that the stone figure had been pushed back into its spot. An inner compulsion drove me to follow the person who had slipped out. Just as he passed an image of the Virgin Mary, he turned his head. By the light of a lamp I recognized Cardillac. I followed the sleepwalker, for so I thought him even though there was no full moon.

"At last he disappeared into a shadow. But I located him in a doorway through a familiar clearing of his throat. I hugged the wall of a house wondering what he would do. In a short while a plumed and spurred nobleman came whistling down the street. Like a tiger Cardillac leaped from his hiding place upon the man who instantaneously sank fatally wounded to the ground. I jumped forward with a cry of horror. 'Damn you,' roared Cardillac, running past me with lightning speed and vanishing. Beyond myself, I approached the man lying on the ground. There was no trace of life in him. In my horror I did not notice the Marechausee surrounding me.

"Someone cried, 'Another person killed by the gang.' They seized me but when a lamp was pushed before my face one of them exclaimed, 'I know him. He is Olivier Brusson, the apprentice who works for honest Master Cardillac. He's just the man to kill in the street and then remain standing next to the corpse lamenting! Tell us what happened, Brusson.'

"'Close in front of me,' I said, 'someone jumped on the man, pushed him down, and ran away when I called out. I wanted to see if he was still alive.'

"'No, my lad,' he answered, 'he's had it through the heart.'

"'The devil,' said another, 'we're too late again.' And with that they carried the body away.

"I felt as if in a nightmare, as if I would have to awaken

at any moment. Cardillac, Madelon's father, a murderer! I
sank down on the steps of a nearby house. By the light of
the dawn I saw a bright plume lying before me. Horrified at
this mute witness of Cardillac's crime, I ran away.

"Completely confused, I returned to my attic room. Suddenly the door opened and Rene Cardillac entered. 'In the
name of Christ,' I shouted, 'what do you want of me?'

"Smiling, he approached, moved an old stool next to me
and sat down. 'Now, Olivier,' he began, 'how are you, poor
boy? I was much too hasty in throwing you out of the house.
Even now I am working on a piece of jewelry that can't be
finished without your help. Come back to work for me. You
don't answer? I know I've insulted you. I won't conceal my
anger at your flirtation with Madelon. But I've thought
about it and find that, with your talent, your industry, your
loyalty, I couldn't possibly find a better son-in-law for myself. Come back with me and win Madelon's hand.'

"Cardillac's words cut through my heart, his maliciousness
horrified me. I couldn't speak a single word. 'You are hesitating. You have other things in mind. You intend to look up
Desgrais or even Regnie. Be careful, my boy, that the claws
you want turned against others don't destroy you instead.'

"Then he changed his tone again. 'You are actually being honored in working for me, the leading master of the
time, known and respected everywhere for his honesty. As
far as Madelon is concerned, you owe my acquiescence
solely to her. She loves you with a passion I would not have
suspected in such a delicate child. No sooner were you gone
than she threw herself at my feet and claimed she couldn't
live without you. At first, I thought she was only imagining
it as all silly young girls do when the first pale youth smiles
at them. But Madelon became ill. What could I do? Last
night I promised to bring you back today. She got well
overnight and is waiting for you now.'

"May the eternal powers of heaven forgive me. I don't
know how it happened. Suddenly I was back in Cardillac's
house, Madelon in my arms."

La Scuderi, horrified by the criminal act of a man she
had considered virtue itself, called out, "How horrible! Car-

dillac belonged to a gang of murderers."

"You say 'gang,' Mademoiselle? There never was any gang. It was Cardillac alone. Let me go on. You can well imagine the position I now found myself in. The step had been taken. I could no longer draw back. At times I felt I had become Cardillac's accomplice. Only in Madelon's love was I able to forget my anguish. Whenever I worked with her father, I could not look him in the face, I could hardly speak a word to him. Madelon doted on him. My heart ached at the thought that the day Cardillac's crimes were revealed would be her last. That by itself caused me to be silent.

"I knew the murderer; I did not know his motive. I was soon to find out. One day Cardillac, who usually was in a good mood while working, threw down a necklace and said, 'Things can't remain the same between us. What the wisdom of Desgrais could not uncover, you have found out by chance. You have seen me at my star-fated nightly labor. Your own evil star caused you to follow me and veiled you in a cloak of invisibility so that I, who can see like a tiger at night, who can hear a gnat in the distance, was not able to see or hear you. Your evil star has made you my companion. You can betray me no more. Therefore I'll tell you my story.

" 'Wise men speak of the strange impressions a pregnant woman is capable of receiving and the profound effect these may have upon her child. I was told a strange story about my mother. During the first months of her pregnancy she was in the company of some other women watching a court festival at the Trianon. Her glance fell upon a cavalier in Spanish costume who wore a magnificent chain around his neck. Her whole being yearned for those sparkling gems. This same courtier had tested my mother's virtue a few years before her marriage. My mother recognized him, but it seemed as if the bright diamonds were the epitome of all beauty. The gentleman noticed her glances and thought he might succeed where before he had not. He approached her and managed to lure her to an isolated spot where he held her in a tight embrace. Whether a sudden stroke hit him or not, I can't say, but he died at that moment and my mother wasn't released until her shrill screams for help were heard by some distant passersby.

" 'Horror brought my mother sick to her bed. She and I were given up for lost. However, she recovered and had a successful delivery. But the terror of that awful moment had affected me. My evil star had risen and shed the baleful light which was to ignite a strange and fatal passion within me. Even in the earliest days of childhood, I was fascinated by gleaming objects, golden chains. It was believed to be a childish preoccupation, but it proved to be otherwise, for even as a boy I used to steal gold and jewels whenever I could put my hands on them. Like the most experienced expert I could distinguish between the real and the imitation. The most dreadful punishments inflicted by my father could not subdue this passion. Finally I became a goldsmith only to be able to handle gold and jewelry. Working passionately, I soon became the foremost master craftsman. Now began a period during which the inborn desire, so long suppressed, burst free. As soon as I completed a piece of jewelry and delivered it, I became miserable. I was robbed of my sleep, health, and the will to live. By day and night the figure of the person to whom I had delivered the gems stood like a ghost before me, adorned by my work, and a voice whispered, "It's yours. It's yours. Take it. What use does a dead man have for diamonds?"

" 'Then I became a thief. No lock withstood my skill, no man my blow to the head. And soon the jewelry I had produced was in my hands again. Soon however that did not diminish my unrest. That eerie voice called to me, "A dead man is wearing your jewelry!" I developed a murderous hatred against those for whom I had produced pieces of jewelry.

" 'At that time I bought this house. After the deal had been closed in the evening, the former owner and I were sitting over a bottle of wine, when he said, "Listen, Master Rene, I must tell you a secret about the house." With that he opened a closet built into the wall, pushed aside the inner wall, slipped into a small room, and lifted a trapdoor. We went down a narrow, steep stairway, came to a low door, which he unlocked, and stepped into the yard. Then he walked up to the wall, pushed a small iron projection, and soon a portion of the wall moved enough so that one person could slip into the street. I'll show you this part of the wall some day, Olivier. It consists of plastered and painted wood. Dark thoughts arose in me when I saw this contraption as if I were seeing events still a secret to me.

" 'I had then just finished a necklace for a courtier. I lay sleepless in my bed. Now the fellow was sneaking to a ballet dancer with my jewelry. Furiously I jumped from my bed, threw a cloak over me, went down the secret staircase, and ran along the Rue Nicaise. He appeared. I fell upon him, pushed the dagger into his heart, and seized the necklace. I suddenly felt at peace with myself. The infernal spirit was gone. The voice of Satan was silent. Now I knew what my evil star demanded. I had to submit or go under.

" 'Now you know the reason for my actions. Yet don't think that because I do what I have to do I am entirely without human pity or sympathy. You know how difficult it is for me to deliver an adornment and that I don't accept orders from those whose death I do not desire.'

"Having said this, Cardillac led me to a secret vault where he showed me all the stolen jewels. On each piece was a tag identifying the owner and the date on which it had been stolen. He wanted me to take an oath on my wedding day to pulverize them after his death.

"Imprisoned in this labyrinth of crime, torn by love and detestation, by delay and despair, I was alike the lost soul upon whom an angel smiles while Satan holds him in his claws, the joy of heaven mirrored by the angel's smile becoming his greatest torment. I thought of flight, suicide; yet there was Madelon. Reproach me, lady. I was too weak to subdue a passion tying me to crime.

"One day Cardillac came home in a good humor. He caressed Madelon, cast me a friendly glance, had an expensive bottle of wine for dinner, and sang most of the evening. After Madelon left us, I arose to go to the workshop. He held me back.

" 'Boy,' Cardillac called, 'drink to the finest lady in Paris.' After we had touched glasses, he asked me how I liked this verse:

> *Un amant qui craint des voleurs*
> *n'est point digne d'amour.*

"He told me what had happened in the chambers of the Marquise de Maintenon, adding that he had honored you for a long time. His evil star could not overcome your virtue. 'Here, Olivier, I have a treasure which was ordered for the unfortunate British princess, Henrietta. I'll have it sent to Mademoiselle de Scuderi in the name of the gang. You'll be my messenger.'

"No sooner had I heard your name than memories of my earliest youth returned. I accepted the assignment, deciding to tell you Cardillac's story. I hoped to throw myself at your feet as Anne Brusson's son. I was certain you in your wisdom would find a way to end Cardillac's evil deeds without having his secret become public. Don't ask me how, but I was certain you'd save Madelon and me. You remember my efforts to see you that night failed. Then it chanced that Cardillac lost all joy. He moved furtively, mumbled softly to himself, and often stared at his hands. His soul seemed tortured by evil thoughts. Once he exclaimed, 'I wish Henrietta of England had worn my jewelry.' These words filled me with horror. The voice of Satan was once more calling him to murder. I saw your life threatened by the devilish killer. If Cardillac had the casket back in his hands, you would be safe. I had to rescue you. That is when I threw the note into your carriage.

"The next night I slipped out of the house. Not long after, Cardillac appeared. He went in the direction of the Rue St. Honore. Suddenly he was gone. I decided to station my-

self at your door. A singing, whistling officer came by me.
In the same moment a black figure leaped out at him. It
was Cardillac. Wanting to prevent this murder, I ran forward with a cry. Not the officer, but Cardillac sank mor-
tally wounded to the street. The officer dropped his dagger, unsheathed his sword, and placed himself across from
me thinking me to be his assailant's accomplice, but he
rushed away when he noticed I was paying him no attention. I pushed the officer's dagger into my belt, put Cardillac on my shoulder, and with great effort carried him
home through the secret passage. The rest is known to you.
My only crime, Mademoiselle, consisted in not betraying
Madelon's father to the courts. No torture will force the secret from me. I do not want the past revealed to the daughter. I do not want the executioner's men to dig up the remains of her father to drag them off to the Place de Greve.

"Mademoiselle, you are convinced of my innocence, I
know you are. How is Madelon?"

La Scuderi called Martiniere and in a few moments Madelon was in the room embracing Olivier. If Mademoiselle
had not been convinced of his innocence she would have
been now while listening to the two murmur to each other.

The first rays of morning touched the windows. Desgrais
knocked on the door, reminding them it was time to return
Olivier to jail, since he could not be taken later without
having people notice him.

Mademoiselle de Scuderi honored the noble sentiments
of the youth who preferred to die rather than betray a secret which would bring death to Madelon. She formulated
countless plans to save Olivier from the authority of the
Chambre Ardente. But hope paled more and more. In order to do something she finally wrote a long letter to Regnie in which she told him Oliver had convinced her of his
innocence and that the heroic decision to take his secret to
the grave kept him from confessing the truth. Regnie's reply came a few hours later. He was happy to hear that
Olivier had justified himself to her but that the Chambre
Ardente could not honor such heroic gestures. All methods
were going to be used to force the secret from him and in

three days he hoped to be able to reveal the solution of the apparent mystery.

Feeling certain that a decision had been reached to torture Olivier, she decided to seek the advice of a lawyer. Pierre Arnaud d'Andilly, to whom she went, was the most famous lawyer in Paris. She told him as much as possible without betraying Olivier's secret. His answer, however, was sharply disappointing. He listened carefully and then quoted Boileau: "The truth at times does not appear truthful." He proved to her that all available evidence spoke against Olivier, that Regnie's conduct was not at all illegal, that he could not act otherwise and still do justice to his duties as a judge. Not even the most clever defense, d'Andilly asserted, could save him from torture.

"Then I shall go before the king."

"Please, Mademoiselle," d'Andilly exclaimed, "I beg of you not to resort to a measure which, if it should fail, will close all avenues to you. The king will never pardon a criminal of this sort. If it were possible to remove suspicion in some way, then would come the time to ask for the king's pardon."

She had to agree with the experienced lawyer. Sorrowfully, despairing for want of a way out of her dilemma, she returned home. Late that night Martiniere announced the Count de Miossens, colonel of the king's guard, who urgently wanted to speak to her.

"Pardon," Miossens said, bowing with military courtesy, "pardon me, my lady, for coming to you at such an untimely hour. We soldiers cannot do otherwise. Moreover, two words will excuse me—Olivier Brusson leads me to you."

Mademoiselle leaned forward tensely. "What do you have to tell me about that unfortunate young man?"

"I thought so," Miossens replied smiling. "I thought that the name of your protege would gain me a hearing. The whole world is convinced of his guilt. I know you believe differently. Your belief is based solely on his confession to you. It is otherwise with me. No one but I can be sure of his innocence."

"Speak," la Scuderi pleaded, "speak!"

"I," Miossens said with emphasis, "I myself slew the gold-smith in the street in front of your house. And I swear to you that I am proud of the deed. Cardillac was the horrible murderer who killed so treacherously at night. I don't know why I came to suspect him when he brought me the jewelry I had ordered from him, but my doubts were aroused when he slyly asked my servant to whom I was giving it and at what time I generally visited her.

"I had noticed a long time ago that the unfortunate vic-tims had all been killed instantly with the same stab. If the first blow failed, the killer and victim would be on equal terms. This fact led me to a safety measure which is so sim-ple I'm surprised no one else thought of it. I wore a light breastplate. Cardillac attacked me from behind. He seized me with great strength, but the blow glanced off the armor. At the same instant I tore myself loose and stabbed him with the dagger I had ready."

"And you are silent? You did not inform the Chambre Ardente of what had actually happened?"

"Permit me, Mademoiselle," Miossens continued, "permit me to remark that such information given to the court could lead to my own destruction or could at least involve me in a long trial. Would Regnie, who noses out crime every-where, have believed me if I had accused the righteous Master Cardillac, the model of all piety and virtue, of at-tempted murder? What if the sword of justice had been turned against me?"

"That would not have been possible—your birth—your rank—"

"Oh, but remember the Marshal whose desire to have his horoscope cast brought him to the Bastille, suspected of poisoning. By St. Denis, I will not sacrifice an hour of free-dom nor the tip of an ear to a raging Regnie."

"You'll allow a guiltless Olivier to mount the scaffold?"

"Guiltless, my lady, guiltless? You call Cardillac's accom-pice guiltless? The man who helped him in all his crimes? No, he bleeds justly. I told Mademoiselle the story so that you might use it to help your charge without revealing my name and without betraying me to the Chambre Ardente."

La Scuderi, overjoyed to find Olivier's innocence proved so clearly, told the entire story to the colonel and asked him to tell his secret to d'Andilly, who would then advise the next move.

D'Andilly, having heard the story, inquired about the most minute details. He especially asked the colonel whether he was convinced it was Cardillac and not Olivier who had attacked him and whether he would be able to identify Brusson as the person who had carried the goldsmith away. Miossens answered that not only had he recognized the goldsmith by the light of the full moon, but he had also seen his own dagger in the possession of Regnie. Moreover, he had stood just one step from Olivier when he bent down over the body of Cardillac.

After a few seconds of thought, d'Andilly said, "Brusson cannot be rescued from the hands of justice in any ordinary manner. He doesn't want to name Cardillac as the killer because of Madelon. Even if he did, and were able to prove his innocence by pointing out the secret passageway and the exit and the hidden jewelry, he would still die as an accomplice. The same would happen if the colonel told the court of his encounter with the goldsmith. A delay is what we must try for at the moment. The count must go to the Conciergerie and ask to be confronted with Olivier. He will recognize him as the man who carried the corpse away. Then he must rush to Regnie and say to him, 'In the Rue St. Honore I saw a man stabbed. I stood close by when another person jumped forward, noticed some life in the body and carried it away. I recognize Olivier Brusson to be this person.'

"This testimony will cause Brusson to be requestioned and to be confronted by the count. Torture will be delayed. The investigation will be continued. By then the time will have come to turn to the king. It would be best to reveal the whole secret to him. Brusson's confession will be supported

by the count's testimony and by a secret search of the
house."

The count did exactly as the lawyer had requested, and
everything happened as foretold. Now la Scuderi had to
approach the king. This was the most difficult part of the
project, for the king had such a hatred of Brusson, whom
he considered to be the murderer who had for so long ter-
rorized Paris, that the very mention of the name angered
him. The Marquise de Maintenon, true to her principle never to speak of unpleasant matters to him, refused to interfere. Thus the fate of Olivier lay entirely in the hands of
la Scuderi.

After long deliberation, she made a decision and then
acted quickly. She donned a black, heavy silken robe, put
on Cardillac's jewels, covered her face with a veil, and then
appeared like this in the chambers of the Marquise. The
noble figure of the venerable lady impressed even the dissolute crowd usually found in the antechambers. Everyone
made way for her and when she entered even the king
arose. The sparkle of the diamonds caught his eye. He exclaimed, "By heaven, Cardillac's jewelry!" And then he
turned to la Maintenon, "See, Madame Marquise, our pretty bride is in mourning for her groom."

"Gracious sire," la Scuderi interrupted him as if continuing the joke, "how proper would it be for a mourning bride
to adorn herself in this splendid fashion? No, I have di-
vorced myself from this goldsmith and would not think of
him any more if the gruesome image of how his corpse was
carried past me did not haunt me."

"What," the king asked, "you saw him, the poor devil?"

La Scuderi told now in a few words how chance had
brought her to Cardillac's house when the murder had just
been discovered. She described Madelon's wild agony, the
deep impression the angelic child had made on her, the
way in which she had saved the poor girl amid the crowd's
shouts of approval. She unfolded the scenes with Desgrais,
Regnie, and Olivier. The king, drawn along by the pulsating

life in la Scuderi's speech, was not aware she was speaking of the hateful Brusson's trial. Before he knew what had happened she lay at his feet asking mercy for Olivier Brusson.

"What are you doing?" the king asked, grasping her hand and pulling her up. "This is indeed a strange story. But who will vouch for the truth of Brusson's fantastic tale?"

"Miossens' testimony—a search of the house—an inner conviction—Madelon's virtuous heart which knew Olivier's virtue."

The king was about to answer when he turned toward a noise at the door. Louvois, who had been working in the other chamber, looked in. The king arose and left the chamber with Louvois. Both la Scuderi and the Marquise considered the interruption dangerous, for, having been surprised once, the king would not be so easily trapped a second time. However, after a few minutes the king returned, walked back and forth a few times, and then remained standing next to la Scuderi saying softly without looking at her, "I should like to see Madelon."

"What happiness your majesty will bestow upon the unhappy child! Only a nod by you is needed to bring her to your feet." She left the room as rapidly as the heavy cloak permitted her to move and announced that the king wanted Madelon Cardillac to appear before him.

Madelon, who had been waiting in an antechamber, appeared with a brief petition which d'Andilly had drawn up for her. In a few moments she lay before the king. Fear, embarrassment, awe, love, and pain caused her blood to rush to her face. The king seemed affected by the rare beauty of the angelic child.

Softly la Maintenon lisped to la Scuderi, "Doesn't the little thing look exactly like la Valliere? The king dwells in memories. You have won your game."

No matter how softly she had spoken, the king seemed to hear her. His face turned red. He glanced at the Marquise, read the petition Madelon handed him, and said mildly, "I well believe, my child, that you are convinced of your beloved's innocence, but let us hear what the Chambre Ardente has to say." A gentle motion of his hand dismissed the little one.

Mademoiselle de Scuderi became aware to her dismay that no matter how advantageous the memories of la Valliere had seemed at first, the king's mind was made up as soon as the Marquise had mentioned her name. Perhaps the king was reminded that he was about to sacrifice justice to beauty, or perhaps he no longer saw his lost love, la Valliere, seeing instead Soeur Louise de la Misericorde, the name she had taken on entering a Carmelite convent. There was nothing left to do now but await the king's decision.

The Count de Miossens' testimony before the Chambre Ardente had by now become generally known, and as so often happens, the people were driven from one extreme to the other. Thus the same person who had been denounced as a bloodthirsty killer was now seen as an innocent victim of a barbaric justice. Only now did the neighbors remember Olivier's virtuous life, his love for Madelon, the loyalty and devotion he had shown for his master. Large mobs appeared before Regnie's palace and cried, "Give us Brusson! He is innocent!" And stones were thrown at the windows so that Regnie was forced to seek the protection of the Marechausee.

Several days days passed without la Scuderi's hearing about Olivier's trial. Disheartened, she went to la Maintenon, who told her the king had been silent about the case and that it did not seem advisable to remind him of it. Then she asked with a strange smile what la Valliere was doing. Mademoiselle realized she could expect nothing more from the Marquise.

Although she heard rumors of an investigation, nearly a month passed before the Marquise sent word that the king wanted to see her in the evening. Her heart beat excitedly. She knew the case would now be decided. Madelon prayed to the Virgin Mother and to all the blessed saints that the king would now be convinced of Olivier's innocence.

And yet it seemed as if the king had forgotten the whole affair, for sitting and chatting as usual with the Marquise and Mademoiselle, he spoke not a syllable concerning Brusson. Finally the king arose, walked toward her, and spoke with a sparkling glance. "I wish you joy, Mademoiselle. Your protege, Olivier Brusson, is free."

Tears fell, wetting her cheek. Unable to speak a word, she wanted to throw herself at the king's feet. He prevented her, saying, "Go, Mademoiselle, go! You ought to be a lawyer pleading cases before parliament, for by St. Denis your eloquence cannot be resisted by anyone in the world. But must the one whom virtue herself defends not be safe from the Chambre Ardente and all the courts of the world?"

She suddenly found the words to thank the king. He interrupted her, telling her that thanks awaited her at home, where a happy Olivier was embracing his Madelon. The king ordered a thousand louis given to Madelon for a dowry. "May she marry Brusson, who really doesn't deserve such happiness, but then both must leave Paris. That is my wish."

Martiniere met la Scuderi with hurried steps, and right behind her was Baptiste. They shouted, their faces beaming, "He is free! He is here! Oh, the dear young people!"

The happy couple knelt before Mademoiselle. "I knew you would save my husband," said Madelon.

"My faith in you, my mother, was always secure," Olivier said, and they kissed her hands and cried. They then embraced each other, again vowing to stay together until death.

Several days later a priest united them. Even if it had not been the king's command, Brusson could not have remained in Paris, where everything reminded him of Cardillac's secret. Immediately after the wedding, he and his bride, accompanied by Scuderi's blessing, moved to Geneva. Enriched by Madelon's dowry, skilled in his craft, a happy, industrious life awaited him there.

A year passed. A public notice signed by Harloy de Chanvalon, Archbishop of Paris, and by the lawyer Pierre Arnaud d'Andilly appeared, proclaiming the recovery of stolen gems from a rueful sinner who had returned a rich treasury under the protective seal of the confessional. Ev-

eryone who had been robbed up to the end of 1680 was to
report to d'Andilly and describe the stolen jewelry. Many
who had been knocked unconscious rather than killed by
Cardillac were able to claim their stolen gems. The remaining jewels became the property of the Church of St. Eu-
stache.

MATEO FALCONE

BY PROSPER MÉRIMÉE

ON LEAVING PORTO-VECCHIO FROM THE northwest and directing his steps towards the interior of the island, the traveller will notice that the land rises rapidly, and after three hours' walking over tortuous paths obstructed by great masses of rock and sometimes cut by ravines, he will find himself on the border of a great mâquis. The mâquis is the domain of the Corsican shepherds and of those who are at variance with justice. It must be known that, in order to save himself the trouble of manuring his field, the Corsican husbandman sets fire to a piece of woodland. If the flame spread farther than is necessary, so much the worse! In any case he is certain of a good crop from the land fertilized by the ashes of the trees which grow upon it. He gathers only the heads of his grain, leaving the straw, which it would be unnecessary labor to cut. In the following spring the roots that have remained in the earth without being destroyed send up their tufts of sprouts, which in a few years reach a height of seven or eight feet. It is this kind of tangled thicket that is called a mâquis. They are made up of different kinds of trees and shrubs, so crowded and mingled together at the caprice of nature that only with an ax in hand can a man open a passage through them, and mâquis are frequently seen so thick and bushy that the wild sheep themselves cannot penetrate them.

If you have killed a man, go into the mâquis of Porto-Vecchio. With a good gun and plenty of powder and balls, you can live there in safety. Do not forget a brown cloak furnished with a hood, which will serve you for both cover and mattress. The shepherds will give you chestnuts, milk and cheese, and you will have nothing to fear from justice nor the relatives of the dead except when it is necessary for you to descend to the city to replenish your ammunition.

When I was in Corsica in 18—, Mateo Falcone had his house half a league from this mâquis. He was rich enough for that country, living in noble style—that is to say, doing nothing—on the income from his flocks, which the shepherds, who are a kind of nomads, lead to pasture here and there on the mountains. When I saw him, two years after the event that I am about to relate, he appeared to me to be about fifty years old or more. Picture to yourself a man, small but robust, with curly hair, black as jet, an aquiline nose, thin lips, large, restless eyes, and a complexion the color of tanned leather. His skill as a marksman was considered extraordinary even in his country, where good shots are so common. For example, Mateo would never fire at a sheep with buckshot; but at a hundred and twenty paces, he would drop it with a ball in the head or shoulder, as he chose. He used his arms as easily at night as during the day. I was told this feat of his skill, which will, perhaps, seem impossible to those who have not travelled in Corsica. A lighted candle was placed at eighty paces, behind a paper transparency about the size of a plate. He would take aim, then the candle would be extinguished, and, at the end of a moment, in the most complete darkness, he would fire and hit the paper three times out of four.

With such a transcendent accomplishment, Mateo Falcone had acquired a great reputation. He was said to be as good a friend as he was a dangerous enemy; accommodating and charitable, he lived at peace with all the world in the district of Porto-Vecchio. But it is said of him that in Corte, where he had married his wife, he had disembarrassed himself very vigorously of a rival who was considered as redoubtable in war as in love; at least, a certain gun-shot which surprized this rival as he was shaving before a little mirror hung in his window was attributed to Mateo. The affair was smoothed over and Mateo was

married. His wife Giuseppa had given him at first three
daughters (which infuriated him), and finally a son, whom
he named Fortunato, and who became the hope of his family, the inheritor of the name. The daughters were well married: their father could count at need on the poignards and
carbines of his sons-in-law. The son was only ten years old,
but he already gave promise of fine attributes.

On a certain day in autumn, Mateo set out at an early
hour with his wife to visit one of his flocks in a clearing of
the mâquis. The little Fortunato wanted to go with them, but
the clearing was too far away; moreover, it was necessary
some one should stay to watch the house; therefore the father refused: it will be seen whether or not he had reason
to repent.

He had been gone some hours, and the little Fortunato
was tranquilly stretched out in the sun, looking at the blue
mountains, and thinking that the next Sunday he was going to dine in the city with his uncle, the Caporal[1], when he
was suddenly interrupted in his meditations by the firing of
a musket. He got up and turned to that side of the plain
whence the noise came. Other shots followed, fired at irregular intervals, and each time nearer; at last, in the path
which led from the plain to Mateo's house, appeared a man
wearing the pointed hat of the mountaineers, bearded, covered with rags, and dragging himself along with difficulty
by the support of his gun. He had just received a wound in
his thigh.

This man was an outlaw, who, having gone to the town
by night to buy powder, had fallen on the way into an am-
buscade of Corsican light-infantry. After a vigorous defense
he was fortunate in making his retreat, closely followed and
firing from rock to rock. But he was only a little in advance
of the soldiers, and his wound prevented him from gaining
the mâquis before being overtaken.

[1]Civic official.

He approached Fortunato and said: "You are the son of
Mateo Falcone?"—"Yes."

"I am Gianetto Saupiero. I am followed by the yellow-
collars[1]. Hide me, for I can go no farther."

"And what will my father say if I hide you without his
permission?"

"He will say that you have done well."

"How do you know?"

"Hide me quickly; they are coming."

"Wait till my father gets back."

"How can I wait? Malediction! They will be here in five
minutes. Come, hide me, or I will kill you."

Fortunato answered him with the utmost coolness:

"Your gun is empty, and there are no more cartridges in
your belt."

"I have my stiletto."

"But can you run as fast as I can?"

He gave a leap and put himself out of reach.

"You are not the son of Mateo Falcone! Will you then let
me be captured before your house?"

The child appeared moved.

"What will you give me if I hide you?" said he, coming
nearer.

The outlaw felt in a leather pocket that hung from his
belt, and took out a five-franc piece, which he had doubtless saved to buy ammunition with. Fortunato smiled at the
sight of the silver piece; he snatched it, and said to Gianetto:

"Fear nothing."

Immediately he made a great hole in a pile of hay that
was near the house. Gianetto crouched down in it and the
child covered him in such a way that he could breathe without it being possible to suspect that the hay concealed a
man. He bethought himself further, and, with the subtlety
of a tolerably ingenious savage, placed a cat and her kit-
tens on the pile, that it might not appear to have been re-

[1] Slang for police.

cently disturbed. Then, noticing the traces of blood on the path near the house, he covered them carefully with dust, and, that done, he again stretched himself out in the sun with the greatest tranquillity.

A few moments afterwards, six men in brown uniforms with yellow collars, and commanded by an Adjutant, were before Mateo's door. This Adjutant was a distant relative of Falcone's. (In Corsica the degrees of relationship are followed much further than elsewhere.) His name was Tiodoro Gamba; he was an active man, much dreaded by the outlaws, several of whom he had already entrapped.

"Good day, little cousin," said he, approaching Fortunato; "how tall you have grown. Have you seen a man go past here just now?"

"Oh! I am not yet so tall as you, my cousin," replied the child with a simple air.

"You soon will be. But haven't you seen a man go by here, tell me?"

"If I have seen a man go by?"

"Yes, a man with a pointed hat of black velvet, and a vest embroidered with red and yellow."

"A man with a pointed hat, and a vest embroidered with red and yellow?"

"Yes, answer quickly, and don't repeat my questions?"

"This morning the curé passed before our door on his horse, Piero. He asked me how papa was, and I answered him—"

"Ah, you little scoundrel, you are playing sly! Tell me quickly which way Gianetto went? We are looking for him, and I am sure he took this path."

"Who knows?"

"Who knows? It is I know that you have seen him."

"Can any one see who passes when they are asleep?"

"You were not asleep, rascal; the shooting woke you up."

"Then you believe, cousin, that your guns make so much noise? My father's carbine has the advantage of them."

"The devil take you, you cursed little scapegrace! I am certain that you have seen Gianetto. Perhaps, even, you have hidden him. Come, comrades, go into the house and

see if our man is there. He could only go on one foot, and
the knave has too much good sense to try to reach the mâquis limping like that. Moreover, the bloody tracks stop
here."

"And what will papa say?" asked Fortunato with a sneer;
"what will he say if he knows that his house has been entered while he was away?"

"You rascal!" said the Adjutant, taking him by the ear,
"do you know that it only remains for me to make you
change your tone? Perhaps you will speak differently after
I have given you twenty blows with the flat of my sword."

Fortunato continued to sneer.

"My father is Mateo Falcone," said he with emphasis.

"You little scamp, you know very well that I can carry
you off to Corte or to Bastia. I will make you lie in a dun-
geon, on straw, with your feet in shackles, and I will have
you guillotined if you don't tell me where Gianetto is."

The child burst out laughing at this ridiculous menace. He
repeated:

"My father is Mateo Falcone."

"Adjutant," said one of the soldiers in a low voice, "let
us have no quarrels with Mateo."

Gamba appeared evidently embarrassed. He spoke in
an undertone with the soldiers who had already visited the
house. This was not a very long operation, for the cabin of
a Corsican consists only of a single square room, furnished
with a table, some benches, chests, housekeeping utensils
and those of the chase. In the meantime, little Fortunato
petted his cat and seemed to take a wicked enjoyment in
the confusion of the soldiers and of his cousin.

One of the men approached the pile of hay. He saw the
cat, and gave the pile a careless thrust with his bayonet,
shrugging his shoulders as if he felt that his precaution was
ridiculous. Nothing moved; the boy's face betrayed not the
slightest emotion.

The Adjutant and his troop were cursing their luck. Already they were looking in the direction of the plain, as if
disposed to return by the way they had come, when their

chief convinced that menaces would produce no impression on Falcone's son, determined to make a last effort, and try the effect of caresses and presents.

"My little cousin," said he, "you are a very wide-awake little fellow. You will get along. But you are playing a naughty game with me; and if I wasn't afraid of making trouble for my cousin, Mateo, the devil take me! but I would carry you off with me."

"Bah!"

"But when my cousin comes back I shall tell him about this, and he will whip you till the blood comes for having told such lies."

"You don't say so!"

"You will see. But hold on!—be a good boy and I will give you something."

"Cousin, let me give you some advice: if you wait much longer Gianetto will be in the mâquis and it will take a smarter man than you to follow him."

The Adjutant took from his pocket a silver watch worth about ten crowns, and noticing that Fortunato's eyes sparkled at the sight of it, said, holding the watch by the end of its steel chain:

"Rascal! you would like to have such a watch as that hung around your neck, wouldn't you, and to walk in the streets of Porto-Vecchio proud as a peacock? People would ask you what time it was, and you would say: 'Look at my watch.' "

"When I am grown up, my uncle, the Caporal, will give me a watch."

"Yes; but your uncle's little boy has one already; not so fine as this either. But then, he is younger than you."

The child sighed.

"Well! Would you like this watch, little cousin?"

Fortunato, casting sidelong glances at the watch, resembled a cat that has been given a whole chicken. It feels that it is being made sport of, and does not dare to use its claws; from time to time it turns its eyes away so as not to be tempted, licking its jaws all the while, and has the appearance of saying to its master, "How cruel your joke is!"

However, the Adjutant seemed in earnest in offering his watch. Fortunato did not reach out his hand for it, but said with a bitter smile:

"Why do you make fun of me?"

"Good God! I am not making fun of you. Only tell me where Gianetto is and the watch is yours."

Fortunato smiled incredulously, and fixing his black eyes on those of the Adjutant tried to read there the faith he ought to have had in his words.

"May I lose my epaulets," cried the Adjutant, "if I do not give you the watch on this condition. These comrades are witnesses; I can not deny it."

While speaking he gradually held the watch nearer till it almost touched the child's pale face, which plainly showed the struggle that was going on in his soul between covetousness and respect for hospitality. His breast swelled with emotion; he seemed about to suffocate. Meanwhile the watch was slowly swaying and turning, sometimes brushing against his cheek. Finally, his right hand was gradually stretched toward it; the ends of his fingers touched it; then its whole weight was in his hand, the Adjutant still keeping hold of the chain. The face was light blue; the cases newly burnished. In the sunlight it seemed to be all on fire. The temptation was too great. Fortunato raised his left hand and pointed over his shoulder with his thumb at the hay against which he was reclining. The Adjutant understood him at once. He dropped the end of the chain and Fortunato felt himself the sole possessor of the watch. He sprang up with the agility of a deer and stood ten feet from the pile, which the soldiers began at once to overturn.

There was a movement in the hay, and a bloody man with a poignard in his hand appeared. He tried to rise to his feet, but his stiffened leg would not permit it and he fell. The Adjutant at once grappled with him and took away his stiletto. He was immediately secured, notwithstanding his resistance.

Gianetto, lying on the earth and bound like a fagot, turned his head towards Fortunato, who had approached.

"Son of—!" said he, with more contempt than anger.

The child threw him the silver piece which he had received, feeling that he no longer deserved it; but the outlaw paid no attention to the movement, and with great coolness said to the Adjutant:

"My dear Gamba, I cannot walk; you will be obliged to carry me to the city."

"Just now you could run faster than a buck," answered the cruel captor; "but be at rest. I am so pleased to have you that I would carry you a league on my back without fatigue. Besides, comrade, we are going to make a litter for you with your cloak and some branches, and at the Crespoli farm we shall find horses."

"Good," said the prisoner. "You will also put a little straw on your litter that I may be more comfortable."

While some of the soldiers were occupied in making a kind of stretcher out of some chestnut boughs and the rest were dressing Gianetto's wound, Mateo Falcone and his wife suddenly appeared at a turn in the path that led to the mâquis. The woman was staggering under the weight of an enormous sack of chestnuts, while her husband was sauntering along, carrying one gun in his hands, while another was slung across his shoulders, for it is unworthy of a man to carry other burdens than his arms.

At the sight of the soldiers Mateo's first thought was that they had come to arrest him. But why this thought? Had he then some quarrels with justice? No. He enjoyed a good reputation. He was said to have a particularly good name, but he was a Corsican and a highlander, and there are few Corsican highlanders who, in scrutinizing their memory, can not find some peccadillo, such as a gun-shot, dagger-thrust, or similar trifles. Mateo more than others had a clear conscience; for more than ten years he had not pointed his carbine at a man, but he was always prudent, and put himself into a position to make a good defense if necessary. "Wife," said he to Giuseppa, "put down the sack and hold yourself ready."

She obeyed at once. He gave her the gun that was slung across his shoulders, which would have bothered him, and, cocking the one he held in his hands, advanced slowly towards the house, walking among the trees that bordered the road, ready at the least hostile demonstration, to hide behind the largest, whence he could fire from under cover. His wife followed closely behind, holding his reserve weapon and his cartridge-box. The duty of a good housekeeper, in case of a fight, is to load her husband's carbines.

On the other side the Adjutant was greatly troubled to see Mateo advance in this manner, with cautious steps, his carbine raised, and his finger on the trigger.

"If by chance," thought he, "Mateo should be related to Gianetto, or if he should be his friend and wish to defend him, the contents of his two guns would arrive amongst us as certainly as a letter in the post; and if he should see me, notwithstanding the relationship!"

In this perplexity he took a bold step. It was to advance alone towards Mateo and tell him of the affair while accosting him as an old acquaintance, but the short space that separated him from Mateo seemed terribly long.

"Hello! old comrade," cried he. "How do you do, my good fellow? It is I, Gamba, your cousin."

Without answering a word, Mateo stopped, and in proportion as the other spoke, slowly raised the muzzle of his gun so that it was pointing upward when the Adjutant joined him.

"Good-day, brother," said the Adjutant, holding out his hand. "It is a long time since I have seen you."

"Good-day, brother."

"I stopped while passing, to say good-day to you and to cousin Pepa here. We have had a long journey to-day, but have no reason to complain, for we have captured a famous prize. We have just seized Gianetto Saupiero."

"God be praised!" cried Giuseppa. "He stole a milch goat from us last week."

These words reassured Gamba.

"Poor devil!" said Mateo, "he was hungry."

"The villain fought like a lion," continued the Adjutant, a little mortified. "He killed one of my soldiers, and not content with that, broke Caporal Chardon's arm; but that matters little, he is only a Frenchman. Then, too, he was so well hidden that the devil couldn't have found him. Without my little cousin, Fortunato, I should never have discovered him."

"Fortunato!" cried Mateo.

"Fortunato!" repeated Giuseppa.

"Yes, Gianetto was hidden under the hay-pile yonder, but my little cousin showed me the trick. I shall tell his uncle, the Caporal, that he may send him a fine present for his trouble. Both his name and yours will be in the report that I shall send to the Attorney-general."

"Malediction!" said Mateo in a low voice.

They had rejoined the detachment. Gianetto was already lying on the litter ready to set out. When he saw Mateo and Gamba in company he smiled a strange smile, then, turning his head towards the door of the house, he spat on the sill, saying:

"House of a traitor."

Only a man determined to die would dare pronounce the word traitor to Falcone. A good blow with the stiletto, which there would be no need of repeating, would have immediately paid the insult. However, Mateo made no other movement than to place his hand on his forehead like a man who is dazed.

Fortunato had gone into the house when his father arrived, but now he reappeared with a bowl of milk which he handed with downcast eyes to Gianetto.

"Get away from me!" cried the outlaw, in a loud voice. Then, turning to one of the soldiers, he said:

"Comrade, give me a drink."

The soldier placed his gourd in his hands, and the prisoner drank the water handed to him by a man with whom he had just exchanged bullets. He then asked them to tie his hands across his breast instead of behind his back.

"I like," said he, "to lie at my ease."

They hastened to satisfy him; then the Adjutant gave the signal to start, said adieu to Mateo, who did not respond, and descended with rapid steps towards the plain.

Nearly ten minutes elapsed before Mateo spoke. The child looked with restless eyes, now at his mother, now at his father, who was leaning on his gun and gazing at him with an expression of concentrated rage.

"You begin well," said Mateo at last with a calm voice, but frightful to one who knew the man.

"Oh, father!" cried the boy, bursting into tears, and making a forward movement as if to throw himself on his knees. But Mateo cried, "Away from me!"

The little fellow stopped and sobbed, immovable, a few feet from his father.

Giuseppa drew near. She had just discovered the watch-chain, the end of which was hanging out of Fortunato's jacket.

"Who gave you that watch?" demanded she in a severe tone.

"My cousin, the Adjutant."

Falcone seized the watch and smashed it in a thousand pieces against a rock.

"Wife," said he, "is this my child?"

Giuseppa's cheeks turned a brick-red.

"What are you saying, Mateo? Do you know to whom you speak?"

"Very well, this child is the first of his race to commit treason."

Fortunato's sobs and gasps redoubled as Falcone kept his lynx-eyes upon him. Then he struck the earth with his gun-stock, shouldered the weapon, and turned in the direction of the mâquis, calling to Fortunato to follow. The boy obeyed. Giuseppa hastened after Mateo and seized his arm.

"He is your son," said she with a trembling voice, fastening her black eyes on those of her husband to read what was going on in his heart.

"Leave me alone," said Mateo, "I am his father."

Giuseppa embraced her son, and, bursting into tears entered the house. She threw herself on her knees before an image of the Virgin and prayed ardently. In the meanwhile Falcone walked some two hundred paces along the path and only stopped when he reached a little ravine which he descended. He tried the earth with the butt-end of his carbine, and found it soft and easy to dig. The place seemed to be convenient for his design.

"Fortunato, go close to that big rock there."

The child did as he was commanded, then he kneeled.

"Say your prayers."

"Oh, father, father, do not kill me!"

"Say your prayers!" repeated Mateo in a terrible voice.

The boy, stammering and sobbing, recited the Pater and the Credo. At the end of each prayer the father loudly answered, "Amen!"

"Are those all the prayers you know?"

"Oh! father, I know the Ave Maria and the litany that my aunt taught me."

"It is very long, but no matter."

The child finished the litany in a scarcely audible tone.

"Are you finished?"

"Oh! my father, have mercy! Pardon me! I will never do so again. I will beg my cousin, the Caporal, to pardon Gianetto."

He was still speaking. Mateo raised his gun, and, taking aim, said:

"May God pardon you!"

The boy made a desperate effort to rise and grasp his father's knees, but there was not time. Mateo fired and Fortunato fell dead.

Without casting a glance on the body, Mateo returned to the house for a spade with which to bury his son. He had gone but a few steps when he met Giuseppa, who, alarmed by the shot, was hastening hither.

"What have you done?" cried she.

"Justice."

"Where is he?"

"In the ravine. I am going to bury him. He died a Christian. I shall have a mass said for him. Have my son-in-law, Tiodoro Bianchi, sent for to come and live with us."

A DESCENT INTO THE MAELSTRÖM

BY EDGAR ALLAN POE

The ways of God in Nature, as in Providence, are not as *our* ways; nor are the models that we frame in any way commensurate to the vastness, profundity, and unsearchableness of His works, *which have a depth in them greater than the well of Democritus.*

—*Joseph Glanvill*

WE HAD NOW REACHED THE SUMMIT OF the loftiest crag. For some minutes the old man seemed too much exhausted to speak.

"Not long ago," said he at length, "and I could have guided you on this route as well as the youngest of my sons; but, about three years past, there happened to me an event such as never happened before to mortal man—or at least such as no man ever survived to tell of—and the six hours of deadly terror which I then endured have broken me up body and soul. You suppose me a *very* old man—but I am not. It took less than a single day to change these hairs from a jetty black to white, to weaken my limbs, and to unstring my nerves, so that I tremble at the least exertion, and am frightened at a shadow. Do you know I can scarcely look over this little cliff without getting giddy?"

The "little cliff," upon whose edge he had so carelessly thrown himself down to rest that the weightier portion of his body hung over it, while he was only kept from falling by the tenure of his elbow on its extreme and slippery edge —this "little cliff" arose, a sheer unobstructed precipice of black shining rock, some fifteen or sixteen hundred feet from the world of crags beneath us. Nothing would have tempted me to be within half a dozen yards of its brink. In truth so deeply was I excited by the perilous position of my companion, that I fell at full length upon the ground, clung to the shrubs around me, and dared not even glance upward at the sky—while I struggled in vain to divest myself of the idea that the very foundations of the mountain were in danger from the fury of the winds. It was long before I could reason myself into sufficient courage to sit up and look out into the distance.

"You must get over these fancies," said the guide, "for I have brought you here that you might have the best possible view of the scene of that event I mentioned—and to tell you the whole story with the spot just under your eyes.

"We are now," he continued, in that particularizing manner which distinguished him—"we are now close upon the Norwegian coast—in the sixty-eighth degree of latitude—in the great province of Nordland—and in the dreary district of Lofoden. The mountain upon whose top we sit is Helseggen, the Cloudy. Now raise yourself up a little higher—hold on to the grass if you feel giddy—so—and look out, beyond the belt of vapor beneath us, into the sea."

I looked dizzily, and beheld a wide expanse of ocean, whose waters wore so inky a hue as to bring at once to my mind the Nubian geographer's account of the *Mare Tenebrarum*. A panorama more deplorably desolate no human imagination can conceive. To the right and left, as far as the eye could reach, there lay outstretched, like ramparts of the world, lines of horridly black and beetling cliff, whose character of gloom was but the more forcibly illustrated by the surf which reared high up against it its white and ghastly crest, howling and shrieking for ever. Just opposite the promontory upon whose apex we were placed, and at a distance of some five or six miles out at sea, there was visible a small, bleak-looking island; or, more properly, its position was discernible through the wilderness of surge in which it was enveloped. About two miles nearer the land, arose another of smaller size, hideously craggy and barren, and encompassed at various intervals by a cluster of dark rocks.

The appearance of the ocean, in the space between the more distant island and the shore, had something very unusual about it. Although, at the time, so strong a gale was blowing landward that a brig in the remote offing lay to under a double-reefed trysail, and constantly plunged her whole hull out of sight, still there was here nothing like a regular swell, but only a short, quick, angry cross dashing of water in every direction—as well in the teeth of the wind as otherwise. Of foam there was little except in the immediate vicinity of the rocks.

"The island in the distance," resumed the old man, "is called by the Norwegians Vurrgh. The one midway is Moskoe. That a mile to the northward is Ambaaren. Yonder are Islesen, Hotholm, Keildhelm, Suarven, and Buckholm. Further off—between Moskoe and Vurrgh—are Otterholm, Flimen, Sandflesen, and Stockholm. These are the true names of the places—but why it has been thought necessary to name them at all, is more than either you or I can understand. Do you hear any thing? Do you see any change in the water?"

We had now been about ten minutes upon the top of Helseggen, to which we had ascended from the interior of Lofoden, so that we had caught no glimpse of the sea until it had burst upon us from the summit. As the old man spoke, I became aware of a loud and gradually increasing sound, like the moaning of a vast herd of buffaloes upon an American prairie; and at the same moment I perceived that what seamen term the *chopping* character of the ocean beneath us, was rapidly changing into a current which set to the eastward. Even while I gazed, this current acquired a monstrous velocity. Each moment added to its speed—to its headlong impetuosity. In five minutes the whole sea, as far as Vurrgh, was lashed into ungovernable fury; but it was between Moskoe and the coast that the main uproar held its sway. Here the vast bed of the waters, seamed and scarred into a thousand conflicting channels, burst suddenly into phrensied convulsion—heaving, boiling, hissing—gyrating in gigantic and innumerable vortices, and all whirling and plunging on to the eastward with a rapidity which water never elsewhere assumes, except in precipitous descents.

In a few minutes more, there came over the scene another radical alteration. The general surface grew somewhat more smooth, and the whirlpools, one by one, disappeared, while prodigious streaks of foam became apparent where none had been seen before. These streaks, at length, spreading out to a great distance, and entering into combination, took unto themselves the gyratory motion of the subsided vortices, and seemed to form the germ of another more vast. Suddenly—very suddenly—this assumed a distinct and definite existence, in a circle of more than a mile in diameter. The edge of the whirl was represented by a broad belt of gleaming spray; but no particle of this slipped into the mouth of the terrific funnel, whose interior, as far as the eye could fathom it, was a smooth, shining, and jet-black wall of water, inclined to the horizon at an angle of some forty-five degrees, speeding dizzily round and round with a swaying and sweltering motion, and sending forth to the winds an appalling voice, half shriek, half roar, such as not even the mighty cataract of Niagara ever lifts up in its agony to Heaven.

The mountain trembled to its very base, and the rock rocked. I threw myself upon my face, and clung to the scant herbage in an excess of nervous agitation.

"This," said I at length, to the old man—"this can be nothing else than the great whirlpool of the Maelström."

"So it is sometimes termed," said he. "We Norwegians call it the Moskoe-ström, from the island of Moskoe in the midway."

The ordinary account of this vortex had by no means prepared me for what I saw. That of Jonas Ramus, which is perhaps the most circumstantial of any, cannot impart the faintest conception either of the magnificence, or of the horror of the scene—or of the wild bewildering sense of *the novel* which confounds the beholder. I am not sure from what point of view the writer in question surveyed it, nor at what time; but it could neither have been from the summit of Helseggen, nor during a storm. There are some passages of his description, nevertheless, which may be quoted for their details, although their effect is exceedingly feeble in conveying an impression of the spectacle.

"Between Lofoden and Moskoe," he says, "the depth of the water is between thirty-six and forty fathoms; but on the other side, toward Ver (Vurrgh) this depth decreases so as

not to afford a convenient passage for a vessel, without
the risk of splitting on the rocks, which happens even in the
calmest weather. When it is flood, the stream runs up the
country between Lofoden and Moskoe with a boisterous rapidity; but the roar of its impetuous ebb to the sea is scarce
equalled by the loudest and most dreadful cataracts; the
noise being heard several leagues off, and the vortices or
pits are of such an extent and depth, that if a ship comes
within its attraction, it is inevitably absorbed and carried
down to the bottom, and there beat to pieces against the
rocks; and when the water relaxes, the fragments thereof
are thrown up again. But these intervals of tranquillity are
only at the turn of the ebb and flood, and in calm weather,
and last but a quarter of an hour, its violence gradually re-
turning. When the stream is most boisterous, and its fury
heightened by a storm, it is dangerous to come within a
Norway mile of it. Boats, yachts, and ships have been carried away by not guarding against it before they were carried within its reach. It likewise happens frequently, that
whales come too near the stream, and are overpowered by
its violence; and then it is impossible to describe their howl-
ings and bellowings in their fruitless struggles to disengage
themselves. A bear once, attempting to swim from Lofoden
to Moskoe, was caught by the stream and borne down,
while he roared terribly, so as to be heard on shore. Large
stocks of firs and pine trees, after being absorbed by the
current, rise again broken and torn to such a degree as if
bristles grew upon them. This plainly shows the bottom to
consist of craggy rocks, among which they are whirled to
and fro. This stream is regulated by the flux and reflux of
the sea—it being constantly high and low water every six
hours. In the year 1645, early in the morning of Sexagesima
Sunday, it raged with such noise and impetuosity that the
very stones of the houses on the coast fell to the ground."

In regard to the depth of the water, I could not see how
this could have been ascertained at all in the immediate
vicinity of the vortex. The "forty fathoms" must have reference only to portions of the channel close upon the shore

either of Moskoe or Lofoden. The depth in the centre of the Moskoe-ström must be unmeasurably greater; and no better proof of this fact is necessary than can be obtained from even the sidelong glance into the abyss of the whirl which may be had from the highest crag of Helseggen. Looking down from this pinnacle upon the howling Phlegethon below, I could not help smiling at the simplicity with which the honest Jonas Ramus records, as a matter difficult of belief, the anecdotes of the whales and the bears, for it appeared to me, in fact, a self-evident thing, that the largest ships of the line in existence, coming within the influence of that deadly attraction, could resist it as little as a feather the hurricane, and must disappear bodily and at once.

The attempts to account for the phenomenon—some of which I remember, seemed to me sufficiently plausible in perusal—now wore a very different and unsatisfactory aspect. The idea generally received is that this, as well as three smaller vortices among the Ferroe Islands, "have no other cause than the collision of waves rising and falling, at flux and reflux, against a ridge of rocks and shelves, which confines the water so that it precipitates itself like a cataract; and thus the higher the flood rises, the deeper must the fall be, and the natural result of all is a whirlpool or vortex, the prodigious suction of which is sufficiently known by lesser experiments."—These are the words of the Encyclopaedia Britannica. Kircher and others imagine that in the centre of the channel of the maelström is an abyss penetrating the globe, and issuing in some very remote part —the Gulf of Bothnia being somewhat decidedly named in one instance. This opinion, idle in itself, was the one to which, as I gazed, my imagination most readily assented; and, mentioning it to the guide, I was rather surprised to hear him say that, although it was the view almost universally entertained of the subject by the Norwegians, it nevertheless was not his own. As to the former notion he confessed his inability to comprehend it; and here I agreed with him—for, however conclusive on paper, it becomes altogether unintelligible, and even absurd, amid the thunder of the abyss.

"You have had a good look at the whirl now," said the old man, "and if you will creep round this crag, so as to get in its lee, and deaden the roar of the water, I will tell you a story that will convince you I ought to know something of the Moskoe-ström."

I placed myself as desired, and he proceeded.

"Myself and my two brothers once owned a schooner-rigged smack of about seventy tons burthen, with which we were in the habit of fishing among the islands beyond Moskoe, nearly to Vurrgh. In all violent eddies at sea there is good fishing, at proper opportunities, if one has only the courage to attempt it; but among the whole of the Lofoden coastmen, we three were the only ones who made a regular business of going out to the islands, as I tell you. The usual grounds are a great way lower down to the southward. There fish can be got at all hours, without much risk, and therefore these places are preferred. The choice spots over here among the rocks, however, not only yield the finest variety, but in far greater abundance; so that we often got in a single day, what the more timid of the craft could not scrape together in a week. In fact, we made it a matter of desperate speculation—the risk of life standing instead of labor, and courage answering for capital.

"We kept the smack in a cove about five miles higher up the coast than this; and it was our practice, in fine weather, to take advantage of the fifteen minutes' slack to push across the main channel of the Moskoe-ström, far above the pool, and then drop down upon anchorage somewhere near Otterholm, or Sandflesen, where the eddies are not so violent as elsewhere. Here we used to remain until nearly time for slack-water again, when we weighed and made for home. We never set out upon this expedition without a steady side wind for going and coming—one that we felt sure would not fail us before our return—and we seldom made a miscalculation upon this point. Twice, during six years, we were forced to stay all night at anchor on account of a dead calm, which is a rare thing indeed just about here; and once we had to remain on the grounds nearly a week, starving to death, owing to a gale which

blew up shortly after our arrival, and made the channel too
boisterous to be thought of. Upon this occasion we should
have been driven out to sea in spite of every thing (for the
whirlpools threw us round and round so violently, that, at
length, we fouled our anchor and dragged it), if it had not
been that we drifted into one of the innumerable cross cur-
rents—here to-day and gone to-morrow—which drove us
under the lee of Flimen, where, by good luck, we brought
up.

"I could not tell you the twentieth part of the difficulties
we encountered 'on the ground'—it is a bad spot to be in,
even in good weather—but we make shift always to run the
gauntlet of the Moskoe-ström itself without accident; although at times my heart has been in my mouth when we
happened to be a minute or so behind or before the slack.
The wind sometimes was not as strong as we thought it at
starting, and then we made rather less way than we could
wish, while the current rendered the smack unmanageable.
My eldest brother had a son eighteen years old, and I had
two stout boys of my own. These would have been of great
assistance at such times, in using the sweeps as well as afterward in fishing—but, somehow, although we ran the risk
ourselves, we had not the heart to let the young ones get
into the danger—for, after all said and done, it *was* a horrible danger, and that is the truth.

"It is now within a few days of three years since what I
am going to tell you occurred. It was on the tenth of July,
18—, a day which the people of this part of the world will
never forget—for it was one in which blew the most terrible
hurricane that ever came out of the heavens. And yet all
the morning, and indeed until late in the afternoon, there
was a gentle and steady breeze from the southwest, while
the sun shone brightly, so that the oldest seaman among us
could not have foreseen what was to follow.

"The three of us—my two brothers and myself—had
crossed over to the islands about two o'clock P.M., and
soon nearly loaded the smack with fine fish, which, we all
remarked, were more plenty that day than we had ever

known them. It was just seven, *by my watch*, when we weighed and started for home, so as to make the worst of the Ström at slack water, which we knew would be at eight.

"We set out with a fresh wind on our starboard quarter, and for some time spanked along at a great rate, never dreaming of danger, for indeed we saw not the slightest reason to apprehend it. All at once we were taken aback by a breeze from over Helseggen. This was most unusual— something that had never happened to us before—and I began to feel a little uneasy, without exactly knowing why. We put the boat on the wind, but could make no headway at all for the eddies, and I was upon the point of proposing to return to the anchorage, when, looking astern, we saw the whole horizon covered with a singular copper-colored cloud that rose with the most amazing velocity.

"In the meantime the breeze that had headed us off fell away and we were dead becalmed, drifting about in every direction. This state of things, however, did not last long enough to give us time to think about it. In less than a minute the storm was upon us—in less than two the sky was entirely overcast—and what with this and the driving spray, it became suddenly so dark that we could not see each other in the smack.

"Such a hurricane as then blew it is folly to attempt describing. The oldest seaman in Norway never experienced any thing like it. We had let our sails go by the run before it cleverly took us; but, at the first puff, both our masts went by the board as if they had been sawed off—the mainmast taking with it my youngest brother, who had lashed himself to it for safety.

"Our boat was the lightest feather of a thing that ever sat upon water. It had a complete flush deck, with only a small hatch near the bow, and this hatch it had always been our custom to batten down when about to cross the Ström, by way of precaution against the chopping seas. But for this circumstance we should have foundered at once— for we lay entirely buried for some moments. How my elder brother escaped destruction I cannot say, for I never had

an opportunity of ascertaining. For my part, as soon as I
had let the foresail run, I threw myself flat on deck, with
my feet against the narrow gunwale of the bow, and with
my hands grasping a ring-bolt near the foot of the fore-
mast. It was mere instinct that prompted me to do this—
which was undoubtedly the very best thing I could have
done—for I was too much flurried to think.

"For some moments we were completely deluged, as I
say, and all this time I held my breath, and clung to the
bolt. When I could stand it no longer I raised myself upon
my knees, still keeping hold with my hands, and thus got my
head clear. Presently our little boat gave herself a shake,
just as a dog does in coming out of the water, and thus rid
herself, in some measure, of the seas. I was now trying to
get the better of the stupor that had come over me, and to
collect my senses so as to see what was to be done, when I
felt somebody grasp my arm. It was my elder brother, and
my heart leaped for joy, for I had made sure that he was
overboard—but the next moment all this joy was turned
into horror—for he put his mouth close to my ear, and
screamed out the word '*Moskoe-ström!*'

"No one ever will know what my feelings were at that
moment. I shook from head to foot as if I had had the most
violent fit of the ague. I knew what he meant by that one
word well enough—I knew what he wished to make me understand. With the wind that now drove us on, we were
bound for the whirl of the Ström, and nothing could save
us!

"You perceive that in crossing the Ström *channel,* we always went a long way up above the whirl, even in the
calmest weather, and then had to wait and watch carefully
for the slack—but now we were driving right upon the pool
itself, and in such a hurricane as this! 'To be sure,' I thought,
'we shall get there just about the slack—there is some little
hope in that'—but in the next moment I cursed myself for
being so great a fool as to dream of hope at all. I knew
very well that we were doomed, had we been ten times a
ninety-gun ship.

"By this time the first fury of the tempest had spent itself, or perhaps we did not feel it so much, as we scudded before it, but at all events the seas, which at first had been kept down by the wind, and lay flat and frothing, now got up into absolute mountains. A singular change, too, had come over the heavens. Around in every direction it was still as black as pitch, but nearly overhead there burst out, all at once, a circular rift of clear sky—as clear as I ever saw— and of a deep bright blue—and through it there blazed forth the full moon with a lustre that I never before knew her to wear. She lit up every thing about us with the greatest distinctness—but, oh God, what a scene it was to light up!

"I now made one or two attempts to speak to my brother —but in some manner which I could not understand, the din had so increased that I could not make him hear a single word, although I screamed at the top of my voice in his ear. Presently he shook his head, looking as pale as death, and held up one of his fingers, as if to say *'listen!'*

"At first I could not make out what he meant—but soon a hideous thought flashed upon me. I dragged my watch from its fob. It was not going. I glanced at its face by the moonlight, and then burst into tears as I flung it far away into the ocean. *It had run down at seven o'clock! We were behind the time of the slack, and the whirl of the Ström was in full fury!*

"When a boat is well built, properly trimmed, and not deep laden, the waves in a strong gale, when she is going large, seem always to slip from beneath her—which appears strange to a landsman—and this is what is called *riding,* in sea phrase.

"Well, so far we had ridden the swells very cleverly; but presently a gigantic sea happened to take us right under the counter, and bore us with it as it rose—up—up—as if into the sky. I would not have believed that any wave could rise so high. And then down we came with a sweep, a slide, and a plunge that made me feel sick and dizzy, as if I was falling from some lofty mountain-top in a dream. But while

we were up I had thrown a quick glance around—and that
one glance was all-sufficient. I saw our exact position in an
instant. The Moskoe-ström whirlpool was about a quarter of
a mile dead ahead—but no more like the every-day Moskoe-ström than the whirl, as you now see it, is like a mill-
race. If I had not known where we were, and what we had
to expect, I should not have recognized the place at all. As
it was, I involuntarily closed my eyes in horror. The lids
clenched themselves together as if in a spasm.

"It could not have been more than two minutes afterwards until we suddenly felt the waves subside, and were
enveloped in foam. The boat made a sharp half turn to
larboard, and then shot off in its new direction like a thun-
derbolt. At the same moment the roaring noise of the water was completely drowned in a kind of shrill shriek—such
a sound as you might imagine given out by the water-pipes
of many thousand steam-vessels letting off their steam all
together. We were now in the belt of surf that always surrounds the whirl; and I thought, of course, that another moment would plunge us into the abyss, down which we could
only see indistinctly on account of the amazing velocity with
which we were borne along. The boat did not seem to sink
into the water at all, but to skim like an air-bubble upon
the surface of the surge. Her starboard side was next the
whirl, and on the larboard arose the world of ocean we
had left. It stood like a huge writhing wall between us and
the horizon.

"It may appear strange, but now, when we were in the
very jaws of the gulf, I felt more composed than when we
were only approaching it. Having made up my mind to
hope no more, I got rid of a great deal of that terror which
unmanned me at first. I supposed it was despair that strung
my nerves.

"It may look like boasting—but what I tell you is truth—
I began to reflect how magnificent a thing it was to die in
such a manner, and how foolish it was in me to think of so
paltry a consideration as my own individual life, in view of
so wonderful a manifestation of God's power. I do believe

that I blushed with shame when this idea crossed my mind. After a little while I became possessed with the keenest curiosity about the whirl itself. I positively felt a *wish* to explore its depths, even at the sacrifice I was going to make; and my principal grief was that I should never be able to tell my old companions on shore about the mysteries I should see. These, no doubt, were singular fancies to occupy a man's mind in such extremity—and I have often thought since, that the revolutions of the boat around the pool might have rendered me a little light-headed.

"There was another circumstance which tended to restore my self-possession; and this was the cessation of the wind, which could not reach us in our present situation—for, as you saw for yourself, the belt of the surf is considerably lower than the general bed of the ocean, and this latter now towered above us, a high, black, mountainous ridge. If you have never been at sea in a heavy gale, you can form no idea of the confusion of mind occasioned by the wind and spray together. They blind, deafen, and strangle you, and take away all power of action or reflection. But we were now, in a great measure, rid of these annoyances—just as death-condemned felons in prison are allowed petty indulgences, forbidden them while their doom is yet uncertain.

"How often we made the circuit of the belt it is impossible to say. We careered round and round for perhaps an hour, flying rather than floating, getting gradually more and more into the middle of the surge, and then nearer and nearer to its horrible inner edge. All this time I had never let go of the ring-bolt. My brother was at the stern, holding on to a small empty water-cask which had been securely lashed under the coop of the counter, and was the only thing on deck that had not been swept overboard when the gale first took us. As we approached the brink of the pit he let go his hold upon this, and made for the ring, from which, in the agony of his terror, he endeavored to force my hands, as it was not large enough to afford us both a secure grasp. I never felt deeper grief than when I saw him attempt this act—although I knew he was a madman

when he did it—a raving maniac through sheer fright. I
did not care, however, to contest the point with him. I knew
it could make no difference whether either of us held on at
all; so I let him have the bolt, and went astern to the cask.
This there was no great difficulty in doing; for the smack
flew round steadily enough, and upon an even keel—only
swaying to and fro with the immense sweeps and swelters
of the whirl. Scarcely had I secured myself in my new position, when we gave a wild lurch to starboard, and rushed
headlong into the abyss. I muttered a hurried prayer to
God, and thought all was over.

"As I felt the sickening sweep of the descent, I had instinctively tightened my hold upon the barrel, and closed
my eyes. For some seconds I dared not open them—while I
expected instant destruction, and wondered that I was not
already in my death-struggles with the water. But moment
after moment elapsed. I still lived. The sense of falling had
ceased; and the motion of the vessel seemed much as it
had been before, while in the belt of foam, with the exception that she now lay more along. I took courage and
looked once again upon the scene.

"Never shall I forget the sensation of awe, horror, and
admiration with which I gazed about me. The boat appeared to be hanging, as if by magic, midway down, upon
the interior surface of a funnel vast in circumference, prodigious in depth, and whose perfectly smooth sides might
have been mistaken for ebony, but for the bewildering rapidity with which they spun around, and for the gleaming
and ghastly radiance they shot forth, as the rays of the full
moon, from that circular rift amid the clouds which I have
already described, streamed in a flood of golden glory
along the black walls, and far away down into the inmost
recesses of the abyss.

"At first I was too much confused to observe any thing
accurately. The general burst of terrific grandeur was all
that I beheld. When I recovered myself a little, however,
my gaze fell instinctively downward. In this direction I was
able to obtain an unobstructed view, from the manner in
which the smack hung on the inclined surface of the pool.

She was quite upon an even keel—that is to say, her deck lay in a plane parallel with that of the water—but this latter sloped at an angle of more than forty-five degrees, so that we seemed to be lying upon our beam-ends. I could not help observing, nevertheless, that I had scarcely more difficulty in maintaining my hold and footing in this situation, than if we had been upon a dead level; and this, I suppose, was owing to the speed at which we revolved.

"The rays of the moon seemed to search the very bottom of the profound gulf; but still I could make out nothing distinctly on account of a thick mist in which every thing there was enveloped, and over which there hung a magnificent rainbow, like that narrow and tottering bridge which Mussulmen say is the only pathway between Time and Eternity. This mist, or spray, was no doubt occasioned by the clashing of the great walls of the funnel, as they all met together at the bottom—but the yell that went up to the Heavens from out of that mist I dare not attempt to describe.

"Our first slide into the abyss itself, from the belt of foam above, had carried us to a great distance down the slope; but our farther descent was by no means proportionate. Round and round we swept—not with any uniform movement—but in dizzying swings and jerks, that sent us sometimes only a few hundred yards—sometimes nearly the complete circuit of the whirl. Our progress downward, at each revolution, was slow, but very perceptible.

"Looking about me upon the wide waste of liquid ebony on which we were thus borne, I perceived that our boat was not the only object in the embrace of the whirl. Both above and below us were visible fragments of vessels, large masses of building-timber and trunks of trees, with many smaller articles, such as pieces of house furniture, broken boxes, barrels and staves. I have already described the unnatural curiosity which had taken the place of my original terrors. It appeared to grow upon me as I drew nearer and nearer to my dreadful doom. I now began to watch, with a strange interest, the numerous things that floated in our company. I *must* have been delirious, for I even sought *amusement* in speculating upon the relative velocities of their several descents toward the foam below. 'This fir-tree,' I found myself at one time saying, 'will certainly be the next thing that takes the awful plunge and disappears,'—and then I was disappointed to find that the wreck of a Dutch merchant ship overtook it and went down before. At length, after making several guesses of this nature, and being deceived in all—this fact—the fact of my invariable miscalculation, set me upon a train of reflection that made my limbs again tremble, and my heart beat heavily once more.

"It was not a new terror that thus affected me, but the dawn of a more exciting *hope*. This hope arose partly from memory and partly from present observation. I called to mind the great variety of buoyant matter that strewed the coast of Lofoden, having been absorbed and then thrown forth by the Moskoe-ström. By far the greater number of the articles were shattered in the most extraordinary way— so chafed and roughened as to have the appearance of being stuck full of splinters—but then I distinctly recollected that there were *some* of them which were not disfigured at all. Now I could not account for this difference except by supposing that the roughened fragments were the only ones which had been *completely absorbed*—that the others had entered the whirl at so late a period of the tide, or, from some reason, had descended so slowly after entering, that they did not reach the bottom before the turn of the flood came, or of the ebb, as the case might be. I conceived it possible, in either instance, that they might thus be whirled up again to the level of the ocean, without undergoing the fate of those which had been drawn in more early or absorbed more rapidly. I made, also, three important observations. The first was, that as a general rule, the larger the bodies were, the more rapid their descent—the second, that, between two masses of equal extent, the one spherical, and the other *of any other shape*, the superiority in speed of descent was with the sphere—the third, that, between two masses of equal size, the one cylindrical, and the other of any other shape, the cylinder was absorbed the more slowly. Since my escape, I have had several conversations on this subject with an old school-master of the district; and it was from him that I learned the use of the words 'cylinder' and 'sphere.' He explained to me—although I have forgotten the explanation—how what I observed was, in fact, the natural consequence of the forms of the floating fragments—and showed me how it happened that a cylinder, swimming in a vortex, offered more resistance to its suction, and was drawn in with greater difficulty than an equally bulky body, of any form whatever.[1]

"There was one startling circumstance which went a great way in enforcing these observations, and rendering me anxious to turn them to account, and this was that, at every revolution, we passed something like a barrel, or else the yard or the mast of a vessel, while many of these things, which had been on our level when I first opened my eyes upon the wonders of the whirlpool, were now high up above us, and seemed to have moved but little from their original station.

"I no longer hesitated what to do. I resolved to lash myself securely to the water-cask upon which I now held, to cut it loose from the counter, and to throw myself with it into the water. I attracted my brother's attention by signs, pointed to the floating barrels that came near us, and did every thing in my power to make him understand what I was about to do. I thought at length that he comprehended my design—but, whether this was the case or not, he shook his head despairingly, and refused to move from his station by the ring-bolt. It was impossible to reach him; the emergency admitted of no delay; and so, with a bitter struggle, I resigned him to his fate, fastened myself to the cask by means of the lashings which secured it to the counter, and precipitated myself with it into the sea, without another moment's hesitation.

"The result was precisely what I had hoped it might be. As it is myself who now tell you this tale—as you see that I *did* escape—and as you are already in possession of the mode in which this escape was effected, and must therefore anticipate all that I have farther to say—I will bring my

---

[1] See Archimedes, "*De Incidentibus in Fluido.*"—lib. 2.

story quickly to conclusion. It might have been an hour, or thereabout, after my quitting the smack, when, having descended to a vast distance beneath me, it made three or four wild gyrations in rapid succession, and, bearing my loved brother with it, plunged headlong, at once and forever, into the chaos of foam below. The barrel to which I was attached sunk very little farther than half the distance between the bottom of the gulf and the spot at which I leaped overboard, before a great change took place in the character of the whirlpool. The slope of the sides of the vast funnel became momently less and less steep. The gyrations of the whirl grew, gradually, less and less violent. By degrees, the froth and the rainbow disappeared, and the bottom of the gulf seemed slowly to uprise. The sky was clear, the winds had gone down, and the full moon was setting radiantly in the west, when I found myself on the surface of the ocean, in full view of the shores of Lofoden, and above the spot where the pool of the Moskoe-ström *had been*. It was the hour of the slack—but the sea still heaved in mountainous waves from the effects of the hurricane. I was borne violently into the channel of the Ström, and in a few minutes, was hurried down the coast into the 'grounds' of the fishermen. A boat picked me up—exhausted from fatigue—and (now that the danger was removed) speechless from the memory of its horror. Those who drew me on board were my old mates and daily companions—but they knew me no more than they would have known a traveller from the spirit-land. My hair, which had been raven black the day before, was as white as you see it now. They say too that the whole expression of my countenance had changed. I told them my story—they did not believe it. I now tell it to *you*—and I can scarcely expect you to put more faith in it than did the merry fishermen of Lofoden."

MR. JUSTICE HARBOTTLE

BY J. SHERIDAN LEFANU

Abridged by the editor

CHAPTER I. *The Judge's House*

THIRTY YEARS AGO, AN ELDERLY MAN, TO whom I paid quarterly a small annuity charged on some property of mine, came on the quarterday to receive it. He was a dry, sad, quiet man, who had known better days, and had always maintained an unexceptionable character. No better authority could be imagined for a ghost story.

He told me one, though with a manifest reluctance; he was drawn into the narration by his choosing to explain what I should not have remarked, that he had called two days earlier than that week after the strict day of payment, which he had usually allowed to elapse. His reason was a sudden determination to change his lodgings, and the consequent necessity of paying his rent a little before it was due.

He lodged in a dark street in Westminster, in a spacious old house, very warm, being wainscoted from top to bottom, and furnished with no undue abundance of windows, and those fitted with thick sashes and small panes.

This house was, as the bills upon the windows testified, offered to be sold or let. But no one seemed to care to look at it.

A thin matron, in rusty black silk, very taciturn, with large, steady, alarmed eyes, that seemed to look in your face, to read what you might have seen in the dark rooms and passages through which you had passed, was in charge of it, with a solitary "maid-of-all-work" under her command. My poor friend had taken lodgings in this house, on account of their extraordinary cheapness. He had occupied

them for nearly a year without the slightest disturbance,
and was the only tenant, under rent, in the house. He had
two rooms; a sitting-room, and a bedroom with a closet
opening from it, in which he kept his books and papers
locked up. He had gone to his bed, having also locked the
outer door. Unable to sleep, he had lighted a candle, and
after having read for a time, had laid the book beside him.
He heard the old clock at the stair-head strike one; and
very shortly after, to his alarm, he saw the closet-door,
which he thought he had locked, open stealthily, and a
slight dark man, particularly sinister, and somewhere about
fifty, dressed in mourning of a very antique fashion, such a
suit as we see in Hogarth, entered the room on tip-toe. He
was followed by an elder man, stout, and blotched with
scurvy, and whose features, fixed as a corpse's, were
stamped with dreadful force with a character of sensuality
and villainy.

This old man wore a flowered-silk dressing-gown and
ruffles, and he remarked a gold ring on his finger, and on
his head a cap of velvet, such as, in the days of perukes,
gentlemen wore in undress.

This direful old man carried in his ringed and ruffled
hand a coil of rope; and these two figures crossed the floor
diagonally, passing the foot of his bed, from the closet-
door at the farther end of the room, at the left, near the
window, to the door opening upon the lobby, close to the
bed's head, at his right.

He did not attempt to describe his sensations as these
figures passed so near him. He merely said, that so far from
sleeping in that room again, no consideration the world
could offer would induce him so much as to enter it again
alone, even in the daylight. He found both doors, that of
the closet, and that of the room opening upon the lobby, in
the morning fast locked, as he had left them before going
to bed.

In answer to a question of mine, he said that neither appeared the least conscious of his presence. They did not
seem to glide, but walked as living men do, but without any
sound, and he felt a vibration on the floor as they crossed

it. He so obviously suffered from speaking about the apparitions, that I asked him no more questions.

There were in his description, however, certain coincidences so very singular, as to induce me, by that very post, to write to a friend much my senior, then living in a remote part of England, for the information which I knew he could give me. He had himself more than once pointed out that old house to my attention, and told me, though very briefly, the strange story which I now asked him to give me in greater detail.

His answer satisfied me; and the following pages convey its substance.

Your letter (he wrote) tells me you desire some particulars about the closing years of the life of Mr. Justice Harbottle, one of the judges of the Court of Common Pleas. You refer, of course, to the extraordinary occurrences that made that period of his life long after a theme for 'winter tales' and metaphysical speculation. I happen to know perhaps more than any other man living of those mysterious particulars.

The old family mansion, when I revisited London, more than thirty years ago, I examined for the last time. During the years that have passed since then, I hear that improvement, with its preliminary demolitions, has been doing wonders for the quarter of Westminster in which it stood. If I were quite certain that the house had been taken down, I should have no difficulty about naming the street in which it stood. As what I have to tell, however, is not likely to improve its letting value, and as I should not care to get into trouble, I prefer being silent on that particular point.

How old the house was, I can't tell. People said it was built by Roger Harbottle, a Turkey merchant, in the reign of King James I. I am not a good opinion upon such questions; but having been in it, though in its forlorn and deserted state, I can tell you in a general way what it was like. It was built of dark-red brick, and the door and windows were faced with stone that had turned yellow by time. It receded some feet from the line of the other houses in the street; and it had a florid and fanciful rail of iron about the broad steps that invited your ascent to the hall-door, in which were fixed, under a file of lamps, among scrolls and twisted leaves, two immense "extinguishers" like the conical caps of fairies, into which, in old times, the footmen used to thrust their flambeaux when their chairs or coaches had set down their great people, in the hall or at the steps, as the case might be. That hall is panelled up to the ceiling, and has a large fire-place. Two or three stately old rooms open from it at each side. The windows of these are tall, with many small panes. Passing through the arch at the back of the hall, you come upon the wide and heavy well-staircase. There is a back staircase also. The mansion is large, and has not as much light, by any means, in proportion to its extent, as modern houses enjoy. When I saw it, it had long been untenanted, and had the gloomy reputation beside of a haunted house. Cobwebs floated from the ceilings or spanned the corners of the cornices, and dust lay thick over everything. The windows were stained with the dust and rain of fifty years, and darkness had thus grown darker.

When I made it my first visit, it was in company with my father, when I was still a boy, in the year 1808. I was about twelve years old, and my imagination impressible, as it always is at that age. I looked about me with great awe. I was here in the very centre and scene of those occurrences which I had heard recounted at the fireside at home, with so delightful a horror.

My father was an old bachelor of nearly sixty when he married. He had, when a child, seen Judge Harbottle on the bench in his robes and wig a dozen times at least before his death, which took place in 1748, and his appearance made a powerful and unpleasant impression, not only on his imagination, but upon his nerves.

The Judge was at that time a man of some sixty-seven years. He had a great mulberry-coloured face, a big, carbuncled nose, fierce eyes, and a grim and brutal mouth. My father, who was young at the time, thought it the most formidable face he had ever seen; for there were evidences of intellectual power in the formation and lines of the forehead. His voice was loud and harsh, and gave effect to the sarcasm which was his habitual weapon on the bench.

This old gentleman had the reputation of being about the wickedest man in England. Even on the bench he now and then showed his scorn of opinion. He had carried cases his own way, it was said, in spite of counsel, authorities, and even of juries, by a sort of cajolery, violence, and bamboozling, that somehow confused and overpowered resistance. He had never actually committed himself; he was too cunning to do that. He had the character of being, however, a dangerous and unscrupulous judge; but his character did not trouble him. The associates he chose for his hours of relaxation cared as little as he did about it.

CHAPTER II. *Mr. Peters*

One night during the session of 1746 this old Judge went down in his chair to wait in one of the rooms of the House of Lords for the result of a division in which he and his order were interested.

This over, he was about to return to his house close by, in his chair; but the night had become so soft and fine that he changed his mind, sent it home empty, and with two footmen, each with a flambeau, set out on foot in preference. Gout had made him rather a slow pedestrian. It took him some time to get through the two or three streets he had to pass before reaching his house.

In one of those narrow streets of tall houses, perfectly silent at that hour, he overtook, slowly as he was walking, a very singular-looking old gentleman.

He had a bottle-green coat on, with a cape to it, and large stone buttons, a broad-leafed low-crowned hat, from under which a big powdered wig escaped; he stooped very much, and supported his bending knees with the aid of a crutch-handled cane, and so shuffled and tottered along painfully.

"I ask your pardon, sir," said this old man in a very quavering voice, as the burly Judge came up with him, and he extended his hand feebly towards his arm.

Mr. Justice Harbottle saw that the man was by no means

poorly dressed, and his manner that of a gentleman.

The Judge stopped short, and said, in his harsh peremptory tones, "Well, sir, how can I serve you?"

"Can you direct me to Judge Harbottle's house? I have some intelligence of the very last importance to communicate to him."

"Can you tell it before witnesses?" asked the Judge.

"By no means; it must reach *his* ear only," quavered the old man earnestly.

"If that be so, sir, you have only to accompany me a few steps farther to reach my house, and obtain a private audience; for I am Judge Harbottle."

With this invitation the infirm gentleman in the white wig complied very readily; and in another minute the stranger stood in what was then termed the front parlour of the Judge's house, *tête-à-tête* with that shrewd and dangerous functionary.

He had to sit down, being very much exhausted, and unable for a little time to speak; and then he had a fit of coughing, and after that a fit of gasping; and thus two or three minutes passed, during which the Judge dropped his roquelaure on an arm-chair, and threw his cocked-hat over that.

The venerable pedestrian in the white wig quickly recovered his voice. With closed doors they remained together for some time.

There were guests waiting in the drawing-rooms, and the sound of men's voices laughing, and then of a female voice singing to a harpsichord, were heard distinctly in the hall over the stairs; for old Judge Harbottle had arranged one of his dubious jollifications, such as might well make the hair of godly men's heads stand upright, for that night.

This old gentleman in the powdered white wig, that rested on his stooped shoulders, must have had something to say that interested the Judge very much; for he would not have parted on easy terms with the ten minutes and upwards which that conference filched from the sort of revelry in which he most delighted, and in which he was the roaring king, and in some sort the tyrant also, of his company.

The footman who showed the aged gentleman out observed that the Judge's mulberry-coloured face, pimples and all, were bleached to a dingy yellow, and there was the abstraction of agitated thought in his manner, as he bid the stranger good night. The servant saw that the conversation had been of serious import, and that the Judge was frightened.

Instead of stumping upstairs forthwith to his scandalous hilarities, his profane company, and his great china bowl of punch—the identical bowl from which a bygone Bishop of London, good easy man, had baptised this Judge's grandfather, now clinking round the rim with silver ladles, and hung with scrolls of lemon peel—instead, I say, of stumping and clambering up the great staircase to the cavern of his Circean enchantment, he stood with his big nose flattened against the window-pane, watching the progress of the feeble old man, who clung stiffly to the iron rail as he got down, step by step, to the pavement.

The hall-door had hardly closed, when the old Judge was in the hall bawling hasty orders, with such stimulating expletives as old colonels under excitement sometimes indulge in nowadays, with a stamp or two of his big foot, and a waving of his clenched fist in the air. He commanded the footman to overtake the old gentleman in the white wig, to offer him his protection on his way home, and in no case to show his face again without having ascertained where he lodged, and who he was, and all about him.

"By—, sirrah! if you fail me in this, you doff my livery tonight!"

Forth bounced the stalwart footman, with his heavy cane under his arm, and skipped down the steps, and looked up and down the street after the singular figure, so easy to recognise.

What were his adventures I shall not tell you just now.

The old man, in the conference to which he had been admitted in that stately panelled room, had just told the Judge a very strange story. He might be himself a conspirator; he might possibly be crazed; or possibly his whole story was straight and true.

The aged gentleman in the bottle-green coat, on finding himself alone with Mr. Justice Harbottle, had become agitated. He said,

"There is, perhaps you are not aware, my lord, a prisoner in Shrewsbury jail, charged with having forged a bill of exchange for a hundred and twenty pounds, and his name is Lewis Pyneweck, a grocer of that town."

"Is there?" says the Judge, who knew well that there was.

"Yes, my lord," says the old man.

"Then you had better say nothing to affect this case. If you do, by—I'll commit you; for I'm to try it," says the Judge, with his terrible look and tone.

"I am not going to do anything of the kind, my lord; of him or his case I know nothing, and care nothing. But a fact has come to my knowledge which it behoves you to well consider."

"And what may that fact be?" inquired the Judge; "I'm in haste, sir, and beg you will use dispatch."

"It has come to my knowledge, my lord, that a secret tribunal is in process of formation, the object of which is to take cognisance of the conduct of the judges; and first, of *your* conduct, my lord: it is a wicked conspiracy."

"Who are of it?" demands the Judge.

"I know not a single name as yet. I know but the fact, my lord; it is most certainly true."

"I'll have you before the Privy Council, sir," says the Judge.

"That is what I most desire; but not for a day or two, my lord."

"And why so?"

"I have not as yet a single name, as I told your lordship; but I expect to have a list of the most forward men in it, and some other papers connected with the plot, in two or three days."

"You said one or two just now."

"About that time, my lord."

"Is this a Jacobite plot?"

"In the main I think it is, my lord."

"Why, then, it is political. I have tried no State prisoners, nor am like to try any such. How, then, doth it concern me?"

"From what I can gather, my lord, there are those in it who desire private revenges upon certain judges."

"What do they call their cabal?"

"The High Court of Appeal, my lord."

"Who are you sir? What is your name?"

"Hugh Peters, my lord."

"That should be a Whig name?"

"It is, my lord."

"Where do you lodge, Mr. Peters?"

"In Thames Street, my lord, over against the sign of the Three Kings."

"Three Kings? Take care one be not too many for you, Mr. Peters! How come you, an honest Whig, as you say, to be privy to a Jacobite plot? Answer me that."

"My lord, a person in whom I take an interest has been seduced to take a part in it; and being frightened at the unexpected wickedness of their plans, he is resolved to become an informer for the Crown."

"He resolves like a wise man, sir. What does he say of the persons? Who are in the plot? Doth he know them?"

"Only two, my lord; but he will be introduced to the club in a few days, and he will then have a list, and more exact information of their plans, and above all of their oaths, and their hours and places of meeting, with which he wishes to be acquainted before they can have any suspicions of his intentions. And being so informed, to whom, think you, my lord, had he best go then?"

"To the king's attorney-general straight. But you say this concerns me, sir, in particular? How about this prisoner, Lewis Pyneweck? Is he one of them?"

"I can't tell, my lord; but for some reason, it is thought your lordship will be well advised if you try him not. For if you do, it is feared 'twill shorten your days."

"So far as I can learn, Mr. Peters, this business smells pretty strong of blood and treason. The king's attorney-general will know how to deal with it. When shall I see you again, sir?"

"If you give me leave, my lord, either before your lordship's court sits, or after it rises, to-morrow. I should like to come and tell your lordship what has passed."

"Do so, Mr. Peters, at nine o'clock to-morrow morning. And see you play me no trick, sir, in this matter; if you do, by ——, sir, I'll lay you by the heels!"

"You need fear no trick from me, my lord; had I not wished to serve you, and acquit my own conscience, I never would have come all this way to talk with your lordship."

"I'm willing to believe you, Mr. Peters; I'm willing to believe you, sir."

And upon this they parted.

"He has either painted his face, or he is consumedly sick," thought the old Judge.

The light had shone more effectually upon his features as he turned to leave the room with a low bow, and they looked, he fancied, unnaturally chalky.

"D— him!" said the Judge ungraciously, as he began to scale the stairs: "he has half-spoiled my supper."

But if he had, no one but the Judge himself perceived it, and the evidence was all, as anyone might perceive, the other way.

CHAPTER III. *Lewis Pyneweck*

In the meantime, the footman dispatched in pursuit of Mr. Peters speedily overtook that feeble gentleman. The old man stopped when he heard the sound of pursuing steps, but any alarms that may have crossed his mind seemed to disappear on his recognising the livery. He very gratefully accepted the proffered assistance, and placed his tremulous arm within the servant's for support. They had not gone far, however, when the old man stopped suddenly, saying,

"Dear me! as I live, I have dropped it. You heard it fall. My eyes, I fear, won't serve me, and I'm unable to stoop low enough; but if *you* will look, you shall have half the find. It is a guinea; I carried it in my glove."

The street was silent and deserted. The footman had hardly descended to what he termed his "hunkers," and begun to search the pavement about the spot which the old man indicated, when Mr. Peters, who seemed very much exhausted, and breathed with difficulty, struck him a violent blow, from above, over the back of the head with a heavy instrument, and then another; and leaving him bleeding and senseless in the gutter, ran like a lamplighter down a lane to the right, and was gone.

When, an hour later, the watchman brought the man in livery home, still stupid and covered with blood, Judge Harbottle cursed his servant roundly, swore he was drunk, threatened him with an indictment for taking bribes to betray his master, and cheered him with a perspective of the broad street leading from the Old Bailey to Tyburn, the cart's tail, and the hangman's lash.

Notwithstanding this demonstration, the Judge was pleased. It was a disguised "affidavit man," or footpad, no doubt, who had been employed to frighten him. The trick had fallen through.

A "court of appeal," such as the false Hugh Peters had indicated, with assassination for its sanction, would be an uncomfortable institution for a "hanging judge" like the Honourable Justice Harbottle. That sarcastic and ferocious administrator of the criminal code of England, at that time a rather pharisaical, bloody, and heinous system of justice, had reasons of his own for choosing to try that very Lewis Pyneweck, on whose behalf this audacious trick was devised. Try him he would. No man living should take that morsel out of his mouth.

Of Lewis Pyneweck of course, so far as the outer world could see, he knew nothing. He would try him after his fashion, without fear, favour, or affection.

But did he not remember a certain thin man, dressed in mourning, in whose house, in Shrewsbury, the Judge's lodgings used to be, until a scandal of his ill-treating his wife came suddenly to light? A grocer with a demure look, a soft step, and a lean face as dark as mahogany, with a nose sharp and long, standing ever so little awry, and a pair of dark steady brown eyes under thinly-traced black brows—a man whose thin lips wore always a faint unpleasant smile.

Had not that scoundrel an account to settle with the
Judge? had he not been troublesome lately? and was not
his name Lewis Pyneweck, some time grocer in Shrewsbury,
and now prisoner in the jail of that town?

The reader may take it, if he pleases, as a sign that
Judge Harbottle was a good Christian, that he suffered
nothing ever from remorse. That was undoubtedly true. He
had nevertheless done this grocer, forger, what you will,
some five or six years before, a grievous wrong; but it was
not that, but a possible scandal, and possible complications,
that troubled the learned Judge now.

Did he not, as a lawyer, know, that to bring a man from
his shop to the dock, the chances must be at least ninety-
nine out of a hundred that he is guilty?

A weak man like his learned brother Withershins was not
a judge to keep the high-roads safe, and make crime tremble. Old Judge Harbottle was the man to make the evil-
disposed quiver, and to refresh the world with showers of
wicked blood, and thus save the innocent, to the refrain of
the ancient saw he loved to quote:

> *Foolish pity*
> *Ruins a city.*

In hanging that fellow he could not be wrong. The eye
of a man accustomed to look upon the dock could not fail
to read "villain" written sharp and clear in his plotting face.
Of course he would try him, and no one else should.

A saucy-looking woman, still handsome, in a mob-cap
gay with blue ribbons, in a saque of flowered silk, with lace
and rings on, much too fine for the Judge's housekeeper,
which nevertheless she was, peeped into his study next
morning, and, seeing the Judge alone, stepped in.

"Here's another letter from him, come by the post this
morning. Can't you do nothing for him?" she said whee-
dlingly, with her arm over his neck, and her delicate finger
and thumb fiddling with the lobe of his purple ear.

"I'll try," said Judge Harbottle, not raising his eyes from
the paper he was reading.

"I knew you'd do what I asked you," she said.

The Judge clapt his gouty claw over his heart, and made her an ironical bow.

"What," she asked, "will you do?"

"Hang him," said the Judge with a chuckle.

"You don't mean to; no, you don't, my little man," said she, surveying herself in a mirror on the wall.

"I'm d—d but I think you're falling in love with your husband at last!" said Judge Harbottle.

"I'm blest but I think you're growing jealous of him," replied the lady with a laugh. "But no; he was always a bad one to me; I've done with him long ago."

"And he with you, by George! When he took your fortune and your spoons and your ear-rings, he had all he wanted of you. He drove you from his house; and when he discovered you had made yourself comfortable, and found a good situation, he'd have taken your guineas and your silver and your ear-rings over again, and then allowed you half a dozen years more to make a new harvest for his mill. You don't wish him good; if you say you do, you lie."

She laughed a wicked saucy laugh, and gave the terrible Rhadamanthus a playful tap on the chops.

"He wants me to send him money to fee a counsellor," she said, while her eyes wandered over the pictures on the wall, and back again to the looking-glass; and certainly she did not look as if his jeopardy troubled her very much.

"Confound his impudence, the *scoundrel!*" thundered the old Judge, throwing himself back in his chair, as he used to do *in furore* on the bench, and the lines of his mouth looked brutal, and his eyes ready to leap from their sockets. "If you answer his letter from my house to please yourself, you'll write your next from somebody else's to please me. You understand, my pretty witch, I'll not be pestered. Come, no pouting; whimpering won't do. You don't care a brass farthing for the villain, body or soul. You came here but to make a row. You are one of Mother Carey's chickens; and where you come, the storm is up. Get you gone, baggage! get you *gone!*" he repeated with a stamp; for a knock at the hall-door made her instantaneous disappearance indispensable.

I need hardly say that the venerable Hugh Peters did not appear again. The Judge never mentioned him. But oddly enough, considering how he laughed to scorn the weak invention which he had blown into dust at the very first puff, his white-wigged visitor and the conference in the dark front parlour was often in his memory.

His shrewd eye told him that allowing for change of tints and such disguises as the playhouse affords every night, the features of this false old man, who had turned out too hard for his tall footman, were identical with those of Lewis Pyneweck.

Judge Harbottle made his registrar call upon the crown solicitor, and tell him that there was a man in town who bore a wonderful resemblance to a prisoner in Shrewsbury jail named Lewis Pyneweck, and to make inquiry through the post forthwith whether anyone was personating Pyneweck in prison, and whether he had thus or otherwise made his escape.

The prisoner was safe, however, and no question as to his identity.

CHAPTER IV. *Interruption in Court*

In due time Judge Harbottle went circuit; and in due time the judges were in Shrewsbury. News travelled slowly in those days, and newspapers, like the wagons and stage-coaches, took matters easily. Mrs. Pyneweck, in the Judge's house, with a diminished household—the greater part of the Judge's servants having gone with him, for he had given up riding circuit, and travelled in his coach in state—kept house rather solitarily at home.

In spite of quarrels, in spite of mutual injuries—some of them, inflicted by herself, enormous—in spite of a married life of spited bickerings—a life in which there seemed no love or liking or forbearance, for years—now that Pyneweck stood in near danger of death, something like remorse came suddenly upon her. She knew that in Shrews-

bury were transacting the scenes which were to determine
his fate. She knew she did not love him; but she could not
have supposed, even a fortnight before, that the hour of
suspense could have affected her so powerfully.

She knew the day on which the trial was expected to
take place. She could not get it out of her head for a minute; she felt faint as it drew towards evening.

Two or three days passed; and then she knew that the
trial must be over by this time. There were floods between
London and Shrewsbury, and news was long delayed. She
wished the floods would last for ever. It was dreadful waiting to hear; dreadful to know that the event was over, and
that she could not hear till self-willed rivers subsided;
dreadful to know that they must subside and the news came
at last.

She had some vague trust in the Judge's good nature,
and much in the resources of chance and accident. She had
contrived to send the money he wanted. He would not be
without legal advice and energetic and skilled support.

At last the news did come—a long arrear all in a gush:
a letter from a female friend in Shrewsbury; a return of the
sentences, sent up for the Judge; and most important, because most easily got at, being told with great aplomb and
brevity, the long-deferred intelligence of the Shrewsbury
Assizes in the *Morning Advertiser*. Like an impatient reader
of a novel, who reads the last page first, she read with
dizzy eyes the list of the executions.

Two were respited, seven were hanged; and in that capital catalogue was this line:

"Lewis Pyneweck—forgery."

She had to read it half a dozen times over before she
was sure she understood it. Here was the paragraph:

> *"Sentence, Death—7.*

"Executed accordingly, on Friday the 13th instant, to wit:
"Thomas Primer, *alias* Duck—highway robbery.
"Flora Guy—stealing to the value of 11*s.* 6*d.*
"Arthur Pounden—burglary.

"Matilda Mummery—riot.

"Lewis Pyneweck—forgery, bill of exchange."

And when she reached this, she read it over and over, feeling very cold and sick.

This buxom housekeeper was known in the house as Mrs. Carwell—Carwell being her maiden name, which she had resumed.

No one in the house except its master knew her history. Her introduction had been managed craftily. No one suspected that it had been concerted between her and the old reprobate in scarlet and ermine.

Flora Carwell ran up the stairs now, and snatched her little girl, hardly seven years of age, whom she met on the lobby, hurriedly up in her arms, and carried her into her bedroom, without well knowing what she was doing, and sat down, placing the child before her. She was not able to speak. She held the child before her, and looked in the little girl's wondering face, and burst into tears of horror.

She thought the Judge could have saved him. I daresay he could. For a time she was furious with him; and hugged and kissed her bewildered little girl, who returned her gaze with large round eyes.

That little girl had lost her father, and knew nothing of the matter. She had been always told that her father was dead long ago.

A woman, coarse, uneducated, vain, and violent, does not reason, or even feel, very distinctly; but in these tears of consternation were mingling a self-upbraiding. She felt afraid of that little child.

But Mrs. Carwell was a person who lived not upon sentiment, but upon beef and pudding; she consoled herself with punch; she did not trouble herself long even with resentments; she was a gross and material person, and could not mourn over the irrevocable for more than a limited number of hours, even if she would.

Judge Harbottle was soon in London again. Except the gout, this savage old epicurean never knew a day's sickness. He laughed and coaxed and bullied away the young woman's faint upbraidings, and in a little time Lewis Pyne-

weck troubled her no more; and the Judge secretly chuckled over the perfectly fair removal of a bore, who might
have grown little by little into something very like a tyrant.

It was the lot of the Judge whose adventures I am now
recounting to try criminal cases at the Old Bailey shortly
after his return. He had commenced his charge to the jury
in a case of forgery, and was, after his wont, thundering
dead against the prisoner, with many a hard aggravation
and cynical gibe, when suddenly all died away in silence,
and, instead of looking at the jury, the eloquent Judge was
gaping at some person in the body of the court.

Among the persons of small importance who stand and
listen at the sides was one tall enough to show with a little
prominence; a slight mean figure, dressed in seedy black,
lean and dark of visage. He had just handed a letter to the
crier, before he caught the Judge's eye.

That Judge descried, to his amazement, the features of
Lewis Pyneweck. He has the usual faint thin-lipped smile;
and with his blue chin raised in air, and as it seemed quite
unconscious of the distinguished notice he has attracted, he
was stretching his low cravat with his crooked fingers, while
he slowly turned his head from side to side—a process
which enabled the Judge to see distinctly a stripe of swollen
blue round his neck, which indicated, he thought, the grip
of the rope.

This man, with a few others, had got a footing on a step,
from which he could better see the court. He now stepped
down, and the Judge lost sight of him.

His lordship signed energetically with his hand in the direction in which this man had vanished. He turned to the
tipstaff. His first effort to speak ended in a gasp. He cleared
his throat, and told the astounded official to arrest that
man who had interrupted the court.

"He's but this moment gone down *there*. Bring him in cus-
tody before me, within ten minutes' time, or I'll strip your
gown from your shoulders and fine the sheriff!" he thundered, while his eyes flashed round the court in search of
the functionary.

Attorneys, counsellors, idle spectators, gazed in the di-

rection in which Mr. Justice Harbottle had shaken his
gnarled old hand. They compared notes. Not one had seen
anyone making a disturbance. They asked one another if
the Judge was losing his head.

Nothing came of the search. His lordship concluded his
charge a great deal more tamely; and when the jury retired, he stared round the court with a wandering mind,
and looked as if he would not have given sixpence to see
the prisoner hanged.

CHAPTER V. *Caleb Searcher*

The Judge had received the letter; had he known from
whom it came, he would no doubt have read it instantaneously. As it was he simply read the direction:

> *To the Honourable*
> *The Lord Justice*
> *Elijah Harbottle,*
> *One of his Majesty's Justices of*
> *the Honourable Court of Common Pleas.*

It remained forgotten in his pocket till he reached home.
When he pulled out that and others from the capacious
pocket of his coat, it had its turn, as he sat in his library in
his thick silk dressing-gown; and then he found its contents
to be a closely-written letter, in a clerk's hand, and an en-
closure in "secretary hand," as I believe the angular scrivi-
nary of law-writings in those days was termed, engrossed
on a bit of parchment about the size of this page. The letter said:

"Mr. Justice Harbottle,—My Lord,

"I am ordered by the High Court of Appeal to acquaint your lordship, in order to your better preparing
yourself for your trial, that a true bill hath been sent
down, and the indictment lieth against your lordship for
the murder of one Lewis Pyneweck of Shrewsbury, citizen, wrongfully executed for the forgery of a bill of ex-

change, on the —th day of —— last, by reason of the wilful perversion of the evidence, and the undue pressure put upon the jury, together with the illegal admission of evidence by your lordship, well knowing the same to be illegal, by all which the promoter of the prosecution of the said indictment, before the High Court of Appeal, hath lost his life.

"And the trial of the said indictment, I am further ordered to acquaint your lordship is fixed for the 10th day of —— next ensuing, by the right honourable the Lord Chief-Justice Twofold, of the court aforesaid, to wit, the High Court of Appeal, on which day it will most certainly take place. And I am further to acquaint your lordship, to prevent any surprise or miscarriage, that your case stands first for the said day, and that the said High Court of Appeal sits day and night, and never rises; and herewith, by order of the said court, I furnish your lordship with a copy (extract) of the record in this case, except of the indictment, whereof, notwithstanding, the substance and effect is supplied to your lordship in this Notice. And further I am to inform you, that in case the jury then to try your lordship should find you guilty, the right honourable the Lord Chief-Justice will, in passing sentence of death upon you, fix the day of execution for the 10th day of ——, being one calendar month from the day of your trial."

It was signed by   "CALEB SEARCHER,
                            "Officer of the Crown Solicitor in
                                   the
                            "Kingdom of Life and Death."

The Judge glanced through the parchment.

" 'Sblood! Do they think a man like me is to be bamboozled by their buffoonery?"

The Judge's coarse features were wrung into one of his sneers; but he was pale. Possibly, after all, there was a conspiracy on foot. It was queer. Did they mean to pistol him in his carriage? or did they only aim at frightening him?

Judge Harbottle had more than enough of animal cour-

age. He was not afraid of highwaymen, and he had fought
more than his share of duels, being a foul-mouthed advo-
cate while he held briefs at the bar. No one questioned his
fighting qualities. But with respect to this particular case of
Pyneweck, he lived in a house of glass. Was there not his
pretty, dark-eyed, over-dressed housekeeper, Mrs. Flora
Carwell? Very easy for people who knew Shrewsbury to
identify Mrs. Pyneweck, if once put upon the scent; and had
he not stormed and worked hard in that case? Had he not
made it hard sailing for the prisoner? Did he not know very
well what the bar thought of it? It would be the worst scandal that ever blasted judge.

So much there was intimidating in the matter, but nothing
more. The Judge was a little bit gloomy for a day or two
after, and more testy with every one than usual.

He locked up the papers; and about a week after he
asked his housekeeper, one day, in the library:

"Had your husband never a brother?"

Mrs. Carwell squalled on this sudden introduction of the
funereal topic, and cried exemplary "piggins full," as the
Judge used pleasantly to say. But he was in no mood for
trifling now, and he said sternly:

"Come, madam! this wearies me. Do it another time; and
give me an answer to my question." So she did.

Pyneweck had no brother living. He once had one; but
he died in Jamaica.

"How do you know he is dead?" asked the Judge.

"Because he told me so."

"Not the dead man?"

"Pyneweck told me so."

"Is that all?" sneered the Judge.

He pondered this matter; and time went on. The Judge
was growing a little morose, and less enjoying. The subject
struck nearer to his thoughts than he fancied it could have
done. But so it is with most undivulged vexations, and there
was no one to whom he could tell this one.

It was now the ninth; and Mr. Justice Harbottle was glad.
He knew nothing would come of it. Still it bothered him; and
to-morrow would see it well over.

[What of the paper, I have cited? No one saw it during his life; no one, after his death. He spoke of it to Dr. Hedstone; and what purported to be "a copy," in the old Judge's handwriting, was found. The original was nowhere. Was it a copy of an illusion, incident to brain disease? Such is my belief.]

CHAPTER VI. *Arrested*

Judge Harbottle went this night to the play at Drury Lane. He was one of those old fellows who care nothing for late hours, and occasionally knocking about in pursuit of pleasure. He had appointed with two cronies of Lincoln's Inn to come home in his coach with him to sup after the play.

They were not in his box, but were to meet him near the entrance, and to get into his carriage there; and Mr. Justice Harbottle, who hated waiting, was looking a little impatiently from the window.

The Judge yawned.

He told the footman to watch for Counsellor Thavies and Counsellor Beller, who were coming; and, with another yawn, he laid his cocked-hat on his knees, closed his eyes, leaned back in his corner, wrapped his mantle closer about him, and began to think of pretty Mrs. Abington.

And being a man who could sleep like a sailor, at a moment's notice, he was thinking of taking a nap. Those fellows had no business to keep a judge waiting.

He heard their voices now. Those rake-hell counsellors were laughing, and bantering, and sparring after their wont. The carriage swayed and jerked, as one got in, and then again as the other followed. The door clapped, and the coach was now jogging and rumbling over the pavement. The Judge was a little bit sulky. He did not care to sit up and open his eyes. Let them suppose he was asleep. He heard them laugh with more malice than good-humour, he thought, as they observed it. He would give them a d——d hard knock or two when they got to his door, and till then he would counterfeit his nap.

The clocks were chiming twelve. Beller and Thavies were silent as tombstones. They were generally loquacious and merry rascals.

The Judge suddenly felt himself roughly seized and thrust from his corner into the middle of the seat, and opening his eyes, instantly he found himself between his two companions.

Before he could blurt out the oath that was at his lips, he saw that they were two strangers—evil-looking fellows, each with a pistol in his hand, and dressed like Bow Street officers.

The Judge clutched at the check-string. The coach pulled up. He stared about him. They were not among houses; but through the windows, under a broad moonlight, he saw a black moor stretching lifelessly from right to left, with rotting trees, pointing fantastic branches in the air, standing here and there in groups, as if they held up their arms and twigs like fingers, in horrible glee at the Judge's coming.

A footman came to the window. He knew his long face and sunken eyes. He knew it was Dingly Chuff, fifteen years ago a footman in his service, whom he had turned off at a moment's notice, in a burst of jealousy, and indicted for a missing spoon. The man had died in prison of the jail-fever.

The Judge drew back in utter amazement. His armed companions signed mutely; and they were again gliding over this unknown moor.

The bloated and gouty old man, in his horror, considered the question of resistance. But his athletic days were long over. This moor was a desert. There was no help to be had. He was in the hands of strange servants, even if his recognition turned out to be a delusion, and they were under the command of his captors. There was nothing for it but submission, for the present.

Suddenly the coach was brought nearly to a standstill, so that the prisoner saw an ominous sight from the window.

It was a gigantic gallows beside the road; it stood three-sided, and from each of its three broad beams at top depended in chains some eight or ten bodies, from several of which the cere-clothes had dropped away, leaving the skeletons swinging lightly by their chains. A tall ladder reached to the summit of the structure, and on the peat beneath lay bones.

On top of the dark transverse beam facing the road, from which, as from the other two completing the triangle of death, dangled a row of these unfortunates in chains, a hangman, with a pipe in his mouth, much as we see him in the famous print of the "Idle Apprentice," though here his perch was ever so much higher, was reclining at his ease and listlessly shying bones, from a little heap at his elbow, at the skeletons that hung round, bringing down now a rib or two, now a hand, now half a leg. A long-sighted man could have discerned that he was a dark fellow, lean; and from continually looking down on the earth from the elevation over which, in another sense, he always hung, his nose, his lips, his chin were pendulous and loose, and drawn down into a monstrous grotesque.

This fellow took his pipe from his mouth on seeing the coach, stood up, and cut some solemn capers high on his beam, and shook a new rope in the air, crying with a voice high and distant as the caw of a raven hovering over a gibbet, "A rope for Judge Harbottle!"

The coach was now driving on at its old swift pace.

So high a gallows as that, the Judge had never, even in his most hilarious moments, dreamed of. He thought he must be raving. And the dead footman! He shook his ears and strained his eyelids; but if he was dreaming, he was unable to awake himself.

There was no good in threatening these scoundrels. A *brutum fulmen* might bring a real one on his head.

Any submission to get out of their hands; and then heaven and earth he would move to unearth and hunt them down.

Suddenly they drove round a corner of a vast white building, and under a *porte-cochère.*

CHAPTER VII. *Chief-Justice Twofold*

The Judge found himself in a corridor lighted with dingy oil-lamps, the walls of bare stone; it looked like a passage in a prison. His guards placed him in the hands of other people. Here and there he saw bony and gigantic soldiers passing to and fro, with muskets over their shoulders. They looked straight before them, grinding their teeth, in bleak fury, with no noise but the clank of their shoes. He saw these by glimpses, round corners, and at the ends of passages, but he did not actually pass them by.

And now, passing under a narrow doorway, he found himself in the dock, confronting a judge in his scarlet robes, in a large courthouse. There was nothing to elevate this temple of Themis above its vulgar kind elsewhere. Dingy enough it looked, in spite of candles lighted in decent abundance. A case had just closed, and the last juror's back was seen escaping through the door in the wall of the jury-box. There were some dozen barristers, some fiddling with pen and ink, others buried in briefs, some beckoning, with the plumes of their pens, to their attorneys, of whom there were no lack; there were clerks to-ing and fro-ing, and the officers of the court, and the registrar, who was handing up a paper to the judge; and the tipstaff, who was presenting a note at the end of his wand to a king's counsel over the heads of the crowd between. If this was the High Court of Appeal, which never rose day or night, it might account for the pale and jaded aspect of everybody in it. An air of indescribable gloom hung upon the pallid features of all the people here; no one ever smiled; all looked more or less secretly suffering.

"The King against Elijah Harbottle!" shouted the officer.

"Is the appellant Lewis Pyneweck in court?" asked Chief-Justice Twofold, in a voice of thunder, that shook the woodwork of the Court, and boomed down the corridors.

Up stood Pyneweck from his place at the table.

"Arraign the prisoner!" roared the Chief; and Judge Harbottle felt the panels of the dock round him, and the floor, and the rails quiver in the vibrations of that tremendous voice.

The prisoner, *in limine,* objected to this pretended court, as being a sham, and non-existent in point of law; and then, that, even if it were a court constituted by law (the

Judge was growing dazed), it had not and could not have any jurisdiction to try him for his conduct on the bench.

Whereupon the chief-justice laughed suddenly, and every one in court, turning round upon the prisoner, laughed also, till the laugh grew and roared all round like a deafening acclamation; he saw nothing but glittering eyes and teeth, a universal stare and grin; but though all the voices laughed, not a single face of all those that concentrated their gaze upon him looked like a laughing face. The mirth subsided as suddenly as it began.

The indictment was read. Judge Harbottle actually pleaded! He pleaded "Not guilty." A jury was sworn. The trial proceeded. Judge Harbottle was bewildered. This could not be real. He must be either mad, or *going* mad, he thought.

One thing could not fail to strike even him. This Chief-Justice Twofold, who was knocking him about at every turn with sneer and gibe, and roaring him down with his tremendous voice, was a dilated effigy of himself; an image of Mr. Justice Harbottle, at least double his size, and with all his fierce colouring, and his ferocity of eye and visage, enhanced awfully.

Nothing the prisoner could argue, cite, or state was permitted to retard for a moment the march of the case towards its catastrophe.

The chief-justice seemed to feel his power over the jury, and to exult and riot in the display of it. He glared at them, he nodded to them; he seemed to have established an understanding with them. The lights were faint in that part of the court. The jurors were mere shadows, sitting in rows; the prisoner could see a dozen pairs of white eyes shining, coldly, out of the darkness; and whenever the judge in his charge, which was contemptuously brief, nodded and grinned and gibed, the prisoner could see, in the obscurity, by the dip of all these rows of eyes together, that the jury nodded in acquiescence.

And now the charge was over, the huge chief-justice leaned back panting and gloating on the prisoner. Every one in the court turned about, and gazed with steadfast hatred on the man in the dock. From the jury-box where

the twelve sworn brethren were whispering together, a
sound in the general stillness like a prolonged "hiss-s-s!"
was heard; and then, in answer to the challenge of the officer, "How say you, gentlemen of the jury, guilty or not
guilty?" came in a melancholy voice the finding, "Guilty."

The place seemed to the eyes of the prisoner to grow
gradually darker and darker, till he could discern nothing
distinctly but the lumen of the eyes that were turned upon
him from every bench and side and corner and gallery of
the building. The prisoner doubtless thought that he had
quite enough to say, and conclusive, why sentence of death
should not be pronounced upon him; but the lord chief-
justice puffed it contemptuously away, like so much smoke,
and proceeded to pass sentence of death upon the prisoner,
having named the 10th of the ensuing month for his execution.

Before he had recovered the stun of this ominous farce,
in obedience to the mandate, "Remove the prisoner," he
was led from the dock. The lamps seemed all to have gone
out, and there were stoves and charcoal-fires here and
there, that threw a faint crimson light on the walls of the
corridors through which he passed. The stones that composed them looked now enormous, cracked and unhewn.

He came into a vaulted smithy, where two men, naked to
the waist, with heads like bulls, round shoulders, and the
arms of giants, were welding red-hot chains together with
hammers that pelted like thunderbolts.

They looked on the prisoner with fierce red eyes, and
rested on their hammers for a minute; and said the elder to
his companion, "Take out Elijah Harbottle's gyves"; and
with a pincers he plucked the end which lay dazzling in the
fire from the furnace.

"One end locks," said he, taking the cool end of the iron
in one hand, while with the grip of a vice he seized the leg
of the Judge, and locked the ring round his ankle. "The
other," he said with a grin, "is welded."

The iron band that was to form the ring for the other
leg lay still red-hot upon the stone floor, with brilliant
sparks sporting up and down its surface.

His companion in his gigantic hands seized the old Judge's other leg, and pressed his foot immovably to the stone floor; while his senior in a twinkling, with a masterly application of pincers and hammer, sped the glowing bar round his ankle so tight that the skin and sinews smoked and bubbled again, and old Judge Harbottle uttered a yell that seemed to chill the very stones, and make the iron chains quiver on the wall.

Chains, vaults, smiths, and smithy all vanished in a moment; but the pain continued. Mr. Justice Harbottle was suffering torture all round the ankle on which the infernal smiths had just been operating.

His friends Thavies and Beller were startled by the Judge's roar in the midst of their elegant trifling about a marriage à la mode case which was going on. The Judge was in panic as well as pain. The street-lamps and the light of his own hall-door restored him.

"I'm very bad," growled he between his set teeth; "my foot's blazing. Who was he that hurt my foot? 'Tis the gout —'tis the gout!" he said, awaking completely. "How many hours have we been coming from the playhouse? 'Sblood, what has happened on the way? I've slept half the night?"

There had been no hitch or delay, and they had driven home at a good pace.

The Judge, however, was in gout; he was feverish too; and the attack, though very short, was sharp; and when, in about a fortnight, it subsided, his ferocious joviality did not return. He could not get this dream, as he chose to call it, out of his head.

CHAPTER VIII. *Somebody Has Got into the House*

People remarked that the Judge was in the vapours. His doctor said he should go for a fortnight to Buxton.

Whenever the Judge fell into a brown study, he was always conning over the terms of the sentence pronounced upon him in his vision—"in one calendar month from the date of this day"; and then the usual form, "and you shall be hanged by the neck till you are dead," &c. "That will be the 10th—I'm not much in the way of being hanged. I know what stuff dreams are, and I laugh at them; but this is continually in my thoughts, as if it forecast misfortune of some sort. I wish the day my dream gave me were passed and over. I wish I were well purged of my gout. I wish I were as I used to be. 'Tis nothing but vapours, nothing but a maggot." The copy of the parchment and letter which had announced his trial with many a snort and sneer he would read over and over again, and the scenery and people of his dream would rise about him in places the most unlikely, and steal him in a moment from all that surrounded him into a world of shadows.

The Judge had lost his iron energy and banter. He was growing taciturn and morose. The Bar remarked the change, as well they might. His friends thought him ill. The doctor said he was troubled with hypochondria, and that his gout was still lurking in his system, and ordered him to that ancient haunt of crutches and chalk-stones, Buxton.

The Judge's spirits were very low; he was frightened about himself; and he described to his housekeeper, having sent for her to his study to drink a dish of tea, his strange dream in his drive home from Drury Lane playhouse. He was sinking into the state of nervous dejection in which men lose their faith in orthodox advice, and in despair consult quacks, astrologers, and nursery story-tellers. Could such a dream mean that he was to have a fit, and so die on the 10th? She did not think so. On the contrary, it was certain some good luck must happen on that day.

The Judge kindled; and for the first time for many days, he looked for a minute or two like himself, and he tapped her on the cheek with the hand that was not in flannel.

"Odsbud! odsheart! you dear rogue! I had forgot. There is young Tom—yellow Tom, my nephew, you know, lies sick at Harrogate; why shouldn't he go that day as well as another, and if he does, I get an estate by it? Why, lookee, I asked Doctor Hedstone yesterday if I was like to take a fit any time, and he laughed, and swore I was the last man in town to go off that way."

The Judge sent most of his servants down to Buxton to

make his lodgings and all things comfortable for him. He was to follow in a day or two.

It was now the 9th; and the next day well over, he might laugh at his visions and auguries.

On the evening of the 9th, Doctor Hedstone's footman knocked at the Judge's door. The doctor ran up the dusky stairs to the drawing room. It was a March evening, near the hour of sunset, with an east wind whistling sharply through the chimney-stacks. A wood fire blazed cheerily on the hearth. And Judge Harbottle, in what was then called a brigadier-wig, with his red roquelaure on, helped the glowing effect of the darkened chamber, which looked red all over like a room on fire.

The Judge had his feet on a stool, and his huge grim purple face confronted the fire, and seemed to pant and swell, as the blaze alternately spread upward and collapsed. He had fallen again among his blue devils, and was thinking of retiring from the Bench, and of fifty other gloomy things.

But the doctor, who was an energetic son of Æsculapius, would listen to no croaking, told the Judge he was full of gout, and in his present condition no judge even of his own case, but promised him leave to pronounce on all those melancholy questions, a fortnight later.

In the meantime the Judge must be very careful. He was overcharged with gout, and he must not provoke an attack, till the waters of Buxton should do that office for him, in their own salutary way.

The doctor did not think him perhaps quite so well as he pretended, for he told him he wanted rest, and would be better if he went forthwith to his bed.

Mr. Gerningham, his valet, assisted him, and gave him his drops; and the Judge told him to wait in his bedroom till he should go to sleep.

Three persons that night had specially odd stories to tell.

The housekeeper had got rid of the trouble of amusing her little girl at this anxious time by giving her leave to run about the sitting-rooms and look at the pictures and china, on the usual condition of touching nothing. It was not until the last gleam of sunset had for some time faded, and the twilight had so deepened that she could no longer discern the colours on the china figures on the chimneypiece or in the cabinets, that the child returned to the housekeeper's room to find her mother.

To her she related, after some prattle about the china, and the pictures, and the Judge's two grand wigs in the dressing-room off the library, an adventure of an extraordinary kind.

In the hall was placed, as was customary in those times, the sedan-chair which the master of the house occasionally used, covered with stamped leather, and studded with gilt nails, and with its red silk blinds down. In this case, the doors of this old-fashioned conveyance were locked, the windows up, and, as I said, the blinds down, but not so closely that the curious child could not peep underneath one of them, and see into the interior.

A parting beam from the setting sun, admitted through the window of a back room, shot obliquely through the open door, and lighting on the chair, shone with a dull transparency through the crimson blind.

To her surprise, the child saw in the shadow a thin man dressed in black seated in it; he had sharp dark features; his nose, she fancied, a little awry, and his brown eyes were looking straight before him; his hand was on his thigh, and he stirred no more than the waxen figure she had seen at Southwark fair.

A child is so often lectured for asking questions and on the propriety of silence, and the superior wisdom of its elders, that it accepts most things at last in good faith; and the little girl acquiesced respectfully in the occupation of the chair by this mahogany-faced person as being all right and proper.

It was not until she asked her mother who this man was, and observed her scared face as she questioned her more minutely upon the appearance of the stranger, that she began to understand that she had seen something unaccountable.

Mrs. Carwell took the key of the chair from its nail over the footman's shelf, and led the child by the hand up to the hall, having a lighted candle in her other hand. She stopped at a distance from the chair, and placed the candlestick in the child's hand.

"Peep in, Margery, again, and try if there's anything there," she whispered; "hold the candle near the blind so as to throw its light through the curtain."

The child peeped, this time with a very solemn face, and intimated at once that he was gone.

"Look again, and be sure," urged her mother.

The little girl was quite certain; and Mrs. Carwell, with her mob-cap of lace and cherry-coloured ribbons, and her dark brown hair, not yet powdered, over a very pale face, unlocked the door, looked in, and beheld emptiness.

"All a mistake, child, you see."

"*There*, ma'am! See there! He's gone round the corner," said the child.

"Where?" said Mrs. Carwell, stepping backward a step.

"Into that room."

"Tut, child! 'twas the shadow," cried Mrs. Carwell angrily, because she was frightened. "I moved the candle." But she clutched one of the poles of the chair, which leant against the wall in the corner, and pounded the floor furiously with one end of it, being afraid to pass the open door the child had pointed to.

The cook and two kitchen-maids came running upstairs, not knowing what to make of this unwonted alarm.

They all searched the room; but it was still and empty, and no sign of anyone's having been here.

Some people may suppose that the direction given to her thoughts by this odd little incident will account for a very strange illusion which Mrs. Carwell herself experienced about two hours later.

CHAPTER IX. *The Judge Leaves His House*

Mrs. Flora Carwell was going up the great staircase with a posset for the Judge in a china bowl, on a little silver tray.

Across the top of the well-staircase there runs a mas-

sive oak rail; and, raising her eyes accidentally, she saw an
extremely odd-looking stranger, slim and long, leaning carelessly over with a pipe between his finger and thumb. Nose,
lips, and chin seemed all to droop downward into extraordinary length, as he leant his odd peering face over the
banister. In his other hand he held a coil of rope, one end
of which escaped from under his elbow and hung over the
rail.

Mrs. Carwell, who had no suspicion at the moment, that
he was not a real person, and fancied that he was someone
employed in cording the Judge's luggage, called to know
what he was doing there.

Instead of answering, he turned about, and walked across
the lobby, at about the same leisurely pace at which she
was ascending, and entered a room, into which she followed him. It was an uncarpeted and unfurnished chamber.
An open trunk lay upon the floor empty, and beside it the
coil of rope; but except herself there was no one in the
room.

Mrs. Carwell was very much frightened, and now concluded that the child must have seen the same ghost that
had just appeared to her. Perhaps, when she was able to
think it over, it was a relief to believe so; for the face, figure, and dress described by the child were awfully like
Pyneweck; and this certainly was not he.

Very much scared and very hysterical, Mrs. Carwell ran
down to her room, afraid to look over her shoulder, and
got some companions about her, and wept, and talked, and
drank more than one cordial, and talked and wept again,
and so on, until, in those early days, it was ten o'clock, and
time to go to bed.

A scullery-maid remained up finishing some of her scour-
ing and "scalding" for some time after the other servants
—who, as I said, were few in number—that night had got
to their beds. This was a low-browed, broad-faced, intrepid
wench with black hair, who did not "vally a ghost not a
button," and treated the housekeeper's hysterics with meas-
ureless scorn.

The old house was quiet, now. It was near twelve o'clock,

no sounds were audible except the muffled wailing of the wintry winds, piping high among the roofs and chimneys, or rumbling at intervals, in under gusts, through the narrow channels of the street.

The spacious solitudes of the kitchen level were awfully dark, and this sceptical kitchen-wench was the only person now up and about, in the house. She hummed tunes to herself, for a time; and then stopped and listened; and then resumed her work again. At last, she was destined to be more terrified than even was the housekeeper.

There was a back-kitchen in this house, and from this she heard, as if coming from below its foundations, a sound like heavy strokes that seemed to shake the earth beneath her feet. Sometimes a dozen in sequence, at regular intervals; sometimes fewer. She walked out softly into the passage, and was surprised to see a dusky glow issuing from this room, as if from a charcoal fire.

The room seemed thick with smoke.

Looking in, she very dimly beheld a monstrous figure, over a furnace, beating with a mighty hammer the rings and rivets of a chain.

The strokes, swift and heavy as they looked, sounded hollow and distant. The man stopped, and pointed to something on the floor, that, through the smoky haze, looked, she thought, like a dead body. She remarked no more; but the servants in the room close by, startled from their sleep by a hideous scream, found her in a swoon on the flags, close to the door, where she had just witnessed this ghastly vision.

Startled by the girl's incoherent asseverations that she had seen the Judge's corpse on the floor, two servants having first searched the lower part of the house, went rather frightened upstairs to inquire whether their master was well. They found him, not in his bed, but in his room. He had a table with candles burning at his bedside, and was getting on his clothes again; and he swore and cursed at them roundly in his old style, telling them that he had business, and that he would discharge on the spot any scoundrel who should dare to disturb him again.

So the invalid was left to his quietude.

In the morning it was rumoured here and there in the street that the Judge was dead. A servant was sent from the house three doors away, by Counsellor Traverse, to inquire at Judge Harbottle's hall-door.

The servant who opened it was pale and reserved, and would only say that the Judge was ill. He had had a dangerous accident; Doctor Hedstone had been with him at seven o'clock in the morning.

There were averted looks, short answers, pale and frowning faces, and all the usual signs that there was a secret that sat heavily upon their minds, and the time for disclosing which had not yet come. That time would arrive when the coroner had arrived, and the mortal scandal that had befallen the house could be no longer hidden. For that morning Mr. Justice Harbottle had been found hanging by the neck from the banister at the top of the great staircase, and quite dead.

There was not the smallest sign of any struggle or resistance. There had not been heard a cry or any other noise in the slightest degree indicative of violence. There was medical evidence to show that, in his atrabilious state, it was quite on the cards that he might have made away with himself. The jury found accordingly that it was a case of suicide. But to those who were acquainted with the strange story which Judge Harbottle had related to at least two persons, the fact that the catastrophe occurred on the morning to the 10th March seemed a startling coincidence.

A few days after, the pomp of a great funeral attended him to the grave; and so, in the language of scripture, "the rich man died, and was buried."

THE TRAVELLER'S STORY
OF A TERRIBLY
STRANGE BED

BY WILKIE COLLINS

SHORTLY AFTER MY EDUCATION AT COL-
lege was finished, I happened to be staying at Paris with an
English friend. We were both young men then, and lived, I
am afraid, rather a wild life, in the delightful city of our
sojourn. One night we were idling about the neighborhood of
the Palais Royal, doubtful to what amusement we should next
betake ourselves. My friend proposed a visit to Frascati's;
but his suggestion was not to my taste. I knew Frascati's, as
the French saying is, by heart; had lost and won plenty of
five-franc pieces there, merely for amusement's sake, until it
was amusement no longer, and was thoroughly tired, in
fact, of all the ghastly respectabilities of such a social
anomaly as a respectable gambling-house. "For Heaven's
sake," said I to my friend, "let us go somewhere where we
can see a little genuine, blackguard, poverty-stricken gaming, with no false gingerbread glitter thrown over it at all.
Let us get away from fashionable Frascati's, to a house
where they don't mind letting in a man with a ragged coat,
or a man with no coat, ragged or otherwise."—"Very
well," said my friend, "we needn't go out of the Palais Royal to find the sort of company you want. Here's the place
just before us; as blackguard a place, by all report, as you
could possibly wish to see." In another minute we arrived
at the door, and entered the house, the back of which you
have drawn in your sketch.[1]

When we got upstairs, and left our hats and sticks with

[1] [The story is supposed to be narrated by its chief actor, to the artist
who is painting his portrait.]

the doorkeeper, we were admitted into the chief gambling-room. We did not find many people assembled there. But, few as the men were who looked up at us on our entrance, they were all types—lamentably true types—of their respective classes.

We had come to see blackguards; but these men were something worse. There is a comic side, more or less appreciable, in all blackguardism—here there was nothing but tragedy—mute, weird tragedy. The quiet in the room was horrible. The thin, haggard, long-haired young man, whose sunken eyes fiercely watched the turning up of the cards, never spoke; the flabby, fat-faced, pimply player, who pricked his piece of pasteboard perseveringly, to register how often black won, and how often red—never spoke; the dirty, wrinkled old man, with the vulture eyes and the darned greatcoat, who had lost his last *sou*, and still looked on desperately, after he could play no longer—never spoke. Even the voice of the croupier sounded as if it were strangely dulled and thickened in the atmosphere of the room. I had entered the place to laugh, but the spectacle before me was something to weep over. I soon found it necessary to take refuge in excitement from the depression of spirits which was fast stealing on me. Unfortunately I sought the nearest excitement, by going to the table, and beginning to play. Still more unfortunately, as the event will show, I won—won prodigiously; won incredibly; won at such a rate, that the regular players at the table crowded round me; and staring at my stakes with hungry, superstitious eyes, whispered to one another that the English stranger was going to break the bank.

The game was *Rouge et Noir*. I had played at it in every city in Europe, without, however, the care or the wish to study the Theory of Chances—that philosopher's stone of all gamblers! And a gambler, in the strict sense of the word, I had never been. I was heart-whole from the corroding passion for play. My gaming was a mere idle amusement. I never resorted to it by necessity, because I never knew what it was to want money. I never practised it so incessantly as to lose more than I could afford, or to gain more than I could coolly pocket without being thrown off my balance by my good luck. In short, I had hitherto frequented gambling-tables—just as I frequented ball-rooms and opera-houses—because they amused me, and because I had nothing better to do with my leisure hours.

But on this occasion it was very different—now, for the first time in my life, I felt what the passion for play really was. My success first bewildered, and then, in the most literal meaning of the word, intoxicated me. Incredible as it may appear, it is nevertheless true, that I only lost when I attempted to estimate chances, and played according to previous calculation. If I left everything to luck, and staked without any care or consideration, I was sure to win—to win in the face of every recognized probability in favour of the bank. At first, some of the men present ventured their money safely enough on my colour; but I speedily increased my stakes to sums which they dared not risk. One after another they left off playing, and breathlessly looked on at my game.

Still, time after time, I staked higher and higher, and still won. The excitement in the room rose to fever pitch. The silence was interrupted by a deep-muttered chorus of oaths and exclamations in different languages, every time the gold was shovelled across to my side of the table—even the imperturbable croupier dashed his rake on the floor in a (French) fury of astonishment at my success. But one man present preserved his self-possession; and that man was my friend. He came to my side, and whispering in English, begged me to leave· the place, satisfied with what I had already gained. I must do him the justice to say that he repeated his warnings and entreaties several times, and only left me and went away, after I had rejected his advice (I was to all intents and purposes gambling-drunk) in terms which rendered it impossible for him to address me again that night.

Shortly after he had gone, a hoarse voice behind me cried: "Permit me, my dear sir!—permit me to restore to their proper place two Napoleons which you have dropped. Wonderful luck, sir! I pledge you my word of honour, as

an old soldier, in the course of my long experience in this
sort of thing, I never saw such luck as yours!—never! Go
on, sir—*Sacré mille bombes!* Go on boldly, and break the
bank!"

I turned round and saw, nodding and smiling at me with
inveterate civility, a tall man, dressed in a frogged and
braided surtout.

If I had been in my senses, I should have considered him,
personally, as being rather a suspicious specimen of an old
soldier. He had goggling blood-shot eyes, mangy musta-
chios, and a broken nose. His voice betrayed a barrack-
room intonation of the worst order, and he had the dirtiest
pair of hands I ever saw—even in France. These little personal peculiarities exercised, however, no repelling influence on me. In the mad excitement, the reckless triumph of
that moment, I was ready to "fraternize" with anybody
who encouraged me in my game. I accepted the old soldier's offered pinch of snuff; clapped him on the back, and
swore he was the honestest fellow in the world—the most
glorious relic of the Grand Army that I had ever met with.
"Go on!" cried my military friend, snapping his fingers in
ecstasy,—"Go on, and win! Break the bank—*Mille tonner-
res!* my gallant English comrade, break the bank!"

And I *did* go on—went on at such a rate, that in another
quarter of an hour the croupier called out: "Gentlemen!
the bank has discontinued for to-night." All the notes, and
all the gold in that "bank," now lay in a heap under my
hands; the whole floating capital of the gambling-house was
waiting to pour into my pockets!

"Tie up the money in your pocket-handkerchief, my
worthy sir," said the old soldier, as I wildly plunged my
hands into my heap of gold. "Tie it up, as we used to tie up
a bit of dinner in the Grand Army; your winnings are too
heavy for any breeches pockets that ever were sewed.
There! that's it—shovel them in, notes and all! *Credié!*
what luck!—Stop! another Napoleon on the floor! *Ah!
sacré petit polisson de Napoléon!* have I found thee at last?
Now then, sir—two tight double knots each way with your
honourable permission, and the money's safe. Feel it! feel

it, fortunate sir! hard and round as a cannon ball—*Ah, bah!*
if they had only fired such cannon balls at us at Austerlitz
—*nom d'une pipe!* if they only had! And now, as an ancient
grenadier, as an ex-brave of the French army, what remains for me to do? I ask what? Simply this: to entreat my
valued English friend to drink a bottle of champagne with
me, and toast the goddess Fortune in foaming goblets before we part!"

Excellent ex-brave! Convivial ancient grenadier! Cham-
pagne by all means! An English cheer for an old soldier!
Hurrah! hurrah! Another English cheer for the goddess
Fortune! Hurrah! hurrah! hurrah!

"Bravo! the Englishman; the amiable, gracious Englishman, in whose veins circulates the vivacious blood of
France! Another glass? *Ah, bah!*—the bottle is empty!
Never mind! *Vive le vin!* I, the old soldier, order another
bottle, and half-a-pound of *bonbons* with it!"

"No, no, ex-brave; never—ancient grenadier! *Your* bottle last time; *my* bottle this. Behold it! Toast away! The
French Army!—the great Napoleon!—the present company! the croupier! the honest croupier's wife and daughters—if he has any! the Ladies generally! Everybody in the
world!"

By the time the second bottle of champagne was emptied, I felt as if I had been drinking liquid fire—my brain
seemed all a-flame. No excess in wine had ever had this effect on me before in my life. Was it the result of a stimu-
lant acting upon my system when I was in a highly excited
state? Was my stomach in a particularly disordered condition? Or was the champagne amazingly strong?

"Ex-brave of the French Army!" cried I, in a mad state
of exhilaration, *"I* am on fire! how are *you?* You have set
me on fire! Do you hear, my hero of Austerlitz? Let us
have a third bottle of champagne to put the flame out!"

The old soldier wagged his head, rolled his goggle eyes,
until I expected to see them slip out of their sockets; placed
his dirty fore-finger by the side of his broken nose; solemnly ejaculated "Coffee!" and immediately ran off into an inner room.

The word pronounced by the eccentric veteran seemed to have a magical effect on the rest of the company present. With one accord they all rose to depart. Probably they had expected to profit by my intoxication; but finding that my new friend was benevolently bent on preventing me from getting dead drunk, had now abandoned all hope of thriving pleasantly on my winnings. Whatever their motive might be, at any rate they went away in a body. When the old soldier returned, and sat down again opposite to me at the table, we had the room to ourselves. I could see the croupier, in a sort of vestibule which opened out of it, eating his supper in solitude. The silence was now deeper than ever.

A sudden change, too, had come over the "ex-brave." He assumed a portentously solemn look! and when he spoke to me again, his speech was ornamented by no oaths, enforced by no finger-snapping, enlivened by no apostrophes or exclamations.

"Listen, my dear sir," said he, in mysteriously confidential tones—"listen to an old soldier's advice. I have been to the mistress of the house (a very charming woman, with a genius for cookery!) to impress on her the necessity of making us some particularly strong and good coffee. You must drink this coffee in order to get rid of your little amiable exaltation of spirits before you think of going home— you *must*, my good and gracious friend! With all that money to take home to-night, it is a sacred duty to yourself to have your wits about you. You are known to be a winner to an enormous extent by several gentlemen present to-night, who, in a certain point of view, are very worthy and excellent fellows, but they are mortal men, my dear sir, and they have their amiable weaknesses! Need I say more? Ah, no, no! you understand me! Now, this is what you must do —send for a cabriolet when you feel quite well again— draw up all the windows when you get into it—and tell the driver to take you home only through the large and well-lighted thoroughfares. Do this; and you and your money will be safe. Do this; and to-morrow you will thank an old soldier for giving you a word of honest advice."

Just as the ex-brave ended his oration in very lachrymose tones, the coffee came in, ready poured out in two cups. My attentive friend handed me one of the cups with a bow. I was parched with thirst, and drank it off at a draught. Almost instantly afterwards, I was seized with a fit of giddiness, and felt more completely intoxicated than ever. The room whirled round and round furiously; the old soldier seemed to be regularly bobbing up and down before me like the piston of a steam-engine. I was half deafened by a violent singing in my ears; a feeling of utter bewilderment, helplessness, idiocy, overcame me. I rose from my chair, holding on by the table to keep my balance; and stammered out, that I felt dreadfully unwell—so unwell that I did not know how I was to get home.

"My dear friend," answered the old soldier—and even his voice seemed to be bobbing up and down as he spoke —"my dear friend, it would be madness to go home in *your* state; you would be sure to lose your money; you might be robbed and murdered with the greatest ease. *I* am going to sleep here: do *you* sleep here, too—they make up capital beds in this house—take one; sleep off the effects of the wine, and go home safely with your winnings to-morrow—to-morrow, in broad daylight."

I had but two ideas left:—one, that I must never let go hold of my handkerchief full of money; the other, that I must lie down somewhere immediately, and fall off into a comfortable sleep. So I agreed to the proposal about the bed, and took the offered arm of the old soldier, carrying my money with my disengaged hand. Preceded by the croupier, we passed along some passages and up a flight of stairs into the bedroom which I was to occupy. The ex-brave shook me warmly by the hand, proposed that we should breakfast together, and then, followed by the croupier, left me for the night.

I ran to the wash-hand stand; drank some of the water in my jug; poured the rest out, and plunged my face into it; then sat down in a chair and tried to compose myself. I soon felt better. The change for my lungs, from the fetid atmosphere of the gambling-room to the cool air of the apartment I now occupied; the almost equally refreshing change for my eyes, from the glaring gas-lights of the "Salon" to the dim, quiet flicker of one bedroom candle, aided wonderfully the restorative effects of cold water. The giddiness left me, and I began to feel a little like a reasonable being again. My first thought was of the risk of sleeping all night in a gambling-house; my second, of the still greater risk of trying to get out after the house was closed, and of going home alone at night, through the streets of Paris, with a large sum of money about me. I had slept in worse places than this on my travels; so I determined to lock, bolt, and barricade my door, and take my chance till the next morning.

Accordingly, I secured myself against all intrusion; looked under the bed, and into the cupboard; tried the fastening of the window; and then, satisfied that I had taken every proper precaution, pulled off my upper clothing, put my light, which was a dim one, on the hearth among a feathery litter of wood ashes, and got into bed, with the handkerchief full of money under my pillow.

I soon felt not only that I could not go to sleep, but that I could not even close my eyes. I was wide awake, and in a high fever. Every nerve in my body trembled—every one of my senses seemed to be preternaturally sharpened. I tossed and rolled, and tried every kind of position, and perseveringly sought out the cold corners of the bed, and all to no purpose. Now, I thrust my arms over the clothes; now, I poked them under the clothes; now, I violently shot my legs straight out down to the bottom of the bed; now, I convulsively coiled them up as near my chin as they would go; now, I shook out my crumpled pillow, changed it to the cool side, patted it flat, and lay down quietly on my back; now, I fiercely doubled it in two, set it up on end, thrust it against the board of the bed, and tried a sitting posture. Every effort was in vain; I groaned with vexation, as I felt that I was in for a sleepless night.

What could I do? I had no book to read. And yet, unless I found out some method of diverting my mind, I felt certain that I was in the condition to imagine all sorts of horrors; to rack my brain with forebodings of every possible and impossible danger; in short, to pass the night in suffering all conceivable varieties of nervous terror.

I raised myself on my elbow, and looked about the room —which was brightened by a lovely moonlight pouring straight through the window—to see if it contained any pictures or ornaments that I could at all clearly distinguish. While my eyes wandered from wall to wall, a remembrance of Le Maistre's delightful little book, *Voyage autour de ma Chambre,* occurred to me. I resolved to imitate the French author, and find occupation and amusement enough to relieve the tedium of my wakefulness, by making a mental inventory of every article of furniture I could see, and by following up to their sources the multitude of associations which even a chair, a table, or a wash-hand stand may be made to call forth.

In the nervous unsettled state of my mind at that moment, I found it much easier to make my inventory than to make my reflections, and thereupon soon gave up all hope of thinking in Le Maistre's fanciful track—or, indeed, of thinking at all. I looked about the room at the different articles of furniture, and did nothing more.

There was, first, the bed I was lying in; a four-post bed, of all things in the world to meet with in Paris!—yes, a thorough clumsy British four-poster, with the regular top lined with chintz—the regular fringed valance all round— the regular stifling unwholesome curtains, which I remembered having mechanically drawn back against the posts without particularly noticing the bed when I first got into the room. Then there was the marble-topped wash-hand stand, from which the water I had spilt, in my hurry to pour it out, was still dripping, slowly and more slowly, on to the brick floor. Then two small chairs, with my coat, waistcoat, and trousers flung on them. Then a large elbow-chair covered with dirty-white dimity, with my cravat and shirt-collar thrown over the back. Then a chest of drawers with two of the brass handles off, and a tawdry, broken china inkstand placed on it by way of ornament for the top. Then the dressing-table, adorned by a very small looking-glass, and a very large pin-cushion. Then the window—an unusually large window. Then a dark old picture, which the feeble candle dimly showed me. It was the picture of a fellow in a high Spanish hat, crowned with a plume of towering feathers. A swarthy sinister ruffian, looking upward, shading his eyes with his hand, and looking intently upward—it might be at some tall gallows at which he was going to be hanged. At any rate, he had the appearance of thoroughly deserving it.

This picture put a kind of constraint upon me to look upward too—at the top of the bed. It was a gloomy and not an interesting object, and I looked back at the picture. I counted the feathers in the man's hat—they stood out in relief—three white, two green. I observed the crown of his hat, which was of a conical shape, according to the fashion supposed to have been favoured by Guido Fawkes. I wondered what he was looking up at. It couldn't be at the stars; such a desperado was neither astrologer nor astronomer. It must be at the high gallows, and he was going to be hanged presently. Would the executioner come into possession of his conical-crowned hat and plume of feathers? I counted the feathers again—three white, two green.

While I still lingered over this very improving and intellectual employment, my thoughts insensibly began to wander. The moonlight shining into the room reminded me of a certain moonlight night in England—the night after a picnic party in a Welsh valley. Every incident of the drive homeward, through lovely scenery, which the moonlight made lovelier than ever, came back to my remembrance, though I had never given the picnic a thought for years; though, if I had *tried* to recollect it, I could certainly have recalled little or nothing of that scene long past. Of all the wonderful faculties that help to tell us we are immortal, which speaks the sublime truth more eloquently than memory? Here was I, in a strange house of the most suspicious character, in a situation of uncertainty, and even of peril, which might seem to make the cool exercise of my recollection almost out of the question; nevertheless, remembering, quite involuntarily, places, people, conversations, minute circumstances of every kind, which I had thought forgotten for ever; which I could not possibly have recalled at will, even under the most favourable auspices. And what cause had produced in a moment the whole of this strange, complicated, mysterious effect? Nothing but some rays of moonlight shining in at my bedroom window.

I was still thinking of the picnic—of our merriment on the drive home—of the sentimental young lady who *would* quote *Childe Harold* because it was moonlight. I was absorbed by these past scenes and past amusements, when, in an instant, the thread on which my memories hung snapped asunder; my attention immediately came back to present things more vividly than ever, and I found myself, I neither knew why nor wherefore, looking hard at the picture again.

Looking for what?

Good God! the man had pulled his hat down on his brows!—No! the hat itself was gone! Where was the conical crown? Where the feathers—three white, two green? Not there? In place of the hat and feathers, what dusky object was it that now hid his forehead, his eyes, his shading hand?

Was the bed moving?

I turned on my back and looked up. Was I mad? drunk? dreaming? giddy again? or was the top of the bed really moving down—sinking slowly, regularly, silently, horribly, right down throughout the whole of its length and breadth —right down upon me, as I lay underneath?

My blood seemed to stand still. A deadly paralysing coldness stole all over me, as I turned my head round on the pillow, and determined to test whether the bed-top was really moving or not, by keeping my eye on the man in the picture.

The next look in that direction was enough. The dull, black, frowsy outline of the valance above me was within an inch of being parallel with his waist. I still looked breathlessly. And steadily, and slowly—very slowly—I saw the figure, and the line of frame below the figure, vanish, as the valance moved down before it.

I am, constitutionally, anything but timid. I have been on more than one occasion in peril of my life, and have not lost my self-possession for an instant; but when the conviction first settled on my mind that the bed-top was really moving, was steadily and continuously sinking down upon me, I looked up shuddering, helpless, panic-stricken, beneath the hideous machinery for murder, which was advancing closer and closer to suffocate me where I lay.

I looked up, motionless, speechless, breathless. The candle, fully spent, went out; but the moonlight still brightened the room. Down and down, without pausing and without sounding, came the bed-top, and still my panic-terror seemed to bind me faster and faster to the mattress on which I lay—down and down it sank, till the dusty odour from the lining of the canopy came stealing into my nostrils.

At that final moment the instinct of self-preservation startled me out of my trance, and I moved at last. There was just room for me to roll myself sideways off the bed. As I dropped noiselessly to the floor, the edge of the murderous canopy touched me on the shoulder.

Without stopping to draw my breath, without wiping the cold sweat from my face, I rose instantly on my knees to watch the bed-top. I was literally spell-bound by it. If I had heard footsteps behind me, I could not have turned round; if a means of escape had been miraculously provided for me, I could not have moved to take advantage of it. The whole life in me was, at that moment, concentrated in my eyes.

It descended—the whole canopy, with the fringe round it, came down—down—close down; so close that there was not room now to squeeze my finger between the bed-top and the bed. I felt at the sides, and discovered that what had appeared to me from beneath to be the ordinary light canopy of a four-post bed, was in a reality a thick, broad mattress, the substance of which was concealed by the valance and its fringe. I looked up and saw the four posts rising hideously bare. In the middle of the bed-top was a huge wooden screw that had evidently worked it down through a hole in the ceiling, just as ordinary presses are worked down on the substance selected for compression. The frightful apparatus moved without making the faintest noise. There had been no creaking as it came down; there was now not the faintest sound from the room above. Amid a dead and awful silence I beheld before me—in the nineteenth century, and in the civilized capital of France—such a machine for secret murder by suffocation as might have existed in the worst days of the Inquisition, in the lonely inns among the Hartz Mountains, in the mysterious tribunals of Westphalia! Still, as I looked on it, I could not move, I could hardly breathe, but I began to recover the power of thinking, and in a moment I discovered the murderous conspiracy framed against me in all its horror.

My cup of coffee had been drugged, and drugged too strongly. I had been saved from being smothered by having taken an overdose of some narcotic. How I had chafed and fretted at the fever-fit which had preserved my life by keeping me awake! How recklessly I had confided myself to the two wretches who had led me into this room, determined, for the sake of my winnings, to kill me in my sleep by the surest and most horrible contrivance for secretly accomplishing my destruction! How many men, winners like me, had slept, as I had proposed to sleep, in that bed, and had never been seen or heard of more! I shuddered at the bare idea of it.

But, ere long, all thought was again suspended by the sight of the murderous canopy moving once more. After it had remained on the bed—as nearly as I could guess—about ten minutes, it began to move up again. The villains who worked it from above evidently believed that their purpose was now accomplished. Slowly and silently, as it had descended, that horrible bed-top rose towards its former place. When it reached the upper extremities of the four posts, it reached the ceiling too. Neither hole nor screw could be seen; the bed became in appearance an ordinary bed again—the canopy an ordinary canopy—even to the most suspicious eyes.

Now, for the first time, I was able to move—to rise from my knees—to dress myself in my upper clothing—and to consider how I should escape. If I betrayed, by the smallest noise, that the attempt to suffocate me had failed, I was certain to be murdered. Had I made any noise already? I listened intently, looking towards the door.

No! no footsteps in the passage outside—no sound of a tread, light or heavy, in the room above—absolute silence everywhere. Besides locking and bolting my door, I had moved an old wooden chest against it, which I had found under the bed. To remove this chest (my blood ran cold as I thought of what its contents *might* be!) without making some disturbance was impossible; and, moreover, to think of escaping through the house, now barred up for the night, was sheer insanity. Only one chance was left me—the window. I stole to it on tiptoe.

My bedroom was on the first floor, above an *entresol,* and looked into the back street, which you have sketched in your view. I raised my hand to open the window, knowing that on that action hung, by the merest hair's-breadth, my chance of safety. They keep vigilant watch in a House of Murder. If any part of the frame cracked, if the hinge creaked, I was a lost man! It must have occupied me at least five minutes, reckoning by time—five *hours,* reckoning by suspense—to open that window. I succeeded in doing it silently—in doing it with all the dexterity of a housebreaker—and then looked down into the street. To leap the distance beneath me would be almost certain destruction! Next, I looked round at the sides of the house. Down the left side ran the thick water-pipe which you have drawn— it passed close by the outer edge of the window. The moment I saw the pipe, I knew I was saved. My breath came and went freely for the first time since I had seen the canopy of the bed moving down upon me!

To some men the means of escape which I had discovered might have seemed difficult and dangerous enough— to *me* the prospect of slipping down the pipe into the street did not suggest even a thought of peril. I had always been accustomed, by the practice of gymnastics, to keep up my schoolboy powers as a daring and expert climber; and knew that my head, hands, and feet would serve me faithfully in any hazards of ascent or descent. I had already got one leg over the window-sill, when I remembered the handkerchief filled with money under my pillow. I could well have afforded to leave it behind me, but I was revengefully determined that the miscreants of the gambling-house should miss their plunder as well as their victim. So I went back to the bed and tied the heavy handkerchief at my back by my cravat.

Just as I had made it tight and fixed it in a comfortable place, I thought I heard a sound of breathing outside the door. The chill feeling of horror ran through me again as I listened. No! dead silence still in the passage—I had only heard the night-air blowing softly into the room. The next moment I was on the window-sill—and the next I had a firm grip on the water-pipe with my hands and knees.

I slid down into the street easily and quietly, as I thought I should, and immediately set off at the top of my speed to a branch "Prefecture" of Police, which I knew was situated in the immediate neighbourhood. A "Sub-prefect," and several picked men among his subordinates, happened to be up, maturing, I believe, some scheme for discovering the perpetrator of a mysterious murder which all Paris was talking of just then. When I began my story, in a breathless hurry and in very bad French, I could see that the Sub-prefect suspected me of being a drunken Englishman who had robbed somebody; but he soon altered his opinion as I went on, and before I had anything like concluded, he shoved all the papers before him into a drawer, put on his hat, supplied me with another (for I was bare-headed), ordered a file of soldiers, desired his expert followers to get ready all sorts of tools for breaking open doors and ripping up brick-flooring, and took my arm, in the most friendly and familiar manner possible, to lead me with him out of the house. I will venture to say, that when the Sub-prefect was a little boy, and was taken for the first time to the play, he was not half as much pleased as he was now at the job in prospect for him at the gambling-house!

Away we went through the streets, the Sub-prefect cross-examining and congratulating me in the same breath as we marched at the head of our formidable *posse comitatus*.

Sentinels were placed at the back and front of the house
the moment we got to it; a tremendous battery of knocks
was directed against the door; a light appeared at a window; I was told to conceal myself behind the police—then
came more knocks, and a cry of "Open in the name of the
law!" At that terrible summons bolts and locks gave way
before an invisible hand, and the moment after the Sub-
prefect was in the passage, confronting a waiter half-
dressed and ghastly pale. This was the short dialogue which
immediately took place:—

"We want to see the Englishman who is sleeping in this
house."

"He went away hours ago."

"He did no such thing. His friend went away; he remained. Show us to his bedroom!"

"I swear to you, Monsieur le Sous-prefect, he is not here!
he—"

"I swear to you, Monsieur le Garçon, he is. He slept
here—he didn't find your bed comfortable—he came to us
to complain of it—here he is among my men—and here am
I ready to look for a flea or two in his bedstead. Renaudin!"
(calling to one of the subordinates, and pointing to the
waiter) "collar that man, and tie his hands behind him.
Now, then, gentlemen, let us walk upstairs!"

Every man and woman in the house was secured—the
"Old Soldier" the first. Then I identified the bed in which I
had slept, and then we went into the room above.

No object that was at all extraordinary appeared in any
part of it. The Sub-prefect looked round the place, commanded everybody to be silent, stamped twice on the floor,
called for a candle, looked attentively at the spot he had
stamped on, and ordered the flooring there to be carefully
taken up. This was done in no time. Lights were produced,
and we saw a deep raftered cavity between the floor of this
room and the ceiling of the room beneath. Through this
cavity there ran perpendicularly a sort of case of iron thick-
ly greased; and inside the case appeared the screw, which
communicated with the bed-top below. Extra lengths of
screw, freshly oiled; levers covered with felt; all the com-

plete upper works of a heavy press—constructed with infernal ingenuity so as to join the fixtures below, and when taken to pieces again to go into the smallest possible compass—were next discovered and pulled out on the floor. After some little difficulty, the Sub-prefect succeeded in putting the machinery together, and leaving his men to work it, descended with me to the bedroom. The smothering canopy was then lowered, but not so noiselessly as I had seen it lowered. When I mentioned this to the Sub-prefect, his answer, simple as it was, had a terrible significance. "My men," said he, "are working down the bed-top for the first time—the men whose money you won were in better practice."

We left the house in the sole possession of two police agents—every one of the inmates being removed to prison on the spot. The Sub-prefect, after taking down my *"procès-verbal"* in his office, returned with me to my hotel to get my passport. "Do you think," I asked, as I gave it to him, "that any men have really been smothered in that bed, as they tried to smother *me?*"

"I have seen dozens of drowned men laid out at the Morgue," answered the Sub-prefect, "in whose pocketbooks were found letters, stating that they had committed suicide in the Seine, because they had lost everything at the gaming-table. Do I know how many of those men entered the same gambling-house that *you* entered? won as *you* won? took that bed as *you* took it? slept in it? were smothered in it? and were privately thrown into the river, with a letter of explanation written by the murderers and placed in their pocket-books? No man can say how many or how few have suffered the fate from which you have escaped. The people of the gambling-house kept their bedstead machinery a secret from *us*—even from the police! The dead kept the rest of the secret for them. Good night, or rather good morning, Monsieur Faulkner! Be at my office again at nine o'clock—in the meantime, *au revoir!*"

The rest of my story is soon told. I was examined and re-examined; the gambling-house was strictly searched all through from top to bottom; the prisoners were separately interrogated; and two of the less guilty among them made a confession. *I* discovered that the Old Soldier was the master of the gambling-house—*justice* discovered that he had been drummed out of the army as a vagabond years ago; that he had been guilty of all sorts of villainies since; that he was in possession of stolen property, which the owners identified; and that he, the croupier, another accomplice, and the woman who had made my cup of coffee, were all in the secret of the bedstead. There appeared some reason to doubt whether the inferior persons attached to the house knew anything of the suffocating machinery; and they received the benefit of that doubt, by being treated simply as thieves and vagabonds. As for the Old Soldier and his two head-myrmidons, they went to the galleys; the woman who had drugged my coffee was imprisoned for I forget how many years; the regular attendants at the gambling-house were considered "suspicious," and placed under "surveillance"; and I became, for one whole week (which is a long time), the head "lion" in Parisian society. My adventure was dramatized by three illustrious playmakers, but never saw theatrical daylight; for the censorship forbade the introduction on the stage of a correct copy of the gambling-house bedstead.

One good result was produced by my adventure, which any censorship must have approved:—it cured me of ever again trying "Rouge et Noir" as an amusement. The sight of a green cloth, with packs of cards and heaps of money on it, will henceforth be for ever associated in my mind with the sight of a bed-canopy descending to suffocate me in the silence and darkness of the night.

THE SQUAW

BY BRAM STOKER

NURNBERG AT THE TIME WAS NOT SO much exploited as it has been since then. Irving had not been playing *Faust*, and the very name of the old town was hardly known to the great bulk of the travelling public. My wife and I being in the second week of our honeymoon, naturally wanted someone else to join our party, so that when the cheery stranger, Elias P. Hutcheson, hailing from Isthmain City, Bleeding Gulch, Maple Tree County, Neb., turned up at the station at Frankfort, and casually remarked that he was going on to see the most all-fired old Methuselah of a town in Yurrup, and that he guessed that so much travelling alone was enough to send an intelligent, active citizen into the melancholy ward of a daft house, we took the pretty broad hint and suggested that we should join forces. We found, on comparing notes afterwards, that we had each intended to speak with some diffidence or hesitation so as not to appear too eager, such not being a good compliment to the success of our married life; but the effect was entirely marred by our both beginning to speak at the same instant—stopping simultaneously and then going on together again. Anyhow, no matter how, it was done; and Elias P. Hutcheson became one of our party. Straightway Amelia and I found the pleasant benefit; instead of quarrelling, as we had been doing, we found that the restraining influence of a third party was such that we now took every opportunity of spooning in odd corners. Amelia declares that ever since she has, as the result of that experience, advised all her friends to take a friend on the honeymoon. Well, we "did" Nurnberg together, and much enjoyed the racy remarks of our Transatlantic friend, who, from his quaint speech and his wonderful stock of adventures, might have stepped out of a novel. We kept for the last object of interest in the city to be visited the Burg, and on the day appointed for the visit strolled round the outer wall of the city by the eastern side.

The Burg is seated on a rock dominating the town, and an immensely deep fosse guards it on the northern side. Nurnberg has been happy in that it was never sacked; had it been it would certainly not be so spick-and-span perfect as it is at present. The ditch has not been used for centuries, and now its base is spread with tea-gardens and orchards, of which some of the trees are of quite respectable growth. As we wandered round the wall, dawdling in the hot July sunshine, we often paused to admire the views spread before us, and in especial the great plain covered with towns and villages and bounded with a blue line of hills, like a landscape of Claude Lorraine. From this we always turned with new delight to the city itself, with its myriad of quaint old gables and acre-wide red roofs dotted with dormer windows, tier upon tier. A little to our right rose the towers of the Burg, and nearer still, standing grim, the Torture Tower, which was, and is, perhaps, the most interesting place in the city. For centuries the tradition of the Iron Virgin of Nurnberg has been handed down as an instance of the horrors of cruelty of which man is capable; we had long looked forward to seeing it; and here at last was its home.

In one of our pauses we leaned over the wall of the moat and looked down. The garden seemed quite fifty or sixty feet below us, and the sun pouring into it with an intense, moveless heat like that of an oven. Beyond rose the grey, grim wall seemingly of endless height, and losing itself right and left in the angles of bastion and counterscarp. Trees and bushes crowned the wall, and above again towered the lofty houses on whose massive beauty Time has only set the hand of approval. The sun was hot and we were lazy; time was our own, and we lingered, leaning on the wall. Just below us was a pretty sight—a great black cat lying stretched in the sun, whilst round her gambolled prettily a tiny black kitten. The mother would wave her tail for the kitten to play with, or would raise her feet and push away the little one as an encouragement to further play. They were just at the foot of the wall, and Elias P. Hutcheson, in order to help the play, stooped and took from the walk a moderate-sized pebble.

"See!" he said, "I will drop it near the kitten, and they will both wonder where it came from."

"Oh, be careful," said my wife; "you might hit the dear little thing!"

"Not me, ma'am," said Elias P. "Why, I'm as tender as a Maine cherry-tree. Lor, bless ye, I wouldn't hurt the poor pooty little critter more'n I'd scalp a baby. An' you may bet your variegated socks on that! See, I'll drop it fur away on the outside so's not to go near her!" Thus saying, he leaned over and held his arm out at full length and dropped the stone. It may be that there is some attractive force which draws lesser matters to greater; or more probably that the wall was not plumb but sloped to its base—we not noticing the inclination from above; but the stone fell with a sickening thud that came up to us through the hot air, right on the kitten's head, and shattered out its little brains then and there. The black cat cast a swift upward glance, and we saw her eyes like green fire fixed an instant on Elias P. Hutcheson; and then her attention was given to the kitten, which lay still with just a quiver of her tiny limbs, whilst a thin red stream trickled from a gaping wound. With a muffled cry, such as a human being might give, she bent over the kitten, licking its wound and moaning. Suddenly she seemed to realise that it was dead, and again threw her eyes up at us. I shall never forget the sight, for she looked the perfect incarnation of hate. Her green eyes blazed with lurid fire, and the white, sharp teeth seemed to almost shine through the blood which dabbled her mouth and whiskers. She gnashed her teeth, and her claws stood out stark and at full length on every paw. Then she made a wild rush up the wall as if to reach us, but when the momentum ended fell back, and further added to her horrible appearance for she fell on the kitten, and rose with her back fur smeared with its brains and blood. Amelia turned quite faint, and I had to lift her back from the wall. There was a seat close by in shade of a spreading plane-tree, and here I placed her whilst she composed herself. Then I went back to Hutcheson, who stood without moving, looking down on the angry cat below.

As I joined him, he said:

"Wall, I guess that air the savagest beast I ever see— 'cept once when an Apache squaw had an edge on a half-breed what they nicknamed 'Splinters' 'cos of the way he fixed up her papoose which he stole on a raid just to show that he appreciated the way they had given his mother the fire torture. She got that kinder look so set on her face that it just seemed to grow there. She followed Splinters more'n three year till at last the braves got him and handed him over to her. They did say that no man, white or Injun, had ever been so long a-dying under the tortures of the Apaches. The only time I ever see her smile was when I wiped her out. I kem on the camp just in time to see Splinters pass in his checks, and he wasn't sorry to go either. He was a hard citizen, and though I never could shake with him after that papoose business—for it was bitter bad, and he should have been a white man, for he looked like one—I see he had got paid out in full. Durn me, but I took a piece of his hide from one of his skinnin posts an' had it made into a pocketbook. It's here now!" and he slapped the breast pocket of his coat.

Whilst he was speaking the cat was continuing her frantic efforts to get up the wall. She would take a run back and then charge up, sometimes reaching an incredible height. She did not seem to mind the heavy fall which she got each time but started with renewed vigour; and at every tumble her appearance became more horrible. Hutcheson was a kind-hearted man—my wife and I had both noticed little acts of kindness to animals as well as to persons—and he seemed concerned at the state of fury to which the cat had wrought herself.

"Wall now!" he said, "I du declare that that poor critter seems quite desperate. There! there! poor thing, it was all an accident—though that won't bring back your little one to you. Say! I wouldn't have had such a thing happen for a thousand! Just shows what a clumsy fool of a man can do when he tries to play! Seems I'm too darned slipperhanded to even play with a cat. Say, Colonel!"—it was a pleasant way he had to bestow titles freely—"I hope your wife don't hold no grudge against me on account of this unpleasantness? Why, I wouldn't have had it occur on no account."

He came over to Amelia and apologized profusely, and she with her usual kindness of heart hastened to assure him that she quite understood that it was an accident. Then we all went again to the wall and looked over.

The cat missing Hutcheson's face had drawn back across the moat, and was sitting on her haunches as though ready to spring. Indeed, the very instant she saw him she did spring, and with a blind unreasoning fury, which would have been grotesque, only that it was so frightfully real. She did not try to run up the wall, but simply launched herself at him as though hate and fury could lend her wings to pass straight through the great distance between them. Amelia, womanlike, got quite concerned, and said to Elias P. in a warning voice:

"Oh! you must be very careful. That animal would try to kill you if she were here; her eyes look like positive murder."

He laughed out jovially. "Excuse me, ma'am," he said, "but I can't help laughin'. Fancy a man that has fought grizzlies an' Injuns bein' careful of bein' murdered by a cat!"

When the cat heard him laugh, her whole demeanour seemed to change. She no longer tried to jump or run up the wall, but went quietly over, and sitting again beside the dead kitten began to lick and fondle it as though it were alive.

"See!" said I, "the effect of a really strong man. Even that animal in the midst of her fury recognises the voice of a master, and bows to him!"

"Like a squaw!" was the only comment of Elias P. Hutcheson, as we moved on our way round the city fosse.

Every now and then we looked over the wall and each time saw the cat following us. At first she had kept going back to the dead kitten, and then as the distance grew greater took it in her mouth and so followed. After a while, however, she abandoned this, for we saw her following all alone; she had evidently hidden the body somewhere. Amelia's alarm grew at the cat's persistence, and more than once she repeated her warning; but the American always laughed with amusement, till finally, seeing that she was beginning to be worried, he said:

"I say, ma'am, you needn't be skeered over that cat. I go heeled, I du!" Here he slapped his pistol pocket at the back of his lumbar region. "Why, sooner'n have you worried, I'll shoot the critter, right here, an' risk the police interferin' with a citizen of the United States for carryin' arms contrairy to reg'lations!" As he spoke he looked over the wall, but the cat, on seeing him, retreated, with a growl, into a bed of tall flowers, and was hidden. He went on: "Blest if that ar critter ain't got more sense of what's good for her than most Christians. I guess we've seen the last of her! You bet, she'll go back now to that busted kitten and have a private funeral of it, all to herself!"

Amelia did not like to say more, lest he might, in mistaken kindness to her, fulfil his threat of shooting the cat: and so we went on and crossed the little wooden bridge leading to the gateway whence ran the steep paved roadway between the Burg and the pentagonal Torture Tower. As we crossed the bridge we saw the cat again down below us. When she saw us her fury seemed to return, and she made frantic efforts to get up the steep wall. Hutcheson laughed as he looked down at her, and said:

"Good-bye, old girl. Sorry I in-jured your feelin's, but you'll get over it in time! So long!" And then we passed through the long, dim archway and came to the gate of the Burg.

When we came out again after our survey of this most beautiful old place which not even the well-intended efforts of the Gothic restorers of forty years ago have been able to spoil—though their restoration was then glaring white—we seemed to have quite forgotten the unpleasant episode of the morning. The old lime tree with its great trunk gnarled with the passing of nearly nine centuries, the deep well cut through the heart of the rock by those captives of old, and the lovely view from the city wall whence we heard, spread over almost a full quarter of an hour, the multitudinous chimes of the city, had all helped to wipe out from our minds the incident of the slain kitten.

We were the only visitors who had entered the Torture Tower that morning—so at least said the old custodian—and as we had the place all to ourselves were able to make a minute and more satisfactory survey than would have otherwise been possible. The custodian, looking to us as the sole source of his gains for the day, was willing to meet our wishes in any way. The Torture Tower is truly a grim place, even now when many thousands of visitors have sent a stream of life, and the joy that follows life, into the place; but at the time I mention it wore its grimmest and most gruesome aspect. The dust of ages seemed to have settled on it, and the darkness and the horror of its memories seem to have become sentient in a way that would have satisfied the Pantheistic souls of Philo or Spinoza. The lower chamber where we entered was seemingly, in its normal state, filled with incarnate darkness; even the hot sunlight streaming in through the door seemed to be lost in the vast thickness of the walls, and only showed the masonry rough as when the builder's scaffolding had come down, but coated with dust and marked here and there with patches of dark stain which, if walls could speak, could have given their own dread memories of fear and pain. We were glad to pass up the dusty wooden staircase, the custodian leaving the outer door open to light us somewhat on our way; for to our eyes the one long-wick'd, evil-smelling candle stuck in a sconce on the wall gave an inadequate light. When we came up through the open trap in the corner of the chamber overhead, Amelia held on to me so tightly that I could actually feel her heart beat. I must say for my own part that I was not surprised at her fear, for this room was even more gruesome than that below. Here there was certainly more light, but only just sufficient to realise the horrible surroundings of the place. The builders of the tower had evidently intended that only they who should gain the top should have any of the joys of light and prospect. There, as we had noticed from below, were ranges of windows, albeit of mediaeval smallness, but elsewhere in the tower were only a very few narrow slits such as were habitual in places of mediaeval defence. A few of these only lit the chamber, and these so high up in the wall that from no part could the sky be seen through the thickness of the walls. In racks, and leaning in disorder against the walls, were a number of headsmen's swords, great double-handed weapons with broad blade and keen edge. Hard by were several blocks whereon the necks of the victims had lain, with here and there deep notches where the steel had bitten through the guard of flesh and shored into the wood. Round the chamber, placed in all sorts of irregular ways, were many implements of torture which made one's heart ache to see—chairs full of spikes which gave instant and excruciating pain; chairs and couches with dull knobs whose torture was seemingly less, but which, though slower, were equally efficacious; racks, belts, boots, gloves, collars, all made for compressing at will; steel baskets in which the head could be slowly crushed into a pulp if necessary; watchmen's hooks with long handle and knife that cut at resistance—this a specialty of the old Nurnberg police system; and many, many other devices for man's injury to man. Amelia grew quite pale with the horror of the things, but fortunately did not faint, for being a little overcome she sat down on a torture chair, but jumped up again with a shriek, all tendency to faint gone. We both pretended that it was the injury done to her dress by the dust of the chair, and the rusty spikes which had upset her, and Mr. Hutcheson acquiesced in accepting the explanation with a kind-hearted laugh.

But the central object in the whole of this chamber of horrors was the engine known as the Iron Virgin, which stood near the centre of the room. It was a rudely-shaped figure of a woman, something of the bell order, or, to make a closer comparison, of the figure of Mrs. Noah in the children's Ark, but without that slimness of waist and perfect *rondeur* of hip which marks the aesthetic type of the Noah family. One would hardly have recognized it as intended for a human figure at all had not the founder shaped on the forehead a rude semblance of a woman's face. This machine was coated with rust without, and covered with dust; a rope was fastened to a ring in the front of the figure, about where the waist should have been, and was drawn through a pulley, fastened on the wooden pillar which sustained the flooring above. The custodian pulling this rope showed that a section of the front was hinged like a door at one side; we then saw that the engine was of considerable thickness, leaving just room enough inside for a man to be placed. The door was of equal thickness and of great weight, for it took the custodian all his strength, aided though he was by the contrivance of the pulley, to open it. This weight was partly due to the fact that the door was of manifest purpose hung so as to throw its weight downwards, so that it might shut of its own accord when the strain was released. The inside was honeycombed with rust —nay more, the rust alone that comes through time would hardly have eaten so deep into the iron walls; the rust of the cruel stains was deep indeed! It was only, however, when we came to look at the inside of the door that the diabolical intention was manifest to the full. Here were several long spikes, square and massive, broad at the base and sharp at the points, placed in such a position that when the door should close the upper ones would pierce the eyes of the victim, and the lower ones his heart and vitals. The sight was too much for poor Amelia, and this time she fainted dead off, and I had to carry her down the stairs, and place her on a bench outside till she recovered. That she felt it to the quick was afterwards shown by the fact that my eldest son bears to this day a rude birthmark on his breast, which has, by family consent, been accepted as representing the Nurnberg Virgin.

When we got back to the chamber we found Hutcheson still opposite the Iron Virgin; he had been evidently philosophising, and now gave us the benefit of his thought in the shape of a sort of exordium.

"Wall, I guess I've been learnin' somethin' here while madam has been gettin' over her faint. 'Pears to me that we're a long way behind the times on our side of the big drink. We uster think out on the plains that the Injun could give us points in tryin' to make a man oncomfortable; but I guess your old mediaeval law-and-order party could raise him every time. Splinters was pretty good in his bluff on the squaw, but this here young miss held a straight flush all high on him. The points of them spikes air sharp enough still, though even the edges air eaten out by what uster be on them. It'd be a good thing for our Indian section to get some specimens of this here play-toy to send round to the Reservations jest to knock the stuffin' out of the bucks, and the squaws too, by showing them as how old civilisation lays over them at their best. Guess but I'll get in that box a minute jest to see how it feels!"

"Oh no! no!" said Amelia. "It is too terrible!"

"Guess, ma'am, nothin's too terrible to the explorin' mind. I've been in some queer places in my time. Spent a night inside a dead horse while a prairie fire swept over me in Montana Territory—an' another time slept inside a dead buffler when the Comanches was on the war path an' I didn't keer to leav my kyard on them. I've been two days in a caved-in tunnel in the Billy Broncho gold mine in New Mexico, an' was one of the four shut up for three parts of a day in the caisson what slid over on her side when we was settin' the foundations of the Buffalo Bridge. I've not funked an odd experience yet, an' I don't propose to begin now!"

We saw that he was set on the experiment, so I said: "Well, hurry up, old man, and get through it quick?"

"All right, General," said he, "but I calculate we ain't quite ready yet. The gentlemen, my predecessors, what stood in that thar canister, didn't volunteer for the office— not much! And I guess there was some ornamental tyin' up before the big stroke was made. I want to go into this thing fair and square, so I must get fixed up proper first. I dare say this old galoot can rise some string and tie me up accordin' to sample?"

This was said interrogatively to the old custodian, but the latter, who understood the drift of his speech, though perhaps not appreciating to the full the niceties of dialect and imagery, shook his head. His protest was, however, only formal and made to be overcome. The American thrust a gold piece into his hand, saying, "Take it, pard! it's your pot: and don't be skeer'd. This ain't no necktie party that you're asked to assist in!" He produced some thin frayed rope and proceeded to bind our companion, with sufficient strictness for the purpose. When the upper part of his body was bound, Hutcheson said:

"Hold on a moment, Judge. Guess I'm too heavy for you to tote into the canister. You jest let me walk in, and then you can wash up regardin' my legs!"

Whilst speaking he had backed himself into the opening which was just enough to hold him. It was a close fit and no mistake. Amelia looked on with fear in her eyes, but she evidently did not like to say anything. Then the custodian completed his task by tying the American's feet together so that he was now absolutely helpless and fixed in his voluntary prison. He seemed to really enjoy it, and the incipient smile which was habitual to his face blossomed into actuality as he said:

"Guess this here Eve was made out of the rib of a dwarf! There ain't much room for a full-grown citizen of the United States to hustle. We uster make our coffins more roomier in Idaho territory. Now, Judge, you just begin to let this door down, slow, on to me. I want to feel the same pleasure as the other jays had when those spikes began to move towards their eyes!"

"Oh no! no! no!" broke in Amelia hysterically. "It is too terrible! I can't bear to see it!—I can't! I can't!"

But the American was obdurate. "Say, Colonel," said he, "Why not take Madame for a little promenade? I wouldn't hurt her feelin's for the world; but now that I am here, havin' kem eight thousand miles, wouldn't it be too hard to give up the very experience I've been pinin' an' pantin' fur? A man can't get to feel like canned goods every time! Me and the Judge here'll fix up this thing in no time, an' then you'll come back, an' we'll all laugh together!"

Once more the resolution that is born of curiosity triumphed, and Amelia stayed holding tight to my arm and shivering whilst the custodian began to slacken slowly inch by inch the rope that held back the iron door. Hutcheson's face was positively radiant as his eyes followed the first movement of the spikes.

"Wall!" he said, "I guess I've not had enjoyment like this since I left Noo York. Bar a scrap with a French sailor at Wapping—an' that warn't much of a picnic neither—I've not had a show fur real pleasure in this dod-rotted Continent, where there ain't no b'ars nor no Injuns, an' wheer nary man goes heeled. Slow there, Judge! Don't you rush this business! I want a show for my money this game—I du!"

The custodian must have had in him some of the blood of his predecessors in that ghastly tower, for he worked the engine with a deliberate and excruciating slowness which after five minutes, in which the outer edge of the door had not moved half as many inches, began to overcome Amelia. I saw her lips whiten, and I felt her hold upon my arm relax. I looked around an instant for a place whereon to lay her, and when I looked at her again found that her eye had become fixed on the side of the Virgin. Following its direction I saw the black cat crouching out of sight. Her green eyes shone like danger lamps in the gloom of the place, and their colour was heightened by the blood which still smeared her coat and reddened her mouth. I cried out:

"The cat! look out for the cat!" for even then she sprang out before the engine. At this moment she looked like a triumphant demon. Her eyes blazed with ferocity, her hair bristled out till she seemed twice her normal size, and her tail lashed about as does a tiger's when the quarry is before it. Elias P. Hutcheson when he saw her was amused, and his eyes positively sparkled with fun as he said:

"Darned if the squaw hain't got on all her war paint! Jest give her a shove off if she comes any of her tricks on me, for I'm so fixed everlastingly by the boss, that durn my skin if I can keep my eyes from her if she wants them! Easy there, Judge! Don't you slack that ar rope or I'm euchered!"

At this moment Amelia completed her faint, and I had to clutch hold of her round the waist or she would have fallen to the floor. Whilst attending to her I saw the black cat crouching for a spring, and jumped up to turn the creature out.

But at that instant, with a sort of hellish scream, she hurled herself, not as we expected at Hutcheson, but straight at the face of the custodian. Her claws seemed to be tearing wildly as one sees in the Chinese drawings of the dragon rampant, and as I looked I saw one of them light on the poor man's eye, and actually tear through it and down his cheek, leaving a wide band of red where the blood seemed to spurt from every vein.

With a yell of sheer terror which came quicker than even his sense of pain, the man leaped back, dropping as he did so the rope which held back the iron door. I jumped for it, but was too late for the cord ran like lightning through the pulley-block, and the heavy mass fell forward from its own weight.

As the door closed I caught a glimpse of our poor companion's face. He seemed frozen with terror. His eyes stared with a horrible anguish as if dazed, and no sound came from his lips.

And then the spikes did their work. Happily the end was quick, for when I wrenched open the door they had pierced so deep that they had locked in the bones of the skull through which they had crushed and actually tore him—it —out of his iron prison till, bound as he was, he fell at full length with a sickly thud upon the floor, the face turning upwards as he fell.

I rushed to my wife, lifted her up and carried her out, for I feared for her very reason if she should wake from her faint to such a scene. I laid her on the bench outside and ran back. Leaning against the wooden column was the custodian moaning in pain whilst he held his reddening handkerchief to his eyes. And sitting on the head of the poor American was the cat, purring loudly as she licked the blood which trickled through the gashed sockets of his eyes.

I think no one will call me cruel because I seized one of the old executioner's swords and shore her in two as she sat.

THE HAND

BY GUY DE MAUPASSANT

THEY MADE A CIRCLE AROUND JUDGE Bermutier, who was giving his opinion of the mysterious affair that had happened at Saint-Cloud. For a month Paris had doted on this inexplicable crime. No one could understand it at all.

M. Bermutier, standing with his back to the chimney, talked about it, discussed the divers opinions but came to no conclusions.

Many women had risen and come nearer, remaining standing, with eyes fixed upon the shaven mouth of the magistrate whence issued these grave words. They shivered and vibrated, crisp through their curious fear, through that eager, insatiable need of terror which haunts their soul, torturing them like a hunger.

One of them, paler than the others, after a silence, said:

"It is frightful. It touches the supernatural. We shall never know anything about it."

The magistrate turned toward her, saying:

"Yes, madame, it is probable that we never shall know anything about it. As for the word 'supernatural,' when you come to use that, it has no place here. We are in the presence of a crime skillfully conceived, very skillfully executed and so well enveloped in mystery that we cannot separate the impenetrable circumstances which surround it. But once in my life I had to follow an affair which seemed truly to be mixed up with something very unusual. However, it was necessary to give it up, as there was no means of explaining it."

Many of the ladies called out at the same time, so quickly that their voices sounded as one:

"Oh, tell us about it."

M. Bermutier smiled gravely, as judges should, and replied:

"You must not suppose, for an instant, that I, at least, believed there was anything superhuman in the adventure. I believe only in normal causes. And if in place of using the word 'supernatural' to express what we cannot compre-

hend we should simply use the word 'inexplicable,' it would
be much better. In any case, the surrounding circumstances
in the affair I am going to relate to you, as well as the pre-
paratory circumstances, have affected me much. Here are
the facts:

"I was then judge of instruction at Ajaccio, a little white
town lying on the border of an admirable gulf that was surrounded on all sides by high mountains.

"What I particularly had to look after there were the affairs of vendetta. Some of them were superb, as dramatic
as possible, ferocious and heroic. We find there the most
beautiful subjects of vengeance that one could dream of,
hatred a century old, appeased for a moment but never extinguished, abominable plots, assassinations becoming mas-
sacres and almost glorious battles. For two years I heard of
nothing but the price of blood, of the terribly prejudiced
Corsican who is bound to avenge all injury upon the person
of him who is the cause of it or upon his nearest descend-
ants. I saw old men and infants, cousins, with their throats
cut, and my head was full of these stories.

"One day we learned that an Englishman had rented
for some years a little villa at the end of the gulf. He had
brought with him a French domestic, picked up at Marseilles on the way.

"Soon everybody was occupied with this singular person
who lived alone in his house, only going out to hunt and
fish. He spoke to no one, never came to the town and every
morning practiced shooting with a pistol and a rifle for an
hour or two.

"Some legends about him were abroad. They pretended
that he was a high personage fled from his own country for
political reasons; then they affirmed that he was concealing himself after having committed a frightful crime. They
even cited some of the particularly horrible details.

"In my capacity of judge I wished to get some information about this man. But it was impossible to learn anything. He called himself Sir John Rowell.

"I contented myself with watching him closely, although
in reality there seemed nothing to suspect regarding him.

"Nevertheless, as rumors on his account continued, grew and became general, I resolved to try and see this stranger myself and for this purpose began to hunt regularly in the neighborhood of his property.

"I waited long for an occasion. It finally came in the form of a partridge which I shot and killed before the very nose of the Englishman. My dog brought it to me, but, immediately taking it, I went and begged Sir John Rowell to accept the dead bird, excusing myself for intrusion.

"He was a tall man with red hair and red beard, very large, a sort of placid, polite Hercules. He had none of the so-called British haughtiness and heartily thanked me for the delicacy in French, with a beyond-the-Channel accent. At the end of a month we had chatted together five or six times.

"Finally one evening, as I was passing by his door, I perceived him astride a chair in the garden, smoking his pipe. I saluted him and he asked me in to have a glass of beer. It was not necessary for him to repeat before I accepted.

"He received me with the fastidious courtesy of the English, spoke in praise of France and of Corsica and declared that he loved that country and that shore.

"Then with great precaution in the form of a lively interest, I put some questions to him about his life and his projects. He responded without embarrassment, told me that he had traveled much, in Africa, in the Indies and in America. He added, laughing:

" 'I have had many adventures, oh yes!'

"I began to talk about hunting, and he gave me many curious details of hunting the hippopotamus, the tiger, the elephant and even of hunting the gorilla.

"I said: 'All these animals are very formidable.'

"He laughed. 'Oh no! The worst animal is man.' Then he began to laugh with the hearty laugh of a big, contented Englishman. He continued:

" 'I have often hunted man also.'

"He spoke of weapons and asked me to go into his house to see his guns of various makes and kinds.

"His drawing room was hung in black, in black silk embroidered with gold. There were great yellow flowers running over the somber stuff, shining like fire.

" 'It is Japanese cloth,' he said.

"But in the middle of a large panel a strange thing attracted my eye. Upon a square of red velvet a black object was attached. I approached and found it was a hand, the hand of a man. Not a skeleton hand, white and characteristic, but a black, desiccated hand with yellow joints, with the muscles bare and on them traces of old blood, of blood that seemed like a scale, over the bones sharply cut off at about the middle of the forearm, as with a blow of a hatchet. About the wrist was an enormous iron chain, riveted, soldered to this unclean member, attaching it to the wall by a ring sufficiently strong to hold an elephant.

"I asked: 'What is that?'

"The Englishman responded tranquilly:

" 'It belonged to my worst enemy. It came from America. It was broken with a saber, cut off with a sharp stone and dried in the sun for eight days. Oh, very good for me, that was!'

"I touched the human relic which must have belonged to a colossus. The fingers were immoderately long and attached by enormous tendons that held the straps of skin in place. This dried hand was frightful to see, making one think, naturally, of the vengeance of a savage.

"I said: 'This man must have been very strong.'

"With gentleness the Englishman answered:

" 'Oh yes, but I was stronger than he. I put this chain on him to hold him.'

"I thought he spoke in jest and replied:

" 'The chain is useless now that the hand cannot escape.'

"Sir John Rowell replied gravely: 'It always wishes to escape. The chain is necessary.'

"With a rapid, questioning glance I asked myself: 'Is he mad or is that an unpleasant joke?'

"But the face remained impenetrable, tranquil and friendly. I spoke of other things and admired the guns.

"Nevertheless, I noticed three loaded revolvers on the pieces of furniture, as if this man lived in constant fear of attack.

"I went there many times after that; then for some time I did not go. We had become accustomed to his presence; he had become indifferent to us.

"A whole year slipped away. Then one morning toward the end of November my domestic awoke me with the announcement that Sir John Rowell had been assassinated in the night.

"A half-hour later I entered the Englishman's house with the central commissary and the captain of police. The servant, lost in despair, was weeping at the door. I suspected him at first but afterward found that he was innocent.

"The guilty one could never be found.

"Upon entering Sir John's drawing room I perceived his dead body stretched out upon its back in the middle of the room. His waistcoat was torn; a sleeve was hanging, and it was evident that a terrible struggle had taken place.

"The Englishman had been strangled! His frightfully black and swollen face seemed to express an abominable fear; he held something between his set teeth, and his neck, pierced with five holes apparently done with a pointed iron, was covered with blood.

"A doctor joined us. He examined closely the prints of fingers in the flesh and pronounced these strange words:

"'One would think he had been strangled by a skeleton.'

"A shiver ran down my back, and I cast my eyes to the place on the wall where I had seen the horrible, torn-off hand. It was no longer there. The chain was broken and hanging.

"Then I bent over the dead man and found in his mouth a piece of one of the fingers of the missing hand, cut off, or rather sawed off, by the teeth exactly at the second joint.

"Then they tried to collect evidence. They could find nothing. No door had been forced, no window opened or piece of furniture moved. The two watch-dogs on the premises had not been aroused.

"Here, in a few words, is the deposition of the servant:

"For a month his master had seemed agitated. He had received many letters which he had burned immediately.

Often, taking a whip in anger which seemed like dementia, he had struck in fury this dried hand fastened to the wall and taken, one knew not how, at the moment of a crime.

"He had retired late and shut himself in with care. He always carried arms. Often in the night he talked out loud, as if he were quarreling with someone. On that night, however, there had been no noise, and it was only on coming to open the windows that the servant had found Sir. John assassinated. He suspected no one.

"I communicated what I knew of the death to the magistrates and public officers, and they made minute inquiries upon the whole island. They discovered nothing.

"One night, three months after the crime, I had a frightful nightmare. It seemed to me that I saw that hand, that horrible hand, running like a scorpion or a spider along my curtains and my walls. Three times I awoke; three times I fell asleep and again saw that hideous relic galloping about my room, moving its fingers like paws.

"The next day they brought it to me, found in the cemetery upon the tomb where Sir John Rowell was interred—for they had not been able to find his family. The index finger was missing.

"This, ladies, is my story. I know no more about it."

The ladies were terrified, pale and shivering. One of them cried:

"But that is not the end, for there was no explanation! We cannot sleep if you do not tell us what was your idea of the reason of it all."

The magistrate smiled with severity and answered:

"Oh, certainly, ladies, but it will spoil all your terrible dreams. I simply think that the legitimate proprietor of the hand was not dead and that he came for it with the one that remained to him. But I was never able to find out how he did it. It was one kind of revenge."

One of the women murmured:

"No, it could not be thus."

And the judge of information, smiling still, concluded:

"I told you in the beginning that my explanation would not satisfy you."

THE ADVENTURE OF THE SPECKLED BAND

BY SIR ARTHUR CONAN DOYLE

ON GLANCING OVER MY NOTES OF THE seventy odd cases in which I have during the last eight years studied the methods of my friend Sherlock Holmes, I find many tragic, some comic, a large number merely strange, but none commonplace; for, working as he did rather for the love of his art than for the acquirement of wealth, he refused to associate himself with any investigation which did not tend towards the unusual, and even the fantastic. Of all these varied cases, however, I cannot recall any which presented more singular features than that which was associated with the well-known Surrey family of the Roylotts of Stroke Moran. The events in question occurred in the early days of my association with Holmes, when we were sharing rooms as bachelors in Baker Street. It is possible that I might have placed them upon record before, but a promise of secrecy was made at the time, from which I have only been freed during the last month by the untimely death of the lady to whom the pledge was given. It is perhaps as well that the facts should now come to light, for I have reasons to know that there are wide-spread rumors as to the death of Dr. Grimesby Roylott which tend to make the matter even more terrible than the truth.

It was early in April in the year '83 that I woke one morning to find Sherlock Holmes standing, fully dressed, by the side of my bed. He was a late riser as a rule, and as the clock on the mantel-piece showed me that it was only a quarter past seven, I blinked up at him in some surprise, and perhaps just a little resentment, for I was myself regular in my habits.

"Very sorry to knock you up, Watson," said he, "but it's the common lot this morning. Mrs. Hudson has been knocked up, she retorted upon me, and I on you."

"What is it, then—a fire?"

"No; a client. It seems that a young lady has arrived in a considerable state of excitement, who insists upon seeing me. She is waiting now in the sitting-room. Now, when young ladies wander about the metropolis at this hour of the morning, and knock sleepy people up out of their beds, I presume that it is something very pressing which they have to communicate. Should it prove to be an interesting case, you would, I am sure, wish to follow it from the outset. I thought, at any rate, that I should call you and give you the chance."

"My dear fellow, I would not miss it for anything."

I had no keener pleasure than in following Holmes in his professional investigations, and in admiring the rapid deductions, as swift as intuitions, and yet always founded on a logical basis, with which he unravelled the problems which were submitted to him. I rapidly threw on my clothes, and was ready in a few minutes to accompany my friend down to the sitting-room. A lady dressed in black and heavily veiled, who had been sitting in the window, rose as we entered.

"Good-morning, madam," said Holmes, cheerily. "My name is Sherlock Holmes. This is my intimate friend and associate, Dr. Watson, before whom you can speak as freely as before myself. Ha! I am glad to see that Mrs. Hudson has had the good sense to light the fire. Pray draw up to it, and I shall order you a cup of hot coffee, for I observe that you are shivering."

"It is not cold which makes me shiver," said the woman, in a low voice, changing her seat as requested.

"What, then?"

"It is fear, Mr. Holmes. It is terror." She raised her veil as she spoke, and we could see that she was indeed in a pitiable state of agitation, her face all drawn and gray, with restless, frightened eyes, like those of some hunted animal.

Her features and figure were those of a woman of thirty, but her hair was shot with premature gray, and her expression was weary and haggard. Sherlock Holmes ran her over with one of his quick, all-comprehensive glances.

"You must not fear," said he, soothingly, bending forward and patting her forearm. "We shall soon set matters right, I have no doubt. You have come in by train this morning, I see."

"You know me, then?"

"No, but I observe the second half of a return ticket in the palm of your left glove. You must have started early, and yet you had a good drive in a dog-cart, along heavy roads, before you reached the station."

The lady gave a violent start, and stared in bewilderment at my companion.

"There is no mystery, my dear madam," said he, smiling. "The left arm of your jacket is spattered with mud in no less than seven places. The marks are perfectly fresh. There is no vehicle save a dog-cart which throws up mud in that way, and then only when you sit on the left-hand side of the driver."

"Whatever your reasons may be, you are perfectly correct," said she. "I started from home before six, reached Leatherhead at twenty past, and came in by the first train to Waterloo. Sir, I can stand this strain no longer; I shall go mad if it continues. I have no one to turn to—none, save only one, who cares for me, and he, poor fellow, can be of little aid. I have heard of you, Mr. Holmes; I have heard of you from Mrs. Farintosh, whom you helped in the hour of her sore need. It was from her that I had your address. Oh, sir, do you not think that you could help me, too, and at least throw a little light through the dense darkness which surrounds me? At present it is out of my power to reward you for your services, but in a month or six weeks I shall be married, with the control of my own income, and then at least you shall not find me ungrateful."

Holmes turned to his desk, and unlocking it, drew out a small case-book, which he consulted.

"Farintosh," said he. "Ah yes, I recall the case; it was concerned with an opal tiara. I think it was before your time, Watson. I can only say, madam, that I shall be happy to devote the same care to your case as I did to that of your friend. As to reward, my profession is its own reward; but you are at liberty to defray whatever expenses I may be put to, at the time which suits you best. And now I beg that you will lay before us everything that may help us in forming an opinion upon the matter."

"Alas!" replied our visitor, "the very horror of my situation lies in the fact that my fears are so vague, and my suspicions depend so entirely upon small points, which might seem trivial to another, that even he to whom of all others I have a right to look for help and advice looks upon all that I tell him about it as the fancies of a nervous woman. He does not say so, but I can read it from his soothing answers and averted eyes. But I have heard, Mr. Holmes, that you can see deeply into the manifold wickedness of the human heart. You may advise me how to walk amid the dangers which encompass me."

"I am all attention, madam."

"My name is Helen Stoner, and I am living with my stepfather, who is the last survivor of one of the oldest Saxon families in England, the Roylotts of Stoke Moran, on the western border of Surrey."

Holmes nodded his head. "The name is familiar to me," said he.

"The family was at one time among the richest in England, and the estates extended over the borders into Berkshire in the north, and Hampshire in the west. In the last century, however, four successive heirs were of a dissolute and wasteful disposition, and the family ruin was eventually completed by a gambler in the days of the Regency. Nothing was left save a few acres of ground, and the two-hundred-year-old house, which is itself crushed under a heavy mortage. The last squire dragged out his existence there, living the horrible life of an aristocratic pauper; but his only son, my step-father, seeing that he must adapt himself to the new conditions, obtained an advance from a relative, which enabled him to take a medical degree, and went out to Calcutta, where, by his professional skill and his force of character, he established a large practice. In a fit of anger, however, caused by some robberies which had been perpetrated in the house, he beat his native butler to death, and narrowly escaped a capital sentence. As it was, he suffered a long term of imprisonment, and afterwards returned to England, a morose and disappointed man.

"When Dr. Roylott was in India he married my mother, Mrs. Stoner, the young widow of Major-general Stoner, of the Bengal Artillery. My sister Julia and I were twins, and we were only two years old at the time of my mother's remarriage. She had a considerable sum of money—not less than £1000 a year—and this she bequeathed to Dr. Roylott entirely while we resided with him, with a provision that a certain annual sum should be allowed to each of us in the event of our marriage. Shortly after our return to England my mother died—she was killed eight years ago in a railway accident near Crewe. Dr. Roylott then abandoned his attempts to establish himself in practice in London, and took us to live with him in the old ancestral house at Stoke Moran. The money which my mother had left was enough for all our wants, and there seemed to be no obstacle to our happiness.

"But a terrible change came over our step-father about this time. Instead of making friends and exchanging visits with our neighbors, who had at first been overjoyed to see a Roylott of Stoke Moran back in the old family seat, he shut himself up in his house, and seldom came out save to indulge in ferocious quarrels with whoever might cross his path. Violence of temper approaching to mania has been hereditary in the men of the family, and in my step-father's case it had, I believe, been intensified by his long residence in the tropics. A series of disgraceful brawls took place, two of which ended in the police-court, until at last he became the terror of the village, and the folks would fly at his approach, for he is a man of immense strength, and absolutely uncontrollable in his anger.

"Last week he hurled the local blacksmith over a parapet

into a stream, and it was only by paying over all the money which I could gather together that I was able to avert another public exposure. He had no friends at all save the wandering gypsies, and he would give these vagabonds leave to encamp upon the few acres of bramble-covered land which represent the family estate, and would accept in return the hospitality of their tents, wandering away with them sometimes for weeks on end. He has a passion also for Indian animals, which are sent over to him by a correspondent, and he has at this moment a cheetah and a baboon, which wander freely over his grounds, and are feared by the villagers almost as much as their master.

"You can imagine from what I say that my poor sister Julia and I had no great pleasure in our lives. No servant would stay with us, and for a long time we did all the work of the house. She was but thirty at the time of her death, and yet her hair had already begun to whiten, even as mine has."

"Your sister is dead, then?"

"She died just two years ago, and it is of her death that I wish to speak to you. You can understand that, living the life which I have described, we were little likely to see any one of our own age and position. We had, however, an aunt, my mother's maiden sister, Miss Honoria Westphail, who lives near Harrow, and we were occasionally allowed to pay short visits at this lady's house. Julia went there at Christmas two years ago, and met there a half-pay major of marines, to whom she became engaged. My step-father learned of the engagement when my sister returned, and offered no objection to the marriage; but within a fortnight of the day which had been fixed for the wedding, the terrible event occurred which has deprived me of my only companion."

Sherlock Holmes had been leaning back in his chair with his eyes closed and his head sunk in a cushion, but he half opened his lids now and glanced across at his visitor.

"Pray be precise as to details," said he.

"It is easy for me to be so, for every event of that dreadful time is seared into my memory. The manor-house is, as I have already said, very old, and only one wing is now inhabited. The bedrooms in this wing are on the ground floor, the sitting-room being in the central block of the buildings. Of these bedrooms the first is Dr. Roylott's, the second my sister's, and the third my own. There is no communication between them, but they all open out into the same corridor. Do I make myself plain?"

"Perfectly so."

"The windows of the three rooms open out upon the lawn. That fatal night Dr. Roylott had gone to his room early, though we knew that he had not retired to rest, for my sister was troubled by the smell of the strong Indian cigars which it was his custom to smoke. She left her room, therefore, and came into mine, where she sat for some time, chatting about her approaching wedding. At eleven o'clock she rose to leave me but she paused at the door and looked back.

" 'Tell me, Helen,' said she, 'have you ever heard any one whistle in the dead of the night?'

" 'Never,' said I.

" 'I suppose that you could not possibly whistle, yourself, in your sleep?'

" 'Certainly not. But why?'

" 'Because during the last few nights I have always, about three in the morning, heard a low, clear whistle. I am a light sleeper, and it has awakened me. I cannot tell where it came from—perhaps from the next room, perhaps from the lawn. I thought that I would just ask you whether you had heard it.'

" 'No, I have not. It must be those wretched gypsies in the plantation.'

" 'Very likely. And yet if it were on the lawn, I wonder that you did not hear it also.'

" 'Ah, but I sleep more heavily than you.'

" 'Well, it is of no great consequence, at any rate.' She smiled back at me, closed my door, and a few minutes later I heard her key turn in the lock."

"Indeed," said Holmes. "Was it your custom always to lock yourselves in at night?"

"Always."

"And why?"

"I think that I mentioned to you that the doctor kept a cheetah and a baboon. We had no feeling of security unless our doors were locked."

"Quite so. Pray proceed with your statement."

"I could not sleep that night. A vague feeling of impending misfortune impressed me. My sister and I, you will recollect, were twins, and you know how subtle are the links which bind two souls which are so closely allied. It was a wild night. The wind was howling outside, and the rain was beating and splashing against the windows. Suddenly, amid all the hubbub of the gale, there burst forth the wild scream of a terrified woman. I knew that it was my sister's voice. I sprang from my bed, wrapped a shawl round me, and rushed into the corridor. As I opened my door I seemed to hear a low whistle, such as my sister described, and a few moments later a clanging sound, as if a mass of metal had fallen. As I ran down the passage, my sister's door was unlocked, and revolved slowly upon its hinges. I stared at it horror-stricken, not knowing what was about to issue from it. By the light of the corridor-lamp I saw my sister appear at the opening, her face blanched with terror, her hands groping for help, her whole figure swaying to and fro like that of a drunkard. I ran to her and threw my arms round her, but at that moment her knees seemed to give way and she fell to the ground. She writhed as one who is in terrible pain, and her limbs were dreadfully convulsed. At first I thought that she had not recognized me, but as I bent over her she suddenly shrieked out in a voice which I shall never forget, 'Oh, my God! Helen! It was the band! The speckled band!' There was something else which she would fain have said, and she stabbed with her finger into the air in the direction of the doctor's room, but a fresh convulsion seized her and choked her words. I rushed out, calling loudly for my step-father, and I met him hastening from his room in his dressing-gown. When he reached my sister's side she was unconscious, and though he poured brandy down her throat and sent for medical aid from the village, all efforts were in vain, for she slowly sank and died without having recovered her consciousness. Such was the dreadful end of my beloved sister."

"One moment," said Holmes; "are you sure about this whistle and metallic sound? Could you swear to it?"

"That was what the county coroner asked me at the inquiry. It is my strong impression that I heard it, and yet, among the crash of the gale and the creaking of an old house, I may possibly have been deceived."

"Was your sister dressed?"

"No, she was in her night-dress. In her right hand was found the charred stump of a match, and in her left a matchbox."

"Showing that she had struck a light and looked about her when the alarm took place. That is important. And what conclusions did the coroner come to?"

"He investigated the case with great care, for Dr. Roylott's conduct had long been notorious in the county, but he was unable to find any satisfactory cause of death. My evidence showed that the door had been fastened upon the inner side, and the windows were blocked by old-fashioned shutters with broad iron bars, which were secured every night. The walls were carefully sounded, and were shown to be quite solid all round, and the flooring was also thoroughly examined, with the same result. The chimney is wide, but is barred up by four large staples. It is certain, therefore, that my sister was quite alone when she met her end. Besides, there were no marks of any violence upon her."

"How about poison?"

"The doctors examined her for it, but without success."

"What do you think that this unfortunate lady died of, then?"

"It is my belief that she died of pure fear and nervous shock, though what it was that frightened her I cannot imagine."

"Were there gypsies in the plantation at the time?"

"Yes, there are nearly always some there."

"Ah, and what did you gather from this allusion to a band—a speckled band?"

"Sometimes I have thought that it was merely the wild talk of delirium, sometimes that it may have referred to some band of people, perhaps to these very gypsies in the plantation. I do not know whether the spotted handkerchiefs which so many of them wear over their heads might have suggested the strange adjective which she used."

Holmes shook his head like a man who is far from being satisfied.

"These are very deep waters," said he; "pray go on with your narrative."

"Two years have passed since then, and my life has been until lately lonelier than ever. A month ago, however, a dear friend, whom I have known for many years, has done me the honor to ask my hand in marriage. His name is Armitage—Percy Armitage—the second son of Mr. Armitage, of Crane Water, near Reading. My step-father has offered no opposition to the match, and we are to be married in the course of the spring. Two days ago some repairs were started in the west wing of the building, and my bedroom wall has been pierced, so that I have had to move into the chamber in which my sister died, and to sleep in the very bed in which she slept. Imagine, then, my thrill of terror when last night, as I lay awake, thinking over her terrible fate, I suddenly heard in the silence of the night the low whistle which had been the herald of her own death. I sprang up and lit the lamp, but nothing was to be seen in the room. I was too shaken to go to bed again, however, so I dressed, and as soon as it was daylight I slipped down, got a dog-cart at the 'Crown Inn,' which is opposite, and drove to Leatherhead, from whence I have come on this morning with the one object of seeing you and asking your advice."

"You have done wisely," said my friend. "But have you told me all?"

"Yes, all."

"Miss Roylott, you have not. You are screening your step-father."

"Why, what do you mean?"

For answer Holmes pushed back the frill of black lace which fringed the hand that lay upon our visitor's knee. Five little livid spots, the marks of four fingers and a thumb, were printed upon the white wrist.

"You have been cruelly used," said Holmes.

The lady colored deeply and covered over her injured wrist. "He is a hard man," she said, "and perhaps he hardly knows his own strength."

There was a long silence, during which Holmes leaned his chin upon his hands and stared into the crackling fire.

"This is a very deep business," he said, at last. "There are a thousand details which I should desire to know before I decide upon our course of action. Yet we have not a moment to lose. If we were to come to Stoke Moran to-day, would it be possible for us to see over these rooms without the knowledge of your step-father?"

"As it happens, he spoke of coming into town to-day upon some most important business. It is probable that he will be away all day, and that there would be nothing to disturb you. We have a house-keeper now, but she is old and foolish, and I could easily get her out of the way."

"Excellent. You are not averse to this trip, Watson?"

"By no means."

"Then we shall both come. What are you going to do yourself?"

"I have one or two things which I would wish to do now that I am in town. But I shall return by the twelve o'clock train, so as to be there in time for your coming."

"And you may expect us early in the afternoon. I have myself some small business matters to attend to. Will you not wait and breakfast?"

"No, I must go. My heart is lightened already since I have confided my trouble to you. I shall look forward to seeing you again this afternoon." She dropped her thick black veil over her face and glided from the room.

"And what do you think of it all, Watson?" asked Sherlock Holmes, leaning back in his chair.

"It seems to me to be a most dark and sinister business."

"Dark enough and sinister enough."

"Yet if the lady is correct in saying that the flooring and walls are sound, and that the door, window, and chimney are impassable, then her sister must have been undoubtedly alone when she met her mysterious end."

"What becomes, then, of these nocturnal whistles, and what of the very peculiar words of the dying woman?"

"I cannot think."

"When you combine the ideas of whistles at night, the presence of a band of gypsies who are on intimate terms with this old doctor, the fact that we have every reason to believe that the doctor has an interest in preventing his step-daughter's marriage, the dying allusion to a band, and, finally, the fact that Miss Helen Stoner heard a metallic clang, which might have been caused by one of those metal bars which secured the shutters falling back into their place, I think that there is good ground to think that the mystery may be cleared along those lines."

"But what, then, did the gypsies do?"

"I cannot imagine."

"I see many objections to any such theory."

"And so do I. It is precisely for that reason that we are going to Stoke Moran this day. I want to see whether the objections are fatal, or if they may be explained away. But what in the name of the devil!"

The ejaculation had been drawn from my companion by the fact that our door had been suddenly dashed open, and that a huge man had framed himself in the aperture. His costume was a peculiar mixture of the professional and of the agricultural, having a black top-hat, a long frock-coat, and a pair of high gaiters, with a hunting-crop swinging in his hand. So tall was he that his hat actually brushed the cross bar of the doorway, and his breadth seemed to span it across from side to side. A large face, seared with a thousand wrinkles, burned yellow with the sun, and marked with every evil passion, was turned from one to the other of us, while his deep-set, bile-shot eyes, and his high, thin, fleshless nose, gave him somewhat the resemblance to a fierce old bird of prey.

"Which of you is Holmes?" asked this apparition.

"My name, sir; but you have the advantage of me," said my companion, quietly.

"I am Dr. Grimesby Roylott, of Stoke Moran."

"Indeed, doctor," said Holmes, blandly. "Pray take a seat."

"I will do nothing of the kind. My step-daughter has been here. I have traced her. What has she been saying to you?"

"It is a little cold for the time of the year," said Holmes.

"What has she been saying to you?" screamed the old man, furiously.

"But I have heard that the crocuses promise well," continued my companion, imperturbably.

"Ha! You put me off, do you?" said our new visitor, taking a step forward and shaking his hunting-crop. "I know you, you scoundrel! I have heard of you before. You are Holmes, the meddler."

My friend smiled.

"Holmes, the busybody!"

His smile broadened.

"Holmes, the Scotland-yard Jack-in-office!"

Holmes chuckled heartily. "Your conversation is most entertaining," said he. "When you go out close the door, for there is a decided draught."

"I will go when I have said my say. Don't you dare to meddle with my affairs. I know that Miss Stoner has been here. I traced her! I am a dangerous man to fall foul of! See here." He stepped swiftly forward, seized the poker, and bent it into a curve with his huge brown hands.

"See that you keep yourself out of my grip," he snarled, and hurling the twisted poker into the fireplace, he strode out of the room.

"He seems a very amiable person," said Holmes, laughing. "I am not quite so bulky, but if he had remained I might have shown him that my grip was not much more feeble than his own." As he spoke he picked up the steel poker, and with a sudden effort straightened it out again.

"Fancy his having the insolence to confound me with the

official detective force! This incident gives zest to our investigation, however, and I only trust that our little friend will not suffer from her impudence in allowing this brute to trace her. And now, Watson, we shall order breakfast, and afterwards I shall walk down to Doctors' Commons, where I hope to get some data which may help us in this matter."

It was nearly one o'clock when Sherlock Holmes returned from his excursion. He held in his hand a sheet of blue paper, scrawled over with notes and figures.

"I have seen the will of the deceased wife," said he. "To determine its exact meaning I have been obliged to work out the present prices of the investments with which it is concerned. The total income, which at the time of the wife's death was little short of £1100, is now, through the fall in agricultural prices, not more than £750. Each daughter can claim an income of £250, in case of marriage. It is evident, therefore, that if both girls had married, this beauty would have had a mere pittance, while even one of them would cripple him to a very serious extent. My morning's work has not been wasted, since it has proved that he has the very strongest motives for standing in the way of anything of the sort. And now, Watson, this is too serious for dawdling, especially as the old man is aware that we are interesting ourselves in his affairs; so if you are ready, we shall call a cab and drive to Waterloo. I should be very much obliged if you would slip your revolver into your pocket. An Eley's No. 2 is an excellent argument with gentlemen who can twist steel pokers into knots. That and a toothbrush are, I think, all that we need."

At Waterloo we were fortunate in catching a train for Leatherhead, where we hired a trap at the station inn, and drove for four or five miles through the lovely Surrey lanes. It was a perfect day, with a bright sun and a few fleecy clouds in the heavens. The trees and way-side hedges were just throwing out their first green shoots, and the air was full of the pleasant smell of the moist earth. To me at least there was a strange contrast between the sweet promise of the spring and this sinister quest upon which we were engaged. My companion sat in the front of the trap, his arms folded, his hat pulled down over his eyes, and his chin sunk upon his breast, buried in the deepest thought. Suddenly, however, he started, tapped me on the shoulder, and pointed over the meadows.

"Look there!" said he.

A heavily-timbered park stretched up in a gentle slope, thickening into a grove at the highest point. From amid the branches there jutted out the gray gables and high roof-tree of a very old mansion.

"Stoke Moran?" said he.

"Yes, sir, that be the house of Dr. Grimesby Roylott," remarked the driver.

"There is some building going on there," said Holmes; "that is where we are going."

"There's the village," said the driver, pointing to a cluster of roofs some distance to the left; "but if you want to get to the house, you'll find it shorter to get over this stile, and so by the foot-path over the fields. There it is, where the lady is walking."

"And the lady, I fancy, is Miss Stoner," observed Holmes, shading his eyes. "Yes, I think we had better do as you suggest."

We got off, paid our fare, and the trap rattled back on its way to Leatherhead.

"I thought it as well," said Holmes, as we climbed the stile, "that this fellow should think we had come here as architects, or on some definite business. It may stop his gossip. Good-afternoon, Miss Stoner. You see that we have been as good as our word."

Our client of the morning had hurried forward to meet us with a face which spoke her joy. "I have been waiting so eagerly for you," she cried, shaking hands with us warmly. "All has turned out splendidly. Dr. Roylott has gone to town, and it is unlikely that he will be back before evening."

"We have had the pleasure of making the doctor's acquaintance," said Holmes, and in a few words he sketched out what had occurred. Miss Stoner turned white to the lips as she listened.

"Good heavens!" she cried, "he has followed me, then."

"So it appears."

"He is so cunning that I never know when I am safe from him. What will he say when he returns?"

"He must guard himself, for he may find that there is some one more cunning than himself upon his track. You must lock yourself up from him to-night. If he is violent, we shall take you away to your aunt's at Harrow. Now, we must make the best use of our time, so kindly take us at once to the rooms which we are to examine."

The building was of gray, lichen-blotched stone, with a high central portion, and two curving wings, like the claws of a crab, thrown out on each side. In one of these wings the windows were broken, and blocked with wooden boards, while the roof was partly caved in, a picture of ruin. The central portion was in little better repair, but the right-hand block was comparatively modern, and the blinds in the windows, with the blue smoke curling up from the chimneys, showed that this was where the family resided. Some scaffolding had been erected against the end wall, and the stone-work had been broken into, but there were no signs of any workmen at the moment of our visit. Holmes walked slowly up and down the ill-trimmed lawn, and examined with deep attention the outsides of the windows.

"This, I take it, belongs to the room in which you used to sleep, the centre one to your sister's, and the one next to the main building to Dr. Roylott's chamber?"

"Exactly so. But I am now sleeping in the middle one."

"Pending the alterations, as I understand. By-the-way, there does not seem to be any very pressing need for repairs at that end wall."

"There were none. I believe that it was an excuse to move me from my room."

"Ah! that is suggestive. Now, on the other side of this narrow wing runs the corridor from which these three rooms open. There are windows in it, of course?"

"Yes, but very small ones. Too narrow for any one to pass through."

"As you both locked your doors at night, your rooms were unapproachable from that side. Now, would you have the kindness to go into your room and bar your shutters."

Miss Stoner did so, and Holmes, after a careful examination through the open window, endeavored in every way to force the shutter open, but without success. There was no slit through which a knife could be passed to raise the bar. Then with his lens he tested the hinges, but they were of solid iron, built firmly into the massive masonry. "Hum!" said he, scratching his chin in some perplexity; "my theory certainly presents some difficulties. No one could pass these shutters if they were bolted. Well, we shall see if the inside throws any light upon the matter."

A small side door led into the whitewashed corridor from which the three bedrooms opened. Holmes refused to examine the third chamber, so we passed at once to the second, that in which Miss Stoner was now sleeping, and in which her sister had met with her fate. It was a homely little room, with a low ceiling and a gaping fireplace, after the fashion of old country-houses. A brown chest of drawers stood in one corner, a narrow white-counterpaned bed in another, and a dressing-table on the left-hand side of the window. These articles, with two small wicker-work chairs, made up all the furniture in the room, save for a square of Wilton carpet in the centre. The boards round and the panelling of the walls were of brown, worm-eaten oak, so old and discolored that it may have dated from the original building of the house. Holmes drew one of the chairs into a corner and sat silent, while his eyes travelled round and round and up and down, taking in every detail of the apartment.

"Where does that bell communicate with?" he asked, at last, pointing to a thick bell-rope which hung down beside the bed, the tassel actually lying upon the pillow.

"It goes to the house-keeper's room."

"It looks newer than the other things?"

"Yes, it was only put there a couple of years ago."

"Your sister asked for it, I suppose?"

"No, I never heard of her using it. We used always to get what we wanted for ourselves."

"Indeed, it seemed unnecessary to put so nice a bell-pull there. You will excuse me for a few minutes while I satisfy myself as to this floor." He threw himself down upon his face with his lens in his hand, and crawled swiftly backward and forward, examining minutely the cracks between the boards. Then he did the same with the wood-work with which the chamber was panelled. Finally he walked over to the bed, and spent some time in staring at it, and in running his eye up and down the wall. Finally he took the bell-rope in his hand and gave it a brisk tug.

"Why, it's a dummy," said he.

"Won't it ring?"

"No, it is not even attached to a wire. This is very interesting. You can see now that it is fastened to a hook just above where the little opening for the ventilator is."

"How very absurd! I never noticed that before."

"Very strange!" muttered Holmes, pulling at the rope. "There are one or two very singular points about this room. For example, what a fool a builder must be to open a ventilator into another room, when, with the same trouble, he might have communicated with the outside air!"

"That is also quite modern," said the lady.

"Done about the same time as the bell-rope?" remarked Holmes.

"Yes, there were several little changes carried out about that time."

"They seem to have been of a most interesting character—dummy bell-ropes, and ventilators which do not ventilate. With your permission, Miss Stoner, we shall now carry our researches into the inner apartment."

Dr. Grimesby Roylott's chamber was larger than that of his step-daughter, but was as plainly furnished. A camp-bed, a small wooden shelf full of books, mostly of a technical character, an arm-chair beside the bed, a plain wooden chair against the wall, a round table, and a large iron safe were the principal things which met the eye. Holmes walked slowly round and examined each and all of them with the keenest interest.

"What's in here?" he asked tapping the safe.

"My step-father's business papers."

"Oh! you have seen inside, then?"

"Only once, some years ago. I remember that it was full of papers."

"There isn't a cat in it, for example?"

"No. What a strange idea!"

"Well, look at this!" He took up a small saucer of milk which stood on the top of it.

"No: we don't keep a cat. But there is a cheetah and a baboon."

"Ah, yes, of course! Well, a cheetah is just a big cat, and yet a saucer of milk does not go very far in satisfying its wants, I dare say. There is one point which I should wish to determine." He squatted down in front of the wooden chair, and examined the seat of it with the greatest attention.

"Thank you. That is quite settled," said he, rising and putting his lens in his pocket. "Hello! Here is something interesting!"

The object which had caught his eye was a small dog-lash hung on one corner of the bed. The lash, however, was curled upon itself, and tied so as to make a loop of whipcord.

"What do you make of that, Watson?"

"It's a common enough lash. But I don't know why it should be tied."

"That is not quite so common, is it? Ah, me! it's a wicked world, and when a clever man turns his brains to crime it is the worst of all. I think that I have seen enough now, Miss Stoner, and with your permission we shall walk out upon the lawn."

I had never seen my friend's face so grim or his brow so dark as it was when we turned from the scene of this investigation. We had walked several times up and down the lawn, neither Miss Stoner nor myself liking to break in upon his thoughts before he roused himself from his reverie.

"It is very essential, Miss Stoner," said he, "that you should absolutely follow my advice in every respect."

"I shall most certainly do so."

"The matter is too serious for any hesitation. Your life may depend upon your compliance."

"I assure you that I am in your hands."

"In the first place, both my friend and I must spend the night in your room."

Both Miss Stoner and I gazed at him in astonishment.

"Yes, it must be so. Let me explain. I believe that that is the village inn over there?"

"Yes, that is the 'Crown.' "

"Very good. Your windows would be visible from there?"

"Certainly."

"You must confine yourself to your room, on pretence of a headache, when your step-father comes back. Then when you hear him retire for the night, you must open the shutters of your window, undo the hasp, put your lamp there as a signal to us, and then withdraw quietly with everything which you are likely to want into the room which you used to occupy. I have no doubt that, in spite of the repairs, you could manage there for one night."

"Oh yes, easily."

"The rest you will leave in our hands."

"But what will you do?"

"We shall spend the night in your room, and we shall investigate the cause of this noise which has disturbed you."

"I believe, Mr. Holmes, that you have already made up your mind," said Miss Stoner, laying her hand upon my companion's sleeve.

"Perhaps I have."

"Then for pity's sake tell me what was the cause of my sister's death."

"I should prefer to have clearer proofs before I speak."

"You can at least tell me whether my own thought is

correct, and if she died from some sudden fright."

"No, I do not think so. I think that there was probably some more tangible cause. And now, Miss Stoner, we must leave you, for if Dr. Roylott returned and saw us, our journey would be in vain. Good-bye, and be brave, for if you will do what I have told you, you may rest assured that we shall soon drive away the dangers that threaten you."

Sherlock Holmes and I had no difficulty in engaging a bedroom and sitting-room at the "Crown Inn." They were on the upper floor, and from our window we could command a view of the avenue gate, and of the inhabited wing of Stoke Moran Manor House. At dusk we saw Dr. Grimesby Roylott drive past, his huge form looming up beside the little figure of the lad who drove him. The boy had some difficulty in undoing the heavy iron gates, and we heard the hoarse roar of the doctor's voice, and saw the fury with which he shook his clinched fists at him. The trap drove on, and a few minutes later we saw a sudden light spring up among the trees as the lamp was lit in one of the sitting-rooms.

"Do you know, Watson," said Holmes, as we sat together in the gathering darkness, "I have really some scruples as to taking you tonight. There is a distinct element of danger."

"Can I be of assistance?"

"Your presence might be invaluable."

"Then I shall certainly come."

"It is very kind of you."

"You speak of danger. You have evidently seen more in these rooms than was visible to me."

"No, but I fancy that I may have deduced a little more. I imagine that you saw all that I did."

"I saw nothing remarkable save the bell-rope, and what purpose that could answer I confess is more than I can imagine."

"You saw the ventilator, too?"

"Yes, but I do not think it is such a very unusual thing to have a small opening between two rooms. It was so small that a rat could hardly pass through."

"I knew that we should find a ventilator before ever we came to Stoke Moran."

"My dear Holmes!"

"Oh yes, I did. You remember in her statement she said that her sister could smell Dr. Roylott's cigar. Now, of course that suggested at once that there must be a communication between the two rooms. It could only be a small one, or it would have been remarked upon at the coroner's inquiry. I deduced a ventilator."

"But what harm can there be in that?"

"Well, there is at least a curious coincidence of dates. A ventilator is made, a cord is hung, and a lady who sleeps in the bed dies. Does not that strike you?"

"I cannot as yet see any connection."

"Did you observe anything very peculiar about that bed?"

"No."

"It was clamped to the floor. Did you ever see a bed fastened like that before?"

"I cannot say that I have."

"The lady could not move her bed. It must always be in the same relative position to the ventilator and to the rope —for so we may call it, since it was clearly never meant for a bell-pull."

"Holmes," I cried, "I seem to see dimly what you are hinting at. We are only just in time to prevent some subtle and horrible crime."

"Subtle enough and horrible enough. When a doctor does go wrong, he is the first of criminals. He has nerve and he has knowledge. Palmer and Pritchard were among the heads of their profession. This man strikes even deeper, but I think, Watson, that we shall be able to strike deeper still. But we shall have horrors enough before the night is over; for goodness' sake let us have a quiet pipe, and turn our minds for a few hours to something more cheerful."

About nine o'clock the light among the trees was extinguished, and all was dark in the direction of the Manor

House. Two hours passed slowly away, and then, suddenly, just at the stroke of eleven, a single bright light shone out right in front of us.

"That is our signal," said Holmes, springing to his feet; "it comes from the middle window."

As we passed out he exchanged a few words with the landlord, explaining that we were going on a late visit to an acquaintance, and that it was possible that we might spend the night there. A moment later we were out on the dark road, a chill wind blowing in our faces, and one yellow light twinkling in front of us through the gloom to guide us on our sombre errand.

There was little difficulty in entering the grounds, for unrepaired breaches gaped in the old park wall. Making our way among the trees, we reached the lawn, crossed it, and were about to enter through the window, when out from a clump of laurel bushes there darted what seemed to be a hideous and distorted child, who threw itself upon the grass with writhing limbs, and then ran swiftly across the lawn into the darkness.

"My God!" I whispered; "did you see it?"

Holmes was for the moment as startled as I. His hand closed like a vise upon my wrist in his agitation. Then he broke into a low laugh, and put his lips to my ear.

"It is a nice household," he murmured. "That is the baboon."

I had forgotten the strange pets which the doctor affected. There was a cheetah, too; perhaps we might find it upon our shoulders at any moment. I confess that I felt easier in my mind when, after following Holmes's example and slipping off my shoes, I found myself inside the bedroom. My companion noiselessly closed the shutters, moved the lamp onto the table, and cast his eyes round the room. All was as we had seen it in the daytime. Then creeping up to me and making a trumpet of his hand, he whispered into my ear again so gently that it was all that I could do to distinguish the words:

"The least sound would be fatal to our plans."

I nodded to show that I had heard.

"We must sit without light. He would see it through the ventilator."

I nodded again.

"Do not go asleep; your very life may depend upon it. Have your pistol ready in case we should need it. I will sit on the side of the bed, and you in that chair."

I took out my revolver and laid it on the corner of the table.

Holmes had brought up a long thin cane, and this he placed upon the bed beside him. By it he laid the box of matches and the stump of a candle. Then he turned down the lamp, and we were left in darkness.

How shall I ever forget that dreadful vigil? I could not hear a sound, not even the drawing of a breath, and yet I knew that my companion sat open-eyed, within a few feet of me, in the same state of nervous tension in which I was myself. The shutters cut off the least ray of light, and we waited in absolute darkness. From outside came the occasional cry of a night-bird, and once at our very window a long drawn cat-like whine, which told us that the cheetah was indeed at liberty. Far away we could hear the deep tones of the parish clock, which boomed out every quarter of an hour. How long they seemed, those quarters! Twelve struck, and one and two and three, and still we sat waiting silently for whatever might befall.

Suddenly there was a momentary gleam of a light up in the direction of the ventilator, which vanished immediately, but was succeeded by a strong smell of burning oil and heated metal. Some one in the next room had lit a dark-lantern. I heard a gentle sound of movement, and then all was silent once more, though the smell grew stronger. For half an hour I sat with straining ears. Then suddenly another sound became audible—a very gentle, soothing sound, like that of a small jet of steam escaping continually from a kettle. The instant that we heard it, Holmes sprang from the bed, struck a match, and lashed furiously with his cane at the bell-pull.

"You see it, Watson?" he yelled. "You see it?"

But I saw nothing. At the moment when Holmes struck the light I heard a low clear whistle, but the sudden glare flashing into my weary eyes made it impossible for me to tell what it was at which my friend lashed so savagely. I could, however, see that his face was deadly pale, and filled with horror and loathing.

He had ceased to strike, and was gazing up at the ventilator, when suddenly there broke from the silence of the night the most horrible cry to which I have ever listened. It swelled up louder and louder, a hoarse yell of pain and fear and anger all mingled in the one dreadful shriek. They say that away down in the village, and even in the distant parsonage, that cry raised the sleepers from their beds. It struck cold to our hearts, and I stood gazing at Holmes, and he at me, until the last echoes of it had died away into the silence from which it rose.

"What can it mean?" I gasped.

"It means that it is all over," Holmes answered. "And perhaps, after all, it is for the best. Take your pistol, and we will enter Dr. Roylott's room."

With a grave face he lit the lamp and led the way down the corridor. Twice he struck at the chamber door without any reply from within. Then he turned the handle and entered, I at his heels, with the cocked pistol in my hand.

It was a singular sight which met our eyes. On the table stood a dark-lantern with the shutter half open, throwing a brilliant beam of light upon the iron safe, the door of which was ajar. Beside this table, on the wooden chair, sat Dr. Grimesby Roylott, clad in a long gray dressing-gown, his bare ankles protruding beneath, and his feet thrust into red heelless Turkish slippers. Across his lap lay the short stock with the long lash which we had noticed during the day. His chin was cocked upward and his eyes were fixed in a dreadful, rigid stare at the corner of the ceiling. Round his brow he had a peculiar yellow band, with brownish speckles, which seemed to be bound tightly round his head. As we entered he made neither sound nor motion.

"The band! the speckled band!" whispered Holmes.

I took a step forward. In an instant his strange head-gear began to move, and there reared itself from among his hair the squat diamond-shaped head and puffed neck of a loathsome serpent.

"It is a swamp adder!" cried Holmes; "the deadliest snake in India. He has died within ten seconds of being bitten. Violence does, in truth, recoil upon the violent, and the schemer falls into the pit which he digs for another. Let us thrust this creature back into its den, and we can then remove Miss Stoner to some place of shelter, and let the county police know what has happened."

As he spoke he drew the dog-whip swiftly from the dead man's lap, and throwing the noose round the reptile's neck, he drew it from its horrid perch, and carrying it at arm's length, threw it into the iron safe, which he closed upon it.

Such are the true facts of the death of Dr. Grimesby Roylott, of Stoke Moran. It is not necessary that I should prolong a narrative which has already run to too great a length, by telling how we broke the sad news to the terrified girl, how we conveyed her by the morning train to the care of her good aunt at Harrow, of how the slow process of official inquiry came to the conclusion that the doctor met his fate while indiscreetly playing with a dangerous pet. The little which I had yet to learn of the case was told me by Sherlock Holmes as we travelled back next day.

"I had," said he, "come to an entirely erroneous conclusion, which shows, my dear Watson, how dangerous it always is to reason from insufficient data. The presence of the gypsies, and the use of the word 'band,' which was used by the poor girl, no doubt to explain the appearance which she had caught a hurried glimpse of by the light of her match, were sufficient to put me upon an entirely wrong scent. I can only claim the merit that I instantly reconsidered my position when, however, it became clear to me that whatever danger threatened an occupant of the room could not come either from the window or the door. My attention was speedily drawn, as I have already remarked to you, to this ventilator, and to the bell-rope which hung down to the bed. The discovery that this was a dummy, and that the bed was clamped to the floor, instantly gave rise to the suspicion that the rope was there as a bridge for something passing through the hole, and coming to the bed. The idea of a snake instantly occurred to me, and when I coupled it with my knowledge that the doctor was furnished with a supply of creatures from India, I felt that I was probably on the right track. The idea of using a form of poison which could not possibly be discovered by any chemical test was just such a one as would occur to a clever and ruthless man who had had an Eastern training. The rapidity with which such a poison would take effect would also, from his point of view, be an advantage. It would be a sharp-eyed coroner, indeed, who could distinguish the two little dark punctures which would show where the poison fangs had done their work. Then I thought of the whistle. Of course he must recall the snake before the morning light revealed it to the victim. He had trained it, probably by the use of the milk which we saw, to return to him when summoned. He would put it through this ventilator at the hour that he thought best, with the certainty that it would crawl down the rope, and land on the bed. It might or might not bite the occupant, perhaps she might escape every night for a week, but sooner or later she must fall a victim.

"I had come to these conclusions before ever I had entered his room. An inspection of his chair showed me that he had been in the habit of standing on it, which of course would be necessary in order that he should reach the ventilator. The sight of the safe, the saucer of milk, and the loop of whipcord were enough to finally dispel any doubts which may have remained. The metallic clang heard by Miss Stoner was obviously caused by her step-father hastily closing the door of his safe upon its terrible occupant. Having once made up my mind, you know the steps which I took in order to put the matter to the proof. I heard the creature hiss, as I have no doubt that you did also, and I instantly lit the light and attacked it."

"With the result of driving it through the ventilator."

"And also with the result of causing it to turn upon its master at the other side. Some of the blows of my cane came home, and roused its snakish temper, so that it flew upon the first person it saw. In this way I am no doubt indirectly responsible for Dr. Grimesby Roylott's death, and I cannot say that it is likely to weigh very heavily upon my conscience."

THE STRANGE RIDE OF MORROWBIE JUKES

BY RUDYARD KIPLING

Alive or dead—there is no other way.

—*Native Proverb.*

THERE IS NO INVENTION ABOUT THIS TALE.
Jukes by accident stumbled upon a village that is well known to exist, though he is the only Englishman who has been there. A somewhat similar institution used to flourish on the outskirts of Calcutta, and there is a story that if you go into the heart of Bikanir, which is in the heart of the Great Indian Desert, you shall come across not a village but a town where the Dead who did not die but may not live have established their headquarters. And, since it is perfectly true that in the same Desert is a wonderful city where all the rich money-lenders retreat after they have made their fortunes (fortunes so vast that the owners cannot trust even the strong hand of the Government to protect them, but take refuge in the waterless sands), and drive sumptuous C-spring barouches, and buy beautiful girls and decorate their palaces with gold and ivory and Minton tiles and mother-o'-pearl, I do not see why Jukes's tale should not be true. He is a Civil Engineer, with a head for plans and distances and things of that kind, and he certainly would not take the trouble to invent imaginary traps. He could earn more by doing his legitimate work. He never varies the tale in the telling, and grows very hot and indignant when he thinks of the disrespectful treatment he received. He wrote this quite straightforwardly at first, but he has touched it up in places and introduced Moral Reflections: thus:—

In the beginning it all arose from a slight attack of fever.

My work necessitated my being in camp for some months between Pakpattan and Mubarakpus—a desolate sandy stretch of country as every one who has had the misfortune to go there may know. My coolies were neither more nor less exasperating than other gangs, and my work demanded sufficient attention to keep me from moping, had I been inclined to so unmanly a weakness.

On the 23rd December 1884, I felt a little feverish. There was a full moon at the time, and, in consequence, every dog near my tent was baying it. The brutes assembled in twos and threes and drove me frantic. A few days previously I had shot one loud-mouthed singer and suspended his carcass *in terrorem* about fifty yards from my tent-door, but his friends fell upon, fought for, and ultimately devoured the body: and, as it seemed to me, sang their hymns of thanksgiving afterwards with renewed energy.

The light-headedness which accompanies fever acts differently on different men. My irritation gave way, after a short time, to a fixed determination to slaughter one huge black and white beast who had been foremost in song and first in flight throughout the evening. Thanks to a shaking hand and a giddy head I had already missed him twice with both barrels of my shotgun, when it struck me that my best plan would be to ride him down in the open and finish him off with a hog-spear. This, of course, was merely the semidelirious notion of a fever-patient; but I remember that it struck me at the time as being eminently practical and feasible.

I therefore ordered my groom to saddle Pornic and bring him round quietly to the rear of my tent. When the pony was ready, I stood at his head prepared to mount and dash out as soon as the dog should again lift up his voice. Pornic, by the way, had not been out of his pickets for a couple of days; the night air was crisp and chilly; and I was armed with a specially long and sharp pair of persuaders with which I had been rousing a sluggish cob that afternoon. You will easily believe, then, that when he was let go he went quickly. In one moment, for the brute bolted as straight as a die, the tent was left far behind, and we were flying over the smooth sandy soil at racing speed. In another we had passed the wretched dog, and I had almost forgotten why it was that I had taken horse and hog-spear.

The delirium of fever and the excitement of rapid motion through the air must have taken away the remnant of my senses. I have a faint recollection of standing upright in my stirrups, and of brandishing my hog-spear at the great white Moon that looked down so calmly on my mad gallop; and of shouting challenges to the camelthorn bushes as they whizzed past. Once or twice, I believe, I swayed forward on Pornic's neck, and literally hung on by my spurs—as the marks next morning showed.

The wretched beast went forward like a thing possessed, over what seemed to be a limitless expanse of moonlit sand. Next, I remember, the ground rose suddenly in front of us, and as we topped the ascent I saw the waters of the Sutlej shining like a silver bar below. Then Pornic blundered heavily on his nose, and we rolled together down some unseen slope.

I must have lost consciousness, for when I recovered I was lying on my stomach in a heap of soft white sand, and the dawn was beginning to break dimly over the edge of the slope down which I had fallen. As the light grew stronger I saw I was at the bottom of a horseshoe-shaped crater of sand, opening on one side directly on to the shoals of the Sutlej. My fever had altogether left me, and, with the exception of a slight dizziness in the head, I felt no bad effects from the fall over night.

Pornic, who was standing a few yards away, was naturally a good deal exhausted, but had not hurt himself in the least. His saddle, a favourite polo one, was much knocked about, and had been twisted under his belly. It took me some time to put him to rights, and in the meantime I had ample opportunities of observing the spot into which I had so foolishly dropped.

At the risk of being considered tedious, I must describe it

at length; inasmuch as an accurate mental picture of its peculiarities will be of material assistance in enabling the reader to understand what follows.

Imagine then, as I have said before, a horseshoe-shaped crater of sand with steeply-graded sand walls about thirty-five feet high. (The slope, I fancy, must have been about 65°.) This crater enclosed a level piece of ground about fifty yards long by thirty at its broadest part, with a rude well in the centre. Round the bottom of the crater, about three feet from the level of the group proper, ran a series of eighty-three semicircular, ovoid, square, and multilateral holes, all about three feet at the mouth. Each hole on inspection showed that it was carefully shored internally with driftwood and bamboos, and over the mouth a wooden drip-board projected, like the peak of a jockey's cap, for two feet. No sign of life was visible in these tunnels, but a most sickening stench pervaded the entire amphitheatre—a stench fouler than any which my wanderings in Indian villages have introduced me to.

Having remounted Pornic, who was as anxious as I to get back to camp, I rode round the base of the horseshoe to find some place whence an exit would be practicable. The inhabitants, whoever they might be, had not thought fit to put in an appearance, so I was left to my own devices. My first attempt to 'rush' Pornic up the steep sand-banks showed me that I had fallen into a trap exactly on the same model as that which the ant-lion sets for its prey. At each step the shifting sand poured down from above in tons, and rattled on the drip-boards of the holes like small shot. A couple of ineffectual charges sent us both rolling down to the bottom, half choked with the torrents of sand; and I was constrained to turn my attention to the river-bank.

Here everything seemed easy enough. The sand hills ran down to the river edge, it is true, but there were plenty of shoals and shallows across which I could gallop Pornic, and find my way back to *terra firma* by turning sharply to the right or the left. As I led Pornic over the sands I was startled by the faint pop of a rifle across the river; and at the same moment a bullet dropped with a sharp 'whit' close to Pornic's head.

There was no mistaking the nature of the missle—a regulation Martini-Henry "picket." About five hundred yards away a country-boat was anchored in midstream; and a jet of smoke drifting away from its bows in the still morning air showed me whence the delicate attention had come. Was ever a respectable gentleman in such an *impasse?* The treacherous sand slope allowed no escape from a spot which I had visited most involuntarily, and a promenade on the river frontage was the signal for a bombardment from some insane native in a boat. I'm afraid that I lost my temper very much indeed.

Another bullet reminded me that I had better save my breath to cool my porridge; and I retreated hastily up the sands and back to the horseshoe, where I saw that the noise of the rifle had drawn sixty-five human beings from the badger-holes which I had up till that point supposed to be untenanted. I found myself in the midst of a crowd of spectators—about forty men, twenty women, and one child who could not have been more than five years old. They were all scantily clothed in that salmon-coloured cloth which one associates with Hindu mendicants, and, at first sight, gave me the impression of a band of loathsome *fakirs*. The filth and repulsiveness of the assembly were beyond all description, and I shuddered to think what their life in the badger-holes must be.

Even in these days, when local self-government has destroyed the greater part of a native's respect for a Sahib, I have been accustomed to a certain amount of civility from my inferiors, and on approaching the crowd naturally expected that there would be some recognition of my presence. As a matter of fact, there was; but it was by no means what I had looked for.

The ragged crew actually laughed at me—such laughter I hope I may never hear again. They cackled, yelled, whis-

tled, and howled as I walked into their midst; some of them
literally throwing themselves down on the ground in convul-
sions of unholy mirth. In a moment I had let go Pornic's
head, and, irritated beyond expression at the morning's adventure, commenced cuffing those nearest to me with all the
force I could. The wretches dropped under my blows like
nine-pins, and the laughter gave place to wails for mercy;
while those yet untouched clasped me round the knees, im-
ploring me in all sorts of uncouth tongues to spare them.

In the tumult, and just when I was feeling very much
ashamed of myself for having thus easily given way to my
temper, a thin, high voice murmured in English from behind
my shoulder: 'Sahib! Sahib! Do you not know me? Sahib, it
is Gunga Dass, the telegraph-master.'

I spun round quickly and faced the speaker.

Gunga Dass (I have, of course, no hesitation in mentioning the man's real name) I had known four years before as
a Deccanee Brahmin lent by the Punjab Government to one
of the Khalsia States. He was in charge of a branch tele-
graph-office there, and when I had last met him was a jovial,
full-stomached, portly Government servant with a marvel-
lous capacity for making bad puns in English—a peculiarity
which made me remember him long after I had forgotten his
services to me in his official capacity. It is seldom that a
Hindu makes English puns.

Now, however, the man was changed beyond all recognition. Caste-mark, stomach, slate-coloured continuations,
and unctuous speech were all gone. I looked at a withered
skeleton, turbanless and almost naked, with long matted hair
and deep-set codfish-eyes. But for a crescent-shaped scar on
the left cheek—the result of an accident for which I was responsible—I should never have known him. But it was in-
dubitably Gunga Dass, and—for this I was thankful—an
English-speaking native who might at least tell me the meaning of all that I had gone through that day.

The crowd retreated to some distance as I turned towards
the miserable figure, and ordered him to show me some
method of escaping from the crater. He held a freshly-

plucked crow in his hand, and in reply to my question climbed slowly on a platform of sand which ran in front of the holes, and commenced lighting a fire there in silence. Dried bents, sand-poppies, and drift-wood burn quickly; and I derived much consolation from the fact that he lit them with an ordinary sulphur match. When they were in a bright glow, and the crow was neatly spitted in front thereof, Gunga Dass began without a word of preamble:—

'There are only two kinds of men, Sar. The alive and the dead. When you are dead you are dead, but when you are alive you live.' (Here the crow demanded his attention for an instant as it twirled before the fire in danger of being burnt to a cinder.) 'If you die at home and do not die when you come to the ghât to be burnt you come here.'

The nature of the reeking village was made plain now, and all that I had known or read of the grotesque and the horrible paled before the fact just communicated by the ex-Brahmin. Sixteen years ago, when I first landed in Bombay, I had been told by a wandering Armenian of the existence, somewhere in India, of a place to which such Hindus as had the misfortune to recover from trance or catalepsy were conveyed and kept, and I recollect laughing heartily at what I was then pleased to consider a traveller's tale. Sitting at the bottom of the sand-trap, the memory of Watson's Hotel, with its swinging punkahs, white-robed servants and the sallow-faced Armenian, rose up in my mind as vividly as a photograph, and I burst into a loud fit of laughter. The contrast was too absurd!

Gunga Dass, as he bent over the unclean bird, watched me curiously. Hindus seldom laugh, and his surroundings were not such as to move him that way. He removed the crow solemnly from the wooden spit and as solemnly devoured it. Then he continued his story, which I give in his own words:—

'In epidemics of the cholera you are carried to be burnt almost before you are dead. When you come to the riverside the cold air, perhaps, makes you alive, and then, if you are only little alive, mud is put on your nose and mouth and

you die conclusively. If you are rather more alive, more mud
is put; but if you are too lively they let you go and take you
away. I was too lively, and made protestation with anger
against the indignities that they endeavoured to press upon
me. In those days I was Brahmin and proud man. Now I am
dead man and eat'—here he eyed the well-gnawed breast
bone with the first sign of emotion that I has seen in him since
we met—'crows, and—other things. They took me from my
sheets when they saw that I was too lively and gave me med-
icines for one week, and I survived successfully. Then they
sent me by rail from my place to Okara Station, with a man
to take care of me; and at Okara Station we met two other
men, and they conducted we three on camels, in the night,
from Okara Station to this place, and they propelled me from
the top to the bottom, and the other two succeeded, and I
have been here ever since two and a half years. Once I was
Brahmin and proud man, and now I eat crows.'

'There is no way of getting out?'

'None of what kind at all. When I first came I made experiments frequently and all the others also, but we have always
succumbed to the sand which is precipitated upon our heads.'

'But surely,' I broke in at this point, 'the river-front is
open, and it is worth while dodging the bullets; while at
night—'

I had already matured a rough plan of escape which a
natural instinct of selfishness forbade me sharing with Gunga
Dass. He, however, divined my unspoken thought almost as
soon as it was formed; and, to my intense astonishment, gave
vent to a long low chuckle of derision—the laughter, be it
understood, of a superior or at least of an equal.

'You will not'—he had dropped the Sir after his first sentence—'make any escape that way. But you can try. I have
tried. Once only.'

The sensation of nameless terror which I had in vain
attempted to strive against, overmastered me completely. My
long fast—it was now close upon ten o'clock, and I had
eaten nothing since tiffin on the previous day—combined

with the violent agitation of the ride had exhausted me, and
I verily believe that, for a few minutes, I acted as one mad.
I hurled myself against the sand-slope. I ran round the base
of the crater, blaspheming and praying by turns. I crawled
out among the sedges of the river-front, only to be driven
back each time in an agony of nervous dread by the rifle-
bullets which cut up the sand round me—for I dared not face
the death of a mad dog among that hideous crowd—and so
fell, spent and raving, at the curb of the well. No one had
taken the slightest notice of an exhibition which makes me
blush hotly even when I think of it now.

Two or three men trod on my panting body as they drew
water, but they were evidently used to this sort of thing, and
had no time to waste upon me. Gunga Dass, indeed, when he
had banked the embers of his fire with sand, was at some
pains to throw half a cupful of fetid water over my head,
an attention for which I could have fallen on my knees and
thanked him, but he was laughing all the while in the same
mirthless, wheezy key that greeted me on my first attempt to
force the shoals. And so, in a half-fainting state, I lay till
noon. Then, being only a man after all, I felt hungry, and
said as much to Gunga Dass, whom I had begun to regard as
my natural protector. Following the impulse of the outer
world when dealing with natives, I put my hand into my
pocket and drew out four annas. The absurdity of the gift
struck me at once, and I was about to replace the money.

Gunga Dass, however, cried: 'Give me the money, all you
have, or I will get help, and we will kill you!'

A Briton's first impulse, I believe, is to guard the contents
of his pockets; but a moment's thought showed me of the folly of differing with the one man who had it in his power to
make me comfortable; and with whose help it was possible
that I might eventually escape from the crater. I gave him all
the money in my possession, Rs. 9-8-5—nine rupees, eight
annas, and five pie—for I always keep small change as
bakshish when I am in camp. Gunga Dass clutched the coins,
and hid them at once in his ragged, loin-cloth, looking round

to assure himself that no one had observed us.

'*Now* I will give you something to eat,' said he.

What pleasure my money could have given him I am unable to say; but inasmuch as it did please him I was not sorry that I had parted with it so readily, for I had no doubt that he would have had me killed if I had refused. One does not protest against the doings of a den of wild beasts; and my companions were lower than any beasts. While I eat what Gunga Dass had provided, a coarse *chapatti* and a cupful of the foul well-water, the people showed not the faintest sign of curiosity—that curiosity which is so rampant, as a rule in an Indian village.

I could even fancy that they despised me. At all events they treated me with the most chilling indifference, and Gunga Dass was nearly as bad. I plied him with questions about the terrible village, and received extremely unsatisfactory answers. So far as I could gather, it had been in existence from time immemorial—whence I concluded that it was at least a century old—and during that time no one had ever been known to escape from it. [I had to control myself here with both hands, lest the blind terror should lay hold of me a second time and drive me raving round the crater.] Gunga Dass took a malicious pleasure in emphasising this point and in watching me wince. Nothing that I could do would induce him to tell me who the mysterious 'They' were.

'It is so ordered,' he would reply, 'and I do not yet know any one who has disobeyed the orders.'

'Only wait till my servant finds that I am missing,' I retorted, 'and I promise you that this place shall be cleared off the face of the earth, and I'll give you a lesson in civility, too, my friend.'

'Your servants would be torn in pieces before they came near this place; and, besides, you are dead, my dear friend. It is not your fault, of course, but none the less you are dead *and* buried.'

At irregular intervals supplies of food, I was told, were dropped down from the land side into the amphitheatre, and the inhabitants fought for them like wild beasts. When a man felt his death coming on he retreated to his lair and died there. The body was sometimes dragged out of the hole and thrown on to the sand, or allowed to rot where it lay.

The phrase 'thrown on to the sand' caught my attention, and I asked Gunga Dass whether this sort of thing was not likely to breed a pestilence.

'That,' said he, with another of his wheezy chuckles, 'you may see for yourself subsequently. You will have much time to make observations.'

Whereat, to his great delight, I winced once more and hastily continued the conversation: 'And how do you live here from day to day? What do you do?' The question elicited exactly the same answer as before—coupled with the information that 'this place is like your European heaven; there is neither marrying nor giving in marriage.'

Gunga Dass had been educated at a Mission School, and, as he himself admitted, had he only changed his religion 'like a wise man,' might have avoided the living grave which was now his portion. But as long as I was with him I fancy he was happy.

Here was a Sahib, a representative of the dominant race, helpless as a child and completely at the mercy of his native neighbours. In a deliberate lazy way he set himself to torture me as a schoolboy would devote a rapturous half-hour to watching the agonies of an impaled beetle, or as a ferret in a blind burrow might glue himself comfortably to the neck of a rabbit. The burden of his conversation was that there was no escape 'of no kind whatever,' and that I should stay here till I died and was 'thrown on to the sand.' If it were possible to forejudge the conversation of the Damned on the advent of a new soul in their abode, I should say that they would speak as Gunga Dass did to me throughout that long afternoon. I was powerless to protest or answer; all my energies being devoted to a struggle against the inexplicable terror that threatened to overwhelm me again and again. I can compare the feeling to nothing except the struggles of a man against the overpowering nausea of the Channel passage—only my agony was of the spirit and infinitely more terrible.

As the day wore on, the inhabitants began to appear in full strength to catch the rays of the afternoon sun, which were now sloping in at the mouth of the crater. They assembled by little knots, and talked among themselves without even throwing a glance in my direction. About four o'clock, so far as I could judge, Gunga Dass rose and dived into his lair for a moment, emerging with a live crow in his hands. The wretched bird was in a most draggled and deplorable condition, but seemed to be in no way afraid of its master. Advancing cautiously to the river-front, Gunga Dass stepped from tussock to tussock until he had reached a smooth patch of sand directly in the line of the boat's fire. The occupants of the boat took no notice. Here he stopped, and, with a couple of dexterous turns of the wrist, pegged the bird on its back with outstretched wings. As was only natural, the crow began to shriek at once and beat the air with its claws. In a few seconds the clamour had attracted the attention of a bevy of wild crows on a shoal a few hundred yards away, where they were discussing something that looked like a corpse. Half a dozen crows flew over at once to see what was going on, and also, as it proved, to attack the pinioned bird. Gunga Dass, who had lain down on a tussock, motioned to me to be quiet, though I fancy this was a needless precaution. In a moment, and before I could see how it happened, a wild crow, who had grappled with the shrieking and helpless bird, was entangled in the latter's claws, swiftly disengaged by Gunga Dass, and pegged down beside its companion in adversity. Curiosity, it seemed, overpowered the rest of the flock, and almost before Gunga Dass and I had time to withdraw to the tussock, two more captives were struggling in the upturned claws of the decoys. So the chase —if I can give it so dignified a name—continued until Gunga Dass had captured seven crows. Five of them he throttled at once, reserving two for further operations another day. I was a good deal impressed by this, to me, novel method of securing food, and complimented Gunga Dass on his skill.

'It is nothing to do,' said he. 'To-morrow you must do it for me. You are stronger than I am.'

This calm assumption of superiority upset me not a little, and I answered peremptorily: 'Indeed, you old ruffian? What do you think I have given you money for?'

'Very well,' was the unmoved reply. 'Perhaps not to-morrow, nor the day after, nor subsequently; but in the end, and for many years, you will catch crows and eat crows, and you will thank your European God that you have crows to catch and eat.'

I could have cheerfully strangled him for this; but judged it best under the circumstances to smother my resentment. A hour later I was eating one of the crows; and, as Gunga Dass had said, thanking my God that I had a crow to eat. Never as long as I live shall I forget that evening meal. The whole population were squatting on the hard sand platform opposite their dens, huddled over tiny fires of refuse and dried rushes. Death, having once laid his hand upon these men and forborne to strike, seemed to stand aloof from them now; for most of our company were old men, bent and worn and twisted with years, and women aged to all appearance as the Fates themselves. They sat together in knots and talked—God only knows what they found to discuss—in low equable tones, curiously in contrast to the strident babble with which natives are accustomed to make day hideous. Now and then an access of that sudden fury which had possessed me in the morning would lay hold on a man or woman; and with yells and imprecations the sufferer would attack the steep slope until, baffled and bleeding, he fell back on the platform incapable of moving a limb. The others would never even raise their eyes when, this happened, as men too well aware of the futility of their fellows' attempts and wearied with their useless repetition. I saw four such outbursts in the course of that evening.

Gunga Dass took an eminently business-like view of my situation, and while we were dining—I can afford to laugh at the recollection now, but it was painful enough at the time—propounded the terms of which he would consent to 'do' for me. My nine rupees eight annas, he argued, at the rate of three annas a day, would provide me with food for fifty-one days, or about seven weeks; that is to say, he would be willing to cater for me for that length of time. At the end of it I was to look after myself. For a further consideration— *videlicet* my boots—he would be willing to allow me to occupy the den next to his own, and would supply me with as much dried grass for bedding as he could spare.

'Very well, Gunga Dass,' I replied; 'to the first terms I cheerfully agree, but, as there is nothing on earth to prevent my killing you as you sit here and taking everything that you have' (I thought of the two invaluable crows at the time), 'I flatly refuse to give you my boots and shall take whichever den I please.'

The stroke was a bold one, and I was glad when I saw that it had succeeded. Gunga Dass changed his tone immediately, and disavowed all intention of asking for my boots. At the time it did not strike me as at all strange that I, a Civil Engineer, a man of thirteen years' standing in the Service, and, I trust, an average Englishman, should thus calmly threaten murder and violence against the man who had, for a consideration it is true, taken me under his wing. I had left the world, it seemed, for centuries. I was as certain then as I am now of my own existence, that in the accursed settlement there was no law save that of the strongest; that the living dead men had thrown behind them every canon of the world which had cast them out; and that I had to depend for my own life on my strength and vigilance alone. The crew of the ill-fated *Mignonette* are the only men who would understand my frame of mind. 'At present,' I argued to myself, 'I am strong and a match for six of these wretches. It is imperatively necessary that I should, for my own sake, keep both health and strength until the hour of my release comes—if it ever does.'

Fortified with these resolutions, I ate and drank as much as I could, and made Gunga Dass understand that I intended to be his master, and that the least sign of insubordination on his part would be visited with the only punishment I had it in my power to inflict—sudden and violent death. Shortly after this I went to bed. That is to say, Gunga Dass gave me a double armful of dried bents which I thrust down the mouth of the lair to the right of his, and followed myself feet foremost; the hole running about nine feet into the sand with a slight downward inclination, and being neatly shored with timbers. From my den, which faced the river-front, I was able to watch the waters of the Sutlej flowing past under the light of a young moon and compose myself to sleep as best I might.

The horrors of that night I shall never forget. My den was nearly as narrow as a coffin, and the sides had been worn smooth and greasy by the contact of innumerable naked bodies, added to which it smelt abominably. Sleep was altogether out of the question to one in my excited frame of mind. As the night wore on, it seemed that the entire amphitheatre was filled with legions of unclean devils that, trooping up from the shoals below, mocked the unfortunates in their lairs.

Personally I am not of an imaginative temperament— very few Engineers are—but on that occasion I was as completely prostrated with nervous terror as any woman. After half an hour or so, however, I was able once more to calmly review my chances of escape. Any exit by the steep sand walls was, of course, impracticable. I had been thoroughly, convinced of this some time before. It was possible, just possible, that I might, in the uncertain moonlight, safely run the gauntlet of the rifle shots. The place was so full of terror for me that I was prepared to undergo any risk in leaving it. Imagine my delight, then, when after creeping stealthily to the river-front I found that the infernal boat was not there. My freedom lay before me in the next few steps!

By walking out to the first shallow pool that lay at the foot of the projecting left horn of the horseshoe, I could wade across, turn the flank of the crater, and make my way inland. Without a moment's hesitation I marched briskly past

the tussocks where Gunga Dass had snared the crows, and
out in the direction of the smooth white sand beyond. My
first step from the tufts of dried grass showed me how utterly
futile was any hope of escape; for, as I put my foot down,
I felt an indescribable drawing, sucking motion of the sand
below. Another moment and my leg was swallowed up nearly to the knee. In the moonlight the whole surface of the sand
seemed to be shaken with devilish delight at my disappoint-
ment. I struggled clear, sweating with terror and exertion,
back to the tussocks behind me and fell on my face.

My only means of escape from the semicircle was protected with a quicksand!

How long I lay I have not the faintest idea; but I was
roused at the last by the malevolent chuckle of Gunga Dass
at my ear. 'I would advise you, Protector of the Poor' (the
ruffian was speaking English) 'to return to your house. It is
unhealthly to lie down here. Moreover, when the boat returns, you will most certainly be rifled at.' He stood over me
in the dim light of the dawn, chuckling and laughing to himself. Suppressing my first impulse to catch the man by the
neck and throw him on to the quicksand, I rose sullenly and
followed him to the platform below the burrows.

Suddenly, and futilely as I thought while I spoke, I asked:
'Gunga Dass, what is the good of the boat if I can't get out
anyhow?' I recollect that even in my deepest trouble I had
been speculating vaguely on the waste of ammunition in
guarding an already well protected foreshore.

Gunga Dass laughed again and made answer: 'They have
the boat only in daytime. It is for the reason that *there is a
way.* I hope we shall have the pleasure of your company for
much longer time. It is a pleasant spot when you have been
here some years and eaten roast crow long enough.'

I staggered, numbed and helpless, towards the fetid burrow allotted to me, and fell asleep. An hour or so later I was
awakened by a piercing scream—the shrill, high-pitched
scream of a horse in pain. Those who have once heard that
will never forget the sound. I found some little difficulty in
scrambling out of the burrow. When I was in the open, I

saw Pornic, my poor old Pornic, lying dead on the sandy soil. How they had killed him I cannot guess. Gunga Dass explained that horse was better than crow, and 'greatest good of greatest number is political maxim. We are now Republic, Mister Jukes, and you are entitled to a fair share of the beast. If you like, we will pass a vote of thanks. Shall I propose?'

Yes, we were a Republic indeed! A Republic of wild beasts penned at the bottom of a pit, to eat and fight and sleep till we died. I attempted no protest of any kind, but sat down and stared at the hideous sight in front of me. In less time almost than it takes me to write this, Pornic's body was divided, in some unclean way or other; the men and women had dragged the fragments on to the platform and were preparing their morning meal. Gunga Dass cooked mine. The almost irresistible impulse to fly at the sand walls until I was wearied laid hold of me afresh, and I had to struggle against it with all my might. Gunga Dass was offensively jocular till I told him that if he addressed another remark of any kind whatever to me I should strangle him where he sat. This silenced him till silence became insupportable, and I bade him say something.

'You will live here till you die like the other Feringhi,' he said coolly, watching me over the fragment of gristle that he was gnawing.

'What other Sahib, you swine? Speak at once, and don't stop to tell me a lie.'

'He is over there,' answered Gunga Dass, pointing to a burrow-mouth about four doors to the left of my own. 'You can see for yourself. He died in the burrow as you will die, and I will die, and as all these men and women and the one child will also die.'

'For pity's sake tell me all you know about him. Who was he? When did he come, and when did he die?'

This appeal was a weak step on my part. Gunga Dass only leered and replied: 'I will not—unless you give me something first.'

Then I recollected where I was, and struck the man between the eyes, partially stunning him. He stepped down from the platform at once, and, cringing and fawning and weeping and attempting to embrace my feet, led me round to the burrow which he had indicated.

'I know nothing whatever about the gentleman. Your God be my witness that I do not. He was as anxious to escape as you were, and he was shot from the boat, though we all did all things to prevent him from attempting. He was shot here.' Gunga Dass laid his hand on his lean stomach and bowed to the earth.

'Well, and what then? Go on!'

'And then—and then, Your Honour, we carried him into his house and gave him water, and put wet cloths on the wound, and he laid down in his house and gave up the ghost.'

'In how long? In how long?'

'About half an hour, after he received his wound. I call Vishn to witness,' yelled the wretched man, 'that I did everything for him. Everything which was possible, that I did!'

He threw himself down on the ground and clasped my ankles. But I had my doubts about Gunga Dass's benevolence, and kicked him off as he lay protesting.

'I believe you robbed him of everything he had. But I can find out in a minute or two. How long was the Sahib here?'

'Nearly a year and a half. I think he must have gone mad. But hear me swear, Protector of the Poor! Won't Your Honour hear me swear that I never touched an article that belonged to him? What is Your Worship going to do?'

I had taken Gunga Dass by the waist and had hauled him on to the platform opposite the deserted burrow. As I did so I thought of my wretched fellow-prisoner's unspeakable misery among all these horrors for eighteen months, and the final agony of dying like a rat in a hole, with a bullet wound in the stomach. Gunga Dass fancied I was going to kill him and howled pitifully. The rest of the population, in the plethora that follows a full flesh meal, watched us without stirring.

'Go inside, Gunga Dass,' said I, 'and fetch it out.'

I was feeling sick and faint with horror now. Gunga Dass nearly rolled off the platform and howled aloud.

'But I am Brahmin, Sahib—a high-caste Brahmin. By your soul, by your father's soul, do not make me do this thing!'

'Brahmin or no Brahmin, by my soul and my father's soul, in you go!' I said, and, seizing him by the shoulders, I crammed his head into the mouth of the burrow, kicked the rest of him in, and, sitting down, covered my face with my hands.

At the end of a few minutes I heard a rustle and a creak; then Gunga Dass in a sobbing, choking whisper speaking to himself; then a soft thud—and I uncovered my eyes.

The dry sand had turned the corpse entrusted to its keeping into a yellow-brown mummy. I told Gunga Dass to stand off while I examined it. The body—clad in an olive-green hunting-suit much stained and worn, with leather pads on the shoulders—was that of a man between thirty and forty, above middle height, with light, sandy hair, long moustache, and a rough unkempt beard. The left canine of the upper jaw was missing, and a portion of the lobe of the right ear was gone. On the second finger of the left hand was a ring—a shield-shaped blood-stone set in gold, with a monogram that might have been either 'B. K.' or 'B. L.' On the third finger of the right hand was a silver ring in the shape of a coiled cobra, much worn and tarnished. Gunga Dass deposited a handful of trifles he had picked out of the burrow at my feet, and, covering the face of the body with my handkerchief, I turned to examine these. I give the full list in the hope that it may lead to the identification of the unfortunate man:—

1. Bowl of a briarwood pipe, serrated at the edge; much worn and blackened; bound with string at the screw.

2. Two patent-lever keys; wards of both broken.

3. Tortoise-shell-handled penknife, silver or nickel, name-plate, marked with monogram 'B. K.'

4. Envelope, postmark undecipherable, bearing a Victorian stamp, addressed to 'Miss Mon——' (rest illegible)— 'ham'—'nt.'

5. Imitation crocodile-skin notebook with pencil. First forty-five pages blank; four and a half illegible; fifteen others filled with private memoranda relating chiefly to three persons—a Mrs. L. Singleton, abbreviated several times to 'Lot Single,' 'Mrs. S. May,' and 'Garmison,' referred to in places as 'Jerry' or 'Jack.'

6. Handle of small-sized hunting-knife. Blade snapped short. Buck's horn, diamond-cut, with swivel and ring on the butt; fragment of cotton cord attached.

It must not be supposed that I inventoried all these things on the spot as fully as I have written them down. The notebook first attracted my attention, and I put it in my pocket with a view to studying it later on. The rest of the articles I conveyed to my burrow for safety's sake, and there, being a methodical man, I inventoried them. I then returned to the corpse and ordered Gunga Dass to help me to carry it out to the river-front. While we were engaged in this, the exploded shell of an old brown cartridge dropped out of one of the pockets and rolled at my feet. Gunga Dass had not seen it; and I fell to thinking that a man does not carry exploded cartridge-cases, especially 'browns,' which will not bear loading twice, about with him when shooting. In other words, that cartridge-case had been fired inside the crater. Consequently there must be a gun somewhere. I was on the verge of asking Gunga Dass, but checked myself, knowing that he would lie. We laid the body down on the edge of the quicksand by the tussocks. It was my intention to push it out and let it be swallowed up—the only possible mode of burial that I could think of. I ordered Gunga Dass to go away.

Then I gingerly put the corpse out on the quicksand. In doing so, it was lying face downward, I tore the frail and rotten khaki shooting-coat open, disclosing a hideous cavity in the back. I have already told you that the dry sand had, as it were, mummified the body. A moment's glance showed that the gaping hole had been caused by a gunshot wound; the gun must have been fired with the muzzle almost touching the back. The shooting-coat, being intact, had been

drawn over the body after death, which must have been instantaneous. The secret of the poor wretch's death was plain
to me in a flash. Some one of the crater, presumably Gunga Dass, must have shot him with his own gun—the gun that
fitted the brown cartridges. He had never attempted to escape in the face of the rifle-fire from the boat.

I pushed the corpse out hastily, and saw it sink from sight
literally in a few seconds. I shuddered as I watched. In a
dazed, half-conscious way I turned to peruse the notebook.
A stained and discoloured slip of paper had been inserted
between the binding and the back, and dropped out as I
opened the pages. This is what it contained: *'Four out from
crow-clump; three left; nine out; two right; three back; two
left; fourteen out; two left; seven out; one left; nine back;
two right; six back; four right; seven back.'* The paper had
been burnt and charred at the edges. What it meant I could
not understand. I sat down on the dried bents turning it
over and over between my fingers, until I was aware of
Gunga Dass standing immediately behind me with glowing
eyes and outstretched hands.

'Have you got it?' he panted. 'Will you not let me look at
it also? I swear that I will return it.'

'Got what? Return what?' I asked.

'That which you have in your hands. It will help us both.'
He stretched out his long, bird-like talons, trembling with
eagerness.

'I could never find it,' he continued. 'He had secreted it
about his person. Therefore I shot him, but nevertheless I
was unable to obtain it.'

Gunga Dass had quite forgotten his little fiction about the
rifle-bullet. I heard him calmly. Morality is blunted by con-
sorting with the Dead who are alive.

'What on earth are you raving about? What is it you want
me to give you?'

'The piece of paper in the notebook. It will help us both.
Oh, you fool! You fool! Can you not see what it will do for
us? We shall escape!'

His voice rose almost to a scream, and he danced with excitement before me. I own I was moved at the chance of getting away.

'Do you mean to say that this slip of paper will help us? What does it mean?'

'Read it aloud! Read it aloud! I beg and I pray to you to read it aloud.'

I did so. Gunga Dass listened delightedly, and drew an irregular line in the sand with his fingers.

'See now! It was the length of his gun-barrels without the stock. I have those barrels. Four gun-barrels out from the place where I caught crows. Straight out; do you mind me? Then three left. Ah! Now well I remember how that man worked it out night after night. Then nine out, and so on. Out is always straight before you across the quicksand to the North. He told me so before I killed him.'

'But if you knew all this why didn't you get out before?'

'I did *not* know it. He told me that he was working it out a year and a half ago, and how he was working it out night after night when the boat had gone away, and he could get out near the quicksand safely. Then he said that we would get away together. But I was afraid that he would leave me behind one night when he had worked it all out, and so I shot him. Besides, it is not advisable that the men who once get in here should escape. Only I, and *I* am a Brahmin.'

The hope of escape had brought Gunga Dass's caste back to him. He stood up, walked about and gesticulated violently. Eventually I managed to make him talk soberly, and he told me how this Englishman had spent six months night after night in exploring, inch by inch, the passage across the quicksand; how he had declared it to be simplicity itself up to within about twenty yards of the river bank after turning the flank of the left horn of the horseshoe. This much he had evidently not completed when Gunga Dass shot him with his own gun.

In my frenzy of delight at the possibilities of escape I recollect shaking hands wildly with Gunga Dass, after we had decided that we were to make an attempt to get away that very night. It was weary work waiting throughout the afternoon.

About ten o'clock, as far as I could judge, when the Moon had just risen above the lip of the crater, Gunga Dass made a move for his burrow to bring out the gun-barrels whereby to measure our path. All the other wretched inhabitants had retired to their lairs long ago. The guardian boat drifted down-stream some hours before, and we were utterly alone by the crow-clump. Gunga Dass, while carrying the gun-barrels, let slip the piece of paper which was to be our guide. I stooped down hastily to recover it, and, as I did so, I was aware that the creature was aiming a violent blow at the back of my head with the gun-barrels. It was too late to turn round. I must have received the blow somewhere on the nape of my neck, for I fell senseless at the edge of the quicksand.

When I recovered consciousness, the Moon was going down, and I was sensible of intolerable pain in the back of my head. Gunga Dass had disappeared and my mouth was full of blood. I lay down again and prayed that I might die without more ado. Then the unreasoning fury which I have before mentioned laid hold upon me, and I staggered inland towards the walls of the crater. It seemed that some one was calling to me in a whisper—'Sahib! Sahib! Sahib!' exactly as my bearer used to call me in the mornings. I fancied that I was delirious until a handful of sand fell at my feet. Then I looked up and saw a head peering down into the amphitheatre—the head of Dunnoo, my dog-boy, who attended to my collies. As soon as he had attracted my attention, he held up his hand and showed a rope. I motioned, staggering to and fro the while, that he should throw it down. It was a couple of leather punkah-ropes knotted together, with a loop at one end. I slipped the loop over my head and under my arms; heard Dunnoo urge something forward; was conscious that I was being dragged, face downward, up the steep sand-slope, and the next instant found myself choked and half-fainting on the sand hills overlooking the crater. Dunnoo, with his face ashy gray in the moonlight, implored me not to stay but to get back to my tent at once.

It seems that he had tracked Pornic's footprints fourteen
miles across the sands to the crater; had returned and told
my servants, who flatly refused to meddle with any one,
white or black, once fallen into the hideous Village of the
Dead; whereupon Dunnoo had taken one of my ponies and
a couple of punkah ropes, returned to the crater, and hauled
me out as I have described.

THE LODGER

BY MARIE BELLOC LOWNDES

"THERE HE IS AT LAST, AND I'M GLAD OF IT, Ellen. 'Tain't a night you would wish a dog to be out in."

Mr. Bunting's voice was full of unmistakable relief. He was close to the fire, sitting back in a deep leather armchair —a clean-shaven, dapper man, still in outward appearance what he had been so long, and now no longer was—a self-respecting butler.

"You needn't feel so nervous about him; Mr. Sleuth can look out for himself, all right." Mrs. Bunting spoke in a dry, rather tart tone. She was less emotional, better balanced, than was her husband. On her the marks of past servitude were less apparent, but they were there all the same—especially in her neat black stuff dress and scrupulously clean, plain collar and cuffs. Mrs. Bunting, as a single woman, had been for long years what is known as a useful maid.

"I can't think why he wants to go out in such weather. He did it in last week's fog, too," Bunting went on complainingly.

"Well, it's none of your business—now, is it?"

"No; that's true enough. Still, 'twould be a very bad thing for us if anything happened to him. This lodger's the first bit of luck we've had for a very long time."

Mrs. Bunting made no answer to this remark. It was too obviously true to be worth answering. Also she was listening —following in imagination her lodger's quick, singularly quiet—"stealthy," she called it to herself—progress through the dark, fog-filled hall and up the staircase.

"It isn't safe for decent folk to be out in such weather—not unless they have something to do that won't wait till to-morrow." Bunting had at last turned round. He was now looking straight into his wife's narrow, colorless face; he was an obstinate man, and liked to prove himself right. "I read you out the accidents in *Lloyd's* yesterday—shocking, they

were, and all brought about by the fog! And then, that
'orrid monster at his work again—"

"Monster?" repeated Mrs. Bunting absently. She was trying to hear the lodger's footsteps overhead; but her husband
went on as if there had been no interruption:

"It wouldn't be very pleasant to run up against such a
party as that in the fog, eh?"

"What stuff you do talk!" she said sharply; and then she
got up suddenly. Her husband's remark had disturbed her.
She hated to think of such things as the terrible series of
murders that were just then horrifying and exciting the neth-
er world of London. Though she enjoyed pathos and sentiment—Mrs. Bunting would listen with mild amusement to
the details of a breach-of-promise action,—she shrank from
stories of either immorality or physical violence.

Mrs. Bunting got up from the straight-backed chair on
which she had been sitting. It would soon be time for supper.

She moved about the sitting-room, flecking off an imper-
ceptible touch of dust here, straightening a piece of furniture there.

Bunting looked around once or twice. He would have
liked to ask Ellen to leave off fidgeting, but he was mild and
fond of peace, so he refrained. However, she soon gave
over what irritated him of her own accord.

But even then Mrs. Bunting did not at once go down to
the cold kitchen, where everything was in readiness for her
simple cooking. Instead, she opened the door leading into
the bedroom behind, and there, closing the door quietly,
stepped back into the darkness and stood motionless, listening.

At first she heard nothing, but gradually there came the
sound of some one moving about in the room just overhead;
try as she might, however, it was impossible for her to guess
what her lodger was doing. At last she heard him open the
door leading out on the landing. That meant that he would
spend the rest of the evening in the rather cheerless room
above the drawing-room floor—oddly enough, he liked
sitting there best, though the only warmth obtainable was
from a gas-stove fed by a shilling-in-the slot arrangement.

It was indeed true that Mr. Sleuth had brought the Buntings luck, for at the time he had taken their rooms it had been touch and go with them.

After having each separately led the sheltered, impersonal, and, above all, the financially easy existence that is the compensation life offers to those men and women who deliberately take upon themselves the yoke of domestic service, these two, butler and useful maid, had suddenly, in middle age, determined to join their fortunes and savings.

Bunting was a widower; he had one pretty daughter, a girl of seventeen, who now lived, as had been the case ever since the death of her mother, with a prosperous aunt. His second wife had been reared in the Foundling Hospital, but she had gradually worked her way up into the higher ranks of the servant class and as useful maid she had saved quite a tidy sum of money.

Unluckily, misfortune had dogged Mr. and Mrs. Bunting from the very first. The seaside place where they had begun by taking a lodging-house became the scene of an epidemic. Then had followed a business experiment which had proved disastrous. But before going back into service, either together or separately, they had made up their minds to make one last effort, and, with the little money that remained to them, they had taken over the lease of a small house in the Marylebone Road.

Bunting, whose appearance was very good, had retained a connection with old employers and their friends, so he occasionally got a good job as waiter. During this last month his jobs had perceptibly increased in number and in profit; Mrs. Bunting was not superstitious, but it seemed that in this matter, as in everything else, Mr. Sleuth, their new lodger, had brought them luck.

As she stood there, still listening intently in the darkness of the bedroom, she told herself, not for the first time, what Mr. Sleuth's departure would mean to her and Bunting. It would almost certainly mean ruin.

Luckily, the lodger seemed entirely pleased both with the rooms and with his landlady. There was really no reason why he should ever leave such nice lodgings. Mrs. Bunting shook off her vague sense of apprehension and unease. She turned round, took a step forward, and, feeling for the handle of the door giving into the passage, she opened it, and went down with light, firm steps into the kitchen.

She lit the gas and put a frying-pan on the stove, and then once more her mind reverted, as if in spite of herself, to her lodger, and there came back to Mrs. Bunting, very vividly, the memory of all that had happened the day Mr. Sleuth had taken her rooms.

The date of this excellent lodger's coming had been the twenty-ninth of December, and the time late afternoon. She and Bunting·had been sitting, gloomily enough over their small banked-up fire. They had dined in the middle of the day—he on a couple of sausages, she on a little cold ham. They were utterly out of heart, each trying to pluck up courage to tell the other that it was no use trying any more. The two had also had a little tiff on that dreary afternoon. A newspaper-seller had come yelling down the Marylebone Road, shouting out, " 'Orrible murder in Whitechapel!" and just because Bunting had an old uncle living in the East End he had gone and bought a paper, and at a time, too, when every penny, nay, every half-penny, had its full value! Mrs. Bunting remembered the circumstances because that murder in Whitechapel had been the first of these terrible crimes— there had been four since—which she would never allow Bunting to discuss in her presence, and yet which had of late begun to interest curiously, uncomfortably, ever her refined mind.

But, to return to the lodger. It was then, on that dreary afternoon, that suddenly there had come to the front door a tremulous, uncertain double knock.

Bunting ought to have got up, but he had gone on reading the paper and so Mrs. Bunting, with the woman's greater courage, had gone out into the passage, turned up the gas, and opened the door to see who it could be. She remembered, as if it were yesterday instead of nigh on a month ago, Mr. Sleuth's peculiar appearance. Tall, dark, lanky, an old-fashioned top hat concealing his high bald forehead, he had stood there, an odd figure of a man, blinking at her.

"I believe—is it not a fact that you let lodgings?" he had asked in a hesitating, whistling voice, a voice that she had known in a moment to be that of an educated man—of a gentleman. As he had stepped into the hall, she had noticed that in his right hand he held a narrow bag—a quite new bag of strong brown leather.

Everything had been settled in less than a quarter of an hour. Mr. Sleuth had at once "taken" to the drawing-room floor, and then, as Mrs. Bunting eagerly lit the gas in the front room above, he had looked around him and said, rubbing his hands with a nervous movement, "Capital—capital! This is just what I've been looking for!"

The sink had specially pleased him—the sink and the gas-stove. "This is quite first-rate!" he had exclaimed, "for I make all sorts of experiments. I am, you must understand, Mrs. —er—Bunting, a man of science." Then he had sat down—suddenly. "I'm very tired," he had said in a low tone, "very tired indeed! I have been walking about all day."

From the very first the lodger's manner had been odd, sometimes distant and abrupt, and then, for no reason at all that she could see, confidential and plaintively confiding. But Mrs. Bunting was aware that eccentricity has always been a perquisite, as it were the special luxury, of the well born and well educated. Scholars and such-like are never quite like other people.

And then, this particular gentleman had proved himself so eminently satisfactory as to the one thing that really matters to those who let lodgings. "My name is Sleuth," he said, "S-l-e-u-t-h. Think of a hound, Mrs. Bunting, and you'll never forget my name. I could give you references," he had added, giving her, as she now remembered, a funny sidewise look, "but I prefer to dispense with them. How much did you say? Twenty-three shillings a week, with attendance? Yes, that will suit me perfectly; and I'll begin by paying my first month's rent in advance. Now, four times twenty-three shillings is"—he looked at Mrs. Bunting, and for the first time he smiled, a queer, wry smile—"ninety-two shillings."

He had taken a handful of sovereigns out of his pocket and put them down on the table. "Look here," he had said, "there's five pounds; and you can keep the change, for I shall want you to do a little shopping for me tomorrow."

After he had been in the house about an hour, the bell had rung, and the new lodger had asked Mrs. Bunting if she could oblige him with the loan of a Bible. She brought up to him her best Bible, the one that had been given to her as a wedding present by a lady with whose mother she had lived for several years. This Bible and one other book, of which the odd name was Cruden's Concordance, formed Mr. Sleuth's only reading: he spent hours each day poring over the Old Testament and over the volume which Mrs. Bunting had at last decided to be a queer kind of index to the Book.

However, to return to the lodger's first arrival. He had had no luggage with him, barring the small brown bag, but very soon parcels had begun to arrive addressed to Mr. Sleuth, and it was then that Mrs. Bunting first became curious. These parcels were full of clothes; but it was quite clear to the landlady's feminine eye that none of these clothes had been made for Mr. Sleuth. They were, in fact, second-hand clothes, bought at good second-hand places, each marked, when marked at all, with a different name. And the really extraordinary thing was that occasionally a complete suit disappeared—became, as it were, obliterated from the lodger's wardrobe.

As for the bag he had brought with him, Mrs. Bunting had never caught sight of it again. And this also was certainly very strange.

Mrs. Bunting thought a great deal about that bag. She often wondered what had been in it; not a nightshirt and comb and brush, as she had at first supposed, for Mr. Sleuth had asked her to go out and buy him a brush and comb and tooth-brush the morning after his arrival. That fact was specially impressed on her memory, for at the little shop, a barber's, where she had purchased the brush and comb, the foreigner who had served her had insisted on telling her some of the horrible details of the murder that had taken place the day before in Whitechapel, and it had upset her very much.

As to where the bag was now, it was probably locked up in the lower part of a chiffonnier in the front sitting-room. Mr. Sleuth evidently always carried the key of the little cupboard on his person, for Mrs. Bunting, though she looked well for it, had never been able to find it.

And yet, never was there a more confiding or trusting gentleman. The first four days that he had been with them he had allowed his money—the considerable sum of one hundred and eighty-four pounds in gold—to lie about wrapped up in pieces of paper on his dressing-table. This was a very foolish, indeed a wrong thing to do, as she had allowed herself respectfully to point out to him; but as only answer he had laughed, a loud, discordant shout of laughter.

Mr. Sleuth had many other odd ways; but Mrs. Bunting, a true woman in spite of her prim manner and love of order, had an infinite patience with masculine vagaries.

On the first morning of Mr. Sleuth's stay in the Buntings' house, while Mrs. Bunting was out buying things for him, the new lodger had turned most of the pictures and photographs hanging in his sitting-room with their faces to the wall! But this queer action on Mr. Sleuth's part had not surprised Mrs. Bunting as much as it might have done; it recalled an incident of her long-past youth—something that had happened a matter of twenty years ago, at a time when Mrs. Bunting, then the still youthful Ellen Cottrell, had been maid to an old lady. The old lady had a favorite nephew, a bright, jolly young gentleman who had been learning to paint animals in Paris; and it was he who had had the impudence, early one summer morning, to turn to the wall six beautiful engravings of paintings done by the famous Mr. Landseer! The old lady thought the world of those pictures, but her nephew, as only excuse for the extraordinary thing he had done, had observed that "they put his eye out."

Mr. Sleuth's excuse had been much the same; for, when Mrs. Bunting had come into his sitting-room and found all her pictures, or at any rate all those of her pictures that happened to be portraits of ladies, with their faces to the wall, he had offered as only explanation, "Those women's eyes follow me about."

Mrs. Bunting had gradually become aware that Mr. Sleuth had a fear and dislike of women. When she was "doing" the staircase and landing, she often heard him reading bits of the Bible aloud to himself, and in the majority of instances the texts he chose contained uncomplimentary reference to her own sex. Only to-day she had stopped and listened while he uttered threateningly the awful words, "A strange woman is a narrow pit. She also lieth in wait as for a prey, and increaseth the transgressors among men." There had been a pause, and then had come, in a high singsong, "Her house is the way to hell, going down to the chambers of death." It had made Mrs. Bunting feel quite queer.

The lodger's daily habits were also peculiar. He stayed in bed all the morning, and sometimes part of the afternoon, and he never went out before the street lamps were alight. Then, there was his dislike of an open fire; he generally sat in the top front room, and while there he always used the large gas-stove, not only for his experiments, which he carried on at night, but also in the daytime, for warmth.

But there! Where was the use of worrying about the lodger's funny ways? Of course, Mr. Sleuth was eccentric; if he hadn't been "just a leetle 'touched' upstairs"—as Bunting had once described it—he wouldn't be their lodger now; he would be living in a quite different sort of way with some of his relations, or with a friend of his own class.

Mrs. Bunting, while these thoughts galloped disconnectedly through her brain, went on with her cooking, doing everything with a certain delicate and cleanly precision.

While in the middle of making the toast on which was to be poured some melted cheese, she suddenly heard a noise, or rather a series of noises. Shuffling, hesitating steps were creaking down the house above. She looked up and listened. Surely Mr. Sleuth was not going out again into the cold, foggy night? But no; for the sounds did not continue down the passage leading to the front door.

The heavy steps were coming slowly down the kitchen stairs. Nearer and nearer came the thudding sounds, and Mrs. Bunting's heart began to beat as if in response. She put out the gas-stove, unheedful of the fact that the cheese would stiffen and spoil in the cold air; and then she turned and faced the door. There was a fumbling at the handle, and a moment later the door opened and revealed, as she had known it would, her lodger.

Mr. Sleuth was clad in a plaid dressing-gown, and in his hand was a candle. When he saw the lit-up kitchen, and the woman standing in it, he looked inexplicably taken aback, almost aghast.

"Yes, sir? What can I do for you, sir? I hope you didn't ring, sir?" Mrs. Bunting did not come forward to meet her lodger; instead, she held her ground in front of the stove. Mr. Sleuth had no business to come down like this into her kitchen.

"No, I—I didn't ring," he stammered; "I didn't know you were down here, Mrs. Bunting. Please excuse my costume. The truth is, my gas-stove has gone wrong, or, rather, that shilling-in-the-slot arrangement has done so. I came down to see if *you* had a gas-stove. I am going to ask leave to use it to-night for an experiment I want to make."

Mrs. Bunting felt troubled—oddly, unnaturally troubled. Why couldn't the lodger's experiment wait till to-morrow? "Oh, certainly, sir; but you will find it very cold down here." She looked round her dubiously.

"It seems most pleasantly warm," he observed, "warm and cozy after my cold room upstairs."

"Won't you let me make you a fire?" Mrs. Bunting's housewifely instincts were roused. "Do let me make you a fire in your bedroom, sir; I'm sure you ought to have one there these cold nights."

"By no means—I mean, I would prefer not. I do not like an open fire, Mrs. Bunting." He frowned, and still stood, a strange-looking figure, just inside the kitchen door.

"Do you want to use this stove now, sir? Is there anything I can do to help you?"

"No, not now—thank you all the same, Mrs. Bunting. I shall come down later, altogether later—probably after you and your husband have gone to bed. But I should be much obliged if you would see that the gas people come to-morrow and put my stove in order."

"Perhaps Bunting could put it right for you, sir. I'll ask him to go up."

"No, no—I don't want anything of that sort done to-night. Besides, he couldn't put it right. The cause of the trouble is quite simple. The machine is choked up with shillings: a foolish plan, so I have always felt it to be."

Mr. Sleuth spoke very pettishly, with far more heat than he was wont to speak; but Mrs. Bunting sympathized with him. She had always suspected those slot-machines to be as dishonest as if they were human. It was dreadful, the way they swallowed up the shillings!

As if he were divining her thoughts, Mr. Sleuth, walking forward, stared up at the kitchen slot-machine. "Is it nearly full?" he asked abruptly. "I expect my experiment will take some time, Mrs. Bunting."

"Oh, no, sir; there's plenty of room for shillings there still. We don't use our stove as much as you do yours, sir. I'm never in the kitchen a minute longer than I can help this cold weather."

And then, with him preceding her, Mrs. Bunting and her lodger made a slow progress to the ground floor. There Mr. Sleuth courteously bade his landlady good night, and proceeded upstairs to his own apartments.

Mrs. Bunting again went down into her kitchen, again she lit the stove, and again she cooked the toasted cheese. But she felt unnerved, afraid of she knew not what. The place seemed to her alive with alien presences, and once she caught herself listening, which was absurd, for of course she could not hope to hear what her lodger was doing two, if not three, flights upstairs. She had never been able to discover what Mr. Sleuth's experiments really were; all she knew was that they required a very high degree of heat.

The Buntings went to bed early that night. But Mrs. Bunting intended to stay awake. She wanted to know at what hour of the night her lodger would come down into the kitchen, and, above all, she was anxious as to how long he would stay there. But she had had a long day, and presently she fell asleep.

The church clock hard by struck two in the morning, and

suddenly Mrs. Bunting awoke. She felt sharply annoyed with herself. How could she have dropped off like that? Mr. Sleuth must have been down and up again hours ago.

Then, gradually, she became aware of a faint acrid odor; elusive, almost intangible, it yet seemed to encompass her and the snoring man by her side almost as a vapor might have done.

Mrs. Bunting sat up in bed and sniffed; and then, in spite of the cold, she quietly crept out of the nice, warm bedclothes and crawled along to the bottom of the bed. There Mr. Sleuth's landlady did a very curious thing; she leaned over the brass rail and put her face close to the hinge of the door. Yes, it was from there that this strange, horrible odor was coming; the smell must be very strong in the passage. Mrs. Bunting thought she knew now what became of those suits of clothes of Mr. Sleuth's that disappeared.

As she crept back, shivering, under the bedclothes, she longed to give her sleeping husband a good shake, and in fancy she heard herself saying: "Bunting, get up! There is something strange going on downstairs that we ought to know about."

But Mr. Sleuth's landlady, as she lay by her husband's side, listening with painful intentness, knew very well that she would do nothing of the sort. The lodger had a right to destroy his clothes by burning if the fancy took him. What if he did make a certain amount of mess, a certain amount of smell, in her nice kitchen? Was he not—was he not such a good lodger! If they did anything to upset him, where could they ever hope to get another like him?

Three o'clock struck before Mrs. Bunting heard slow, heavy steps creaking up her kitchen stairs. But Mr. Sleuth did not go straight up to his own quarters, as she expected him to do. Instead, he went to the front door, and, opening it, put it on the chain. At the end of ten minutes or so he closed the front door, and by that time Mrs. Bunting had divined why the lodger had behaved in this strange fashion— it must have been to get the strong acrid smell of burning wool out of the passage. But Mrs. Bunting felt as if she herself would never get rid of the horrible odor. She felt herself to be all smell.

At last the unhappy woman fell into a deep, troubled sleep; and then she dreamed a most terrible and unnatural dream; hoarse voices seemed to be shouting in her ear, " 'Orrible murder off the Edgeware Road!" Then three words, indistinctly uttered, followed by "—at his work again! Awful details!"

Even in her dream Mrs. Bunting felt angered and impatient; she knew so well why she was being disturbed by this horrid nightmare. It was because of Bunting—Bunting, who insisted on talking to her of those frightful murders, in which only morbid, vulgar-minded people took any interest. Why, even now, in her dream, she could hear her husband speaking to her about it.

"Ellen,"—so she heard Bunting say in her ear,—"Ellen, my dear, I am just going to get up to get a paper. It's after seven o'clock."

Mrs. Bunting sat up in bed. The shouting, nay, worse, the sound of tramping, hurrying feet smote on her ears. It had been no nightmare, then, but something infinitely worse—reality. Why couldn't Bunting have lain quietly in bed awhile longer, and let his poor wife go on dreaming? The most awful dream would have been easier to bear than this awakening.

She heard her husband go to the front door, and, as he bought the paper, exchange a few excited words with the newspaper boy. Then he came back and began silently moving about the room.

"Well!" she cried. "Why don't you tell me about it?"

"I thought you'd rather not hear."

"Of course I like to know what happens close to our own front door!" she snapped out.

And then he read out a piece of the newspaper—only a few lines, after all—telling in brief, unemotional language that the body of a woman, apparently done to death in a peculiarly atrocious fashion some hours before, had been found in a passage leading to a disused warehouse off the Marylebone Road.

"It serves that sort of hussy right!" was Mrs. Bunting's

only comment.

When Mrs. Bunting went down into the kitchen, everything there looked just as she had left it, and there was no trace of the acrid smell she had expected to find there. Instead, the cavernous whitewashed room was full of fog, and she noticed that, though the shutters were bolted and barred as she had left them, the windows behind them had been widely opened to the air. She, of course, had left them shut.

She stooped and flung open the oven door of her gas-stove. Yes, it was as she had expected; a fierce heat had been generated there since she had last used the oven, and a mass of black, gluey soot had fallen through to the stone floor below.

Mrs. Bunting took the ham and eggs that she had bought the previous day for her own and Bunting's breakfast, and broiled them over the gas-ring in their sitting-room. Her husband watched her in surprised silence. She had never done such a thing before.

"I couldn't stay down there," she said, "it was so cold and foggy. I thought I'd make breakfast up here, just for to-day."

"Yes," he said kindly; "that's quite right, Ellen. I think you've done quite right, my dear."

But, when it came to the point, his wife could not eat any of the nice breakfast she had got ready; she only had another cup of tea.

"Are you ill?" Bunting asked solicitously.

"No," she said shortly; "of course I'm not ill. Don't be silly! The thought of that horrible thing happening so close by has upset me. Just hark to them, now!"

Through their closed windows penetrated the sound of scurrying feet and loud, ribald laughter. A crowd, nay, a mob, hastened to and from the scene of the murder.

Mrs. Bunting made her husband lock the front gate. "I don't want any of those ghouls in here!" she exclaimed angrily. And then, "What a lot of idle people there must be in the world," she said.

The coming and going went on all day. Mrs. Bunting stayed indoors; Bunting went out. After all, the ex-butler was human—it was natural that he should feel thrilled and excited. All their neighbors were the same. His wife wasn't reasonable about such things. She quarreled with him when he didn't tell her anything, and yet he was sure she would have been angry with him if he had said very much about it.

The lodger's bell rang about two o'clock, and Mrs. Bunting prepared the simple luncheon that was also his breakfast. As she rested the tray a minute on the drawing-room floor landing, she heard Mr. Sleuth's high, quavering voice reading aloud the words:

"She saith to him, Stolen waters are sweet, and bread eaten in secret is pleasant. But he knoweth not that the dead are there; and that her guests are in the depths of hell."

The landlady turned the handle of the door and walked in with the tray. Mr. Sleuth was sitting close by the window, and Mrs. Bunting's Bible lay open before him. As she came in he hastily closed the Bible and looked down at the crowd walking along the Marylebone Road.

"There seem a great many people out to-day," he observed, without looking round.

"Yes, sir, there do." Mrs. Bunting said nothing more, and offered no other explanation; and the lodger, as he at last turned to his landlady, smiled pleasantly. He had acquired a great liking and respect for this well-behaved, taciturn woman; she was the first person for whom he had felt any such feeling for many years past.

He took a half sovereign out of his waistcoat pocket; Mrs. Bunting noticed that it was not the same waistcoat Mr. Sleuth had been wearing the day before. "Will you please accept this half sovereign for the use of your kitchen last night?" he said. "I made as little mess as I could, but I was carrying on a rather elaborate experiment."

She held out her hand, hesitated, and then took the coin.

As she walked down the stairs, the winter sun, a yellow ball hanging in the smoky sky, glinted in on Mrs. Bunting, and lent blood-red gleams, or so it seemed to her, to the piece of gold she was holding in her hand.

It was a very cold night—so cold, so windy, so snow-laden the atmosphere, that every one who could do so stayed indoors. Bunting, however, was on his way home from what had proved a very pleasant job; he had been acting as waiter at a young lady's birthday party, and a remarkable piece of luck had come his way. The young lady had come into a fortune that day, and she had had the gracious, the surprising thought of presenting each of the hired waiters with a sovereign.

This birthday treat had put him in mind of another birthday. His daughter Daisy would be eighteen the following Saturday. Why shouldn't he send her a postal order for half a sovereign, so that she might come up and spend her birthday in London?

Having Daisy for three or four days would cheer up Ellen. Mr. Bunting, slackening his footsteps, began to think with puzzled concern of how queer his wife had seemed lately. She had become so nervous, so "jumpy," that he didn't know what to make of her sometimes. She had never been a really good-tempered woman,—your capable, self-respecting woman seldom is,—but she had never been like what she was now. Of late she sometimes got quite hysterical; he had let fall a sharp word to her the other day, and she had sat down on a chair, thrown her black apron over her face, and burst out sobbing violently.

During the last ten days Ellen had taken to talking in her sleep. "No, no, no!" she had cried out, only the night before. "It isn't true! I won't have it said! It's a lie!" And there had been a wail of horrible fear and revolt in her unusually quiet, mincing voice. Yes, it would certainly be a good thing for her to have Daisy's company for a bit. Whew! It *was* cold; and Bunting had stupidly forgotten his gloves. He put his hands in his pockets to keep them warm.

Suddenly he became aware that Mr. Sleuth, the lodger who seemed to have "turned their luck," as it were, was walking along on the opposite side of the solitary street.

Mr. Sleuth's tall, thin figure was rather bowed, his head bent toward the ground. His right arm was thrust into his long Inverness cape; the other occasionally sawed the air, doubtless in order to help him keep warm. He was walking rather quickly. It was clear that he had not yet become aware of the proximity of his landlord.

Bunting felt pleased to see his lodger; it increased his feeling of general satisfaction. Strange, was it not, that that odd, peculiar-looking figure should have made all the difference to his (Bunting's) and Mrs. Bunting's happiness and comfort in life?

Naturally, Bunting saw far less of the lodger than did Mrs. Bunting. Their gentleman had made it very clear that he did not like either the husband or wife to come up to his rooms without being definitely asked to do so, and Bunting had been up there only once since Mr. Sleuth's arrival five weeks before. This seemed to be a good opportunity for a little genial conversation.

Bunting, still an active man for his years, crossed the road, and, stepping briskly forward, tried to overtake Mr. Sleuth; but the more he hurried, the more the other hastened, and that without even turning to see whose steps he heard echoing behind him on the now freezing pavement.

Mr. Sleuth's own footsteps were quite inaudible—an odd circumstance, when you came to think of it, as Bunting did think of it later, lying awake by Ellen's side in the pitch-darkness. What it meant was, of course, that the lodger had rubber soles on his shoes.

The two men, the pursued and the pursuer, at last turned into the Marylebone Road. They were now within a hundred yards of home; and so, plucking up courage, Bunting called out, his voice echoing freshly on the still air:

"Mr. Sleuth, sir! Mr. Sleuth!"

The lodger stopped and turned round. He had been walking so quickly, and he was in so poor a physical condition, that the sweat was pouring down his face.

"Ah! So it's you, Mr. Bunting? I heard footsteps behind me, and I hurried on. I wish I'd known that it was only you; there are so many queer characters about at night in London."

"Not on a night like this, sir. Only honest folk who have business out of doors would be out such a night as this. It *is* cold, sir!" And then into Bunting's slow and honest mind there suddenly crept the query as to what Mr. Sleuth's own business out could be on this cold, bitter night.

"Cold?" the lodger repeated. "I can't say that I find it cold, Mr. Bunting. When the snow falls the air always becomes milder."

"Yes, sir; but to-night there's such a sharp east wind. Why, it freezes the very marrow in one's bones!"

Bunting noticed that Mr. Sleuth kept his distance in a rather strange way: he walked at the edge of the pavement, leaving the rest of it, on the wall side, to his landlord.

"I lost my way," he said abruptly. "I've been over Primrose Hill to see a friend of mine, and then, coming back, I lost my way."

Bunting could well believe that, for when he had first noticed Mr. Sleuth he was coming from the east, and not, as he should have done if walking home from Primrose Hill, from the north.

They had now reached the little gate that gave on to the shabby, paved court in front of the house. Mr. Sleuth was walking up the flagged path, when, with a "By your leave, sir," the ex-butler, stepping aside, slipped in front of his lodger, in order to open the front door for him.

As he passed by Mr. Sleuth, the back of Bunting's bare left hand brushed lightly against the long Inverness cape the other man was wearing, and, to his surprise, the stretch of cloth against which his hand lay for a moment was not only damp, damp from the flakes of snow that had settled upon it, but wet—wet and gluey. Bunting thrust his left hand into his pocket; it was with the other that he placed the key in the lock of the door.

The two men passed into the hall together. The house seemed blackly dark in comparison with the lighted up road outside; and then, quite suddenly, there came over Bunting a feeling of mortal terror, an instinctive knowledge that some terrible and immediate danger was near him. A voice —the voice of his first wife, the long-dead girl to whom his mind so seldom reverted nowadays—uttered in his ear the words, "Take care!"

"I'm afraid, Mr. Bunting, that you must have felt something dirty, foul, on my coat? It's too long a story to tell you now, but I brushed up against a dead animal—a dead rabbit lying across a bench on Primrose Hill."

Mr. Sleuth spoke in a very quiet voice, almost in a whisper.

"No, sir; no, I didn't notice nothing. I scarcely touched you, sir." It seemed as if a power outside himself compelled Bunting to utter these lying words. "And now, sir, I'll be saying good night to you," he added.

He waited until the lodger had gone upstairs, and then he turned into his own sitting-room. There he sat down, for he felt very queer. He did not draw his left hand out of his pocket till he heard the other man moving about in the room above. Then he lit the gas and held up his left hand; he put it close to his face. It was flecked, streaked with blood.

He took off his boots, and then, very quietly, he went into the room where his wife lay asleep. Stealthily he walked across to the toilet-table, and dipped his hand into the water-jug.

The next morning Mr. Sleuth's landlord awoke with a start; he felt curiously heavy about the limbs and tired about the eyes.

Drawing his watch from under his pillow, he saw that it was nearly nine o'clock. He and Ellen had overslept. Without waking her, he got out of bed and pulled up the blind. It was snowing heavily, and, as is the way when it snows, even in London, it was strangely, curiously still.

After he had dressed he went out into the passage. A newspaper and a letter were lying on the mat. Fancy having slept through the postman's knock! He picked them both up and went into the sitting-room; then he carefully shut the door behind him, and, tossing the letter aside, spread the newspaper wide open on the table and bent over it.

As Bunting at last looked up and straightened himself, a look of inexpressible relief shone upon his stolid face. The item of news he had felt certain would be there, printed in big type on the middle sheet, was not there.

He folded the paper and laid it on a chair, and then eagerly took up his letter.

Dear Father [it ran]: I hope this finds you as well as it leaves me. Mrs. Puddle's youngest child has got scarlet fever, and aunt thinks I had better come away at once, just to stay with you for a few days. Please tell Ellen I won't give her no trouble.

> Your loving daughter,
> Daisy.

Bunting felt amazingly light-hearted; and, as he walked into the next room, he smiled broadly.

"Ellen," he cried out, "here's news! Daisy's coming today. There's scarlet fever in their house, and Martha thinks she had better come away for a few days. She'll be here for her birthday!"

Mrs. Bunting listened in silence; she did not even open her eyes. "I can't have the girl here just now," she said shortly; "I've got just as much as I can manage to do."

But Bunting felt pugnacious, and so cheerful as to be almost light-headed. Deep down in his heart he looked back to last night with a feeling of shame and self-rebuke. Whatever had made such horrible thoughts and suspicions come into his head?

"Of course Daisy will come here," he said shortly. "If it comes to that, she'll be able to help you with the work, and she'll brisk us both up a bit."

Rather to his surprise, Mrs. Bunting said nothing in answer to this, and he changed the subject abruptly. "The lodger and me came in together last night," he observed. "He's certainly a funny kind of gentleman. It wasn't the sort of night one would choose to go for a walk over Primrose Hill, and yet that was what he had been doing—so he said."

It stopped snowing about ten o'clock, and the morning wore itself away.

Just as twelve was striking, a four-wheeler drew up to the gate. It was Daisy—pink-cheeked, excited, laughing-eyed Daisy, a sight to gladden any father's heart. "Aunt said I was to have a cab if the weather was bad," she said.

There was a bit of a wrangle over the fare. King's Cross, as all the world knows, is nothing like two miles from the

Marylebone Road, but the man clamored for one-and-six-pence, and hinted darkly that he had done the young lady a favor in bringing her at all.

While he and Bunting were having words, Daisy, leaving them to it, walked up the path to the door where her step-mother was awaiting her.

Suddenly there fell loud shouts on the still air. They sounded strangely eerie, breaking sharply across the muffled, snowy air.

"What's that?" said Bunting, with a look of startled fear. "Why, whatever's that?"

The cabman lowered his voice: "Them are crying out that 'orrible affair at King's Cross. He's done for two of 'em this time! That's what I meant when I said I might have got a better fare; I wouldn't say anything before Missy there, but folk 'ave been coming from all over London—like a fire; plenty of toffs, too. But there—there's nothing to see now!"

"What! Another woman murdered last night?" Bunting felt and looked convulsed with horror.

The cabman stared at him, surprised. "Two of 'em, I tell yer—within a few yards of one another. He 'ave got a nerve—"

"Have they caught him?" asked Bunting perfunctorily.

"Lord, no! They'll never catch 'im! It must 'ave happened hours and hours ago—they was both stone-cold. One each end of an archway. That's why they didn't see 'em before."

The hoarse cries were coming nearer and nearer—two news-venders trying to outshout each other.

" 'Orrible discovery near King's Cross!" they yelled ex-ultantly. And as Bunting, with his daughter's bag in his hand, hurried up the path and passed through his front door, the words pursued him like a dreadful threat.

Angrily he shut out the hoarse, insistent cries. No, he had no wish to buy a paper. That kind of crime wasn't fit reading for a young girl, such a girl as was his Daisy, brought up as carefully as if she had been a young lady by her strict Methody aunt.

As he stood in his little hall, trying to feel "all right" again, he could hear Daisy's voice—high, voluble, excited—

giving her stepmother a long account of the scarlet-fever case to which she owed her presence in London. But, as Bunting pushed open the door of the sitting-room, there came a note of sharp alarm in his daughter's voice, and he heard her say: "Why, Ellen! Whatever is the matter? You do look bad!" and his wife's muffled answer: "Open the window—do."

Rushing across the room, Bunting pushed up the sash. The newspaper-sellers were now just outside the house. "Horrible discovery near King's Cross—a clue to the murderer!" they yelled. And then, helplessly, Mrs. Bunting began to laugh. She laughed and laughed and laughed, rocking herself to and fro as if in an ecstasy of mirth.

"Why, father, whatever's the matter with her?" Daisy looked quite scared.

"She's in 'sterics—that's what it is," he said shortly. "I'll just get the water-jug. Wait a minute."

Bunting felt very put out, and yet glad, too, for this queer seizure of Ellen's almost made him forget the sick terror with which he had been possessed a moment before. That he and his wife should be obsessed by the same fear, the same terror, never crossed his simple, slow-working mind.

The lodger's bell rang. That, or the threat of the water-jug, had a magical effect on Mrs. Bunting. She rose to her feet, still trembling, but composed.

As Mrs. Bunting went upstairs she felt her legs trembling under her, and put out a shaking hand to clutch at the bannister for support. She waited a few minutes on the landing, and then knocked at the door of her lodger's parlor.

But Mr. Sleuth's voice answered her from the bedroom. "I'm not well," he called out querulously; "I think I caught a chill going out to see a friend last night. I'd be obliged if you'll bring me up a cup of tea and put it outside my door, Mrs. Bunting."

"Very well, sir."

Mrs. Bunting went downstairs and made her lodger a cup of tea over the gas-ring, Bunting watching her the while in heavy silence.

During their midday dinner the husband and wife had a

little discussion as to where Daisy should sleep. It had already been settled that a bed should be made up for her in the sitting-room, but Bunting saw reason to change this plan. As the two women were clearing away the dishes, he looked up and said shortly: "I think 'twould be better if Daisy were to sleep with you, Ellen, and I were to sleep in the sitting room."

Ellen acquiesced quietly.

Daisy was a good-natured girl; she liked London, and wanted to make herself useful to her stepmother. "I'll wash up; don't you bother to come downstairs," she said.

Bunting began to walk up and down the room. His wife gave him a furtive glance; she wondered what he was thinking about.

"Didn't you get a paper?" she said at last.

"There's the paper," he said crossly, "the paper we always do take in, the *Telegraph*." His look challenged her to a further question.

"I thought they was shouting something in the street—I mean just before I was took bad."

But he made no answer; instead, he went to the top of the staircase and called out sharply: "Daisy! Daisy, child, are you there?"

"Yes, father," she answered from below.

"Better come upstairs out of that cold kitchen."

He came back into the sitting-room again.

"Ellen, is the lodger in? I haven't heard him moving about. I don't want Daisy to be mixed up with him."

"Mr. Sleuth is not well to-day," his wife answered; "he is remaining in bed a bit. Daisy needn't have anything to do with him. She'll have her work cut out looking after things down here. That's where I want her to help me."

"Agreed," he said.

When it grew dark, Bunting went out and bought an evening paper. He read it out of doors in the biting cold, standing beneath a street lamp. He wanted to see what was the clue to the murderer.

The clue proved to be a very slender one—merely the imprint in the snowy slush of a half-worn rubber sole; and it

was, of course, by no means certain that the sole belonged
to the boot or shoe of the murderer of the two doomed wom-
en who had met so swift and awful a death in the arch near
King's Cross station. The paper's special investigator
pointed out that there were thousands of such soles being
worn in London. Bunting found comfort in that obvious fact.
He felt grateful to the special investigator for having stated
it so clearly.

As he approached his house, he heard curious sounds
coming from the inner side of the low wall that shut off
the courtyard from the pavement. Under ordinary circumstances Bunting would have gone at once to drive whoever
was there out into the roadway. Now he stayed outside, sick
with suspense and anxiety. Was it possible that their place
was being watched—already?

But it was only Mr. Sleuth. To Bunting's astonishment, the
lodger suddenly stepped forward from behind the wall on
to the flagged path. He was carrying a brown-paper parcel,
and, as he walked along, the new boots he was wearing
creaked and the tap-tap of wooden heels rang out on the
stones.

Bunting, still hidden outside the gate, suddenly understood what his lodger had been doing the other side of the
wall. Mr. Sleuth had been out to buy himself a pair of boots,
and had gone inside the gate to put them on, placing his old
footgear in the paper in which the new boots had been
wrapped.

Bunting waited until Mr. Sleuth had let himself into the
house; then he also walked up the flagged pathway, and
put his latch-key in the door.

In the next three days each of Bunting's waking hours
held its meed of aching fear and suspense. From his point of
view, almost any alternative would be preferable to that
which to most people would have seemed the only one open
to him. He told himself that it would be ruin for him and for
his Ellen to be mixed up publicly in such a terrible affair. It
would track them to their dying day.

Bunting was also always debating within himself as to
whether he should tell Ellen of his frightful suspicion. He

could not believe that what had become so plain to himself could long be concealed from all the world, and yet he did not credit his wife with the same intelligence. He did not even notice that, although she waited on Mr. Sleuth as assiduously as ever, Mrs. Bunting never mentioned the lodger.

Mr. Sleuth, meanwhile, kept upstairs, he had given up going out altogether. He still felt, so he assured his landlady, far from well.

Daisy was another complication, the more so that the girl, whom her father longed to send away and whom he would hardly let out of his sight, showed herself inconveniently inquisitive concerning the lodger.

"Whatever does he do with himself all day?" she asked her stepmother.

"Well, just now he's reading the Bible," Mrs. Bunting had answered, very shortly and dryly.

"Well, I never! That's a funny thing for a gentleman to do!" Such had been Daisy's pert remark, and her stepmother had snubbed her well for it.

Daisy's eighteenth birthday dawned uneventfully. Her father gave her what he had always promised she should have on her eighteenth birthday—a watch. It was a pretty little silver watch, which Bunting had bought second-hand on the last day he had been happy; it seemed a long time ago now.

Mrs. Bunting thought a silver watch a very extravagant present, but she had always had the good sense not to interfere between her husband and his child. Besides, her mind was now full of other things. She was beginning to fear that Bunting suspected something, and she was filled with watchful anxiety and unease. What if he were to do anything silly—mix them up with the police, for instance? It certainly would be ruination to them both. But there—one never knew, with men! Her husband, however, kept his own counsel absolutely.

Daisy's birthday was on Saturday. In the middle of the morning Ellen and Daisy went down into the kitchen. Bunting didn't like the feeling that there was only one flight of stairs between Mr. Sleuth and himself, so he quietly slipped

out of the house and went to buy himself an ounce of tobacco.

In the last four days Bunting had avoided his usual haunts.
But to-day the unfortunate man had a curious longing for
human companionship—companionship, that is, other than
that of Ellen and Daisy. This feeling led him into a small,
populous thoroughfare hard by the Edgeware Road. There
were more people there than usual, for the housewives of
the neighborhood were doing their marketing for Sunday.

Bunting passed the time of day with the tobacconist, and
the two fell into desultory talk. To the ex-butler's surprise,
the man said nothing at all to him on the subject of which
all the neighborhood must still be talking.

And then, quite suddenly, while still standing by the
counter, and before he had paid for the packet of tobacco
he held in his hand, Bunting, through the open door, saw,
with horrified surprise, that his wife was standing outside a
green-grocer's shop just opposite. Muttering a word of apol-
ogy, he rushed out of the shop and across the road.

"Ellen!" he gasped hoarsely. "You've never gone and left
my little girl alone in the house?"

Mrs. Bunting's face went chalky white. "I thought you
were indoors," she said. "You *were* indoors. Whatever made
you come out for, without first making sure I was there?"

Bunting made no answer; but, as they stared at each other in exasperated silence, *each knew that the other knew.*

They turned and scurried down the street.

"Don't run," he said suddenly; "we shall get there just
as quickly if we walk fast. People are noticing you, Ellen.
Don't run."

He spoke breathlessly, but it was breathlessness induced
by fear and excitement, not by the quick pace at which they
were walking.

At last they reached their own gate. Bunting pushed past
in front of his wife. After all, Daisy was his child—Ellen
couldn't know how he was feeling. He made the path almost in one leap, and fumbled for a moment with his latch-
key. The door opened.

"Daisy!" he called out in a wailing voice. "Daisy, my dear,

where are you?"

"Here I am, father; what is it?"

"She's all right!" Bunting turned his gray face to his wife. "She's all right, Ellen!" Then he waited a moment, leaning against the wall of the passage. "It did give me a turn," he said; and then, warningly, "Don't frighten the girl, Ellen."

Daisy was standing before the fire in the sitting-room, admiring herself in the glass. "Oh, father," she said, without turning round, "I've seen the lodger! He's quite a nice gentleman—though, to be sure, he does look a cure! He came down to ask Ellen for something, and we had quite a nice little chat. I told him it was my birthday, and he asked me to go to Madame Tussaud's with him this afternoon." She laughed a little self-consciously. "Of course I could see he was 'centric, and then at first he spoke so funnily. 'And who be you?' he says, threatening-like. And I says to him, 'I'm Mr. Bunting's daughter, sir.' 'Then you're a very fortunate girl'—that's what he said, Ellen—'to 'ave such a nice stepmother as you've got. That's why,' he says, 'you look such a good, innocent girl.' And then he quoted a bit of the prayer-book at me. 'Keep innocency,' he says, wagging his head at me. Lor'! It made me feel as if I was with aunt again."

"I won't have you going out with the lodger—that's flat." He was wiping his forehead with one hand, while with the other he mechanically squeezed the little packet of tobacco, for which, as he now remembered, he had forgotten to pay.

Daisy pouted. "Oh, father, I think you might let me have a treat on my birthday! I told him Saturday wasn't a very good day—at least, so I'd heard—for Madame Tussaud's. Then he said we could go early, while the fine folk are still having their dinners. He wants you to come, too." She turned to her stepmother, then giggled happily. "The lodger has a wonderful fancy for you, Ellen; if I was father, I'd feel quite jealous!"

Her last words were cut across by a loud knock on the door. Bunting and his wife looked at each other apprehensively.

Both felt a curious thrill of relief when they saw that it was only Mr. Sleuth—Mr. Sleuth dressed to go out: the tall hat he had worn when he first came to them was in his hand, and he was wearing a heavy overcoat.

"I saw you had come in,"—he addressed Mrs. Bunting in his high, whistling, hesitating voice,—"and so I've come down to ask if you and Miss Bunting will come to Madame Tussaud's now. I have never seen these famous waxworks, though I've heard of the place all my life."

As Bunting forced himself to look fixedly at his lodger, a sudden doubt, bringing with it a sense of immeasurable relief, came to him. Surely it was inconceivable that this gentle, mild-mannered gentleman could be the monster of cruelty and cunning that Bunting had but a moment ago believed him to be!

"You're very kind, sir, I'm sure." He tried to catch his wife's eye, but Mrs. Bunting was looking away, staring into vacancy. She still, of course, wore the bonnet and cloak in which she had just been out to do her marketing. Daisy was already putting on her hat and coat.

Madame Tussaud's had hitherto held pleasant memories for Mrs. Bunting. In the days when she and Bunting were courting they often spent part of their "afternoon out" there. The butler had an acquaintance, a man named Hopkins, who was one of the waxworks' staff, and this man had sometimes given him passes for "self and lady." But this was the first time Mrs. Bunting had been inside the place since she had come to live almost next door, as it were, to the big building.

The ill-sorted trio walked up the great staircase and into the first gallery; and there Mr. Sleuth suddenly stopped short. The presence of those curious, still figures, suggesting death in life, seemed to surprise and affright him.

Daisy took quick advantage of the lodger's hesitation and unease.

"Oh, Ellen," she cried, "do let us begin by going into the Chamber of Horrors! I've never been in there. Aunt made father promise he wouldn't take me, the only time I've ever been here. But now that I'm eighteen I can do just as I like; besides, aunt will never know!"

Mr. Sleuth looked down at her.

"Yes," he said, "let us go into the Chamber of Horrors; that's a good idea, Miss Bunting."

They turned into the great room in which the Napoleonic relics are kept, and which leads into the curious, vaultlike chamber where waxen effigies of dead criminals stand grouped in wooden docks. Mrs. Bunting was at once disturbed and relieved to see her husband's old acquaintance, Mr. Hopkins, in charge of the turnstile admitting the public to the Chamber of Horrors.

"Well, you *are* a stranger," the man observed genially. "I do believe this is the very first time I've seen you in here, Mrs. Bunting, since you married!"

"Yes," she said; "that is so. And this is my husband's daughter, Daisy; I expect you've heard of her, Mr. Hopkins. And this"—she hesitated a moment—"is our lodger, Mr. Sleuth."

But Mr. Sleuth frowned and shuffled away. Daisy, leaving her stepmother's side, joined him.

Mrs. Bunting put down three sixpences.

"Wait a minute," said Hopkins; "you can't go into the Chamber of Horrors just yet. But you won't have to wait more than four or five minutes, Mrs. Bunting. It's this way, you see; our boss is in there, showing a party round." He lowered his voice. "It's Sir John Burney—I suppose you know who Sir John Burney is?"

"No," she answered indifferently; "I don't know that I ever heard of him." She felt slightly—oh, very slightly— uneasy about Daisy. She would like her stepdaughter to keep well within sight and sound. Mr. Sleuth was taking the girl to the other end of the room.

"Well, I hope you never *will* know him—not in any personal sense, Mrs. Bunting." The man chuckled. "He's the Head Commissioner of Police—that's what Sir John Burney is. One of the gentlemen he's showing round our place is the Paris Prefect of Police, whose job is on all fours, so to speak, with Sir John's. The Frenchy has brought his daughter with him, and there are several other ladies. Ladies always like 'orrors, Mrs. Bunting; that's our experience here.

'Oh, take me to the Chamber of 'Orrors!'—that's what they say the minute they gets into the building."

A group of people, all talking and laughing together, were advancing from within toward the turnstile.

Mrs. Bunting stared at them nervously. She wondered which of them was the gentleman with whom Mr. Hopkins had hoped she would never be brought into personal contact. She quickly picked him out. He was a tall, powerful, nice-looking gentleman with a commanding manner. Just now he was smiling down into the face of a young lady. "Monsieur Barberoux is quite right," he was saying; "the English law is too kind to the criminal, especially to the murderer. If we conducted our trials in the French fashion, the place we have just left would be very much fuller than it is to-day! A man of whose guilt we are absolutely assured is oftener than not acquitted, and then the public taunt us with 'another undiscovered crime'!"

"D'you mean, Sir John, that murderers sometimes escape scot-free? Take the man who has been committing all those awful murders this last month. Of course, I don't know much about it, for father won't let me read about it, but I can't help being interested!" Her girlish voice rang out, and Mrs. Bunting heard every word distinctly.

The party gathered round, listening eagerly to hear what the Head Commissioner would say next.

"Yes." He spoke very deliberately. "I think we may say —now, don't give me away to a newspaper fellow, Miss Rose—that we do know perfectly well who the murderer in question is—"

Several of those standing near by uttered expressions of surprise and incredulity.

"Then why don't you catch him?" cried the girl indignantly.

"I didn't say we know *where* he is; I only said we know *who* he is; or, rather, perhaps I ought to say that we have a very strong suspicion of his identity."

Sir John's French colleague looked up quickly. "The Hamburg and Liverpool man?" he said interrogatively.

The other nodded. "Yes; I suppose you've had the case turned up?"

Then, speaking very quickly, as if he wished to dismiss the subject from his own mind and from that of his auditors, he went on:

"Two murders of the kind were committed eight years ago—one in Hamburg, the other just afterward in Liverpool, and there were certain peculiarities connected with the crimes which made it clear they were committed by the same hand. The perpetrator was caught, fortunately for us red-handed, just as he was leaving the house of his victim, for in Liverpool the murder was committed in a house. I myself saw the unhappy man—I say unhappy, for there is no doubt at all that he was mad,"—he hesitated, and added in a lower tone—"suffering from an acute form of religious mania. I myself saw him, at some length. But now comes the really interesting point. Just a month ago this criminal lunatic, as we must regard him, made his escape from the asylum where he was confined. He arranged the whole thing with extraordinary cunning and intelligence, and we should probably have caught him long ago were it not that he managed, when on his way out of the place, to annex a considerable sum of money in gold with which the wages of the staff were about to be paid."

The Frenchman again spoke. "Why have you not circulated a description?" he asked.

"We did that at once,"—Sir John Burney smiled a little grimly,—"but only among our own people. We dare not circulate the man's description among the general public. You see, we may be mistaken, after all."

"That is not very probable!" The Frenchman smiled a satirical little smile.

A moment later the party were walking in Indian file through the turnstile, Sir John Burney leading the way.

Mrs. Bunting looked straight before her. Even had she wished to do so, she had neither time nor power to warn her lodger of his danger.

Daisy and her companion were now coming down the room, bearing straight for the Head Commissioner of Police.

In another moment Mr. Sleuth and Sir John Burney would be face to face.

Suddenly Mr. Sleuth swerved to one side. A terrible change came over his pale, narrow face; it became discomposed, livid with rage and terror.

But, to Mrs. Bunting's relief,—yes, to her inexpressible relief,—Sir John Burney and his friends swept on. They passed by Mr. Sleuth unconcernedly, unaware, or so it seemed to her, that there was any one else in the room but themselves.

"Hurry up, Mrs. Bunting," said the turnstile-keeper; "you and your friends will have the place all to yourselves." From an official he had become a man, and it was the man in Mr. Hopkins that gallantly addressed pretty Daisy Bunting. "It seems strange that a young lady like you should want to go in and see all those 'orrible frights," he said jestingly.

"Mrs. Bunting, may I trouble you to come over here for a moment?" The words were hissed rather than spoken by Mr. Sleuth's lips.

His landlady took a doubtful step forward.

"A last word with you, Mrs. Bunting." The lodger's face was still distorted with fear and passion. "Do you think to escape the consequences of your hideous treachery? I trusted you, Mrs. Bunting, and you betrayed me! But I am protected by a higher power, for I still have work to do. Your end will be bitter as wormwood and sharp as a two-edged sword. Your feet shall go down to death, and your steps take hold on hell." Even while Mr. Sleuth was uttering these strange, dreadful words, he was looking around, his eyes glancing this way and that, seeking a way of escape.

At last his eyes became fixed on a small placard placed about a curtain. "Emergency Exit" was written there. Leaving his landlady's side, he walked over to the turnstile. He fumbled in his pocket for a moment, and then touched the man on the arm. "I feel ill," he said, speaking very rapidly; "very ill indeed! It's the atmosphere of this place. I want you to let me out by the quickest way. It would be a pity for me to faint here—especially with ladies about." His left hand shot out and placed what he had been fumbling for in his pocket on the other's bare palm. "I see there's an emergency exit over there. Would it be possible for me to get out that way?"

"Well, yes, sir; I think so." The man hesitated; he felt a slight, a very slight, feeling of misgiving. He looked at Daisy, flushed and smiling, happy and unconcerned, and then at Mrs. Bunting. She was very pale; but surely her lodger's sudden seizure was enough to make her feel worried. Hopkins felt the half sovereign pleasantly tickling his palm. The Prefect of Police had given him only half a crown—mean, shabby foreigner!

"Yes, I can let you out that way," he said at last, "and perhaps when you're standing out in the air on the iron balcony you'll feel better. But then, you know, sir, you'll have to come round to the front if you want to come in again, for those emergency doors only open outward."

"Yes, yes," said Mr. Sleuth hurriedly; "I quite understand! If I feel better I'll come in by the front way, and pay another shilling—that's only fair."

"You needn't do that if you'll just explain what happened here."

The man went and pulled the curtain aside, and put his shoulder against the door. It burst open, and the light for a moment blinded Mr. Sleuth. He passed his hand over his eyes.

"Thank you," he said; "thank you. I shall get all right here."

Five days later Bunting identified the body of a man found drowned in the Regent's Canal as that of his late lodger; and, the morning following, a gardener working in the Regent's Park found a newspaper in which were wrapped, together with a half-worn pair of rubber-soled shoes, two surgical knives. This fact was not chronicled in any newspaper; but a very pretty and picturesque paragraph went the round of the press, about the same time, concerning a small box filled with sovereigns which had been forwarded anonymously to the Governor of the Foundling Hospital.

Mr. and Mrs. Bunting are now in the service of an old lady, by whom they are feared as well as respected, and whom they make very comfortable.

THE ESCAPE
BY HEREWARD CARRINGTON

ALL DAY LONG ORLOFF HAD PACED HIS cell. The blackness of the sky outside was equalled only by the blackness of his thoughts. The deep rolling of the thunder reverberated through the thick stone walls of his prison, and every now and then a fitful gust of rain swirled through the tiny broken window, wetting his face as he stared out into the night. Orloff cursed, wiped the water from his face with his grimy fingers, and turned to pacing his cell once more.

For seven long years Orloff had been thus confined—but a small fraction of the life sentence he was serving for the horrible crime he had committed. But at times he had asked himself, 'Was it not worth it, after all?' He could still feel the wet, warm blood trickling between his fingers, and see the whites of his victim's eyes. Then, too, there was that great day of the trial, when so many officials, in their splendid uniforms and gold braid, and so many beautiful women, clad in their furs and satins, had gazed at him, horror-struck, unable to avert their eyes from his face, or miss one word that fell from his lips. . . . At such times Orloff would rub his hands and smile to himself, in memory of that great day.

But tonight Orloff was in a different mood. Black despair and vengeance reigned supreme in his soul; he wished only to escape, in order that he might seek out his destroyers and in turn destroy them. His steps became more feverishly agitated; perspiration gathered on his forehead and he clenched his hands until the nails bit into his flesh and little trickles of blood oozed from between his fingers.

A brilliant lightning flash illuminated the far wall of his cell—lighting it as it had never been lighted before. Orloff's

eyes became riveted upon a huge stone, on the lowest tier.
. . . Were his eyes deceiving him, or had he in truth seen a
tiny crack surrounding it, as though the cement had been
scraped away or altogether removed. Hardly daring to
breathe he tip-toed across the room and fell on his knees before the stone, feeling its edges with his blood-stained fingers.

Yes, there was a deep crevice surrounding it. And, what
was more, the stone was loose. Orloff tugged at it, scraping
the flesh from his fingers, sweat pouring from his face and
matted hair. . . . It moved. . . . He pulled the great stone
from its place and peered into the blackness beyond. Another lightning flash showed him what he had hardly dared
hope for—a passage in the rock, leading downward from
his place of torment.

On the floor was a piece of paper, folded and yellow
with age. With trembling fingers he carried it to the window,
through which shone the faint rays of a lamp in the courtyard below, and there unfolded it. On it was a brief mes-
sage, apparently written with some dark red fluid. For the
first time in his life Orloff was glad that he had been made
to read, if only a little. For on the paper before him was
written:

"I escaped by this passage. May he who finds this share
my good fortune!"

It was signed S.K.

The tramp of the sentry's feet resounded outside the door
of his cell. Orloff threw himself over the stone till the footsteps had died away; then he thrust his head and shoulders
into the opening, and began slowly to worm his way along
the narrow passage before him.

The walls of the passage were wet with slime and mould,
and sharp, jagged rocks protruded, tearing Orloff's clothes
and scratching deep into his flesh. . . . But of all this Orloff
knew nothing. His eyes were gleaming, but one thought present in his mind—escape. He dug his bloody fingers into the
mud and pushed himself steadily forward, flat on his stomach, like a serpent.

As he advanced the floor of the passage became steeper

and steeper, sloping at an ever-greater angle. The walls became yet wetter and more slimy and the jagged rocks bit deeper into his writhing limbs. Foot after foot Orloff propelled himself along this narrow, sloping path. His breath came in short gasps, while the darkness seemed to become ever more intense. For one moment he paused, an agonizing fear shooting through him. He realized that it would be impossible for him ever to ascend that sloping passage to regain his cell. A cold shiver ran down his spine. Then, he clenched his teeth and propelled himself forward with the superhuman strength of despair.

A sharp bend in the passage revealed a sight which made him gasp. A faint, circular opening in the distance permitted the rays of the moon—which had fitfully begun to shine—to penetrate the stygian blackness. The end of the passage lay before him. Victory—escape! The cold night air fanned his face; he urged himself onward in a last desperate effort.

The passage became ever more sloping as he advanced. His body was inclined at a sickening angle. Strange streaks of blackness seemed to cross his vision, as he half fell, half slid the few feet which yet remained to be traversed. . . . Orloff's head crashed into something hard, which half stunned him. A moment later he opened his eyes, and saw before him a heavily barred iron grating, and—a skeleton.

THE VANISHING LADY
BY ALEXANDER WOOLLCOTT

THEN THERE WAS THE STORY—TOLD ME
some years ago as a true copy of a leaf from the dread secret
archives of the Paris police—of the woman who disappeared
during the World Exposition as suddenly, as completely, and
as inexplicably as did Dorothy Arnold ten years later from
the sidewalks of New York.

As I first heard the story, it began with the arrival from
Marseilles of an Englishwoman and her young, inexperi-
enced daughter, a girl of seventeen or thereabouts. The
mother was the frail, pretty widow of an English officer who
had been stationed in India, and the two had just come
from Bombay, bound for home. In the knowledge that, after
reaching there, she would soon have to cross to Paris to sign
some papers affecting her husband's estate, she decided at
the last minute to shift her passage to a Marseilles steam-
er, and, by going direct to Paris, look up the lawyers there
and finish her business before crossing the Channel to settle
forever and a day in the Warwickshire village where she
was born.

Paris was so tumultuously crowded for the Exposition that
they counted themselves fortunate when the *cocher* deposited
them at the Crillon, and they learned that their precautionary
telegram from Marseilles had miraculously caught a room
on the wing—a double room with a fine, spacious sitting-
room looking out on the Place de la Concorde. I could wish
that they had wired one of those less magnificent caravan-
saries, if only that I might revel again in such a name as the
Hotel of Jacob and of England, or, better still, the Hotel of
the Universe and of Portugal. But, as the story reached me, it
was to the Crillon that they went.

The long windows of their sitting-room gave on a narrow,

stone-railed balcony and were half-shrouded in heavy curtains of plum-colored velvet. As again and again the girl later on had occasion to describe the look of that room when first she saw it, the walls were papered in old rose. A high-backed sofa, an oval satinwood table, a mantel with an ormolu clock that had run down—these also she recalled.

The girl was the more relieved that there would be no need of a house-to-house search for rooms, for the mother had seemed unendurably exhausted from the long train ride, and was now of such a color that the girl's first idea was to call the house physician, hoping fervently that he spoke English, for neither she nor her mother spoke any French at all.

The doctor, when he came—a dusty, smelly little man with a wrinkled face lost in a thicket of whiskers, and a reassuring Legion of Honor ribbon in the buttonhole of his lapel—did speak a little English. After a long, grave look and a few questions put to the tired woman on the bed in the shaded room, he called the girl into the sitting-room and told her frankly that her mother's condition was serious; that it was out of the question for them to think of going on to England next day; that on the morrow she might better be moved to a hospital, etc., etc.

All these things he would attend to. In the meantime he wanted the girl to go at once to his home and fetch him a medicine that his wife would give her. It could not be as quickly prepared in any chemist's. Unfortunately, he lived on the other side of Paris and had no telephone, and with all Paris *en fête* it would be perilous to rely on any messenger. Indeed, it would be a saving of time and worry if she could go, armed with a note to his wife he was even then scribbling in French at a desk in the sitting-room. In the lobby below, the manager of the hotel, after an excited colloquy with the doctor, took charge of her most sympathetically, himself putting her into a *sapin* and, as far as she could judge, volubly directing the driver how to reach a certain house in the Rue Val du Grâce, near the Observatoire.

It was then that the girl's agony began, for the ramshackle victoria crawled through the festive streets and, as she afterwards realized, more often than not crawled in the wrong direction. The house in the Rue Val du Grâce seemed to stand at the other end of the world, when the carriage came at last to a halt in front of it. The girl grew old in the time which passed before any answer came to her ring at the bell. The doctor's wife, when finally she appeared, read his note again and again, then with much muttering and rattling of keys stationed the girl in an airless waiting room and left her there so long that she was weeping for very desperation, before the medicine was found, wrapped, and turned over to her.

A hundred times during that wait she rose and started for the door, determined to stay no longer but to run back empty-handed through the streets to her mother's bedside. A thousand times in the wretched weeks that followed she loathed herself for not having obeyed that impulse. But always there was the feeling that having come so far and having waited so long, she must not leave without the medicine just for lack of the strength of will to stick it out a little longer—perhaps only a few minutes longer.

Then the snail's pace trip back to the Right Bank was another nightmare, and it ended only when, at the *cocher's* mulish determination to deliver her to some hotel in the Place Vendôme, she leaped to the street and in sheer terror appealed for help to a passing young man whose alien tweeds and boots told her he was a compatriot of hers.

He was still standing guard beside her five minutes later when, at long last, she arrived at the desk of the Crillon and called for her key, only to have the very clerk who had handed her a pen to register with that morning look at her without recognition and blandly ask, "Whom does Mademoiselle wish to see?" At that a cold fear clutched her heart, a sudden surrender to a panic that she had fought back as preposterous when first it visited her as she sat and twisted her handkerchief in the waiting room of the doctor's office on the Left Bank; a panic born when, after the doctor had casually told her he had no telephone, she heard the fretful ringing of its bell on the other side of his walnut door.

This then was the predicament of the young English girl

as she stood there at the desk of the hotel in Paris—a stranger in the city and a stranger to its bewildering tongue. She had arrived that morning from India and had left her ailing mother in charge of the house physician while she went out in quest of medicine for her—a quest in which, through a malignant conspiracy between perverse circumstances and apparently motiveless passers-by, she had lost four hours.

But now with the bottle of medicine clutched in her hand, she reached the hotel at last, only to be stared down by the clerk at the desk, only to have the very man who had shown them their rooms with such a flourish that morning now gaze at her opaquely as though she were some slightly demented creature demanding admission to someone else's apartment.

But, no, Mam'zelle must be mistaken. Was it not at some other hotel she was descended? Two more clerks came fluttering into the conference. They all eyed her without a flicker of recognition. Did Mam'zelle say her room was No. 342? Ah, but 342 was occupied by M. Quelquechose. Yes, a French client of long standing. He had been occupying it these past two weeks and more. Ah, no, it would be impossible to disturb him. All this while the lobby, full of hurrying, polyglot strangers, reeled around her.

She demanded the registration slips only to find in that day's docket no sign of the one she herself had filled out that morning on their arrival, the while her tired mother leaned against the desk and told her how. And even as the clerk now shuffled the papers before her eyes, the stupefying bloodstone which she had noticed on his ring-finger when he handed her the pen five hours before, winked at her in confirmation.

From then on she came only upon closed doors. The same house physician who had hustled her off on her tragic wild-goose chase across Paris protested now with all the shrugs and gestures of his people that he had dispatched her on no such errand, that he had never been summoned to attend her mother, that he had never seen her before in all his life. The same hotel manager who had so sympathetically helped her into the carriage when she set forth on her fruitless mission, denied her now as flatly and somehow managed to do it with the same sympathetic solicitude, suggesting that Mam'zelle must be tired, that she should let them provide another chamber where she might repose herself until such time as she could recollect at what hotel she really belonged or until some inquiries should bring in news of where her mother and her luggage were, if—

For always there was in his ever polite voice the unspoken reservation that the whole mystery might be a thing of her own disordered invention. Then, and in the destroying days that followed, she was only too keenly aware that these evasive people—the personnel of the hotel, the attachés of the embassy, the reporters of the Paris *Herald,* the officials at the Sûreté—were each and everyone behaving as if she had lost her wits. Indeed there were times when she felt that all Paris was rolling its eyes behind her back and significantly tapping its forehead.

Her only aid and comfort was the aforesaid Englishman who, because a lovely lady in distress had come up to him in the street and implored his help, elected thereafter to believe her against all the evidence which so impressed the rest of Paris. He proved a pillar of stubborn strength because he was some sort of well-born junior secretary at the British Embassy with influence enough to keep her agony from gathering dust in the official pigeon-holes.

His faith in her needed to be unreasoning because there slowly formed in his mind a suspicion that for some unimaginable reason all these people—the hotel attendants and even the police—were part of a plot to conceal the means whereby the missing woman's disappearance had been effected. This suspicion deepened when, after a day's delay, he succeeded in forcing an inspection of Room 342 and found that there was no detail of its furnishing which had not been altered from the one etched into the girl's memory.

It remained for him to prove the mechanism of that plot and to guess at its invisible motive—a motive strong enough to enlist all Paris in the silent obliteration of a woman of no importance, moreover a woman who, as far as her daughter knew, had not an enemy in the world. It was the purchased confession of one of the paper-hangers, who had worked all night in the hurried transformation of Room 342, that started the unraveling of the mystery.

By the time the story reached me, it had lost all its content of grief and become as unemotional as an anagram. Indeed, a few years ago it was a kind of circulating parlor game and one was challenged to guess what had happened to the vanished lady. Perhaps you yourself have already surmised that the doctor had recognized the woman's ailment as a case of the black plague smuggled in from India; that his first instinctive step, designed only to give time for spiriting her out of the threatened hotel, had, when she died that afternoon, widened into a conspiracy on the part of the police to suppress, at all costs to this one girl, an obituary notice which, had it ever leaked out, would have emptied Paris overnight and spread ruin across a city that had gambled heavily on the great Exposition for which its gates were even then thrown wide.

The story of this girl's ordeal long seemed to me one of the great nightmares of real life and I was, therefore, the more taken aback one day to have its historicity faintly impaired by my discovering its essence in a novel called *The End of Her Honeymoon* which the incomparable Mrs. Belloc Lowndes wrote as long ago as 1913. Then I find myself wondering if she unearthed it in the archives of the Paris police or whether she spun its mystery out of her own macabre fancy, making from whole cloth a tale of such felicitous invention that, like Stockton's *The Lady or the Tiger* or Anatole France's *The Procurator of Judea*, it had moved from land to land with the seven-league boots of folk-music and so been told and retold at hearths the world around by people who had never read it anywhere.

THE SMALL ASSASSIN
BY RAY BRADBURY

JUST WHEN THE IDEA OCCURRED TO HER that she was being murdered she could not tell. There had been little subtle signs, little suspicions for the past month; things as deep as sea tides in her, like looking at a perfectly calm stretch of tropic water, wanting to bathe in it and finding, just as the tide takes your body, that monsters dwell just under the surface, things unseen, bloated, many-armed, sharp-finned, malignant and inescapable.

A room floated around her in an effluvium of hysteria. Sharp instruments hovered and there were voices, and people in sterile white masks.

My name, she thought, what is it?

Alice Leiber. It came to her. David Leiber's wife. But it gave her no comfort. She was alone with these silent, whispering white people and there was great pain and nausea and death-fear in her.

I am being murdered before their eyes. These doctors, these nurses don't realize what hidden thing has happened to me. David doesn't know. Nobody knows except me and—the killer, the little murderer, the small assassin.

I am dying and I can't tell them now. They'd laugh and call me one in delirium. They'll see the murderer and hold him and never think him responsible for my death. But here I am, in front of God and man, dying, no one to believe my story, everyone to doubt me, comfort me with lies, bury me in ignorance, mourn me and salvage my destroyer.

Where is David? she wondered. In the waiting room, smoking one cigarette after another, listening to the long tickings of the very slow clock? Sweat exploded from all of her body at once, and with it an agonized cry. Now! Try and kill me, she screamed. Try, but I won't die! I won't!

There was a hollowness. A vacuum. Suddenly the pain fell away. Exhaustion, and dusk came around. It was over. Oh, God! She plummeted down and struck a black nothingness which gave way to nothingness and nothingness and another and still another. . . .

Footsteps. Gentle, approaching footsteps.

Far away, a voice said, "She's asleep. Don't disturb her."

An odor of tweeds, a pipe, a certain shaving lotion. David was standing over her. And beyond him the immaculate smell of Dr. Jeffers.

She did not open her eyes. "I'm awake," she said, quietly. It was a surprise, a relief to be able to speak, to not be dead.

"Alice," someone said, and it was David beyond her closed eyes, holding her tired hands.

Would you like to meet the murderer, David? she thought. I hear your voice asking to see him, so there's nothing but for me to point him out to you. David stood over her. She opened her eyes. The room came into focus. Moving a weak hand, she pulled aside a coverlet.

The murderer looked up at David Leiber with a small, red-faced, blue-eyed calm. Its eyes were deep and sparkling.

"Why!" cried David Leiber, smiling. "He's a *fine* baby!"

Dr. Jeffers was waiting for David Leiber the day he came to take his wife and new child home. He motioned Leiber to a chair in his office, gave him a cigar, lit one for himself, sat on the edge of his desk, puffing solemnly for a long moment. Then he cleared his throat, looked David Leiber straight on and said, "Your wife doesn't like her child, Dave."

"What!"

"It's been a hard thing for her. She'll need a lot of love this next year. I didn't say much at the time, but she was hysterical in the delivery room. The strange things she said—I won't repeat them. All I'll say is that she feels alien to the child. Now, this may simply be a thing we can clear up with one or two questions." He sucked on his cigar another moment, then said, "Is this child a 'wanted' child, Dave?"

"Why do you ask?"

"It's vital."

"Yes. Yes, it is a 'wanted' child. We planned it together. Alice was so happy, a year ago, when——"

"Mmmm— That makes it more difficult. Because if the child was unplanned, it would be a simple case of a woman hating the idea of motherhood. That doesn't fit Alice." Dr. Jeffers took his cigar from his lips, rubbed his hand across his jaw. "It must be something else, then. Perhaps something buried in her childhood that's coming out now. Or it might be the simple temporary doubt and distrust of any mother who's gone through the unusual pain and near-death that Alice has. If so, then a little time should heal that. I thought I'd tell you, though, Dave. It'll help you be easy and tolerant with her if she says anything about—well—about wishing the child had been born dead. And if things don't go well, the three of you drop in on me. I'm always glad to see old friends, eh? Here, take another cigar along for the baby."

It was a bright spring afternoon. Their car hummed along wide, tree-lined boulevards. Blue sky, flowers, a warm wind. Dave talked a lot, lit his cigar, talked some more. Alice answered directly, softly, relaxing a bit more as the trip progressed. But she held the baby not tightly or warmly or motherly enough to satisfy the queer ache in Dave's mind. She seemed to be merely carrying a porcelain figurine.

"Well," he said, at last, smiling. "What'll we name him?"

Alice Leiber watched green trees slide by. "Let's not decide yet. I'd rather wait until we get an exceptional name for him. Don't blow smoke in his face." Her sentences ran together with no change of tone. The last statement held no motherly reproof, no interest, no irritation.

The husband, disquieted, dropped the cigar from the window. "Sorry," he said.

The baby rested in the crook of his mother's arm, shadows of sun and tree changing his face. His blue eyes opened like fresh blue spring flowers. Moist noises came from the tiny, pink, elastic mouth.

Alice gave her baby a quick glance. Her husband felt her shiver against him.

"Cold?" he asked.

"A chill. Better raise the window, David."

It was more than a chill. He rolled the window slowly up. Suppertime.

Dave had brought the child from the nursery, propped him at a tiny, bewildered angle, supported by many pillows, in a newly purchased high chair.

Alice watched her knife and fork move. "He's not highchair size," she said.

"Fun having him here, anyway," said Dave, feeling fine. "Everything's fun. At the office, too. Orders up to my nose. If I don't watch myself I'll make another fifteen thousand this year. Hey, look at Junior, will you? Drooling all down his chin!" He reached over to wipe the baby's mouth with his napkin. From the corner of his eye he realized that Alice wasn't even watching. He finished the job.

"I guess it wasn't very interesting," he said, back again at his food. "But one would think a mother'd take some interest in her own child!"

Alice jerked her chin up. "Don't speak that way! Not in front of him! Later, if you must."

"Later?" he cried. "In front of, in back of, what's the difference?" He quieted suddenly, swallowed, was sorry. "All right. Okay. I know how it is."

After dinner she let him carry the baby upstairs. She didn't tell him to; she *let* him.

Coming down, he found her standing by the radio, listening to music she didn't hear. Her eyes were closed, her whole attitude one of wondering, self-questioning. She started when he appeared.

Suddenly, she was at him, against him, soft, quick; the same. Her lips found him, kept him. He was stunned. Now that the baby was gone, upstairs, out of the room, she began to breathe again, live again. She was free. She was whispering, rapidly, endlessly.

"Thank you, thank you, darling. For being yourself, always. Dependable, so very dependable!"

He had to laugh. "My father told me, 'Son, provide for your family!'"

Wearily, she rested her dark, shining hair against his neck. "You've overdone it. Sometimes I wish we were just the way we were when we were first married. No responsibilities, nothing but ourselves. No—no babies."

She crushed his hand in hers, a supernatural whiteness in her face.

"Oh, Dave, once it was just you and me. We protected each other, and now we protect the baby, but get no protection from it. Do you understand? Lying in the hospital I had time to think a lot of things. The world is evil—"

"Is it?"

"Yes. It is. But laws protect us from it. And when there aren't laws, then love does the protecting. You're protected from my hurting you, by my love. You're vulnerable to me, of all people, but love shields you. I feel no fear of you, because love cushions all your irritations, unnatural instincts, hatreds and immaturities. But—what about the baby? It's too young to know love, or a law of love, or anything, until we teach it. And in the meantime be vulnerable to it."

"Vulnerable to a baby?" He held her away and laughed gently.

"Does a baby know the difference between right and wrong?" she asked.

"No. But it'll learn."

"But a baby is so new, so amoral, so conscience-free." She stopped. Her arms dropped from him and she turned swiftly. "That noise? What was it?"

Leiber looked around the room. "I didn't hear—"

She stared at the library door. "In there," she said, slowly.

Leiber crossed the room, opened the door and switched the library lights on and off. "Not a thing." He came back to her. "You're worn out. To bed with you—right now."

Turning out the lights together, they walked slowly up the soundless hall stairs, not speaking. At the top she apologized. "My wild talk, darling. Forgive me. I'm exhausted."

He understood, and said so.

She paused, undecided, by the nursery door. Then she fingered the brass knob sharply, walked in. He watched her approach the crib much too carefully, look down, and stiffen as if she'd been struck in the face. "David!"

Leiber stepped forward, reached the crib.

The baby's face was bright red and very moist; his small pink mouth opened and shut, opened and shut; his eyes were a fiery blue. His hands leapt about on the air.

"Oh," said Dave, "he's just been crying."

"Has he?" Alice Leiber seized the crib-railing to balance herself. "I didn't hear him."

"The door was closed."

"Is that why he breathes so hard, why his face is red?"

"Sure. Poor little guy. Crying all alone in the dark. He can sleep in our room tonight, just in case he cries."

"You'll spoil him," his wife said.

Leiber felt her eyes follow as he rolled the crib into their bedroom. He undressed silently, sat on the edge of the bed. Suddenly he lifted his head, swore under his breath, snapped his fingers. "Damn it! Forgot to tell you. I must fly to Chicago Friday."

"Oh, David." Her voice was lost in the room.

"I've put this trip off two months, and now it's so critical I just *have* to go."

"I'm afraid to be alone."

"We'll have the new cook by Friday. She'll be here all the time. I'll only be gone a few days."

"I'm afraid. I don't know of what. You wouldn't believe me if I told you. I guess I'm crazy."

He was in bed now. She darkened the room; he heard her walk around the bed, throw back the cover, slide in. He smelled the warm woman-smell of her next to him. He said, "If you want me to wait a few days, perhaps I could—"

"No," she said, unconvinced. "You go. I know it's important. It's just that I keep thinking about what I told you. Laws and love and protection. Love protects you from me. But, the baby—" She took a breath. "What protects you from him, David?"

Before he could answer, before he could tell her how silly it was, speaking of infants, she switched on the bed light, abruptly.

"Look," she said, pointing.

The baby lay wide-awake in its crib, staring straight at him, with deep, sharp blue eyes.

The lights went out again. She trembled against him.

"It's not nice being afraid of the thing you birthed." Her whisper lowered, became harsh, fierce, swift. "He tried to kill me! He lies there, listens to us talking, waiting for you to go away so he can try to kill me again! I swear it!" Sobs broke from her.

"Please," he kept saying, soothing her. "Stop it. Please."

She cried in the dark for a long time. Very late she relaxed, shakingly, against him. Her breathing came soft, warm, regular, her body twitched its worn reflexes and she slept.

He drowsed.

And just before his eyes lidded wearily down, sinking him into deeper and yet deeper tides, he heard a strange little sound of awareness and awakeness in the room.

The sound of small, moist, pinkly elastic lips.

The baby.

And then—sleep.

In the morning, the sun blazed. Alice smiled.

David Leiber dangled his watch over the crib. "See, baby? Something bright. Something pretty. Sure. Sure. Something bright. Something pretty."

Alice smiled. She told him to go ahead, fly to Chicago, she'd be very brave, no need to worry. She'd take care of baby. Oh, yes, she'd take care of him, all right.

The airplane went east. There was a lot of sky, a lot of sun and clouds and Chicago running over the horizon. Dave was dropped into the rush of ordering, planning, banqueting, telephoning, arguing in conference. But he wrote letters each day and sent telegrams to Alice and the baby.

On the evening of his sixth day away from home he received the long-distance phone call. Los Angeles.

"Alice?"

"No, Dave. This is Jeffers speaking."

"Doctor!"

"Hold onto yourself, son. Alice is sick. You'd better get the next plane home. It's pneumonia. I'll do everything I can, boy. If only it wasn't so soon after the baby. She needs strength."

Leiber dropped the phone into its cradle. He got up, with no feet under him, and no hands and no body. The hotel room blurred and fell apart.

"Alice," he said, blindly, starting for the door.

The propellers spun about, whirled, fluttered, stopped; time and space were put behind. Under his hand, David felt the doorknob turn; under his feet the floor assumed reality, around him flowed the walls of a bedroom, and in the late-afternoon sunlight Dr. Jeffers stood, turning from a window, as Alice lay waiting in her bed, something carved from a fall of winter snow. Then Dr. Jeffers was talking, talking continuously, gently, the sound rising and falling through the lamplight, a soft flutter, a white murmur of voice.

"Your wife's too good a mother, Dave. She worried more about the baby than herself. . . ."

Somewhere in the paleness of Alice's face, there was a sudden constriction which smoothed itself out before it was realized. Then, slowly, half-smiling, she bagan to talk and she talked as a mother should about this, that and the other thing, the telling detail, the minute-by-minute and hour-by-hour report of a mother concerned with a dollhouse world and the miniature life of that world. But she could not stop; the spring was wound tight, and her voice rushed on to anger, fear and the faintest touch of revulsion, which did not change Dr. Jeffers' expression, but caused Dave's heart to match the rhythm of this talk that quickened and could not stop:

"The baby wouldn't sleep. I thought he was sick. He just lay, staring, in his crib, and late at night he'd cry. So loud, he'd cry, and he'd cry all night and all night. I couldn't quiet him, and I couldn't rest."

Dr. Jeffers' head nodded slowly, slowly. "Tired herself right into pneumonia. But she's full of sulfa now and on the safe side of the whole damn thing."

David felt ill. "The baby, what about the baby?"

"Fit as a fiddle; cock of the walk!"

"Thanks, Doctor."

The doctor walked off away and down the stairs, opened the front door faintly, and was gone.

"David!"

He turned to her frightened whisper.

"It was the baby again." She clutched his hand. "I try to lie to myself and say that I'm a fool, but the baby knew I was weak from the hospital, so he cried all night every night, and when he wasn't crying he'd be too quiet. I knew if I switched on the light he'd be there, staring up at me."

David felt his body close in on itself like a fist. He remembered seeing the baby, feeling the baby, awake in the dark, awake very late at night when babies should be asleep. Awake and lying there, silent as thought, not crying, but watching from its crib. He thrust the thought aside. It was insane.

Alice went on. "I was going to kill the baby. Yes, I was. When you'd been gone only a day on your trip I went to his room and put my hands about his neck; and I stood there, for a long time, thinking, afraid. Then I put the covers up over his face and turned him over on his face and pressed him down and left him that way and ran out of the room."

He tried to stop her.

"No, let me finish," she said, hoarsely, looking at the wall. "When I left his room I thought, It's simple. Babies smother every day. No one'll ever know. But when I came back to see him dead, David, he was alive! Yes, alive, turned over on his back, alive and smiling and breathing. And I couldn't touch him after that. I left him there and I didn't come back, not to feed him or look at him or do anything. Perhaps the cook tended to him. I don't know. All I know is that his crying kept me awake, and I thought all through the night, and walked around the rooms and now I'm sick." She was almost finished now. "The baby lies there and thinks of ways to kill me. Simple ways. Because he knows I know so much about him. I have no love for him; there is no protection between us; there never will be."

She was through. She collapsed inward on herself and finally slept. David Leiber stood for a long time over her, not able to move. His blood was frozen in his body, not a cell stirred anywhere, anywhere at all.

The next morning there was only one thing to do. He did it. He walked into Dr. Jeffers' office and told him the whole thing, and listened to Jeffers' tolerant replies:

"Let's take this thing slowly, son. It's quite natural for mothers to hate their children, sometimes. We have a label for it, ambivalence. The ability to hate, while loving. Lovers hate each other, frequently. Children detest mothers—"

Leiber interrupted. "I never hated my mother."

"You won't admit it, naturally. People don't enjoy admitting hatred for their loved ones."

"So Alice hates her baby."

"Better say she has an obsession. She's gone a step further than plain, ordinary ambivalence. A Caesarian operation brought the child into the world and almost took Alice out of it. She blames the child for her near-death and her pneumonia. She's projecting her troubles, blaming them on the handiest object she can use as a source of blame. We *all* do it. We stumble into a chair and curse the furniture, not our own clumsiness. We miss a golf-stroke and damn the turf or our club, or the make of ball. If our business fails we blame the gods, the weather, our luck. All I can tell you is what I told you before. Love her. Finest medicine in the world. Find little ways of showing your affection, give her security. Find ways of showing her how harmless and innocent the child is. Make her feel that the baby was worth the risk. After awhile, she'll settle down, forget about death, and begin to love the child. If she doesn't come around in the next month or so, ask me. I'll recommend a good psychiatrist. Go on along now, and take that look off your face."

When summer came, things seemed to settle, become easier. Dave worked, immersed himself in office detail, but found much time for his wife. She, in turn, took long walks, gained strength, played an occasional light game of badminton. She rarely burst out any more. She seemed to have rid herself of her fears.

Except on one certain midnight when a sudden summer wind swept around the house, warm and swift, shaking the trees like so many shining tambourines. Alice wakened, trembling, and slid over into her husband's arms, and let him console her, and ask her what was wrong.

She said, "Something's here in the room, watching us."

He switched on the light. "Dreaming again," he said. "You're better, though. Haven't been troubled for a long time."

She sighed as he clicked off the light again, and suddenly she slept. He held her, considering what a sweet, weird creature she was, for about half an hour.

He heard the bedroom door sway open a few inches.

There was nobody at the door. No reason for it to come open. The wind had died.

He waited. It seemed like an hour he lay silently, in the dark.

Then, far away, wailing like some small meteor dying in the vast inky gulf of space, the baby began to cry in his nursery.

It was a small, lonely sound in the middle of the stars and the dark and the breathing of this woman in his arms and the wind beginning to sweep through the trees again.

Leiber counted to one hundred, slowly. The crying continued.

Carefully disengaging Alice's arm he slipped from bed, put on his slippers, robe, and moved quietly from the room.

He'd go downstairs, he thought, fix some warm milk, bring it up, and—

The blackness dropped out from under him. His foot slipped and plunged. Slipped on something soft. Plunged into nothingness.

He thrust his hands out, caught frantically at the railing. His body stopped falling. He held. He cursed.

The "something soft" that had caused his feet to slip, rustled and thumped down a few steps. His head rang. His heart hammered at the base of his throat, thick and shot with pain.

Why do careless people have things strewn about a house? He groped carefully with his fingers for the object that had almost spilled him headlong down the stairs.

His hand froze, startled. His breath went in. His heart held one or two beats.

The thing he held in his hand was a toy. A large cumbersome, patchwork doll he had bought as a joke, for—

For the baby.

Alice drove him to work the next day.

She slowed the car halfway downtown; pulled to the curb and stopped it. Then she turned on the seat and looked at her husband.

"I want to go away on a vacation. I don't know if you can make it now, darling, but if not, please let me go alone. We can get someone to take care of the baby, I'm sure. But I just have to get away. I thought I was growing out of this—this *feeling*. But I haven't. I can't stand being in the room with him. He looks up at me as if he hates me, too. I can't put my finger on it; all I know is I want to get away before something happens."

He got out on his side of the car, came around, motioned to her to move over, got in. "The only thing you're going to do is see a good psychiatrist. If he suggests a vacation, well, okay. But this can't go on; my stomach's in knots all the time." He started the car. "I'll drive the rest of the way."

Her head was down; she was trying to keep back tears. She looked up when they reached his office building. "All right. Make the appointment. I'll go talk to anyone you want, David."

He kissed her. "Now, you're talking sense, lady. Think you can drive home okay?"

"Of course, silly."

"See you at supper, then. Drive carefully."

"Don't I always? 'Bye."

He stood on the curb, watching her drive off, the wind taking hold of her long, dark, shining hair. Upstairs, a minute later, he phoned Jeffers and arranged an appointment with a reliable neuropsychiatrist.

The day's work went uneasily. Things fogged over; and in the fog he kept seeing Alice lost and calling his name. So much of her fear had come over to him. She actually had him convinced that the child was in some ways not quite natural.

He dictated long, uninspired letters. He checked some shipments downstairs. Assistants had to be questioned, and kept going. At the end of the day he was exhausted, his head throbbed, and he was very glad to go home.

On the way down in the elevator he wondered, What if I told Alice about the toy—that patchwork doll—I slipped on on the stairs last night? Lord, wouldn't *that* back her off? No, I won't ever tell her. Accidents are, after all, accidents.

Daylight lingered in the sky as he drove home in a taxi. In front of the house he paid the driver and walked slowly up the cement walk, enjoying the light that was still in the sky and the trees. The white colonial front of the house looked unnaturally silent and uninhabited, and then, quietly, he remembered this was Thursday, and the hired help they were able to obtain from time to time were all gone for the day.

He took a deep breath of air. A bird sang behind the house. Traffic moved on the boulevard a block away. He twisted the key in the door. The knob turned under his fingers, oiled, silent.

The door opened. He stepped in, put his hat on the chair with his briefcase, started to shrug out of his coat, when he looked up.

Late sunlight streamed down the stairwell from the window near the top of the hall. Where the sunlight touched it took on the bright color of the patchwork doll sprawled at the bottom of the stairs.

But he paid no attention to the toy.

He could only look, and not move, and look again at Alice.

Alice lay in a broken, grotesque, pallid gesturing and angling of her thin body, at the bottom of the stairs, like a crumpled doll that doesn't want to play any more, ever.

Alice was dead.

The house remained quiet, except for the sound of his heart.

She was dead.

He held her head in his hands, he felt her fingers. He held her body. But she wouldn't live. She wouldn't even try to live. He said her name, out loud, many times, and he tried, once again, by holding her to him, to give her back some of the warmth she had lost, but that didn't help.

He stood up. He must have made a phone call. He didn't remember. He found himself, suddenly, upstairs. He opened the nursery door and walked inside and stared blankly at the crib. His stomach was sick. He couldn't see very well.

The baby's eyes were closed, but his face was red, moist

with perspiration, as if he'd been crying long and hard.

"She's dead," said Leiber to the baby. "She's dead."

Then he started laughing low and soft and continuously for a long time until Dr. Jeffers walked in out of the night and slapped him again and again across his face.

"Snap out of it! Pull yourself together!"

"She fell down the stairs, doctor. She tripped on a patchwork doll and fell. I almost slipped on it the other night, myself. And now—"

The doctor shook him.

"Doc, Doc, Doc," said Dave, hazily. "Funny thing. Funny. I—I finally thought of a name for the baby."

The doctor said nothing.

Leiber put his head back in his trembling hands and spoke the words. "I'm going to have him christened next Sunday. Know what name I'm giving him? I'm going to call him Lucifer."

It was eleven at night. A lot of strange people had come and gone through the house, taking the essential flame with them—Alice.

David Leiber sat across from the doctor in the library.

"Alice wasn't crazy," he said, slowly. "She had good reason to fear the baby."

Jeffers exhaled. "Don't follow after her! She blamed the child for her sickness, now you blame it for her death. She stumbled on a toy, remember that. You can't blame the child."

"You mean Lucifer?"

"Stop calling him that!"

Leiber shook his head. "Alice heard things at night, moving in the halls. You want to know what made those noises, Doctor? They were made by the baby. Four months old, moving in the dark, listening to us talk. Listening to every word!" He held to the sides of the chair. "And if I turned the lights on, a baby is so small. It can hide behind furniture, a door, against a wall—below eye-level."

"I want you to stop this!" said Jeffers.

"Let me say what I think or I'll go crazy. When I went to Chicago, who was it kept Alice awake, tiring her into pneu-

monia? The baby! And when Alice didn't die, then he tried
killing me. It was simple; leave a toy on the stairs, cry in the
night until your father goes downstairs to fetch your milk,
and stumbles. A crude trick, but effective. It didn't get me.
But it killed Alice dead."

David Leiber stopped long enough to light a cigarette. "I
should have caught on. I'd turn on the lights in the middle of
the night, many nights, and the baby'd be lying there, eyes
wide. Most babies sleep all the time. Not this one. He stayed
awake, thinking."

"Babies don't think."

"He stayed awake doing whatever he *could* do with his
brain, then. What in hell do we know about a baby's mind?
He had every reason to hate Alice; she suspected him for
what he was—certainly not a normal child. Something—
different. What do you know of babies, doctor? The general
run, yes. You know, of course, how babies kill their mothers
at birth. Why? Could it be resentment at being forced into
a lousy world like this one?"

Leiber leaned toward the doctor, tiredly. "It all ties up.
Suppose that a few babies out of all the millions born are
instantaneously able to move, see, hear, think, like many
animals and insects can. Insects are born self-sufficient. In a
few weeks most mammals and birds adjust. But children take
years to speak and learn to stumble around on their weak
legs.

"But suppose one child in a billion is—strange? Born
perfectly aware, able to think, instinctively. Wouldn't it be
a perfect setup, a perfect blind for anything the baby might
want to do? He could pretend to be ordinary, weak, crying,
ignorant. With just a *little* expenditure of energy he could
crawl about a darkened house, listening. And how easy to
place obstacles at the top of stairs. How easy to cry all
night and tire a mother into pneumonia. How easy, right at
birth, to be so close to the mother that *a few deft maneuvers
might cause peritonitis!*"

"For God's sake!" Jeffers was on his feet. "That's a repulsive thing to say!"

"It's a repulsive thing I'm speaking of. How many mothers

have died at the birth of their children? How many have
suckled strange little improbabilities who cause death one
way or another? Strange, red little creatures with brains
that work in a bloody darkness we can't even guess at. Ele-
mental little brains, aswarm with racial memory, hatred, and
raw cruelty, with no more thought than self-preservation.
And self-preservation in this case consisted of eliminating a
mother who realized what a horror she had birthed. I ask
you, doctor, what is there in the world more selfish than a
baby? Nothing!"

Jeffers scowled and shook his head, helplessly.

Leiber dropped his cigarette down. "I'm not claiming any
great strength for the child. Just enough to crawl around a
little, a few months ahead of schedule. Just enough to listen
all the time. Just enough to cry late at night. That's enough,
more than enough."

Jeffers tried ridicule. "Call it murder, then. But murder
must be motivated. What motive had the child?"

Leiber was ready with the answer. "What is more at peace,
more dreamfully content, at ease, at rest, fed, comforted,
unbothered, than an unborn child? Nothing. It floats in a
sleepy, timeless wonder of nourishment and silence. Then,
suddenly, it is asked to give up its berth, is forced to va-
cate, rushed out into a noisy, uncaring, selfish world
where it is asked to shift for itself, to hunt, to feed from the
hunting, to seek after a vanishing love that once was its un-
questionable right, to meet confusion instead of inner silence and conservative slumber! And the child *resents* it!
Resents the cold air, the huge spaces, the sudden departure
from familiar things. And in the tiny filament of brain the
only thing the child knows is selfishness and hatred because
the spell has been rudely shattered. Who is responsible for
this disenchantment, this rude breaking of the spell? The
mother. So here the new child has someone to hate with all
its unreasoning mind. The mother has cast it out, rejected it.
And the father is no better, kill him, too! He's responsible in
his way!"

Jeffers interrupted. "If what you say is true, then every
woman in the world, would have to look on her baby as

something to dread, something to wonder about."

"And why not? Hasn't the child a perfect alibi? A thousand years of accepted medical belief protects him. By all natural accounts he is helpless, not responsible. The child is born hating. And things grow worse, instead of better. At first the baby gets a certain amount of attention and mothering. But then as time passes, things change. When very new, a baby has the power to make parents do silly things when it cries or sneezes, jump when it makes a noise. As the years pass, the baby feels even that small power slip rapidly, forever away, never to return. Why shouldn't it grasp all the power it can have? Why shouldn't it jockey for position while it has all the advantages? In later years it would be too late to express its hatred. *Now* would be the time to strike."

Leiber's voice was very soft, very low.

"My little boy baby, lying in his crib nights, his face moist and red and out of breath. From crying? No. From climbing slowly out of his crib, from crawling long distances through darkened hallways. My little boy baby. I want to kill him."

The doctor handed him a water glass and some pills. "You're not killing anyone. You're going to sleep for twenty-four hours. Sleep'll change your mind. Take this."

Leiber drank down the pills and let himself be led upstairs to his bedroom, crying, and felt himself being put to bed. The doctor waited until he was moving deep into sleep, then left the house.

Leiber, alone, drifted down, down.

He heard a noise. "What's *that?*" he demanded, feebly.

Something moved in the hall.

David Leiber slept.

Very early the next morning, Dr. Jeffers drove up to the house. It was a good morning, and he was here to drive Leiber to the country for a rest. Leiber would still be asleep upstairs. Jeffers had given him enough sedative to knock him out for at least fifteen hours.

He rang the doorbell. No answer. The servants were probably not up. Jeffers tried the front door, found it open, stepped in. He put his medical kit on the nearest chair.

Something white moved out of sight at the top of the stairs, a suggestion of a movement. Jeffers hardly noticed it.

The smell of gas was in the house.

Jeffers ran upstairs, crashed into Leiber's bedroom.

Leiber lay motionless on the bed, and the room billowed with gas, which hissed from a released jet at the base of the wall near the door. Jeffers twisted it off, then forced up all the windows and ran back to Leiber's body.

The body was cold. It had been dead quite a few hours.

Coughing violently, the doctor hurried from the room, eyes watering. Leiber hadn't turned on the gas himself. He *couldn't* have. Those sedatives had knocked him out, he wouldn't have wakened until noon. It wasn't suicide. Or was there the faintest possibility?

Jeffers stood in the hall for five minutes. Then he walked to the door of the nursery. It was shut. He opened it. He walked inside and to the crib.

The crib was empty.

He stood swaying by the crib for half a minute, then he said something to nobody in particular.

"The nursery door blew shut. You couldn't get back into your crib where it was safe. You didn't plan on the door blowing shut. A little thing like a slammed door can ruin the best of plans. I'll find you somewhere in the house, hiding, pretending to be something you are not." The doctor looked dazed. He put his hand to his head and smiled palely. "Now I'm talking like Alice and David talked. But, I can't take any chances. I'm not sure of anything, but I can't take any chances."

He walked downstairs, opened his medical bag on the chair, took something out of it and held it in his hands.

Something rustled down the hall. Something very small and very quiet. Jeffers turned rapidly.

I had to operate to bring you into this world, he thought. Now I guess I can operate to take you out of it. . . .

He took half-a-dozen slow, sure steps forward into the hall. He raised his hand into the sunlight.

"See, baby! Something bright—something pretty!"

A scalpel.